A Hazardous Game

THE ALICE CHRONICLES

JUST CAUSES

A HAZARDOUS GAME

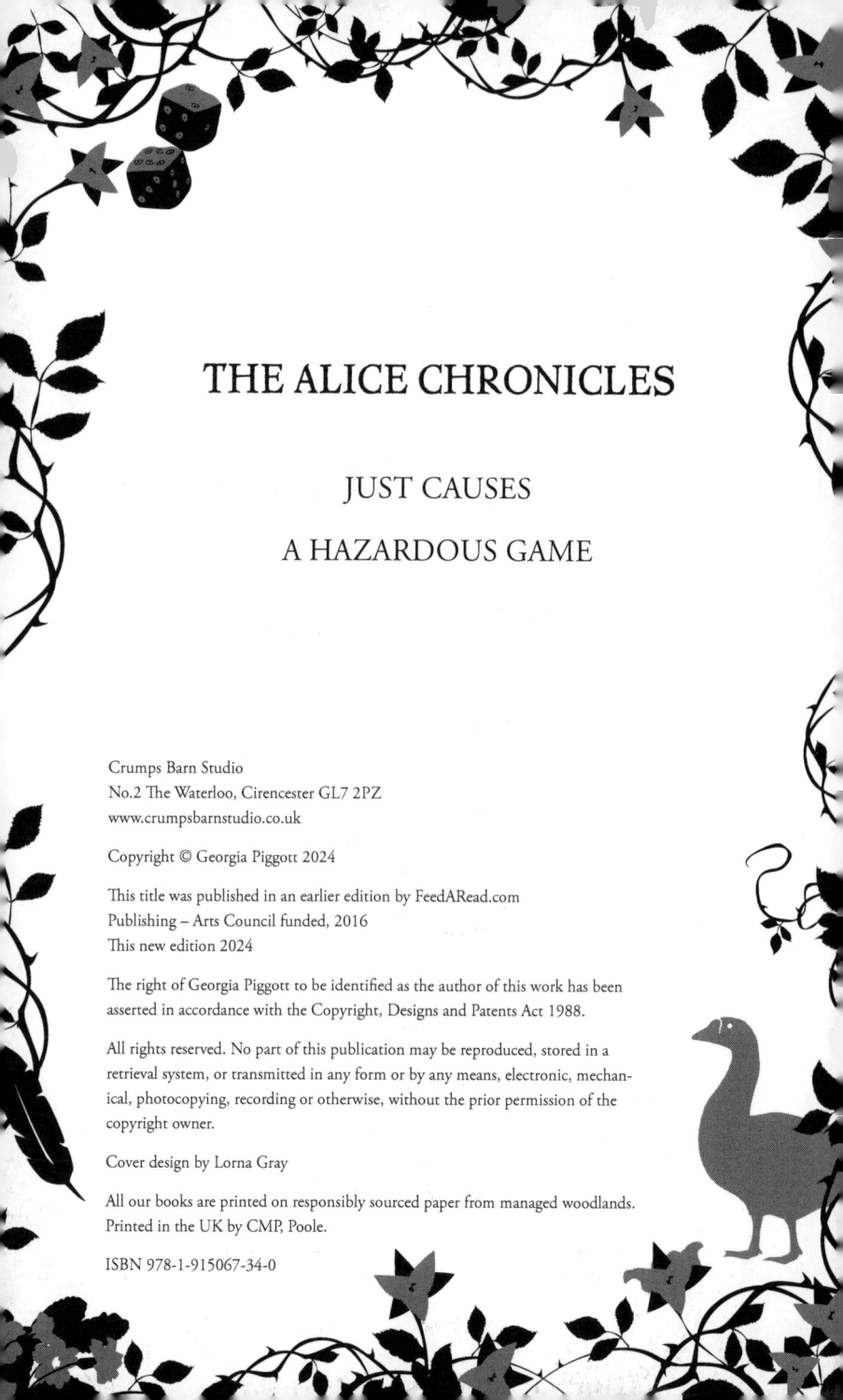

Crumps Barn Studio
No.2 The Waterloo, Cirencester GL7 2PZ
www.crumpsbarnstudio.co.uk

Copyright © Georgia Piggott 2024

This title was published in an earlier edition by FeedARead.com Publishing – Arts Council funded, 2016
This new edition 2024

The right of Georgia Piggott to be identified as the author of this work has been asserted in accordance with the Copyright, Designs and Patents Act 1988.

All rights reserved. No part of this publication may be reproduced, stored in a retrieval system, or transmitted in any form or by any means, electronic, mechanical, photocopying, recording or otherwise, without the prior permission of the copyright owner.

Cover design by Lorna Gray

All our books are printed on responsibly sourced paper from managed woodlands. Printed in the UK by CMP, Poole.

ISBN 978-1-915067-34-0

A Hazardous Game

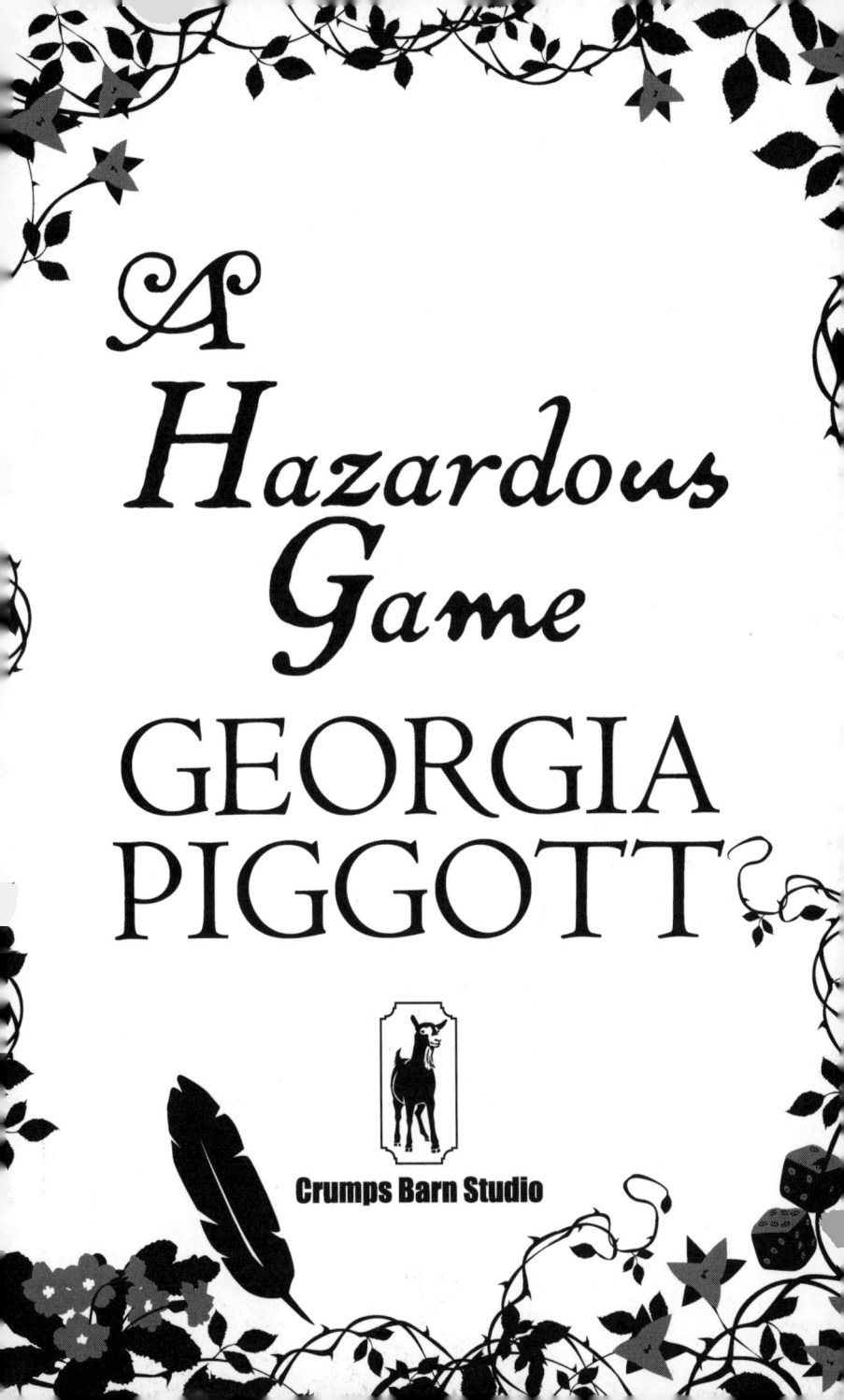

GEORGIA PIGGOTT

Crumps Barn Studio

Who is Sylvia? What is she,
That all our swains commend her?

William Shakespeare

PROLOGUE

OCTOBER 1624

Leaning against his barrels, the landlord of the Red Lion Inn yawned and squeezed tobacco-stained fingers against his eyes. A long and unprofitable evening was turning into a long and unprofitable night. In ones and twos, most of the regulars had long since drained their drinks and gone to their beds. The landlord propped his chin on his hand and morosely regarded the core of five persisting by the fire, playing at Hazard. Their bids and counterbids, their sporadic jests and curses, returned slight echoes from the dark void of the taproom.

A creak as the door to the stable yard settled on its hinges appeared to rouse them from their absorption. The players sat back, and the landlord began to look hopeful as one or two protested that the play was getting deep. Experience prompted him nimbly forward, proffering cloaks and gauntlets as three rose more or less collectively. He bellowed for the stable lad in the hay loft to fetch mounts, and ushered his trio of departing guests, lurching like one of the landlady's loose blancmanges, towards the door.

Having seen them mounted, and as secure in the saddle as several pints of Old Leo's would allow, the landlord returned to the taproom. For a few minutes he bustled around, collecting empties. 'Another ale for yourself, Master Tillotson?' to a lone drinker in the shadows. 'No? Godspeed you on your way, then, sir.' He completed his pointed wiping of tables and stopped by the two players.

'A mug of ale before you depart, Sir Malcolm? Master Jerrard?' he asked hopefully.

Sir Malcolm Wipley, Knight, screwed round, the feather on his high-crowned hat dancing a flourish. From under the rolling brim he fixed the landlord with a stare. 'Who said anything about departing? Bring another jug of Old Leo's, man.'

'Only, it would be kindly in you to let me know how long you might be, Sir Malcolm,' the landlord replied. 'It being late, and …' He trailed off as Sir Malcolm continued to stare. 'Very well, sir.'

Fresh ale supplied, the landlord announced his retreat to wait in his chair by the kitchen fire. There he lit a pipe and the smoke drifted languidly through the taproom.

The scene was not uncommon in the Red Lion, any more than the Crown, the Angel or any other of the inns gracing Guildford's High Street. The notable feature here was that one of the two players now started to cheat.

Except for the hearth, the only light was a greasy radiance from the solitary rush on the Hazard table. It oozed drops of pig fat into a congealed puddle. Scratches on the wood bore witness to sundry tapsters' past efforts to scrape up the lard for further rush lights. The flame barely lit the faces of the two men seated opposite each other. Jerrard wore a closely tucked, straight-brimmed hat and a short cloak pushed back over a striped woollen doublet and straight, calf-length breeches. Sir Malcolm, his great thighs splayed, sported full-skirted trunk hose and a woollen doublet of heavy cloth. He had draped his long cloak widely over the next table.

Neither bothered with the courtesies they had observed towards each other in company, and they spoke but little. Ruffs loosened, ale cups to hand, their concentration centred on each roll of the dice. Every now and then, one or other paused to raise the rush in its clip as it burned down, while beside them the fire diminished to a flickering glow amongst the ash in the hearth. From the kitchen drifted the sound of the landlord's open-mouthed dozing, the aroma of pipe smoke.

Time passed, the play veering to and fro without resolution.

The landlord's juddering snores were cut rudely short by the tinkle of clay shattering on brick hearth, followed by the creak of chair legs and a muttered curse. A few seconds later he appeared at the door to the taproom. His jerkin was open, shirt hanging out over his working breeches. He yawned, scratching an armpit where the seams had parted company. 'You wish for more ale, Sir Malcolm?' he asked.

The knight was monosyllabic. 'No.'

'Or you, Master Jerrard?'

'We have sufficient,' the other said, holding up his cup.

'Shall I rouse the lad to saddle up, then?' the landlord asked, brightening.

Without turning, Sir Malcolm said again, 'No.' Seated opposite, Jerrard addressed the landlord now approaching. 'We're not finished yet, Melbury. Another rush light, if you will.' He moved to raise and re-clip the rush.

'And paper,' Sir Malcolm said, 'and ink.'

'Paper,' Melbury repeated.

'I take it you have paper?'

'I expect so, Sir Malcolm,' Melbury said, scratching his head where the hair was thinning, as though puzzlement was his habitual state, and its remedy the cause of his baldness. 'I shall have to ask my wife. She being lettered, you see.' He paused, as though waiting for one or other to deny the need. When neither responded, he added, 'I may be a little while, she does not like to be roused.'

Sir Malcolm gave a shout of laughter. 'Frightened she'll cast missiles at your head, Melbury?' The landlord vouchsafed no answer. With set mouth, he shuffled away to the kitchen, and the sound of his reluctant steps mounting the back stairs filtered through to the players.

'Glad I'm not married,' the knight grunted. He flapped a hand in front of his nose. 'God's death, that rush stinks.'

'We could have gone to The Angel,' Jerrard answered shortly.

'Fancy all that new-fangled woodwork, do you?'

'I was thinking of the mutton-fat lights, less stench.'

Sir Malcolm did not answer and the two fell once more to their play, silence between them beyond the periodic calls, or the occasional suppressed curse as the play veered badly for one or other. Outside, an owl hooted its predatory warning into the night.

In due course landlord Melbury returned, having unearthed ink, a quill and some thin sheets of paper. He laid these and a further rush on the table.

Sir Malcolm took a leaf between two fingers, inspecting.

'Tis our best paper, Sir Malcolm,' the landlord assured him.

'I can believe that.'

'Good enough for notes of hand, Wipley,' Jerrard said. 'Are you playing or not?'

The knight dropped the sheet back on the table and turned to the hovering innkeeper. 'Well?'

'Sir Malcolm, I'm sorry to be asking you again, but will you be requiring my services much longer?' Melbury ventured. 'Only, I have to be up in the morning and—'

'Back to your kitchen, man,' Sir Malcolm ordered. 'We'll tell you when we're done.'

The night dragged on. The last embers in the hearth turned to ash. Discarded notes multiplied; the calling of mains, the casting of dice, continued. The game of Hazard being exactly that, the skill was in the numerical memory of the player, the instinct for the arithmetic of chance, when to raise the stakes, when to hold back.

The landlord's snores rumbled from the kitchen. Outside, the owl hooted again.

The notes of hand grew. Conversationally, Sir Malcolm murmured, 'So, is it true about you and Isabel Mullen?'

Jerrard made his throw and looked. 'Out.' He took up the dice again. 'What about Mistress Mullen?'

Wipley chuckled. 'Leave out "Mullen". Just "mistress" …'

'Your mind is a midden, Wipley.' He threw a second time. 'I do not make it my business to ruin a virtuous woman.'

Wipley brought the rush close to where the dice lay. 'Oh dear. Out … again.' He sat back. 'Warming your bed for you tonight, is she?'

'I have never had any designs on Mistress Mullen. She is my cousin, no less, no more. If you ever suggest otherwise in public, I'll call you out.'

'Mercy me. A terrifying prospect.'

'And I'm ten times the swordsman you are.'

'What makes you think I'd choose swords? Ever heard of flintlocks?'

'Flintlocks!' Jerrard scoffed. 'You'd be hard put to hit anything at twenty paces with one of them.' He threw again. 'Aha! Chance.'

'If not the esteemed Isabel, maybe you're akin to Tillotson's son. I hear he prefers young men.' Wipley picked up the dice and dropped them just short of Jerrard's outstretched palm so that they clattered onto the table. Jerrard gave him a straight look. 'Whatever Jeremy Tillotson is or is not,' he countered, 'you've no cause to make trouble for him, Wipley.' His fingers closed on the dice. 'And while you're being so righteous, we all know about your squalid fancy for young women who can't fight back.' He threw, looked and frowned.

'Oh, bad luck. Out again,' Wipley said. 'The thing is, I know women, Jerrard.'

Jerrard made another throw – another out. 'You flatter yourself.'

'Wrong. I flatter *them*. With power. It's why they choose me. Let me give you a hint, Jerrard.' He leaned forward in conspiratorial fashion, whispered, 'They don't want little men.'

Jerrard ignored him and went to throw. Wipley reached across, grasping his wrist. 'Abandon this point. I'll make you an offer. I'll wager two wins out of my next three throws – if I lose you get your grey stallion back. If I win, I get your demesne.'

Jerrard threw off his hold. 'That's a ridiculous wager.'

'Very well, my chestnut as well as your grey.'

'I don't want your chestnut.'

'But you want your grey,' Wipley goaded.

'You always do this when you're drunk, Wipley.'

'Do what?'

'Overreach yourself.'

'I'll even let you choose the main. Six or eight. Which is it to be?'

'We've decided the game we're playing.'

'Ah, Jerrard, you fear changing the game – I wonder why that is?'

'What maggot's got into your head tonight, Wipley?'

'Two wins out of three, the same combination, main or nick, no chances. Can't say fairer than that,' Wipley persisted.

'It won't happen. Withdraw.'

'Jerrard, Jerrard,' the knight said, smiling, scribbling a fresh note of hand. 'What a dull opponent you make.' He added his signature. 'Haven't the balls to go higher.' He placed the sheet on the table between them. 'Gutless.'

The two looked hard at each other.

At last, 'Very well,' Jerrard answered. 'If that's the way you want it.' He took a fresh sheet. 'Two wins out of three casts. He scribbled quickly, tossed it on top of the other. 'There's my pledge. Main is eight. So that's five and three or six and two.'

'And nick is twelve.' Sir Malcolm took the dice. 'So, let us be clear. Two wins out of three casts. If my cast adds up to eight, or I throw double six, that's a win. Anything else is Out. Two wins and the wager is mine. We are agreed?'

'Get on with it.'

'First throw, then.' A louder bubbling snore from the kitchen and Sir Malcolm paused momentarily, then cast. Four and five.

'Out.' Jerrard leaned back. 'Second throw.'

The knight gathered the dice up. He too leaned back in his chair and a wooden creak made an answering echo in the darkness of the taproom. Had either man glanced aside at that moment he might have discerned the glimmer of a face in the shadows, intent, watchful. Sir Malcolm linked his fingers together as though praying. His knuckles and the broad cube of his face under the curling brim were all that showed in the flicker of the rush light. He straightened, shook the dice in his large palm and threw.

Six and two.

'Eight. A win,' Wipley breathed.

Jerrard sat silent, his face impassive.

Wipley picked up. For a few seconds he seemed to gather himself. He took a deep breath. Shook the dice. Cast.

The short clatter of wood on wood and both leaned forward. For a few seconds there was silence as each absorbed the shift in fortune. Jerrard sat stock-still, disbelief writ large in his frowning stare, his face in the lurid light the colour of old cheese. A two and a six, and for him, time had tipped into the irretrievable.

Sir Malcolm Wipley rose, the legs of his chair scraping on the boards as he reached for Jerrard's final note of hand. 'That'll teach you. You'll get a day's notice when I'm moving in.'

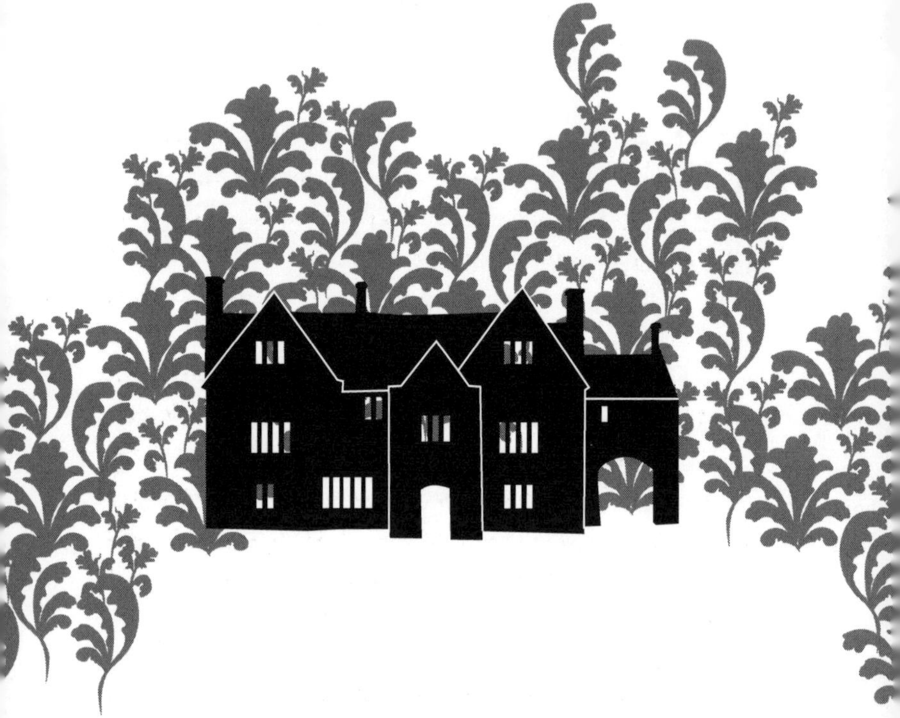

1

APRIL 1626

EIGHTEEN MONTHS LATER

'So this is High Stoke.' She takes her first look at her married home. It's huge. And wide. And three storeys high. *Three.* Gabled wings either side. Chimneys all over the place. She had expected something larger than Hill House, the farmhouse in Dorset where she grew up. Her idea of a gentleman's home was something double-fronted, close-timbered, a jutting upper floor. But this …

From the clearing where they stand, Alice looks up at the frontage of High Stoke House. The 'X' pattern, picked out in protruding bricks along its length, has been crafted to give the impression of continuity. On each side of the protruding front door is a many-paned window, the one on the left broader, higher, double her height, so that must be the hall. Two gable-topped wings at north and south ends lend balance to the line of the house. An elegant home generously proportioned, and for a few seconds she is overwhelmed by the match she has made. Daughter of a Dorset yeoman, will she know how to take such a house under her care and give it the attention it merits? Yet Alice is not so dazzled that she fails to note the air of grace neglected; the stain of mossy water-runs from the roof, a broken drift of clouds in the cracked panes of the hall window.

'What do you think?' her husband asks.

Alice regards the soft madder of the brickwork, the simple, three-plank garden door in a wall adjoining the end of the house, the long shadows cast by the chimneys across the clearing as the sun sinks. High Stoke, Henry has told her, was altered and enlarged as so many were fifty or more years ago, its 'E' shape designed to flatter their sovereign lady, its style boasting the confidence of the wool trade as it then was. Not any more.

'I think you are very fortunate.'

'In more ways than one, now you're here.' He draws her within his arm, adding, 'It's a mite tumbledown.'

'Nothing that cannot be rectified. Your home is beautiful, Henry,' she says, and means it.

'Our home. You are mistress of High Stoke now, Mistress Jerrard.'

Her married home. It sounds strange, she is still getting used to being married. It is only a matter of days. But Henry is right, it is tumbledown. Slipped slates, cracked glass, plants clinging where no plants should be. These days no one has any money, it seems. She shivers, not only from the sharp spring breeze.

'Let's go in, you're chilled,' Henry says, opening the door, which swings wide on greased hinges. They step into a passageway leading straight ahead, doors off. It is dim, cool, with a stone-flagged floor. Pale plaster walls glimmer between upright studs of wood. He pushes at a door on their left.

'Come into the hall, there's a fire,' he says. 'Where's Isabel, I wonder?'

Together they walk the length of the great room, Henry matching his long stride to her shorter pace, one arm protectively round her shoulders while the other removes his wide-brimmed, feathered hat, tossing it on a long table running half the length of the room. The floor is stone-flagged like the passage and her guess is that the passage was created when the house was altered, by screening off the end of the hall. A screens passage is intended to cut down the draughts. She hopes it is effective. She is chilled, the fatigue of the long journey, the anticipation, are telling on her. The blaze in the hearth is welcoming, she can feel its warmth as they approach.

'Isabel knows we're arriving today,' Henry is saying. 'She should be waiting to welcome you.'

'I expect she's busy,' Alice says, curious about this relation who 'does this and that in the house' as Henry described her. Like a wispy aunt pottering with linens.

'Here, make yourself comfortable and I'll find her. She can't be far,' Henry says, pulling the settle nearer the hearth. 'Are you all right there? Shall I put another log on?'

Alice sags onto the settle before the blaze, leaning back against the wood. God be thanked, she thinks, no gaggle of servants is gathered peering to catch a glimpse of me. At this moment, I am so weary, I could fall asleep.

'Are you too close to the fire? Would you like a cushion?'

She smiles and raises a staying hand. 'I am very well, Henry. I am glad of the fire. I shall try not to drop off before you find your relation.'

Henry chuckles as he re-crosses the hall. 'She will be so vexed with herself not to have been here, Isabel hates to be caught out.' And off he strides into the nether regions of the house, opening doors and calling. The squeak of a chimney hook filters into the hall, the clap of metal on earthenware. Someone is preparing a meal.

An enduring sense of rocking and jolting makes Alice lightheaded. They have been travelling for three days since they were married in Dorset on Tuesday, stopping overnight and starting early. Involuntarily she grasps the arm of the settle to steady herself, in the same way she grabbed Henry's arm when the little coach lurched through deep ruts. Plenty of those today on the slow pull up the rise from Farnham, along the breezy top for what seemed like miles, then down the steep slope at the end, to ford the river and climb through the middle of Guildford, bustling with people, lined with inns and shops, punctuated by narrow passages. They had left the town far behind by the time they turned off the road through the trees and arrived here. The dust! Her face feels tight, her eyes gritty.

Before her the fire crackles, flames leap from the splitting wood. Nevertheless, she is aware of a draught around her ankles. She pulls her cloak close and screws round to the wide, tall window, which she now sees has not only cracks but also some missing panes. She scans the rest of the hall. My hall, she reminds herself, her gaze moving from the plaster strapwork running round the ceiling, to the long table flanked by benches, and at its head a handsome carved-back chair with arms. The fireplace before her is bordered on the right by a door standing ajar to a sunlit room and on the left, by a stone staircase set into the corner.

A light slap-slap interrupts Alice's musing. She cocks her head, the better to trace its direction. It is here in the hall. As she peers, a grey-coloured goose makes its flat-footed way over the stone flags. A noble-looking creature, head held high. Alice has never seen one like it. Where she comes from in the heart of Dorset, she knows only white ones. She wonders if this is the rare marvel called the barnacle goose. They say such geese are born out of shells that grow on the barnacle tree, not that Alice has ever seen a barnacle tree either.

While Alice ponders this mystery, a draggle-haired girl pokes her head round the door and slides into the hall. She is small and thin, just a child really, in a yellowed shift crushed under a cut-down bodice. Her much-patched skirts are going to threads at the hem and she is barefoot. She edges towards the bird, alternately waving her arms and backing away. She has not seen Alice, so intent is she in her timid pursuit of the goose. Unfazed, the bird hisses at her, beating its wings and chasing her to a distance. As though to underline its contempt, it then turns its back and waddles to the massive fireplace, taking up its station not four paces from where Alice sits. The girl catches sight of Alice at the same moment as the goose ejects a wet black-green splat onto the floor.

The girl looks at Alice, and looks at the goose. Her face screws up in an agony of indecision, and she half curtsies, half-herds, hopping sideways across the floor with outstretched arms. The effect is that of a player trying to take a bow and embrace her audience at the same time. The goose returns hissing to the attack and the child retreats to the flight of stairs where, several steps up, she finds sanctuary.

Alice rises, pulls off her gauntlets, unties her cloak strings and tosses the lot on the table. 'Let us catch it between us,' she says, and hurries to close the door to the sunlit room. Intimidated by the movement of another person, the goose slaps hurriedly away from the stairs. The girl says nothing but appears emboldened, perhaps by the goose's retreat, or by the offer of aid, or both. She descends, bobs another wide-armed curtsey at Alice and dodges across the hall lunging for the bird's tail feathers. But the goose is wise to such clumsy tactics, it breaks into a flapping run and heads under the table. At that moment the hall door flies open and a sturdy young man in leather jerkin and worn kersey breeches strides into the hall.

'Close the door, can you?' Alice calls. 'We'll keep it in here, at least.' As he turns to do her bidding, she calculates how to catch the bird. She turns to the girl. 'If you go and stand on the stairs, it can't get past you.' The girl will be better there than trying to herd a goose that is well aware of her diffidence. 'You and I,' she says to the young man, 'we can surely get it between us.'

He nods. 'Drive it towards the corner,' he says. His voice has an unfamiliar burr, flatter, less pronounced than the village men in Alice's native Dorset. His brows meeting over his eyes, coupled with his jutting jaw, give him an air of determination.

They make their way, jointly herding. Odours of manure and old sweat seep from his thick linen shirt, his tawny breeches. Moving ahead of her, he has the goose cornered within seconds and grabs it behind the head. The bird hisses and flaps in vain as he brings its neck to the floor and immobilises it. Alice is on the point of commending his speed when he pulls a small axe from his belt, his hand rises and falls, and metal meets stone with a chopping crunch. To Alice's astounded gaze he rises holding a beaked head on a short length of neck. The rest of the goose kicks and flaps where it lies, sending blood splashing on his nether hose and streaking across the floor. Speechless, all Alice can think is that she has seen the first and last of this unique and wondrous creature hatched from a shell produced by the barnacle tree.

'Lost its head, stupid bird,' the young man comments. 'Goose for the steward, I suppose. Not for us, that's certain.' He drops the head and wipes the axe-blade on his breeches. 'You'd better clean that up, Mollie,' he orders the young girl, turning on his heel. The smell of blood now mingles in his wake with the odours of sweat and stables.

From the door, Henry says, 'Well done, Joe!' Alice pulls her gaze away from the bloody remains to see Henry clap Joe on the shoulder in passing. 'Good clean job,' he says and turns to the child called Mollie. 'Wipley's goose, is it?' To Alice, he adds, 'We're forever finding the birds his girl loses.'

'There are more of them?' Alice wonders how many of these marvellous creatures exist in this strange region of England.

'Couple of dozen or so, she's always losing them.'

'This is his goose-girl?' Alice asks.

'No, this is Mollie, our scullion.' To the maidservant he calls, 'This is your new mistress, Mollie.' Mollie makes another curtsey. Alice, crossing to greet the girl, resolves to say nothing of barnacle geese in case it was not such and Henry thinks her a bumpkin.

'Geese can be frightening, I know,' she says to the girl. 'I've been chased by them too. Did it peck you?' Mollie does not speak but shakes her head vigorously. 'The thing is,' Alice says, turning back to Henry, 'it's not our goose.'

Henry shrugs. 'It is, now, thanks to Joe. Wipley only has himself to blame.'

'Shouldn't we return it to the goose-girl?' Alice asks.

Henry looks at the two pieces of goose and grins. 'It'd have a job keeping up with the others, don't you think?'

'What will your Master Wipley say?'

'*Sir Malcolm* Wipley, our Noble Knight,' Henry dips his head, tugging at his forelock. 'Not supposed to let geese off the tether, tis the law, as his great friend Justice Townsend would remind him.'

'Doesn't Lady Wipley keep a check on her goose girl?'

'There is no Lady Wipley. Wipley pays his goose-girl a pittance so she is forever going off collecting kindling and suchlike to scratch a living. The geese wander as they please. He can hardly complain if he loses one.'

Alice's gaze follows Mollie as she retreats from the hall clutching the parts of goose in her red-blotched apron. 'Talking of losing one,' she says, 'I assume we've lost Sam to the stables, have we?'

Sam, the stick-like orphan Alice discovered terrified and starving after the plague hit her village last autumn, has filled out and gained assurance in Alice's care. She has no idea when he was born but reckons him around four or five. Horses are his love and when they arrived here he begged to be allowed to watch the coach being uncoupled, the horses led away to their stables behind the house.

'He'll be helping to groom and feed them by now, I should think,' Henry says. 'In fact I seem to recall that his agreement to our marriage was conditional on my taking him up for a ride on the grey. I must honour that soon.'

She moves towards him, leaning into his shoulder. 'What a long time ago that all seems,' she says, smiling. 'What would I have done without you? I still shudder to think.'

They stand, arms round each other, each with their own thoughts. Without Henry, Alice knows she would have faced a very different future with a very different man, cornered into a dutiful marriage that would have robbed her of Hill House and its farm, her inheritance. Choosing to marry Henry instead, a man she hardly knew, was a risk, she realised that at the time. But from that day, not a moment's doubt has assailed her. She is still smiling as she says, 'Well, I must find Sam. He'll be hungry and—'

'He'll say when he's hungry.'

'We've been travelling all day, Henry. He must eat before I put him to bed. And I'd also like to unlace, now that we're within doors.' She thinks longingly of a loose-gown of lightweight wool packed in her coffer that will be more comfortable than the tightness of doublet and bodice. But it would be ill-mannered to retire to their chamber without meeting his relation. 'Did you find Isabel?' she asks.

'No one has seen her; I don't know where she is.' He trails his fingers up and down her neck. 'While we're waiting, Mistress Jerrard …' He pulls her towards him.

'Yes, Master Jerrard?' She scans his face as she runs her fingers through the long hair at his nape. 'What did you have in mind?' A month ago, she wouldn't have dared act in this way. A month ago nothing had prepared her for this ease, this undreamed-of delight that has bloomed in those few days since she and Henry were wed, this confidence in reaching out to her man, the thrill as he reaches out to her, desire matching desire. As their lips meet, her hat slips off and falls with a soft plop onto the stone flags, rolling slightly on its narrow brim.

From the screens passage, a woman's voice sharp with irritation. 'Is that Mollie? What are you doing, girl?' Henry mutters, 'So, at last.' Alice hastily steps back, checks her hair, tucks away a lock.

A tight-laced figure gowned all in black but for a narrow gathering of lace close about the neck, stops dead in the doorway, heavy skirts swinging, unseen keys clinking. Her form is spare. The light glances off her silk gown at the gaunt shoulders, the bony elbows. The eyes are black above cheek-hollows, the lines of nose and mouth straight, the jaw angular. For the space of a drawn breath, the two women regard each other. Then Alice watches the transformation as the other's glance lights on Henry, the severity dissolves, eyes brightening, smile blossoming.

'Cousin! They did not say you were arrived!' Her greeting is honeyed with pleasure. He steps towards her and she advances, stretching out welcoming hands. Placing them on his shoulders, she kisses his cheek. Unlike Alice, she does not have to stand on tiptoe; this woman is close to Henry's height.

'Isabel!' He returns the kiss. 'I was looking all over for you. Allow me to introduce my—'

'I hardly looked for your coming before nightfall,' Isabel hurries on, 'but what joy to see you already.' Alice smiles to herself that she imagined meeting a sort of elderly aunt. Older than herself, but not by that much. Somewhere around Henry's age?

Isabel is clutching Henry's arm, gazing into his face. High on her sallow cheeks, two spots of pink glow. 'I hope I see you well, cousin, and I thank God you are returned safe.' She kisses him again. 'We have been cooking against your arrival. We have your favourite, oysters brought up specially from the coast. And here you are—' She stops as though bereft of speech at the vision of Henry. She is still holding his arm, and he extricates himself to stretch out to Alice. She steps forward and extends her hands and a smile to this cousin of Henry's. 'Isabel, I am pleased to make your acquaintance.'

Isabel steps back clasping bony fingers against her skirt at the end of the long V of her arms. She gives a formal dip of the head. 'Mistress.'

Taken aback by the formality, Alice hesitates, abruptly aware she is being assessed. Isabel's pin-point eyes are engaged in swiftly raking over the dark worsted of Alice's skirt, the close-fitting doublet with its embroidered panes sitting out around the waist, the gauntlets lying on the woollen cloak tossed across the table.

Isabel's glance takes in the hat that fell to the ground as Henry kissed his wife, and finally her gaze arrives at Alice's face.

'High Stoke greets you,' Isabel announces, and Alice wonders if this is the way this household works. She hopes not, she is used to the easy family ways she was brought up to in Dorset. While she is wondering, Isabel turns back to Henry, reaching to straighten the wings of his doublet. 'Look at you, travel-weary and crumpled,' she reproves fondly. In the way of an older sibling with an unruly brother, she makes to smooth the lawn collar which is neither crushed nor crooked.

Henry disengages himself, gently chiding, 'Come now, Isabel.'

A frown creases Isabel's forehead. She leans close. 'From one who knows you, I see you are out of temper.'

'No indeed, Isabel,' he assures her, 'you see nothing of the sort.'

'As you wish, cousin.' She eyes him knowingly. She looks, Alice thinks, as though she would like to welcome Henry all over again, to sprinkle further kisses and smoothings. Evidently Isabel enjoys much licence in this household, the licence of a relation holding a privileged position.

Henry turns to Alice. 'My love, Isabel is steward to the household, the cousin I told you of. I have known her forever.'

'I am sure there is much I can learn of High Stoke with your help, Isabel,' Alice says, and adds for form's sake, 'I thank you for your welcome.'

Isabel inclines her head. 'No need of thanks, mistress.' It might be a courtesy, it feels more like a reproof for presumption, as though Alice is of that order of guests unlikely to be invited again.

'Come, Isabel, stir yourself,' Henry prompts. 'What about a drink by way of welcome?'

'Indeed, cousin.' Isabel brightens. 'I shall fetch you the red Gascony wine you like so much.'

She turns and is already retreating as Henry calls, 'Wait, Isabel!' and says to Alice. 'White Gascony for you, I think?'

'White Gascony would be refreshing,' Alice agrees, and together they turn in enquiry to Isabel.

From the doorway, Henry's cousin says, 'How unfortunate. The white Gascony is finished.'

'What, the one that came in the autumn?' Henry asks. 'I can't believe that's all gone.'

'It was finished some time back, cousin. If it is refreshment that is required, the working men favour a pint of small-ale.' The discourtesy is brazen, and too late Isabel tries to turn it aside. 'That is—'

'You forget yourself, Isabel!' Henry declares. 'Get some of the Rhenish. We've still some of that, I suppose?'

'Indeed, cousin.'

'Bring a glass of that. The London Rhenish, mind you, the one from the Steelyard in Thames Street, not the Bristol stuff.'

The atmosphere has turned sharp, and Alice tries to soften it by adding a request. 'And I should be glad if you would have a jug of water sent upstairs, please, Isabel?' she asks. 'I need to wash off the travel dust.'

'Very well,' Isabel says. The expressionless tone has returned. 'It will take a while.'

'Is there a difficulty?' Alice asks, wondering if clean water is in short supply in Surrey.

'The bed must be changed.'

Henry frowns. 'What's that to do with anything?'

'The silly girl has used the wrong sheets,' Isabel explains, tutting. 'Harden-linen. I ask you!'

'Please do not trouble on that score, Isabel,' Alice says. 'I've slept in harden-linen before now. It is a mite scratchy but will not harm us.'

'Perhaps I should explain, my cousin sleeps in fine linen,' Isabel says, the emphasis heavy with implication about Alice's habits. 'Not flax-crop discards.'

'God-a-mercy, Isabel, go to, go to!' Henry says. 'Tell the girl to take up warm water directly.'

'But your sheets, cousin! What about your sheets?'

'She can change the bed later. Now fetch us those drinks.'

'Of course, cousin.' Isabel, quietly compliant, turns to go.

'And if you're looking for Mollie, she's dealing with one of Sir Malcolm's runaway geese.'

A scowl of irritation crosses Isabel's face. 'She shouldn't be anywhere near his geese. She's forever wandering off and leaving her work.'

'It made its way in here.' Alice impulsively defends the absent. 'She was trying to catch it.'

'It's all right, Isabel,' Henry says. 'Joe solved the problem by executing it. Maureen can hang it or jug it or whatever dark arts she practises on fowl.'

'Maureen is a sober, God-fearing cook, cousin!' Isabel protests. 'She would never practise dark arts, I assure you.'

'Yes, yes,' Henry waves a dismissive hand. 'And not a word to Wipley.' In a warning tone, he adds, 'Cousin?'

Isabel inclines her head but the smile has not returned.

ALICE takes a last look to satisfy herself that Sam's little chamber is ready for him when he has eaten, before she returns to the hall to sup with Henry. She pulls the door to and approaches the main chamber. Within, a maidservant flaps out a fresh sheet and tucks the corner neatly. As Alice enters, the girl turns. She is short, with plump arms and a round face, with enviably long lashes fringing her grey eyes. Her bodice and linen skirt stand dark against a plain white chemise, the neckline of which is modest without primness. Strands of escaped honey-gold hair slip from under the girl's cap and stick to her neck. Her nose and forehead are sheened, and sweat pearls above her lip. A flush of heat or embarrassment, or both, mantles the girl's cheeks with rose as she bobs a hurried curtsey.

'I'm so sorry the water was cold, mistress. There was warm water in the wash-house but Isabel said there was no time to fetch it.'

'It matters not,' Alice assures her, recalling the shock of well-water as she bent her face to the basin.

'And I am sorry about the sheets. I am a dairymaid really, and I have not ... I am new here, you see, and I didn't know which sheets to use.'

'How could you? I'd not have known myself where to find the right sheets.' *A certain someone should have shown you. Called a steward and cannot direct the maidservant to heat water, find sheets?* She picks up a pillowcase. 'Here, let me help.'

The girl gapes. 'You – help?' she blurts. Recollecting herself, she adds quickly, 'Thank you, no, mistress. Isabel would not like it.'

Alice sees the moist eyes, feels a surge of sympathy for this girl still fresh to her position, clearly frightened by the ways of this household. 'Nevertheless, I shall help you and we shall have it done in no time. Isabel does not need to be fretted with such a detail. Tell me, what is your name?'

And while Grace the dairymaid talks of herself and her family in Chilworth a few miles away, Alice mulls over Isabel's jealous allegiance towards Henry.

IN the High Stoke servants' parlour, Sylvia is carrying supper to table in a covered pot. Joe's eyes track her. With good reason. Sylvia is an arresting sight, her large, brown eyes dance under dark lashes and finely tilted brows. Her generous mouth is just now widening into the suggestion of a smile.

Alongside Joe at the table, Allan looks down and busies himself by wiping his hands down his breeches and checking them as if for working dirt. Having driven the High Stoke coach down to Farnham to collect his master, the new mistress and the little boy, his breeches are as dusty as the rest of him and unlikely to improve the condition of his hands. His rough linen shirt would have made a better means of wiping off the dirt. He keeps his head down as Sylvia stops and leans to position the pot on the table. After a moment, she mops the rim with her cloth, her tongue mirroring the movement round her lips. Joe gazes open-mouthed. Allan is still wiping and checking his hands. Leaning on the board, Sylvia asks, 'Something to satisfy a man's appetite, Allan?'

'Satisfy indeed,' Joe cuts in. 'A man could go a long way on that.' The axe he used to behead the goose hangs from his belt and he moves it round out of the way. 'Why don't you come and sit here, Sylvia?'

'Because you smell of the midden, if you want to know.' She turns back to Allan. 'Just as you like it?' She removes the lid. Steam rises. 'Go on, take a good look.'

Ignored, Joe looks from Sylvia to Allan and his heavy brows fold up against each other. At last Allan looks, pulls a face. 'About as grey and boring as all Maureen's pottages.'

Sylvia looks. 'You're right, it looks like the run-off from Betsy's wash-house.'

Joe tries to look roguish. 'But it's always nicer when *you* bring it to table, Sylvia.'

Sylvia kneels on the bench and leans her elbows on the board. Beneath her chemise, the flesh swells in shadowed crescents over the confining bodice. Joe leans across Allan. 'Sylvia—?'

'Get off!' Allan digs an elbow into Joe's ribs.

'So how was your day away from the woodshed?' Sylvia asks Allan. 'Must have been a welcome change from wading through sawdust.'

'I like working with wood.'

'Don't I know it. Every time you used to come up to Tillotsons it was, *Ah, here's a bit of wood to saw. Ah, here's another bit of wood to saw.*'

Allan smiles. 'I was making things.'

'Like heaps of sawdust. Ever heard of stopping for a gossip?'

'If you want to gossip, Sylvia, I'm surprised you haven't asked about the new mistress.'

'What about her, then?' touching a hand to the gleaming chestnut curls peeping from under her cap. 'Is she as pretty as me?'

'Not possible!' Joe declares. He reaches a brawny arm to help himself from the pile of lumpy grey bread trenchers, tears off a piece and stuffs it in his mouth.

'She's got nice eyes,' Allan says.

'Oh, nice eyes, has she?' Sylvia says. 'That's nice for her.'

'Master says she's ordered her own household these five years.'

'Where's that, then?'

'Dorset,' Allan says. 'She's lived there all her life.'

'Ooh, fancy, the wilds of Dorset!' Sylvia giggles. 'Are her hands red? Does she talk all ooh-arrr?'

'Shut up, Sylvia.'

'The master's one for taking chances, by all I've heard,' Sylvia goes on. 'She must have had something he wanted. Not that,' she says, quelling Joe's dawning leer, and looks back at Allan. 'Something else.'

'What would you know?' Allan says.

'You'd be surprised what I know. Still, a country rustic? You wait, she'll have us all eating turnips and wearing clogs.'

It draws a reluctant grin from Allan.

Sylvia grins back and slips off the bench to return to the kitchen. 'That's better,' she murmurs.

2

Alice surfaces from sleep, and for a moment the light coming from the wrong direction confuses her. It is a few seconds before she remembers where she is.

The climbing sun shines through the yellowed bed curtains onto the form lying beside her, bare arm resting on the coverlet. His flesh is patterned light and dark with sunlit echoes of the bed hangings, stitched long ago with the tree-of-life design, now worn thin with age and use. Alice reaches out to rest her hand on her husband's chest as he stirs in the feathered warmth. She moves towards him, savouring the seductive feel as the fine linen sheet slides over her body. She smiles to herself. Very well, Isabel was right. Harden-linen, which Alice is more used to than she admitted, is scratchy, whereas these sheets, this pillowcase, are soft and smooth.

Henry's arm reaches round her, drawing her close, and she unwinds, arching the length of her body against him, wrapping a leg round his. She pulls him into a kiss, feeling the warmth of his chest, the hairs that tickle her skin, before she nestles back to sleep.

LATER, while Henry slumbers on, she slips out of bed and stands by the window on this her first morning and looks down on the wide sunlit clearing before the house. High Stoke, Henry has told her, sits a little way north of Guildford, between the London and Leatherhead ways. He has lived here all his life. By God's grace, he says, I shall still be here when I die. She can see why he loves it so much, the peace of it, like her own Hill House in Dorset, neighboured but not closely, away from the road yet near the town. The bright spring rays streaming through the diamonds of glass fill the air with golden, dancing dust motes. This chamber with its window jutting out above the front door faces roughly east, and morning's long beams reach across the floorboards.

Shading her eyes, she revels in the scene outside. A dozen ewes graze the short turf of the clearing while their lambs chase each other in woolly play. Every now and then one charges at another, which jumps off all fours in pretence of panic and rushes to the teat, there to nudge insistently for milk, before its dam tires of the demand and turns away to new grazing. And the youngster skips back to the others, to begin the game all over again. The wide clearing is their world for the time being, bounded on one side by the house and the garden wall, and a curve of trees some two hundred paces away to south, east and north, a green curl of bursting leaf.

And there below, hop-skipping alongside a mounted man and deep in animated conversation is four-year-old Sam. He is barefoot, his breeches are on the wrong way round, and his shirt hangs out. Times beyond counting, her heart has ached with love for this plague orphan she found and took in during those dark days after last autumn's pestilence swept through her village.

Up betimes and ever curious, on his first morning at High Stoke Sam is clearly enjoying talking horses, pointing out the praiseworthy aspects of the man's big-boned bay. Not a particularly well-looking man, Alice notices. He is finely clad in russet doublet and breeches, and appears to be taking equal pleasure in Sam's company. She can hear the tone of his voice though not his words as he responds in courteous and forthcoming manner, as he might man to man. He is hatless and his dark tousled hair resting on his shoulders catches gleams of bronze in the sun. Together they pass round the house and out of sight, Sam hopping and chattering all the way.

Behind her, Henry slides his legs out of bed and treads across the chamber. His arm slips round her shoulder, fingers brushing her nipple, and her toes curl against the warmth of the sunlit floorboards. The shadows of the lattice draw sinuous grids on their twined flesh.

'Good morning, my strumpet of a wife.'

'You say so? Such discourtesy, sir,' she answers, leaning languidly against him. 'Strumpet indeed!'

'Of course. Look at this hair.' He reaches to ruffle the red-brown kinked curls spreading in bedded disorder over her shoulders.

'I never found the trick of confining it.' She tries to flatten it under her hand. 'It always escapes.'

'I'm glad of it,' he murmurs, possessing himself of her hand. 'It's a cakes-and-ale wife I married, not a purse-mouthed puritan.' They stand thus locked together, Henry nuzzling her neck, his chest warm against her back while she gazes out, still thinking of Sam. And that stranger. He was not overly stout, no, but by her reckoning he is nowhere near as tall as Henry, probably little more than her own height. All in all, she decides, not as fine-looking as her husband … with a rush of secret pride she twists round and clasps Henry.

'What's this for, then?' he says, his arm tightening around her in response.

She smiles up at him. 'Oh, merely that I am glad I am married to you.'

'Now, if that's not an invitation—'

'Henry!' Alice squirms in his hold.

'What?'

'Shouldn't we get dressed?'

Henry's fingertips brush soft as feathers down her back. 'Whatever for?'

'It is full morning. We cannot sleep all day.'

His eyes brighten, looking down at her. 'Sleep, no.'

'I mean, there are things to do.'

'I couldn't agree more.' He lifts her such that her feet dangle just clear of the floor. 'Cakes-and-ale wife.' Laughing, she rests her head on his shoulder and lets herself be carried back to bed.

'YOUR new dairymaid is called Grace,' Alice says across the breakfast dishes. She is realising how much she, like Grace, has to learn about this house. She would have headed for the kitchen to eat as she always did at home, except that she was on Henry's arm and he brought her here. She has never known a separate parlour solely for eating. It is small, just of a size to be furnished with a small oblong table by the front-facing window, flanked by stools and two chairs, and a side-board opposite of similar dark wood, its upper and lower shelves holding pewter tableware and two candlesticks. Last night they dined at the long table in the hall, but that was special, it was their homecoming. Or at least it was Henry's homecoming. Isabel hovered at his elbow throughout, ministering to his every need.

'*Our* new dairymaid,' Henry corrects her.

'Oh, yes.' This is not yet her home. She has let go of Hillbury, her childhood village, but Guildford, it seems, will need time to accept her.

'Isabel introduced her?' he asks.

'Isabel sent her to change the sheets last night. Poor girl – she's a little overwhelmed here, and she's homesick.' Alice looks around at the offerings on the table.

'She said she was homesick?'

'No. Nor did she say she's overwhelmed, but she is, both. And diligent. Isabel must find her a great asset.'

'Isabel, my love, makes a point of finding very few an asset.'

'Then life must be somewhat of a trial for Isabel,' she says. 'For sure, she doesn't find me much of an asset.'

'Oh, I'm sure she will.'

'I hope I shall get on with her, Henry.'

'Give her time; she's always something stiff with strangers.'

But is it just stiffness within that bony frame, Alice wonders, or is it something more? Carefully, she says, 'Tell me about Isabel. I saw her again last night when I took Sam to bed. She looked very upright, very still.' An unnerving episode it was, like a silent passage of arms, the steward standing there, encased in that black gown, following Alice with her pin-point eyes, her arms in their close-fitting sleeves held straight in a long black V to the clasped hands. Alice felt Sam move closer, clutching her skirt.

Her husband considers the fare on the table. 'What can I tell you about Isabel?'

'Where does she come from? How long has she been here?' Alice tests a damson cheese and rejects its dense bounciness in favour of dried figs. 'How did she come to be your, er, your ...' she feels silly saying the word.

'Steward.'

'Indeed. Henry, is she really a cousin of yours?' *Why would a middling sort of household like this need an indoor steward? They are for earls and the like.*

Henry cuts himself slices of ham, pointing at it with his knife. 'Egerton sent this from himself and his lady, handsome of them. Yes, Isabel's a cousin. Her mother was cousin to my mother. Aunt Mullen, I called her. Isabel's an only child.'

'Did your mother bring Isabel here, then?'

'No, she only came three or four years ago. Grew up in Devonshire. I've known her forever, though not as close kin.'

'So, you needed someone to direct the household?'

'I wasn't looking for anyone, the household seemed to run itself after my mother died, though I am the first to admit I wouldn't notice the things a mistress would. But after Aunt died, my Uncle Mullen sent word. He was in difficulties for Isabel. Needed a position for her.'

'Why? Could she not find work in Devonshire?' Alice sips her small ale. It is bland and colourless but, she supposes, better than nothing.

'Isabel had gone from home to be a maidservant. But she found various roles did not suit. She would come home and my aunt and uncle would find another position for her. But then—'

'Why did her roles not suit?'

Henry finishes a mouthful of ham before replying. 'It seems they did not treat her well, she felt unwelcome.'

'Why? What had they done?'

Henry gives a short laugh. 'It was nothing they had *done*, exactly. People always took against her. She has a somewhat severe mien, I will admit, no fault of hers. But their courtesy towards her was not what it should have been, apparently, and made it impossible for her to stay.' He picks up the ale jug and makes pouring gestures.

'No, I thank you,' Alice declines. 'In all her roles?' she asks.

While he pours for himself, 'I can only go by what she told my Uncle Mullen,' he says, 'and he was desperate by the time I got there. He cannot support a daughter at home, he's a poor man, and he felt they had reached a point where Isabel had to leave and find work further afield. He appealed to me.'

'So you brought her here?'

'So I brought her here.'

Alice can only think to say, 'She must have been so grateful to you.' Indeed Isabel, a maidservant raised to virtual head of a household in one step should be deeply grateful. But four years on, it hardly explains her conspicuous affection.

'Looking back,' Henry goes on, 'I think I have as much to be grateful for. No doubt it would all have gone to ruin here but for Isabel. Her firm hand ensures things continue well.'

Alice seeks that fleeting glance she is coming to know in her husband's face, that hint of a curve to his mouth that says he is in jest, but Henry continues to concentrate on his plate. Continue well? she thinks. That first impression yesterday has told her that no repairs have been attempted for years. What has the steward done about it? As Henry goes to take a draught of ale, he glances at her. 'What?'

'Nothing.'

'It's not nothing. I know that look.'

She thinks fast. 'Well ... I was wondering, what of the title "steward"? Where does that come from?'

Henry shrugs. 'She directs the household – women servants, the men around the kitchen court – exactly as a steward does.'

'A steward does rather more than that. What experience does Isabel have, to be raised to the station of steward?'

'She was a maidservant as I say, but in large, respectable houses, mind you.' He laughs sheepishly. 'Oh, very well, she chose "steward" herself.'

So it is ambition, Alice thinks. A steward is also secretary, bailiff, messenger, ambassador, confidential go-between, overseer of buildings and demesne. At the very least, Isabel is failing in those last two. 'What do you intend for her now that I'm here?'

He frowns in puzzlement. 'What should I intend?'

'You have said to me several times, Henry, I am mistress of High Stoke and I may run my own household. Are you thinking of a pension for Isabel? A position in another household? We cannot turn her off unaided.'

'I'm not thinking to turn her off. She knows the house, she can go on running it. You needn't do anything.'

Alice gives a short laugh. 'Forgive me, but we are not so plump of pocket that I can play the fine lady. Nor do I wish to.'

'But don't you do ... embroidery, sewing, something of that sort?'

'I seem to remember that whenever you visited me at Hill House I was nearly always in disreputable work wear.'

'Ah, the seam-rent rug-gown.' He smiles. 'I remember it well.'

'And you've not seen my attempts at embroidery or you wouldn't suggest it. In truth, Henry, there are things that need attention here that are being neglected at present.'

'Such as?'

'Such as slipped roof tiles, cracked panes. It makes the hall terribly draughty, especially with a good fire going.'

'Well, I'll get Allan to attend to it.'

'Not only that.'

His face takes on a hunted look. 'Alice!'

'Look at this bread, Henry. Do you always have five-day-old bread? Or that fruit cheese, it's so solid you could plug the holes in the roof with it. The only food worth its name on this table is that ham from … from …?'

'Egerton.'

'And in truth, do you know what your stocks of wine are?'

'Isabel knows all that.' He waves a dismissive hand.

Alice knows she should stop, and knows she must speak. 'Well, does she? You said yesterday you could not believe the white Gascony was finished.'

A look of irritation crosses his face. 'I was surprised. I'd forgotten.'

She looks at him.

He puts down his knife. 'Alice. Understand me. All that is for Isabel to direct. Drop a word in her ear now and again.'

'I am to teach her her role? She's much older than me. How do you think she will like that?'

'Just mention it. Now listen, why don't we ride this afternoon? This morning I must go into town to see my attorney. I'll take Sam with me, he'll enjoy the ride. This afternoon I'll bid Joe saddle up Cassie for you after we've eaten. We'll go up the hill and along the Long Down towards Albury. Fine views all around from there.' He lifts his last slice of ham to his mouth and takes a draught of ale. 'I shall see you later.' The subject is closed, especially since he has so adroitly navigated round her with that offer to take Sam. They both know young Sam will jump at the chance of sitting up in front of Henry on the grey.

He rises, kisses her and is gone. She listens to his step receding down the screens passage, his voice calling in the kitchen, then the outer door slams and the house is quiet.

Alice balls her fists. 'Oh, God-a-mercy, woman! Married only days and already you're a scold.' She leans her elbows on the table, rests her chin in her palms, and regards the remains of breakfast. Neither of them touched the dark yellow slab like a lump of beeswax on the table. She pulls it towards her, picks it up, eyes it, sniffs. Its sour whiff is enough to identify cheese made from skimmed milk, tough and hard. It must be last year's over-wintering cheese, but surely they have soft cheese by now. Easter is past, and what is the new dairymaid for but to make butter and cheese?

Then there is the red wine. She knows Henry favours a wine with some barrel age, but his red Gascony last night was at death's door. Fortunately he did not finish his glass. That crimson-brown sediment was the very stuff of stomach disorder, a sign that too much is being bought, too long stored. The Rhenish that Isabel reluctantly provided – that at least was fresh and clear; a pity it was not served with breakfast instead of this cloudy liquor passing itself off as small ale – even the sun shining through her glass casts only a tired puddle of light on the table. And if all the preserves are like the so-called damson cheese, there is a deal of education needed in the still room arts. And he thinks I can "drop a word" and all will be well. The degree of ignorance is worrying, this household is failing. A house that warrants its own dairymaid, cook, scullion and menservants, and from what Henry has told her, supports a number of tenants on the demesne, has responsibilities towards all of them. They depend on its survival. Even though these are difficult times, a way of reviving High Stoke's fortunes must be found.

Alice sits long at the table, turning over the problem in her mind, unable to form even the bare bones of a workable idea. All she can think is that any solution must save face for Isabel, but

Isabel clearly likes to be top of the tree.

She is gazing out of the window musing on her quandary when Henry passes by on his grey heading across the clearing for the track through the trees. Sam sits up in front pointing to something ahead. Thanks be to God, Sam slept well on his first night here, the excitement of the long journey ensuring a good night's sleep. Even before she had finished telling him a little story as she always does, his eyelids were drooping.

Now, up on the grey, Sam is chattering to Henry in the same way he did with that stranger earlier this morning. And she stood at the chamber window, she realises, in nothing but her hair, no thought crossing her mind that the man might idly look up. Recalling it, she instinctively raises her hands as though to cover bare breasts. The thought causes a low laugh to rise in her throat. Behind her a sharply indrawn breath jolts her back to the present.

'Isabel! I didn't realise you had come in.' The steward stands in the doorway, utterly still, hands clasped in front of her at the end of the long, black V of her arms. Alice bites down on the impulse to ask her how long she has been standing there, why she did not make her presence known. As the self-styled steward proceeds to collect dishes, Alice tries. 'I understand you are a relation of Henry on his mother's side, is that right?'

'He and I are cousins,' Isabel says, as though correcting Alice.

It will need much patience, Alice reminds herself, a delicate touch, give and take on both sides. 'And you have been here several years, he tells me. You must know every nook and cranny of this house.'

'No, indeed,' Isabel says with a little laugh. 'In houses such as High Stoke, it is the maidservants who know the nooks and crannies. The Steward oversees their work.'

'Of course, Isabel.' Alice winces. A *very* delicate touch. 'I mean that you must be familiar with all the workings of the household.'

'In a senior capacity, that is so,' Isabel responds, adding, 'Unlike a farmhouse, I imagine.'

'Unlike the farmhouse where I come from, certainly,' Alice retorts. 'There, I made sure the maids knew where the correct sheets were to be found.'

There is a little silence, while Alice chides herself for irritability. This will not do, if she is to live peaceably with Isabel. Things are going to be hard enough with the way the place has fallen into disrepair, the savings and economies to be made in the months ahead. She starts again.

'This house was built on the wool trade, I understand?'

'This is a gentleman's home,' Isabel corrects her. 'Not a tradesman's.'

Alice laughs. 'Many gentlemen's fathers or grandfathers rose on trade, and all due credit to them,' she says. 'At what point do you think the Jerrards transformed from the one into the other?' Isabel does not respond. 'I have seen quite a few of these lovely houses lose their lustre over my lifetime,' Alice goes on. 'It is a misfortune that our heavy English wool cannot compete with the New Woollens coming from foreign parts. It's a struggle to maintain standards when incomes shrink.'

'We do not scrimp here,' Isabel explains. 'My cousin instructs on the expenditure he requires and I keep full accounts of monetary transactions for his perusal.'

Alice becomes hopeful for the first time in this exchange. 'Really? I should be very interested to see your accounts. I feel sure you will have ideas for economies, ways of controlling waste—'

'It is for my cousin to say if he requires a change in expenditure,' Isabel explains.

'Up till now, yes, I agree. But between you and me we could probably find areas of saving. I too have knowledge of running a household.'

'Not a gentleman's household,' Isabel says.

'Much the same arts are required in farmhouse as in gentleman's house.'

Isabel says, 'I do my duty as stipulated by my cousin. If you have any complaint, he will be the correct person to approach.'

There is another silence while Alice thinks what else to say. Isabel continues to clear the table. She indicates Alice's unfinished small ale. 'Will you be finishing your breakfast?'

'I don't want any more, thank you Isabel.'

Isabel picks up the glass and a thought seems to occur to her. 'I could save that for midday meal, it will reduce waste.'

Alice ignores the gibe. 'Tell me about life here,' she suggests.

'What is it you wish to know of my life?'

Alice feels like an intruder, as she suspects she was meant to. 'Not *your* life expressly, Isabel. What I should like to know is how my household works, and how best you and I may work together.'

'Allow me to explain,' Isabel says with overt patience. 'In a household such as this, it would be the normal practice for you to lodge any enquiry you have with my cousin.'

'We are both here, Isabel,' Alice insists. 'It seems clear to me it is not easy for you to have a mistress in the house when there has been none in all these years. So let us talk, you and I.'

'The difficulty is not mine,' Isabel replies. 'How could it be, when my cousin has never found fault?'

Alice leans forward, looking up at the other woman. 'What if you were to show me the house and outbuildings, so that I can see the accommodations and learn how you arrange things? Shall we do that now?'

Isabel stands as though undecided or unwilling, and for a frozen moment, it seems to Alice that the steward will turn her down flat. Then, 'Which particular room do you wish to see?'

'All of them.'

'Is the hall to be included?'

'No, I've seen the hall. It's the other rooms I should like you to show me.'

'And my cousin's chamber?'

Alice pauses. *The chamber I share with your cousin.* 'Very well, all the rest, then.'

'And the boy's chamber?'

'Isabel, I think you know what I am saying.'

'Indeed, I am not sure I do. You have not yet told me which rooms you wish to inspect.'

Before Alice can refute the word 'inspect', a hesitant tap comes on the door. Isabel's eyes flicker away, she puts down the plates she has gathered and opens the door. 'But of course, girl!' she snaps. 'Have I instructed you to stop tending the fires?'

Alice leans to see who Isabel is addressing. Little shoeless Mollie stands there, hearth brush and shovel in hand. Alice can just see her peering wide-eyed round Isabel. 'Give you good morning, Mollie. Isabel, do we keep a fire all day in the hall?'

'Fires are always lit every morning in the hall and winter parlour.'

'It was a kind gesture to welcome us yesterday, but isn't it a little warm today?'

'My cousin instructs me when he wishes it otherwise.'

Alice sighs. How can any change take place with such a fortress of a woman? Give her time, she tells herself, remembering Henry's words, *she's always something stiff with strangers.*

3

With a weary sigh, Grace lowers her aching arms and sinks down on the stool. She flexes her back and hunches her shoulders. Despite the cool of the dairy, the task of churning is hot and tiring. She has already pushed up her sleeves and kilted her skirt. Now she reaches to unstrap her pattens and then works off her shoes, setting them neatly aside. Pressing her bare soles on the cold stone flags feels as good as if she were dangling her feet in a stream. On the shelf lies her cap, long since discarded though carefully folded. She pushes loose strands of hair from her overheated face, determined to take only a short rest and then try again. Or perhaps all the vigorous pounding is to no purpose. She lifts aside the lid and peers into the depths of the churn. Sometimes when the weather is warm the devil gets into the cream and stops it turning to butter. Grace prays not, she is already in enough trouble with Isabel over those sheets last night without having to tell her that the butter will not come. She sits back. A minute, no more, and then she will try again.

It is quiet in the dairy. This, Grace reflects, is the only thing about this house that she likes. Here, the dairy is separated from the kitchen and all its comings and goings by a length of passage. She closed the door earlier, wanting to be on her own. The opposite door, leading out to the dairy court, is also closed. The thickness of it is enough to deaden most sounds, though the drainage channel in the floor betrays any tread of feet outside. And so it is a quiet place with few disturbances, and today that suits Grace's humours. At her home, the dairy was a tiny space barely larger than a cupboard, where Grace made butter and cheese. In the main room, her bustling mother was forever scraping ladles in iron pots, rasping dry bread to crumbs or pounding some preparation in the heavy wooden mortar. But for all that rattle and clatter, Grace yearns to be back there, wishes she had never come to this cold, unfeeling place where everything she does is viewed with suspicion and contempt by everyone. Well, almost everyone …

Footsteps approach across the dairy court, covert, cautious, halting outside the door. A pause, silence, and her heartbeat quickens in hope. She gazes at the door as though by sheer force of will she might see through it. The lightest of knocks and she rises quickly. God send that Isabel is at the far end of the house and not about to snoop on her dairymaid, because Grace knows that knock. She reaches for the latch and edges open the door. The sight of his brown tangled hair, his thin face, warms her heart. Under the dark lashes his rich brown eyes, wide-set with a straight gaze, seem to look life trustingly in the face and find honest dealing in return. She has seen him frown once or twice, but only when concentrating on fine work with the adze. Never has he frowned at her. And that smile does strange things to her stomach, like turning a cartwheel. Not for the first time, Grace knows a jolt of surprise that she can feel so strongly on such a short acquaintance.

'Allan!' She knows she ought to be modest and cast down her eyes, but she cannot resist looking into his smiling face, cannot keep the beaming joy from her own.

'I brought you these,' he says. He slips past her into the dairy, spare of build, weathered from working out of doors. His hand comes from behind his back, holding out a little bunch of woodland flowers, all cream and blue and wafting scent.

'Oh, how kind!' Overwhelmed, she reaches to accept the tribute. 'How kind,' she says again. His slim brown fingers touch hers briefly as she takes the primroses and sweet violets into her cradling hands. She buries her face in the bunch and inhales luxuriously.

Footsteps approach along the kitchen passage and both jump a guilty distance as the door swings open. Grace grabs for her cap.

'Am I interrupting something?'

'Sylvia!' Grace blows out a breath of relief. 'I thought it was Isabel.' She returns the cap to the shelf. Sylvia looks at Allan and her voice is cold. 'No men in the dairy. You know it taints the cheese.'

'I was just passing,' he mumbles. 'I'll see you at midday meal.' Grace is unsure whether he is speaking to Sylvia or herself. He backs out into the dairy court and the door closes.

'Cap off, eh, Grace?' Sylvia says. 'And showing your legs?' She gives a light laugh and closes the door to the kitchen passage. 'You'll be getting a name for a fast one, you will.'

Grace hurriedly unkilts her skirt, feet fishing for her shoes, her pattens. 'Don't say that, Sylvia.'

'Just as well I came by when I did,' Sylvia says. She picks up Grace's cap, toys with the short, rounded lappets that hug the sides of the face, drops it back. 'You want to watch that one.'

'Allan?' Even to herself, Grace's indifference sounds forced.

Sylvia grins. 'You're blushing! I've touched a soft spot.'

'Not at all!' Grace struggles for disinterest. 'I'm heated with working this churn.'

'Worming his way into your favour.'

'That's what you said yesterday when he brought me the pie.' He found her doing the evening milking after Isabel had dragged her from her supper to do as she was bid and change the sheets. Wordlessly he slipped her a piece of pie hidden in a napkin, smiled and was gone. 'And by the way, Sylvia, that was my supper and you ate it!'

'I was hungry.'

'What about me?'

'I did you a favour,' Sylvia tells her. 'He'll expect something in return for these little gifts.' Leaning against the lime-washed wall of the dairy, Sylvia re-ties the strings at the neck of her shift in a pretty bow. 'Ever a weather eye for a bit of leg or a low-cut bodice, that's Allan.'

'I don't believe it!' Grace answers hotly.

'Nor did Mary, till she found herself with child.' She tweaks the bow, contemplating its symmetry.

'Mary?' Grace is momentarily baffled.

'She who was dairying here before.'

'I know who Mary was! But nobody said she—'

'Haven't you heard? I suppose not, best not to talk about it. That's why she had to leave.'

Grace stares. 'He got her with child? No!'

Sylvia picks up Grace's cap again. 'Oh, if I don't sit down, I'll fall down.' She plumps onto Grace's stool. 'Making beds is so tiring.'

'There's only one, Sylvia.'

'And the little boy's! Anyway, as I was saying, Allan tried it with me. "Ooh, Sylvia!"' she says in a sing-song voice. '"You work so hard. Ooh, Sylvia, come and rest with me in the granary." I was having none of it, but poor Mary had already been caught. Everybody denies it, of course, for Mary's sake.' She laughs and starts to roll the lappets of Grace's cap round her finger.

A flush, not of heat, colours Grace's cheeks. 'He was only giving me these flowers,' she says in a low voice. 'They smell so sweet, he must have taken a lot of trouble to collect them.'

'He'll have done his toadying to Mary the same way.' She reaches to ruffle the petals. 'Just a few sad flowers and he got into her skirts in return.'

'How do you know so much about it?' Grace flashes back. 'You weren't even here.'

'I was, I came in December and Mary left after New Year. As soon as Isabel realised her condition, she turned her off. Ask Isabel.'

Grace knows that, for her, asking Isabel is impossible. 'Why was Allan not turned off as well?'

Sylvia laughs. 'Don't be silly, Grace. Dismiss a craftsman of his skill?'

Grace knows what Sylvia means. In a snatched moment one day Allan told her how he was apprenticed to a cartwright, but his master died suddenly and so Allan, still a novice, is barred from practising his craft. He had to do something to make his living, he told Grace, so he put himself out for general labouring. 'You misjudge him, Sylvia,' Grace says. 'He didn't expect anything in return from me.'

Sylvia looks up from the cap in her hands. 'You didn't see how he jumped back, so guilty, when I came in?'

Grace is silent, recalling how Allan jumped back. But so did she …

'Sorry, Grace,' Sylvia says. 'You need to give that one a wide berth, he's trouble for a nice girl like you.'

'What are you doing with my cap?'

'Rolling the lappets of course, to make them curve round your face. You don't want them hanging down like a bloodhound, do you?'

It is strange, Grace thinks, how she always feels torn with Sylvia. Like now. Sylvia doing the kindness of rolling her cap lappets for her, yet at the same time saying these things about Allan that cannot possibly be true … can they? 'Well, these flowers shan't suffer. I shall get some water for them.'

Sylvia stands, holding up a silencing finger, and backs towards the passageway door. 'Get back to work, Grace, I think I hear Isabel! Give those to me, I'll hide them, put them in water for you.' She tosses Grace's cap back onto the shelf, takes the posy and leans her ear to the door, listening. 'No, all's well, she must have gone the other way. Now, tell me, I came for butter. How much have you done so far?'

'So far?' Grace looks up in dismay, indicating the churn. 'But … this is the first. It's not ready … quite,' she stammers.

'Let's have a look.' Grace opens the churn and Sylvia dips

daintily into its depths, regards the liquid dripping off her finger. 'What have you been doing, Grace?'

'I'm going as fast as I can. It just won't turn.'

'You should be on your second batch easily by now.' From the pocket tied at her waist, Sylvia draws out a tiny scrap of freshly laundered kerchief to wipe her fingers. 'I'd help, but you're the dairymaid.'

'Where were you earlier when Isabel couldn't find you? I had to take wine up to the main chamber. And I had to heat water and scald this churn before I could start; you said you'd do it last night—'

'Well, it's no good me taking excuses to Isabel. Aren't you used to this work? I thought you came experienced in the dairy arts.'

'Of course I am,' Grace defends herself. 'I looked after our two cows at home from a little girl. And on top of that—'

'Well, High Stoke has rather more than two kine, Grace, as you know. You must stir yourself if you're to keep your place here. Oh, and be my own sweet Grace, will you? Now we've got a goose, Isabel says to use some of the fat to—'

'Is it true Joe killed it in the hall?'

Sylvia's laughter strikes brightly off the walls of the dairy. 'He said it looked so funny kicking about with no head!'

Grace winces. 'Poor thing. He didn't have to kill it.'

'Well, it's dead,' Sylvia says with finality. 'And Isabel says take the fat and grease the hinges to the master's chamber.'

'Can't you do that, Sylvia?'

Sylvia gives a shudder. 'It's the slick feel of it on my fingers I so hate. And anyway, you can do it when you strew the floors upstairs this afternoon. If you'd done that yesterday, I wouldn't be asking you to do the hinges now.'

'But none of us knew they were coming so early, not even Isabel. Allan thought he was going to have to wait hours for them at Farnham and they rode in just minutes after he got there.'

Sylvia pulls a face. 'You have to find ways to do things, Grace. You cannot sit around thinking what a surprise it all is.' She looks at Grace's crestfallen face, and continues as though chastened, 'Listen, you do the hinges and I'll find a story to weave to Isabel about the butter, trust me.'

'Very well, Sylvia. It should be on the turn soon, I've been at it long enough.' Grace bends with renewed vigour to the churn.

'That's right. You keep at it, Grace. Er ... don't bring it out to Isabel. I'll come and get it when the time's right.'

Grace nods, concentrating on the churn.

'Oh! I forgot,' Sylvia says. 'I came to bring you a message.'

'Not another task from Isabel?'

'From your father. Isabel said I may tell you now.'

'My father? Is he here then?' Grace's face brightens as she looks up. 'Where is he?'

'No, he sent a message by the carter. Your mother is not well, he says. He wants you to go home but Isabel says—'

'Mother? What's wrong with her?'

Sylvia shrugs. 'How would I know? He says she is confined to her bed. What's the matter?' she asks as Grace's hand goes to her mouth.

'My mother confined to her bed? She is never confined to her bed, Sylvia. If my father wants me at home, I must go immediately.'

'Well you can't, you've got the cows to milk.'

'But you could do them for a few days, couldn't you?'

'In truth, Grace, you only ever think of yourself! How many times do I have to tell you my hands are not strong like yours?' She holds up slim white fingers. 'Squeezing those teats. Ugh!'

'You did them after Mary left, before I came.'

'Oh, you silly!' Sylvia laughs. 'You know I'm not at my best in the mornings. When I think how early I had to get up every day to get Mollie awake and milking. Imagine how hard that was for me.'

Grace does not stop to imagine. 'You say the carter brought

my father's message?'

'That's right.'

'But the carter comes on Wednesday, I saw him. That's three days ago!'

'Don't blame me, Grace! You're lucky to have it at all. Isabel said she was relenting as a special favour because the master has come home.'

Grace frowns at Sylvia. 'She kept it quiet all this time? How dare she?' A militant red smoulders on each cheek. 'I must leave immediately. Where is she?' Grace crams her cap on her head and is out of the door, hastening along the passage. She leans into the kitchen, sees the cook. 'Maureen? Do you know where Isabel is?'

'I dare say she'll be checking Mollie has cleaned the hearths properly,' the cook replies, looking up from her pots. 'But if I were you I wouldn't—'

Grace does not stop to hear what Maureen would not do. She scurries up the screens passage, her pattens clicking on the stone. At the door of the hall she sketches a quick curtsey to the steward at the other end by the fire, and blurts out her request. 'Isabel, I am sorry to disturb you, but I must go home. My mother—' She stops, seeing the look the steward is turning on her. 'I'm sorry—'

'What are you doing in this part of the house?' the steward thunders, starch-stiff, eyes flashing, and Grace realises that once again she has transgressed. 'Are you quite determined to be dismissed your place here?' Isabel bears down on Grace, turning her bodily round and prodding her out of the hall.

'I ... no, I'm sorry Isabel,' Grace stammers. 'But you have only now permitted Sylvia to give me the message. You see, my mother is poorly and—'

'Why is your cap in that ill-conditioned state?'

'My cap?' Grace's hand flies to her head. She feels the lappets sticking out like jug ears.

'Do you think to ridicule this household by wearing a cap in that state?'

Grace groans inwardly. Sylvia cannot have been thinking, she has rolled the lappets the wrong way. 'I'm sorry,' she hears herself saying again. 'But, Isabel—?' Retreating down the screens passage in the face of the steward's fury, she ploughs on. 'My father begs my return. And this is so worrying about my mother; she is always well—'

'So now you make up another excuse to malinger? Yesterday you went out of your way to shame me by using the wrong sheets, today you try this cock and bull pretence over a little cold. Get back to your work and be grateful I do not dismiss you out of hand!'

'I promise you, Isabel,' Grace is becoming desperate. By now they are outside the kitchen. 'Father will have seen the carter on Tuesday last, and you have only allowed me to have the message today. I have come to you straight away—'

Isabel stands implacable. 'Your trouble, miss, is that you do not like to be discovered in your slovenliness. You've been here five minutes and think to trick me into indulging you with a holiday. You have gall indeed.'

'Please, Isabel!' Grace fights back tears. 'I promise you, this is no holiday!'

Isabel is unmoved. 'You have admitted it yourself. Your mother is always well. Now get back to the dairy and stop whining. You may send word to your father by the carter on Wednesday.'

'Isabel, please!'

The kitchen door bangs shut behind the steward. Grace stands staring at the wood in disbelief. She turns this way and that, pleats and unpleats her apron, bites her lip. 'I don't know what to do,' she whispers to the dimness of the dairy passage. 'I don't know what to do.'

4

Alice endures Isabel's introduction to High Stoke, discovering in herself undreamed-of reserves of forbearance. In each room, Isabel stands at the door, hands clasped at the end of the straight V of her black-clad arms, a gesture Alice is already coming to know. In wooden tones the steward makes each announcement. 'This is the kitchen,' she says and adds, pointing to one of the doors off it, 'That is the still room. A still room,' she proceeds to explain, 'is where the various preserves and waters—'

'Yes, thank you Isabel, I know what a still room is,' Alice says.

'This is Maureen. She is the cook.' Isabel is martyring herself to Alice's wish to walk the house with her, to meet the women and men who work under the steward's rule. By the time they are halfway through, Alice is heartily wishing she had simply made her own way into the nooks and crannies Isabel so disdains. With the steward at her side, it is as though the entire body of servants has been warned against verbal communication with the intruder parading as the new mistress. What information she receives, scant at best, is provided by Isabel. Not one of them ventures a word in response to Alice's interested questions, though the language of silence is in itself a revelation.

The cook, Maureen, sketches a meagre curtsey and avoids Alice's eye. Little shoeless Mollie makes several curtseys, alternately casting uncertain smiles at Alice and terrified glances at Isabel. Meeting Grace in the dairy, Alice is careful not to refer to their shared making of the bed yesterday, and Grace stands silent and subdued while Isabel answers for her. And so it goes on. In the woodshed is Allan, who drove their coach yesterday. He was talkative enough during breaks in their journey, and happy to bear with Sam's innumerable questions about the horses. Today Allan stands in silence next to an older man called Angus. Both shuffle their feet and look at each other or the ground. In the stables Alice recognises the young man called Joe who despatched the goose. He studies her from under his dark brows, chin jutting under a mouth tight shut. Others they meet all have those same morose eyes, the same reticence.

Some rooms, some of the buildings, have no one in them; granary, barn, cow byre, buttery, storerooms. Isabel is meticulous about showing every single one, including the necessary-house on the kitchen court. She opens the door, announces, it is viewed and they pass on. Alice would willingly call a halt, but this she will not do, convinced that it is exactly what Isabel wishes.

They arrive at the last outbuilding before returning to the kitchen. Alice braces herself once more. The long, low structure is built out from the house and divides the kitchen court from the dairy court. Faint smoke drifts from its little chimney and the door stands wide, thick vapours of starch afloat on the air. Within, the glow of embers shows a fire dying down, but a large three-legged cauldron stands amongst the ashes, wisps of steam rising ragged from under its wooden lid. Barely halting, Isabel indicates, 'Wash-house. That's the washerwoman.'

Standing at one of the sinks, rinsing a shirt or shift, is a short woman of massive girth, with sturdy arms and reddened hands. She looks up as Alice pauses in the doorway and beams a gappy smile. Beneath a rosy bulbous chin swells another rosy bulbous chin, the flush of perspiration spreading down the folds of her short neck.

Three paces away, the steward's foot taps as she waits for Alice to follow. But Alice is intrigued by the first sign of welcome she has had this morning. The woman's amply cut linen shift covers well-rounded shoulders and an abundance of bosom behind the straining bodice. A thick square of linen apron that would encircle Alice's waist twice, barely covers the front of her grey skirts, and she sways from side to side as she approaches, grasping a handful of apron to dry her reddened hands.

'God bless you, dear, I'm Betsy. Let's have a look at you.' She takes Alice's hands, giving her a frank look from head to toe. 'That's a pretty cap you're wearing. Is that a Dorset style, then?' Covering her own head is a square of cloth wrapped the old-fashioned way over her hair and pinned to a wide linen fillet tied round her forehead. She goes on, 'I didn't think you'd be so young. He could give you several years, I dare say.'

'He is a little older, it's true, Betsy. But we're close in other ways, which is all I care about.' She senses the air behind her bristling with black-clad disapproval.

'And quite right, too,' Betsy comments as she tucks away wisps of greying hair with a work-worn hand. 'How long have you known him?'

'Barely a month,' Isabel breaks into the exchange.

'I first met him in late autumn last year,' Alice says, and feels rather than sees Isabel's start of surprise. 'My father met him—'

'My cousin was in Devon in late autumn,' Isabel corrects her.

Alice turns to her. 'And he called on his way west, hoping to renew his acquaintance with my father.' Isabel looks blackly but says nothing. Alice turns back to Betsy. 'My father and he met by chance last spring in London, along with two other neighbours from round here. There was a Master Tillotson, I remember that name—'

'Oh, yes. Master Frederick Tillotson.' The laundress' voice warms as she adds, 'Everyone liked old Master Frederick.' She returns to the sink, still talking, her skirt swaying to her walk. 'We miss him. Poor man, he died at Hallowmas, you know.'

Alice did not know. 'I'm sorry for it,' she says, following Betsy. 'I was hoping to meet someone else who knew my father. He too died last Autumn, my mother as well.'

'You poor child.' Betsy stretches out a hand to briefly touch

Alice's cheek. 'Well, for what we're worth, you must needs take us for family now, dear.'

'I hope so indeed.' Strange how a small gesture of sympathy can so easily bring the tears to her eyes. She is reminded of Henry back in the winter, a casual question that had the same effect, asking who looked after "orphan Alice".

'You'd have liked Master Frederick,' Betsy is saying. 'A stern man when roused, but always fair he was, people went to him to solve their disputes. Quite sudden, him going like that.'

'My parents were taken very suddenly also,' Alice says. 'By plague. Was it the same for Master Tillotson? I know the plague was in London last Summer.'

'No, it didn't touch us,' Betsy says. 'He died a natural death in his bed. Coroner tried to make something out of it, forever going back to poke around. But poor Master Frederick, he'd had one or two seizures before, and then this one carried him off.' Betsy draws a delicate chemise from the water and plunges it back in. 'It was still a surprise when it came. Especially for young Master Jeremy, that's his son. He'd never have stayed up north the past couple of years if he'd guessed his father was ailing. Took him weeks to get back home. You never think, do you?'

'Why did the coroner keep going back, then?' Alice asks.

Betsy chuckles. 'Coroner lives on the Long Down road at Poyle, just a step away from Tillotsons. Rumour has it he coveted his neighbour's chattels!'

Behind Alice, Isabel intervenes. 'Sir Malcolm Wipley is a great benefactor of the poor – such a man does not cast covetous eyes at his neighbour's goods!'

'If you say so, Isabel.' Betsy shows no sign of being impressed as she raises and plunges the chemise.

'He subscribed to His Grace's new hospital at the top of the town, I would remind you.'

'And didn't we all hear about it,' Betsy mutters. In a louder voice, she adds, 'It seems to me he's fond of turning up at all times of the day and night looking for plots and devices that aren't there.'

'Sir Malcolm is diligent and thorough or he would not make such a superior coroner,' Isabel retorts.

'He had to admit in the end that the Lord had gathered Master Tillotson without a helping hand, I believe?' Isabel does not answer. Betsy wrings out the chemise and drops it into the basket at her feet.

Alice breaks the silence. 'And there was another of that London party last spring,' she says. 'His name escapes me.'

'That's right, dear, young Master Jack. Egerton, that is. I nursed him from a babe. Lives over by Merrow.' Betsy points out past the woodshed. 'His land runs alongside ours for a space.'

Betsy's easy use of the word "ours" pleases Alice. Here is a woman who knows she belongs. 'They were all in London for the great event,' Alice says, 'though I suspect,' picking her next words carefully, 'that there were those who were not as sorrowful about it as some.'

'I remember it well,' Betsy says. 'Master Jack declared it was a shameful waste of money.'

'It was King James's funeral!' Isabel bursts out.

'So what?' Betsy continues her rinsing without looking up. 'The Lord won't think better of him for spending good money on a pompous burying.'

While Alice privately revels in Betsy's plain speaking, the laundress continues, 'The Egertons sent over a ham this morning. Did Isabel serve it for breakfast or has she squirreled it away somewhere?'

The steward chokes. 'I do not—'

'Oh, go to, go to, Isabel, it was a jest.'

'We had some for breakfast,' Alice cuts in quickly. So that was the Egertons' man she saw talking with Sam. 'And very good it is. I should like to send a note of thanks this afternoon, Isabel. Perhaps

Mollie could take it.'

'Sadly, not this afternoon,' Isabel says.

'Why is that?'

'She is busy. There are things for her to do.'

'Very well, when can she go?'

'Nonsense, Isabel!' Betsy says. 'You know well that the master says Mollie's to be free on Saturday afternoons.' She addresses Alice. 'It's because she spends Sunday morning preparing midday dinner while we're all at church. Mollie will love to take a note for you, she likes it at Freemans, that's the Egertons' place.'

Surely an ally.

'And that reminds me,' Betsy says to Alice. 'I wanted to ask you, dear. Young Master Tillotson, Jeremy that is, Master Frederick's son. He's running the land now. I saw him in town the other day. He's been turning out the house as both his parents are gone. Found a lot of things he can't use, old clothes and the like, hoarded for decades—'

Isabel interrupts the flow. 'My cousin has no use for throw-outs from the Tillotsons. I told you that last week.'

'I know you did Isabel, when the master was not even here to decide. So now I'm asking the *mistress.*' Betsy turns to address Alice. 'There are things dating back to his parents' grandparents at least, when they used to be the wealthiest family around here. They're made of decent cloths but very worn. He wants me to find good use for them. They'll be a godsend for some of the needy folk around here.'

'Is he quite sure he wants to give such things away, Betsy?' Alice asks.

'Oh, yes. They're very old, he says, of a sort nobody wears now, trunk hose and gable hoods enough to laugh yourself into stitches. But there's good cloth in amongst it all, and plenty of old linen that can be pieced and re-fashioned. He asked me to find homes for them. I've said to him to send the cart next week unless he hears otherwise. Will you be content for me to sort them out here?'

'Very content.' Alice turns to the steward. 'Isabel, I think that as long as this does not interfere with Betsy's work here it will be well for her to sort them and share them out. And it need not disturb my husband, we will make sure the things are not in his way.' Alice is reminded of her home village in Dorset where even the most restrained poor will fight for a discarded pair of breeches or a worn-out shift. A whole collection of clothes will be like manna from Heaven. 'It's a handsome gift Master Tillotson is making.' She is still addressing Isabel but it is Betsy who responds.

'It's the sort of thoughtfulness I'd expect from Jeremy Tillotson. Poor enough he is himself, but he knows it's much worse for smaller folk. It was a hard winter, and last year's harvest didn't help.'

'You know the deserving poor in these parts, Betsy?'

'Oh, yes, and I also know who's too idle to do more than hold out a begging hand.'

Betsy's lack of reverence for the conventions, her unconcealed sidestepping of Isabel's authority, her familiar references to their neighbours, bear all the signs of a servant who has become answerable only to the master. In that last way, she's like Isabel, Alice thinks, and yet Betsy endears herself, where Isabel alienates. Give her time, she reminds herself, she's always something stiff with strangers. 'And you will have time to do this as well as your own work, Betsy?'

'I'm in and out of here, mistress, but surely I'll sort them when I'm around. I'll know who needs what when I see the things.'

'When you're around?' Alice queries.

'I do for Mistress Egerton as well,' Betsy explains. 'So I go over there, and sometimes I do for Master Renwick down the road too, and others when I can.'

'I gave her leave to do so,' Isabel affirms from the doorway.

Betsy is undaunted. 'No you didn't, Isabel, I asked the master, and he only told you later when you complained that – ooh!' Betsy suddenly stands on one leg and kicks off her wooden patten. 'Ooh! Cramp.' She screws up her face and flexes her leg. 'Ooh!' The lines on her face deepen into grimace as she leans forward trying to reach her foot. 'I tell you, I'm getting too old for this.'

Alice takes Betsy's arm. 'Come, sit down, Betsy.' She turns the laundress round to sit on the edge of the sink. 'It's tiring work, standing all day.' Alice stands before Betsy. The foot, the ankle, are blue with cold.

'Oh, don't you fret, mistress,' Betsy says, wincing. 'You don't have to fuss over the likes of me.' She leans forward trying to take hold of her toes, to pull back against the spasm, but she cannot reach.

'May I?' Alice reaches for the foot. Surprised, Betsy only stares as her new mistress takes the twisted toes, holding them against her skirt. Alice pummels vigorously with her warm hands. 'You need stockings, Betsy,' Alice tells her. 'That would help keep your legs warm.'

'I did have some once,' Betsy says, 'but they went to holes.' She adds with a laugh, 'Got old, like me. There, it's easing already.'

'Who helps you here, Betsy?'

Her voice colourless, Betsy says, 'Sylvia used to come in.'

'Sylvia? I've yet to meet—'

'Sylvia has ever been a willing worker,' Isabel cuts in. Caught unawares by the commendation, Alice starts and turns. The steward's pin-point eyes target Betsy. 'But the poor girl is affected by the gross vapours of the starch, as you well know.'

Alice nearly misses Betsy's muttered, 'And the great big cows, and the dirty dust …' while Isabel continues, 'Sylvia has modest manners, and' – with raised emphasis – 'due deference to her seniors.' Betsy rolls her eyes.

Outside, Alice allows her curiosity to get the better of her. 'You find Sylvia amenable, Isabel?'

'There are few maidservants of good character and honest industry in these days,' Isabel answers. 'Betsy may sneer but Sylvia is forever here and there doing whatever she can. You should see her struggling with the weight of the milk pails.'

'A paragon indeed,' is the best Alice feels she can say. 'How long has she been here?'

'She used to work for Master Tillotson,' Isabel says, and adds, 'Master Frederick Tillotson, that is.'

'The man who died?'

'After his death that shiftless son of his came home and swore he had no money to pay the servants. At the time I was about to turn off an unsatisfactory girl, so I summoned Sylvia and very quickly approved her. She has been a fortunate choice for High Stoke.'

And now Alice is more than curious to know this maidservant who engenders such opposing reports, who has convinced Isabel of her high worth, but failed miserably to impress Betsy.

5

Joe delves into his pocket to retrieve a dog-eared sheet of paper. Carefully he smoothes out the letter and in the half-light of the stables regards his handiwork. It is several years since he sat bleakly unwilling in Guildford's Free School arduously shaping his letters and repeatedly beaten for his trouble. Angry and disheartened he took to truanting until they gave up expecting him to attend. None of the other boys saw writing as worth doing, Joe remembers, except the ones with stick legs and no chins, the ones who always ran away when Joe and his friends confronted them. He could do with one of those chinless boys now, he thinks wryly, looking at his work. But although the lines slope away, it is a letter, and far better than a prepared speech. The last time he approached Sylvia his mouth suddenly went dry, and instead of his thought-out lines he blurted a lot of rambling nonsense. She told him to go away until he was grown up, and later he saw Maureen pausing in her cooking as Sylvia whispered, and the two of them burst out laughing.

Well, he is grown up now. *Melt her heart with missives and storm your prize with kisses.* He got that from Nol Simpson, one of the regulars in the Red Lion, in return for buying the man a drink. Well, three or four drinks, but so what? This is the way to do it, Nol says, and he should know, he is forever talking about his successes with women.

Joe's eyes follow his slowly guiding finger as he checks one last time, mouthing the words he has so arduously penned. Pleased with his toil, he tenderly refolds the sheet and slips it back in his pocket. Sylvia, his shining Sylvia. He saw her glide past, skirt swaying, as the master and mistress left for their ride. She was heading for the drying bushes behind the stables, which is just what he needs, it is secluded there. His own Sylvia. He hops about in a little dance of glee. Well, she is not quite his own yet, but she soon will be. He checks both ways, slips out of the stables and makes his furtive way round to the back where clothes for drying are spread out on clumps of bushes. And there she is, gracefully leaning forward to feel whether three daintily worked kerchiefs are yet dry.

'Look.' Proudly Joe holds out his letter, but Sylvia does not turn immediately. He is obliged to wait, hand outstretched, while Sylvia finishes re-arranging the damp wisps of linen on the bush, ensuring that no parts are caught on twigs. Finally she turns.

'I wrote this – for you.' He gestures to her to take it.

She regards first his face, then the dog-eared and finger-marked sheet in his hands. Her eyebrows twitch but with a shrug she takes it, unfolds and looks. A hand goes up to conceal her mouth.

'I knew you'd like a courtly letter, like a real lady,' Joe says, anxiously hopeful. She carries on reading until to his astonishment, instead of commending his manly feelings she turns furious eyes on him. 'Is this your idea of a jest?'

'Jest? What's wrong, Sylvia?'

'What's wrong? "My best delight is having you",' she reads, pointing at a line. 'What do you mean, *having?*'

He looks. 'No, I – that's not what—'

'And this? "Feeling you every day". How dare you?'

And he took so much care. 'No, Sylvia, please.' He points. 'That's *My best delite is loving you. Loving,* not *having.*'

'This word here, then?' she demands.

'That's *seeing you every day.*' He feels ridiculous, explaining the words.

She gives a short laugh. 'Seeing? Then in that case, well done, Joe, very prettily written.' She crumples it in her palm. 'Was there something else?'

'I spent a long time getting it right,' he continues, gazing at her. 'A labour of love, you might say.'

'Laboured, certainly.'

He finds himself giving a tense laugh. 'Well, yes, I laboured indeed.' The man in the Red Lion warned Joe he might have to bear scorn. Beautiful women are always scornful towards their lovers, he said; it means they feel their defences weakening. Joe sends up a small prayer that she will not keep him waiting long, he is keen to get to the part where he storms his prize with kisses.

'I offer you my heart, Sylvia.'

She stares. 'Your heart?' It almost sounds like she is laughing.

'You're the only woman in all of Christendom for me. Will you marry me, Sylvia?'

She halts, she seems to be thinking. He is encouraged that she smoothes out his letter and reads it through a second time. An idea seems to come to her. She gives a small, secret smile. Surely she is about to say ...

'No.'

'No?'

'No. I told you when you asked before, I'd let you know. Have I let you know?' She pushes the paper into the pocket tied at her waist and goes back to arranging the kerchiefs.

'Then if you do not wish to, I'll take back my letter.'

She turns, eyebrows raised. 'You want it back?' She has that nearly-smile on her face. He isn't sure it's friendly; he isn't sure what it is, but he certainly does not want Sylvia reading that letter to Maureen. He takes a deep breath and extends his hand.

'If ... if you're not going to marry me, yes, I want it back.'

She is silent, considering him. After a pause, she says, 'All right. I'll marry you. How's that?'

He's done it! It's true, her defences were weakening all the time! 'I really love you, Sylvia!' he blurts. 'And I didn't mean to harass you, and it was only because I want you so much that I—'

'All right! I've said yes,' she snaps. 'And keep your voice down!'

'You mean it? You really want to marry me? Oh, Sylvia!' He

springs towards her, arms spread wide, but already she is turning from him.

'Not yet, though. Now, I must be getting on.' She reaches to pat his shoulder and walks away to another bush.

'So ... when, then?' Joe asks, following her. Two chemises share the bush, a fresh white one and a smaller, much patched and yellowed one. Mollie's, he guesses, contemptuous. Mollie's are not pretty like Sylvia's.

'When what?' Sylvia asks.

Joe indicates the pocket at Sylvia's waist where a crumpled corner of the letter sticks out. 'When shall we be married?'

'Oh, not for a while,' she says. She pushes the little yellowed chemise aside and its sleeve catches on a twig, the other sleeve drops in the mire. Sylvia proceeds to re-lay the white one to her satisfaction.

'When, then?' he repeats.

'Not for the time being.' Gently she slides her hand underneath and teases the fabric to lie flat. 'I'll tell you when.'

'Oh!' He claps his hands together in excess of ecstasy. 'Just wait till I tell Allan and Angus and—'

'Shhh!' Sylvia swings round. 'You tell nobody, do you hear me, Joe? Nobody at all!'

'But Sylvia, we are betrothed. Of course I'm going to tell them.'

'Not till I say!'

He knows he is scowling at her but how can he help it? Now that they are betrothed she has to start obeying him. He is expected to lead, he can't let a woman tell him what to do. But just as he resolves to overrule her, her voice softens. 'Joe, dear Joe, let us keep this wonderful secret between us for now.' She comes up to him and stands there, inches away. 'It will mean so much to me.'

He catches a delicious waft of her shining hair. Well, he thinks, I mustn't be too hasty. She is like a finely bred mare, she must be broken in gently. I will not overrule her just yet.

'Don't you think,' she continues, 'it would be such a precious thing to look back on when we are married?'

When we are married. To hear that from her lips. When that time comes, everything will be resolved, Sylvia will bow to his command and every man will be envious of him. *When?* How long will he have to wait? Rebellion tugs at his heart. 'But, Sylvia …'

'Joe, think what pleasure to exchange secret glances when we meet by chance, when the sermon goes on and on tomorrow, across the table at meals, knowing they are all ignorant? Promise me, Joe.' He feels the caress in her tones as though she is stroking his face. There will be plenty of time later to show her who rules the roost. This close, all he wants to think about is the fragrance of her, that and the tiny blue vein pulsing just above the ruffled neckline.

'You must be very careful,' she murmurs. 'Promise me you will tell nobody until I say.'

Oh God, through the fabric he can see down between—

She draws the letter out of her pocket. Open-mouthed he meets her look as she puts it to her lips, watches her loosen the ties of her chemise, exposing the rise of bosom above the bodice. From unknown chasms within him a blood-driven instinct surges, dark, untried. He lets her grasp his hand, clamp the letter in his stiff fingers, lets her thrust his fingers down between the twin swells of bosom, now up a little, now down, up, down, each time a little deeper, watches the paper and then his fingers disappear. She holds him willing captive in the warm abyss. 'Now let go.' He surrenders the letter. 'Promise me, Joe.' He tries to twist his fingers round to feel the soft warmth of her breast, but winces as her nails dig in. 'Promise me.'

THEY arrive back at the stables together, panting and exhilarated from the gallop down the long slope off the downs, pursued by a chill breeze out of a purple sky. By the time Henry reaches

Alice's side she has already slid off Cassie's back and he has only to hand the reins of both horses to Joe, standing straight and tall and grinning. Before she suffers Joe to lead Cassie away, Alice makes a fuss of the leggy little mare, her friend of many years. Then hand in hand, Alice matching her run to Henry's stride, they cross the courtyard and pass through the kitchen and the hall to the stone stairs where Mollie found sanctuary from the goose yesterday. At the top Alice halts momentarily to glance out of the end window where looming cloud has obliterated the sun, and they both approach the glass to watch the gathering squall. In a strange confluence of the senses, Alice imagines the storm brings with it the scent of rosemary, she can see the bushes in the herb garden below, and smell it on the air. For a moment they stand watching the green-sprouting trees bend in gusty waves.

'Mistress?' A soft voice draws Alice's head round. Without the sun the passage is dim, but halfway along, at the top of a little spiral staircase that rises from the dairy passage, a figure steps forward. Around the edges of the white linen cap, luscious curls peep, a dainty bow sits at the neck of the chemise under the tight-laced bodice, and linen skirts swing just clear of the ground. The figure takes a step forward as Henry turns. 'Sylvia? Is that you? What do you want?'

So this is Sylvia.

Hands clasped at her bosom, Sylvia answers, 'Forgive my trespass.'

'Come on, then, Sylvia,' Henry says. 'Say your piece.'

'Is it permitted to speak with the mistress?' Sylvia casts down her eyes, waiting.

'Yes, of course,' Alice says, feeling a vague desire for brisk practicality. Behind her, she hears the rain fling its first long slashes down the glass. 'Come here by the window, Sylvia. We didn't meet earlier when Isabel was showing me the house.' Sylvia approaches, a graceful figure, seeming not so much to walk as to glide. As she comes forward, Alice realises that the scent of rosemary rises not from the garden but from the floor. 'How pleasing,' she says. 'Someone has strewn rosemary along with the fresh rushes.'

'I hoped you would like it,' Sylvia says. 'And the chamber door hinges have been greased to silence the squeak.'

'Thank you, Sylvia, that was thoughtful,' Alice says. She turns back to the window. 'Look at that rain. We were lucky to escape it.' This girl, she thinks, is blessed with such perfection of line and shadow in every respect, from the delicately flushed cheeks to the graceful curve of the neck and the fine proportions of her form. What irony – had Sylvia been gently born, her beauty would long since have prompted fervent offers from many a son of illustrious blood. Even as a maidservant, she cannot be short of admirers who could raise her station. That is, as long as they don't notice that under the modestly downcast lids, the eyes slide sideways. Alice's observation is not untinged with irritation as she watches Sylvia watch Henry move away into the chamber. When the door has closed, 'So, Sylvia, what is it you'd like to say to me?'

''Tis for Grace I speak, mistress.'

'For Grace?'

'She has had a message from home, mistress. Her mother is ill. She is needed at home to nurse her.'

'Then for sure she must go,' Alice replies. 'Why does she not say? Is she chary of asking?'

'She asked Isabel, but Isabel will not permit it. She has to ask Isabel, you see, as house steward.'

'I perfectly see that, Sylvia. Where is the problem?' Was it only that predatory glance at Henry, Alice wonders, or something more, that puts me on my guard with Sylvia?

'Isabel told me to give Grace the message today, but it came by the carter on Wednesday. He comes on Wednesdays.'

'I don't understand. A message came on Wednesday but Grace only had it today?'

'Isabel held it back because of Grace's poor work, but now Grace is distracted because of the delay. Isabel is adamant, and Grace is desperate.' Sylvia raises moist eyes to Alice, who instantly chides herself for uncharitable thoughts. 'I shall be happy to stand in for Grace in addition to my other duties,' Sylvia adds.

Here is a clear attempt to help a fellow maidservant; what possible advantage can that be to Sylvia? Alice reasons. She is well aware of the extra workload in a dairymaid's absence. 'Very well, Sylvia, thank you for telling me. I shall take the matter up and we shall see what can be done for Grace.'

IT is dim in the dairy, not only from the clouded sky, but also from the mesh shutter drawn across the window to exclude flies. Alice feels her heart contract at the lines of hurt on Grace's tear-streaked face. Memories of her own mother's last illness rise in Alice's mind, threatening to overwhelm her. Then the rain blowing a great gust against the window pulls her back to the present.

'Sylvia tells me you need to go home to nurse your mother, is that right?'

Grace nods, choking back tears as she draws the skimming ladle time and again across the milk. 'She's ill.'

'How many days do you need, do you know?'

'I don't know,' Grace sobs. Eyes down, she skims and skims. 'Father sent word last Tuesday; he would be expecting me to return with the carter on Wednesday afternoon, Thursday at the latest, and now it's Saturday and I do not even know what ails Mother; and we cannot afford the apothecary. She's never sickly. I fear … I fear …' Grace's voice breaks apart, she cries heartily.

There is only so much cream in any bowl of milk and Grace has already skimmed it blue. Gently Alice takes the ladle, lays it aside and possesses herself of Grace's hands. 'Grace, listen to me a moment. I shall speak with Isabel and arrange it for you. In a case like this, I feel sure she will understand.'

Grace shakes her head and sobs a series of misery-laden phrases. 'Isabel says I am slovenly ... that I am trying to get a holiday ... and I took the wrong sheets on purpose ... and I disarranged my cap but I didn't ... and I was slow with the butter and—'

'Grace,' Alice says, understanding less than half of this confused narrative. 'It matters not what errors there have been. You shall go home this afternoon. Can you ride?'

Grace nods, drawing shuddering breaths.

'This shower won't last. Take Cassie, my horse. I can spare her for a few days. Cassie's had a short run so she won't be frisky, and she can take you straight home today. Can you graze her with the kine you told me about?'

Grace nods. 'She can go in with them, and there's a small byre.'

'Then it's settled. You shall see your mother before nightfall. How does that sound?'

Grace's head comes up; wondering eyes above a wavering smile betray the struggle between doubt and hope.

A soft knock on the door from the dairy court, and both women turn to look as the latch lifts and a draggled, tousled head peers cautiously in. His hair hangs dripping over his forehead, flattened on neck and shoulder. The jerkin on which it rests is shiny wet and he blinks the rain from his eyes. Grace immediately turns her back and grabs the ladle.

'Allan!' Alice says, 'Give you good day. Are you looking for someone?'

Allan immediately starts to back out. 'No, mistress. Only came to see ... if Grace needs anything. I was just passing, and I thought ... If there's anything you need, Grace ...?' The words limp to a halt. Grace, busying herself with bowls to no effect whatsoever, gives a strangled sound and shakes her head.

'I believe Grace has all she needs now, thank you, Allan.' He nods but still hovers, glancing at Grace who resolutely keeps her back turned. Finally, meeting Alice's enquiring look, he withdraws. So, Alice thinks, there is one at least who does not share Isabel's opinion of her dairymaid. Quite the opposite, in fact. And Grace must needs try a lot harder before she convinces me that she is unaffected by his visit. And Alice has another thought. While Allan was talking, her attention was drawn to Grace's skirt where a small sprig of rosemary clings. She stores away the revelation of Sylvia accepting thanks for what Grace has done.

With the retreat of Allan, Grace turns to Alice once again with a more collected face. 'Did you mean it, about going home?'

'Of course,' Alice assures her, 'or I should not have said it. And you must tell your father to send for the apothecary and I shall settle his fee.'

Grace gasps. 'I could not accept that, mistress.'

'I think for your mother's sake you can, Grace. I shall write you a note to give him by way of surety. No, better still, if I give you a shilling, you'll find that will more than cover his fee. Now, if you need to stay beyond Tuesday, send me a message by the carter; will you do that?'

Grace wipes fingers across her cheeks now glowing with hope and takes a deep breath. 'Yes, mistress, oh, thank you, mistress. It is such a relief to be believed!'

'As soon as I have talked with Isabel, I shall tell Joe to saddle up for you, then you may leave as soon as you like. Sylvia can take over here, and Isabel will perfectly understand the situation.'

But later, Alice has to admit that was not quite true, for perfect understanding does not figure in the steward's response. Isabel's tight lips and averted glance convey their own impression of less than enthusiasm. 'The girl chose to wait her moment, thinking to catch me unawares, but I am not easily cozened. You don't know these girls, they can be crafty.'

'I understand she is new,' Alice says. 'How long has she been here?'

'She came soon after my cousin ... went away.'

Alice bites back the words that rise, *to get married to me, and you cannot bring yourself to say it.* She says, 'Not very long to attain the standards you set here, Isabel.'

'She has shown neither promise nor willingness in all that time. You weren't here yesterday when she—'

Before Isabel can launch into a litany of Grace's perceived faults, Alice interjects, 'I too have found that not all servants fit easily into new surroundings. I believe there is no question as to the truth of the statement that her mother is ill?'

'Except for the lapse of time since the message was sent.'

'Yes, and I understand Grace received the news only today. I think that in her shoes, I should be frenzied with concern. Grace's family feelings are much to her credit, do you not think?'

Albeit unwilling, Isabel concedes, 'It shows some feeling, I grant. Though the woman is probably better by now.'

'So that it would not be impossible to allow her a few days to go and relieve her mind of the worry?'

'I don't see how—'

'In order that she may return in more sanguine humour and apply herself to her work here. Surely that's plain, Isabel?' And Alice adds, 'I do not wish her distraction to be a burden on yourself or the rest of the household, Isabel, when it can so easily be remedied.'

'That leaves no one to do the milking. Are the kine to be left to suffer?'

'Sylvia will do the milking.'

'It is not Sylvia's task to do the dairying.'

'Sylvia has offered and I have accepted.'

The steward eyes her with disfavour. 'If my cousin wishes it,' she says.

'*I* wish it, Isabel. And there's an end to it.'

6

The newly emerged sun is burning the rain off the tiled stable roof in wisps of vapour. Grace paces in and out, watching Joe take as long as he can to saddle up the mare. She would rather do it herself, it is clear he is only doing it because the mistress said. He'd saddle up eagerly enough for Sylvia, she thinks; Joe's eyes shout his worship whenever they light on Sylvia. At this moment, Grace herself would do any favour for Sylvia, who so gallantly supported her need to visit her mother.

'Joe, will it take much longer?' she asks finally, after he has tried and rejected three bridles.

'Have to get it right for Milady Dairymaid,' he says. 'Heaven forbid that Milady Dairymaid gets the wrong tack.'

Grace is silent, wishing it were not Joe but Allan saddling up for her. But Allan is out in the fields with Angus and the others. If he were in the woodshed, she feels sure he would have got rid of Joe and done the job himself. He wouldn't carp like Joe, he would hasten for her sake, would probably suggest seeing her through the woods up to the road. The idea of precious minutes alone with Allan enchants her. She has no idea what she would talk about, but what matter? It would be such pleasure just to be with him.

Ever a weather eye for a bit of leg or a low-cut bodice. Sylvia's warning cuts across Grace's pleasant fancies. How vulnerable she would be, alone with Allan. She has heard stories of dairymaids being attacked and ravished in the fields as they milked, yet she cannot imagine Allan thinking such a thing, far less doing it. He isn't that sort of man; she feels it in her bones. Even so, she has to admit there is a tempting lure, a yielding sweetness about the words *alone with Allan.* She cannot help liking the idea. What would it feel like to be caught in his embrace, her body pressed against his? What would his smile taste like, warm and moist to her kiss, perhaps a tang of salt above his lip where traces of sweat always glisten after a day's work? And those hands of his, if they rested on her, she would surely melt! Those lean, strong hands that so lightly brushed hers when she accepted his fragrant posy. Part of the reason she buried her face in the flowers was to conceal the jolting thrill that stabbed through her at that moment of contact. To hold him in her arms in some sunlit glade, stroking his dark tousled hair from his face while he loosens her bodice and kisses her, picks her up and lays her on the warm, scented—

'Hey!'

'What?' Grace is jerked rudely back to the stable, Joe an arm's length away, eyes glowering under dark brows.

'You deaf? You're going to need feed for her, aren't you? Get some from the bin, instead of standing there grinning like a lob,' he grumbles. 'Can't be expected to do everything myself.'

7

It is that time of the day when the sun has lost its warmth but the early evening sky still glows through the trees beyond ridge tile and chimney. Lengthening shadows spread across the empty kitchen court as Alice completes a round of the house and outbuildings with Sam at her side. Above them the starlings in their dozens chatter on the coping stones atop the granary and a blackbird skims past, clacking its noisy way to roost. Beside her, Sam rattles on about anything that comes to mind, his usual way of warding off the moment of bedtime.

The door of the wash-house stands slightly ajar and Alice pulls it open. Within, Betsy is sorting and folding a pile of washed linen. Wise to the tedium of a wash-house, Sam declares his intention of going to look for Henry. Alice watches him cross the court and push open the kitchen door, and turns back to the laundress. 'It's Sabbath, Betsy. Is there such a deal to do that it cannot wait till tomorrow?'

'I go to Master Renwick's tomorrow,' Betsy replies, 'so I might as well finish what I can here.' She rolls a chemise and adds it to the basket by her side.

Alice steps over the run-off gutter in the floor and perches on one of the sinks, looking around her. A faint tang of lye lingers as though it seeps from the very plaster. The fireplace stands cold, hearth brushed clean. Beside it, a lone cauldron and several buckets are stacked ready for their next use and on the floor under the window sits the wooden box for ash. In the sink behind her, a small chemise yellowed with age lies soaking in a few inches of water, a faint mud stain soiling one sleeve. Crude tucks in the fabric show where it has been shortened to fit little Mollie. Alice takes it up and rubs at the stain. With patience it will come out.

She rubs again. 'Where is everyone, Betsy? What do they do on the Lord's Day?'

'You'd be surpri—' Betsy checks herself. 'Angus, he's in the woodshed, and Mollie's on late milking as Grace is away.'

Ah, thinks Alice, so Sylvia has roped in Mollie to help. 'Mollie seems to say very little,' she comments. 'Is it me, or is she shy with everyone?'

'Mollie says nothing. To anybody,' Betsy answers, and at Alice's look, 'The child came to us like that. Most people assume she's dumb. Over at Freemans, the Egertons' place, they say she talks with the head man's children. I don't know, I've never heard her.'

'What about Joe? How does he amuse himself on his day off?'

'He won't be doing much amusing of himself, is my guess.' Betsy says, tight-lipped. Alice waits. Betsy's profile against the golden funnel of light through the opposite window is unreadable, her expression impossible to gauge.

'Why is that, Betsy?'

Betsy stops her folding and looks at Alice. 'I see you've not heard of the betrothal, have you?'

'Betrothal? Who?'

'Allan and Sylvia got betrothed today.'

Alice stares. 'Allan and *Sylvia?* I thought he and Grace—' she breaks off. 'But why haven't I heard? Does the master know?'

Betsy shrugs again. 'Isabel said there was to be no talk. I think she wants Sylvia to think again and for once I agree with her, but there's little chance. Sylvia declares she's holding fast.'

'When did this start, Betsy? Isabel said Sylvia was at Tillotsons before.'

''Twas December when she came here.'

'So it started with Allan then? In December?'

'I don't know about that. Allan already knew her. He's often gone up to help at Tillotsons with this and that.'

Alice rinses and checks the cuff of the little chemise. Gradually, the stain is fading. 'A lucky opening for Sylvia at that time of year. In Dorset, servants usually change households at Lady Day.'

'Same here,' Betsy agrees. 'Coroner hinted that young Jeremy Tillotson might cut down on servants, and told Isabel she should make a place for Sylvia and not wait till spring.'

'*Told* Isabel to take Sylvia?'

Betsy pulls a face. 'Maybe I shouldn't say this but when Coroner speaks, Isabel jumps.' She drags the filled basket aside and reaches an empty one off a hook to replace it. 'Then, soon after, Twelfth Night it was, Isabel dismissed Mary out of hand.'

'Mary … ?'

'Dairymaid.'

Alice frowns. 'The dairymaid was dismissed, and a maidservant taken on? Why?'

Betsy shrugs. 'Isabel wanted Sylvia. Didn't want Mary.'

'I mean,' Alice goes on, 'was Mary – you know – in trouble?'

'God-a-mercy, no!' Betsy exclaims. 'Mary's far too sharp to be cozened by a cheating lover. Mistress Sanderson in town was waiting for Lady Day to engage her anyway, and has been very good, noising it abroad that High Stoke's loss is her gain. I've seen Mary quite a few times down there and I have to say, she's much happier.'

In the silence that follows, Alice reaches into Betsy's basket and holds up a handful of pockets with waist ties. On each is a neatly stitched three-petalled flower. 'These are prettily made, I am almost envious.'

Betsy pulls a face. 'Sylvia's.'

'She is a fastidious dresser, very neat at all points. And a fine needlewoman, it seems.'

Betsy looks sceptical. 'I doubt the fine needlework is Sylvia's. My guess is she talked old Florence at Tillotsons into doing them, the kerchiefs too. But whatever else, I have to say Sylvia keeps herself clean and neat. A delight to the eye.'

'Indeed, she seems to have caught Allan's eye.'

Betsy snorts.

'Are you as surprised as I am, Betsy or did you have an inkling?'

'There was a murmur of something around Valentine's Day, but it never came to anything that I saw.'

'And suddenly love has blossomed, is that it?' Alice drops the pockets into the basket.

'Something's blossomed, that's for sure.' Betsy has her back to Alice now.

'While Grace is not here,' Alice finishes for her. 'Is that what you're saying?'

For a moment Betsy is silent. Her shoulders droop. Then, 'I don't know what I'm saying.' She shakes her head and resumes her smoothing, except that now she flattens and punches the clothes against her lap as she works.

'Allan was free to make his choice,' Alice reminds her.

Betsy turns to her. 'Then why's he so sour-faced about it? If you'd seen him at midday meal you'd know what I mean. In all the time I've known Allan he's never looked so grim.'

'And what of Grace? I can't believe I misread the signs of Allan's affection for her, but perhaps I mistook her feelings for him. What were your thoughts of Grace and Allan?'

'Doesn't need much time when heart talks to heart – twas obvious those two were stricken with each other, they couldn't conceal it.'

Alice nods, recalling Allan's appearance at the dairy door, Grace's blushing confusion. Betsy points at the window onto the dairy court where the evening sun floods through. 'Does he think I don't notice him talking with her when she's in trouble, taking food for her when she's denied her meal, stealing across to slip flowers to her, and her so delighted and blushing and all?'

'Betsy, he did not have to plight his troth to Sylvia if he didn't want to. Why would he betroth himself to one where he supposedly loves another? What is he thinking of?'

Betsy says nothing.

'It may be a vain hope but perhaps Grace's feelings are not as engaged as Allan's seemed to be, and she will not take this news to heart.' When Betsy still declines to reply, Alice asks, 'So where does Joe come into this?'

'Joe?'

'You said Joe will not be feeling very amused.'

Betsy folds the last shirt and pushes it onto the pile. She sits up, hands on her knees and sighs. 'Heartsick for her, he's been, poor lad, though he's far too green for one of her stamp. Follows her around like a little dog, you can almost see his tongue hanging out, silly boy.'

'Joe is heartsick for Sylvia?'

Betsy nods. 'They forget, I see much from here.' She glances towards the open door.

'This winds itself into ever stranger coils! And does she show a fondness for him?'

Betsy puts her hand on Alice's arm and lowers her voice. 'When you were out on your ride yesterday, I saw Sylvia steal out from the drying bushes, tying her chemise strings, if you please. Then out comes Joe, looking very cock-a-hoop, and stands there gazing after her with his chest puffed out and his thumbs stuck in his armholes.'

'You're not saying he'd been tumbling her?'

'I wouldn't go so far as that. But I don't suppose they were admiring the linen, were they?' Betsy prods Alice's arm as she speaks. 'That one's a taking one and she knows it, but she should be careful how she lets young men dangle after her. There's little love lost between Allan and Joe.'

'And now Sylvia is betrothed to Allan, despite her fondness for secret visits to the drying bushes with Joe? Excellent!' Alice says. 'This bodes well for future peace and harmony.'

THE daylight is all but gone and her candle casts little light off the panelling, causing her to slow in her descent to the hall. The tableau there by the fire might have been arranged for her edification. Sylvia leans towards Allan, hands on his shoulders, whispering smiling words. He stands straight and correct, chin drawn back, looking at her. As Alice greets the two of them, she watches Sylvia place herself by Allan's side, link his arm and clasp his hand. Does the lowering of her head conceal a blush, Alice wonders, and decides it is unlikely, given those sliding eyes. Briskly she greets them, indicates the settle. Allan hands Sylvia to the end nearest the fire before sitting down himself. The gap he leaves between them is promptly closed by Sylvia.

Alice comes straight to the point. 'I asked the two of you to come to the hall to wish you joy on your betrothal.' Sylvia shimmers. Allan nods.

'This has all been a great secret has it not?' Alice asks. 'You seem to have taken the household by surprise.'

'We first knew in February, did we not, Allan?' Sylvia rests her head on his shoulder. 'On Valentine's Eve, you remember?'

Allan looks at her. 'Yes.'

Sylvia turns wide-eyed to Alice. 'That night, when I rolled papers in a bowl of water, the first slip that rose to the surface was the one in which I had concealed a snowdrop petal!'

There is a short silence while Alice wonders what response is expected of her.

'To signify the purity of my feelings!' Sylvia lowers her lashes along with her voice. 'From that moment I knew it was a sure sign of matrimony.' She breathes a small sigh of content. Alice groans inwardly. How long does the maiden plan to gush? Sylvia continues, 'We have been as good as betrothed from that moment!' Her fond hand moves to Allan's chin, bringing his face round to hers.

'A very touching story, Sylvia,' Alice says. 'In which case I wonder your betrothal was not announced before. However' – forestalling further flutterings of eager reticence – 'I asked you both here to speak of practical matters. We should like to offer the two of you a gift to mark your betrothal.' Not quite true. When she told Henry, he said, 'God's teeth, Allan can count himself lucky. When first she came here she was hanging out for George Renwick down the road with his house and lands. At the very least I thought she'd skewer some greenhorn with more silver than sense. A gift? There isn't that sort of money around, Alice, as you know.' But when she persisted, he eventually come up with an idea, one which she feels is fair, even generous. But before Alice gets any further,

'We need somewhere to live,' Sylvia says. 'The lodge would be ideal, would it not, Allan?'

'Lodge?' Alice asks. Are they asking for a house to be put at their disposal?

'It's not far from here,' Sylvia explains. 'It needs a little renovation, but nobody lives there and it would be the right size for us.' She squeezes Allan's arm, 'Especially as we may one day be blessed with a family.' Allan looks down.

'I did not have in mind a house, Sylvia,' Alice says. 'I was thinking rather of some bolts of fabric that lie in one of the upstairs chambers. I understand there is some good twill, some serge. You may wish to make up cloaks for each of you. And Allan, the master says you may help yourself to some wood in the woodshed if you wish to make a coffer, stools, things of that sort.' She watches Sylvia's annoyed frown. 'As to somewhere to live, of course you two must have your own chamber and I have in mind the end room of the passage, beyond the dairy. It is a good size, and light, facing the sun most of the day. I wonder it is not used more.'

'But it will not be large enough—' Sylvia starts to say.

'We do not need to take the room,' Allan says quickly. 'We each have our rooms here and can continue like that until I am able to find us a place.'

Sylvia looks aghast, she bursts out, 'We can't do that!'

'And if there is a bolt of wool, mistress,' Allan continues as though there has been no interruption, 'I should much like a cloak for winter use. And is there something for a gown for Sylvia? You would like to make up a gown for best, would you not, Sylvia?'

'I don't do sewing,' Sylvia declares.

Blunt as it is, the pronouncement strikes Alice with her first spark of kinship with Sylvia. Her own attempts at needlework have always been crowned with disaster. She can still recall the sense of doom she experienced hemming her first kerchief. 'Do we know someone who can sew?' she asks.

Allan says, 'A girl called Mary used to be dairymaid here. She does sewing – she has a position with Mistress Sanderson in the town now, perhaps she will make such things.'

Sylvia's smile shines forth once more. 'I have a better idea. You may ask Mary to make your cloak, if you wish, Allan dear, but she only does plain sewing. Grace is good at fine needlework. Grace may make up a gown for me.'

'Oh dear,' Alice says quickly, 'it would be a pity to delay your wedding.'

'She won't take that long.' Sylvia replies. 'She can work at it in the light evenings.'

'That's not what is in my mind,' Alice says. 'The point is, when Grace returns, she will need to apply herself. You spoke true when you told me that Isabel has not been satisfied with Grace's work. I cannot allow her to take on extra work at this time.' She watches the thwarted look in Sylvia's eyes, and something like ashamed relief in Allan's. 'It is settled then. You and I shall visit Mistress Sanderson tomorrow, Sylvia.'

8

'I know where the lodge is,' Sam announces.

'Sylvia said it's not far,' Alice says.

She came in search of Sam on her return from the Sandersons. The ladies there, mother and three garrulous daughters, were enchanted with Sylvia, running for string to measure her for the gown, voluble with ideas for tucking and trimming and pinching in at the waist. Until Sylvia abruptly changed her mind and requested a cloak to match Allan's. Too well-bred to question this sudden reversal, Mistress Sanderson hushed her girls and sent for Mary. Alice took to Mary immediately, to her square, kindly face, brown hair and capable hands. She nodded her understanding of the task, smilingly offering felicitations to Sylvia, and confirmed she could easily produce two cloaks within the month.

Alice immediately rose to leave, despite the protestations of all four Sanderson ladies, their offer of refreshments. Expressing her regrets at her hasty departure she explained her concern at leaving Sam overlong, even in the willing care of Mollie or Allan. Sam's four-year-old's mind is endlessly curious. He wants to try everything, and he is innocently unaware of the hazards of a busy kitchen or a tool-filled woodshed. Not that he was in either place on her return.

Climbing the spiral backstairs and calling for him, she first heard him cry her name, and then watched him fly out of his chamber to cannon into her as she reached the head of the steep little steps. She relishes his joy at seeing her, and her pleasure at each rediscovery is as great as his. But hers, she knows, will grow, whereas his over the years will moderate as he approaches manhood. And rightly so, she tells herself, yes, rightly so. She hugs him closer, breathing the soft, baby smell.

'I didn't know when you were coming back,' he accuses her, arms round her neck. Orphanhood still holds a rawness for Sam. His dreams for months were haunted by people abandoning him. Clutched in his hands and digging into her back are the two little wooden figures that his friend and hero Daniel the blacksmith whittled for him back in Dorset. The figures, Samuel and Zachariah he calls them, are his constant comfort as well as his pleasure.

'I'm back now, and we'll spend some time together,' she promises him. 'We'll go and find this place they call the lodge, just you and me.' Sam, still hugging her, does a small jig. She has not mentioned the matter of the lodge to Henry, she has no intention of giving away a free home at Sylvia's bidding. Nevertheless, if there is an empty house on High Stoke's land there is need to see what it might be used for.

'We went there,' Sam tells her.

'To the lodge? Who did you go with?'

'Mollie, when you were all at church yesterday.'

'I thought she was preparing midday meal.'

Sam wriggles with secret glee. 'Mollie didn't tell Isabel she'd already done it. Isabel's always vexed, she'd make her go to church twice. Mollie says it's dull.' Recalling the lengthy and monotonous sermonising they endured yesterday, Alice cannot help agreeing. Henry dropped off, his head on her shoulder. Alice, accustomed to the uplifting ideas of Vicar Rutland in her home village, was hard put to maintain a polite listening air in the face of Vicar Fitzsimmons' wearisome berating of sins more imagined than real. The entire household was subdued, melancholy even, on returning to High Stoke. Dull is the least of it.

Alice allows Sam to lead her out of the house by the kitchen court and past the woodshed. While he runs and skips around her, she exults in the spring sunshine warm on her back and breathes in the smell of the grasses bending and springing back as her skirts swish through. The belt of woodland round the extensive clearing at the front of the house comes to an end by the woodshed, and once they have passed that, open land stretches with not a building in sight. Before them the ground gently dips and rises, dotted with trees, their still-bare twigs making scribbles against the sky. Further on, a small wood straggles across their view. Distantly on their left down a long incline stretches a thicker belt of woodland betraying the flow of the river they crossed three days ago when they arrived in Guildford.

High Stoke is out of sight behind, and the small wood ahead turns out to be an unkempt copse. They push through scrubby undergrowth and pick their way between sprouting clumps of hazel. As they emerge, Sam stops and points. 'This is the way,' he says. 'It goes to the lodge.'

ALLAN slouches into the woodshed and throws aside his mattock.

'Have a care, lad!' Angus protests behind him, 'You'll be taking my foot off.'

Allan slumps onto the bench, elbows on knees, chin on his fists. He watches Angus, joints stiff with age, bend to pick up the mattock and put a hand to his back as he slowly straightens. He places it carefully with the other tools in the box. An orderly man by nature, Angus tut-tuts at the sight of a crookedly propped ladder and lays it down to lean against the wall. He re-stacks some hurdles, commenting, 'Looks like we'll be needing these to replace the ones in the top field, d'you think?'

Allan stares unseeing.

'Sheep'll be breaking out of the old hurdles soon,' Angus says, shovelling words into a silence that would normally be perfectly companionable to both. 'The wood's that brittle it won't hold them.' Angus crosses the woodshed to stand in front of Allan. 'You should go and see vicar, decide a date, Allan my lad. Twill settle your nervous humours to fix the day.'

Allan lifts his head, as though only now noticing Angus, and looks away again. 'How did I get into this?' he murmurs.

'Tis natural a young man is jumpy when he's put the question, been accepted. You should go and see vicar. Mistress gave you leave, don't know why you don't simply go and do it.'

'I think I have gone and done it,' Allan says under his breath.

'A fair maid like her. Any man'd be keen to tie the knot.'

'The only knot I'd like to tie is round her neck!' Allan's voice is unwontedly vicious.

'Ah, come now, lad. Go this afternoon,' Angus advises. 'Go and see vicar like we agreed.' Allan sighs. Angus continues, 'Twill surely cure your melancholy, you see if it don't. Anyway tis mealtime now; that should cheer you, your sweetheart'll be there.'

'No she won't,' Allan mumbles.

'Ah, but I just saw her go in.'

Allan rises, brushes past Angus and strides out of the door. In the kitchen court, he leans against the woodshed wall and sinks down on his haunches, folding his arms hard across his chest. 'Why don't you just stop going on about it, Angus?' he mutters through clenched teeth, 'All morning it's been *sweet and twenty ... lovers' meeting ... patter of tiny feet,* till I'm ready to punch your face through the back of your head!'

Angus comes out. 'I'd be jealous of you if I were ten year younger,' he says, artlessly twisting the knife. 'Her always around with her pretty face and winning ways; first thing in the morning, last thing at night.' He nudges Allan with the toe of his boot. 'You're a lucky dog and you don't know it, Allan. Joe's green as a frog you got in there first.' Angus chuckles, Allan seethes. 'Where is he, come to think on it? There's the master coming along the track from town and he'll want the grey stabled.'

'Joe's walking the pasture with Ned,' Allan says, rising. He goes to stand by the stables as Jerrard approaches. And good riddance to Joe, he thinks. The stupid little puppy has been full of bile ever

81

since yesterday's announcement, though Allan is at a loss to know why. Sylvia has never shown any fancy in that direction. Allan wishes she had, it might be a way out. He goes to take the reins as Jerrard dismounts. Sylvia has set her heart on himself. And he? He has made his bed, but heaven knows what he would give not to lie on it. Why did he agree to this sorry betrothal? But he knows the answer to that.

'Did you hear me, Allan?' Jerrard's question jerks him from his thoughts. 'I said, do you know where the mistress is?'

Allan rouses. 'She took young Master Sam walking.' He points up the track that diminishes into tufty grass beyond the woodshed. 'I heard her say Isabel should tell you not to wait for your midday meal.'

Jerrard nods. He turns and walks across the kitchen court, calling to the steward. 'What's for my meal today, then, Isabel?' When she appears smiling at the door, he says, 'I gather the mistress is out, so you're feeding only me this time.' Isabel's smile widens and she stands back to let Jerrard into the kitchen. 'There are some game chewits if you fancy them, cousin. Shall I help you off with your boots?' The door closes.

As Allan removes the grey's saddle, Angus comes into the stable. 'You coming to midday meal, then?'

'Not yet. I'll catch you up.' Allan places water for the horse and waits in the stable until Angus has gone into the kitchen. He checks nobody is around, then slips out past the wash-house into the dairy court. Cautiously he approaches the dairy. He knows it is a fool's errand; Grace has been laughing behind his back and spending stolen days with her lover. He would never have believed it but for that letter Sylvia showed him. All his hopes so easily torn down. He knows he is being unreasonable that his wrath is against Sylvia for finding the letter, for showing it to him.

Grace has fooled them all, pretending her mother is ill. *My best delite is having you,* the letter said. The words are like talons, clawing his flesh to the bone. But for all that, if she is back, he would just like to see her face, the curve of her cheek, that determined set of her jaw when she nears the tough part of the churning. He will tell her of his betrothal, of course; he wants her to hear it from him. He wants to see for himself if it raises the smallest sign of remorse in her eyes, because even that would be something. He is morosely aware that the comfort he seeks is of the order of table sweepings, but he will scrabble for it on his knees if it is there. In his dreams she remains his dear love. Always she reaches for those flowers, the pushed-up sleeves revealing the creamy skin of her plump arms; always she has that look of inexpressible pleasure on her face.

Feeling you every day. He gorges on the sickening idea, fuelling his disgust, fearful that otherwise he could fall back under Grace's spell. Just one in the queue for her favours. He peers in through the little window. The dairy is empty. He is halfway back across the dairy court when he hears the latch carefully raised. Heart jolting, he turns.

'Looking for me, are you, Allan dear?'

He has to brace himself to conceal his disenchantment. Sylvia steps down from the doorway and approaches him, head on one side, playing with a lock of her hair. 'I saw you peering in the window,' she says, leaning and kissing him before he has a chance to think. 'But I hid, so that you would not see me!' She tweaks a curl of his hair. 'Don't you want to know what I have been doing this morning?'

He supposes he ought to want to know. 'What was that, then, Sylvia?'

'I went to the Sandersons.'

'You saw Mary? How is she?'

'Plain, square Mary is as plain and square as ever she was.'

'That's not kind, Sylvia.'

''Twas your description, if I remember aright.'

He recalls with mortification a jest with Sylvia months back that Mary's hands were as square as her face. He wonders what other errors he has committed that will be brought out to flay him in years to come. 'Is she going to make your gown?'

'No, I have asked her to make me a cloak only, as she will for you.'

'Why a cloak? I thought you wanted a good gown for best?'

'I decided I should not take advantage of Mary's goodwill by asking her to make a gown in only three weeks. It must be close-fitted and becoming to my figure and she would not have the time when she is busy with her own work. It would be self-seeking and I do not wish you to think ill of me.'

Allan is momentarily taken aback at this unexpected selflessness. 'That's very thoughtful of you, Sylvia.' Then the message behind the words surfaces. Three weeks. Once he sees the vicar, it will be only three weeks. He feels his resolve waver as a thought tempts him. 'But, Sylvia, perhaps you can still have your gown. If we delayed getting married – only by a little,' he says hurriedly, as he sees her open her mouth to object. 'Say a month – two months, perhaps, Mary will have plenty of time with the summer evenings to make you a gown.'

'I would rather give up ten gowns than delay marrying you by a day, Allan, my dearest,' declares Sylvia, whose chances of ever owning ten gowns, as they both know, are vanishingly small.

'But it might be sensible to wait a little anyway, Sylvia.'

'You know that is not possible.'

'After all, we have no money.'

'What need have we of money,' Sylvia asks, wide-eyed, 'when we have each other?'

'We've no roof over our heads,' Allan reminds her. 'Only that one there,' pointing in the direction of the end room beyond the dairy. 'And you don't want that, do you?'

'We'll get the lodge,' Sylvia says with conviction. 'I've only to keep asking and she'll see the sense of giving it to us. Nobody else wants it, it hasn't been lived in for ages. Why shouldn't we have it?'

For Sylvia, Allan thinks, wanting becomes owning purely by strength of desire. 'It's in very poor condition,' he says. 'Have you seen inside?'

'A few repairs to the roof and it will be fine. You could do that, you're good with your hands.'

'But thatch costs money,' he reminds her. Will nothing deter her?

'Then we'll get money. I know a way. Come on.' She takes his hand and draws him into the dairy. Allan allows himself to be led in a daze of reluctant admiration. Nothing seems to daunt Sylvia, nothing is going to stand in her way. He tells himself yet again how grateful he ought to be for such unconditional love, and wishes he did not feel this persistent dread at being tied to her for life. For life! To this strangling, suffocating existence.

9

It is an odd sort of dwelling, Alice thinks, that has no track leading to it. Perhaps it is an old shepherd's hut or pig-keeper's shelter, either would provide lodging of a sort.

'Tell me about this lodge, Sam. What is it like?' He walks ahead of her for some while in silence. He shrugs. 'It's like a house,' he says at last.

'A big house?'

'Quite big.'

'Does it have windows?'

'Of course it has windows,' he says as though explaining to a dull-wit.

'And a door?'

'You can't get in through the door, you have to climb in the window.'

'I see. And does the roof have holes in it?'

'Yes!' he says, clearly delighted that at last she understands. 'The birds fly in and out, like this.' He waves his hand to and fro in the air. So at the very least it is in need of new tiles or thatch, and has been left to weather. Perhaps it can be repaired.

'Did Mollie say who used to live there?' But Sam does not remember, or Mollie did not know.

'You just have to come and see it,' is all he will say. They breast a rise and skirt a patch of high brambles pushing out thorny new shoots. Sam points. 'There, Alice, there!' and jumps up and down, urging her to catch up. She follows his pointing finger. The ground slopes gently down and a hundred paces away stands a small sad dwelling, its thatched roof dark with age. Pock-marks betray thievery by birds for nest material, many are the inroads they have made in its surface. As if summoned, two fly out of adjacent holes and a third flutters down to disappear inside.

The gable end of the cottage is mired with bird droppings streaking down window and wall. At the other end a brick stack rises, sprouting a chimney much pitted where the mortar has dropped out, though otherwise it looks sound enough. Alice follows Sam down the slope towards the lodge. On one long side is a dark door flanked by two unglazed, wood-mullioned windows at ground level and another upstairs over the door. Little more than two rooms and a sleeping space, but at least that chimney at the end means it has provision for cooking. The lime-washed wall is barely recognisable as such, its surface cracked and pitted and streaked with dirt.

Together they circle the house. The back of it stands in even worse condition than the front. On this side, moss has spread on the remains of the roof. Two windows along its length and one above correspond with those at the front, each supported by two wooden mullions much chewed by time and weather. Internal shutters, where they exist, hang crookedly, hampering the view within, but Alice guesses that acquisitive hands will long since have stripped this place of anything worth having.

All around the house, the ground is crossed with tangled growth, clumps of grass, rustling stalks of long dead seasons, new brambles clawing their way over anything that provides purchase. Some sort of fruit tree, its branches and twigs furred with grey-green lichen, sports scant sprays of blossom.

Rounding the house to the front, they come to another tree playing host to ivy that winds snake-like up its trunk. A square patch of ground before the door seems to suggest an effort at cultivation in the past, but it is now covered in tussocks of grass and weeds. Alice twitches her skirt clear of snagging thorns and reaches the big stone doorstep. The door, four broad planks, the dark wood cracked down its grain, has seen as many winters as the house. The door frame sags and the door stands slightly ajar but will not move to her touch. Clearly it has been like this for some time, for she can make out a drift of dried leaves across the floor within.

Sam points to the window by the front door, one of whose mullions is rotted away. 'You have to go in here, Alice.' The sill and the wall below are encrusted with bird droppings.

'I think I'll try the door first.' By pushing her weight against it she makes it creak, but it stays put. Sam shoves at it, then takes a step back and makes a run at it. It defies his four-year-old's efforts and he kicks it, which also makes no impact. An idea occurs to Alice.

'A moment, Sam.' She reaches round the door, gingerly testing with her fingers until she finds what she seeks. The bracing on the inside will give her the purchase she needs. By dint of lifting and pushing, she can feel a slight shift but still it will not open. She stands back and looks again. The door is not only dropped on its hinges, the sagging frame has come to rest on the top of it and the two are jammed together. It groans and grates as Alice pushes again, and bit by bit it creaks open a few inches. On all fours Sam edges past her legs and she is just able to squeeze through the narrow gap she has opened up.

Inside is a large room. On the end wall is the fireplace, smoke stains on the chimney breast, and in its dark corners cobwebs sag with soot. The rotting shutter on the back window is so overlaid with dirt-filled cobwebs it lends a misty, milky light to the room. To the side, where a smaller room leads off, is the window by which Sam and Mollie entered. Leaves have blown into both rooms, dried and curled, but in places the brown of a packed earth floor shows through. A ladder staircase in the corner of the main room leads up through a square hole in the ceiling. All around, the plaster walls have flaked and fallen away like flesh from a wound, exposing the bones of wattle. Sam dances around, kicking up rustling skirmishes of leaves and darting between the two rooms.

'I wonder who lived here,' she murmurs. Sam runs past her to the ladder, calling. 'Come on, there's more upstairs.' Sam is used to ladders. In the hovel he briefly occupied with his mother in Alice's Dorset village, a ladder like this led from the ground floor room to the sleeping space above. With vague distaste, Alice wonders what they might find upstairs. Birds' nests? Droppings? Bats? And what state are the roof beams in, the thatch so opened up to the weather? She follows Sam up the creaking rungs, checking above as she goes.

10

Sylvia pulls Allan along the kitchen passage. From the servants' parlour comes Isabel's voice, ordering Mollie to bring the bread trenchers. Well, Allan thinks, at least I shall have time to think how to delay this wretched wedding while we eat our meal. But Sylvia suddenly turns and pulls him along the forbidden screens passage.

'No! Sylvia, we can't!' Allan whispers, glancing back in case Isabel with her uncanny sense for wrongdoing should be alerted to their whereabouts. But Sylvia brooks no objection and hushes him as she keeps going. She knocks quietly at the door to the dining parlour and walks in. Jerrard, his knife half-way to his mouth, looks up in surprise. 'Sylvia? And Allan? What's to do?'

Sylvia bobs a dutiful curtsey and stands before him, eyes downcast, hands linked. 'Allan and I wish to say how grateful we are for the betrothal gift you and the mistress are giving us.'

'Oh.' Jerrard says vaguely. 'Yes.' Allan can see he is casting around in his mind to remember what gift he has given. Sylvia gives him his cue.

'The cloaks will be most welcome to us.'

'Ah yes, indeed. Cloaks are useful things.' Jerrard sits looking at the pair, eyebrows raised.

Allan pulls at Sylvia's hand. 'Come along, Sylvia.'

'Very useful indeed,' Sylvia goes on. 'Especially walking to and from our work, morning and evening.'

'Oh?' Jerrard looks surprised. 'Are you taking a cottage then, Allan?'

'No—'

'Yes, we should like to,' Sylvia says. 'And if we had a small consideration in recognition of our marriage, we could afford to do so.'

Allan holds his breath. Jerrard sits back and regards Sylvia with amusement. 'You want money.'

Sylvia bats long lashes. 'It is not unknown for a master to be generous on the occasion of a marriage.'

Between gritted teeth, 'Sylvia!' Allan whispers.

Jerrard smiles widely. 'This is a pleasant comedy, Sylvia, but you're wasting your time. Was there anything else? If so, be quick, I'm going out again soon.'

'It could be of advantage to the manor that Allan improves one of your dwellings,' Sylvia persists. She is still forging ahead but to Allan's ears a note of nervousness has crept in as this interview fails to go her way.

Jerrard lays down his knife. 'And which particular dwelling did you have in mind for Allan to work on, Sylvia?' Allan recognises the tell-tale signs of Jerrard's approaching boredom. Again he pulls at her hand; she snatches it back.

'The mistress said she thinks to let us have the lodge,' Sylvia declares.

'Sylvia, she didn't say—'

'So you covet the lodge do you?' Jerrard says. 'What are you planning to do to it?'

'The thatch needs work,' Sylvia says. 'Allan can do that.'

'Yes?'

Sylvia takes encouragement from his tone. 'And the windows need glass.'

'Just so.'

'He can repair the plaster, and give it a lime wash, and …' Allan watches in horror as she casts around to recollect anything else that might attract funds. '… and make a new front door.' Despairing, Allan feels the ground being cut from under his feet as Sylvia and his master plan his life for him.

Jerrard says, 'While you are about all this worthy activity in the lodge, I might as well ask you whether you know about the rotten floorboards upstairs. Tell me, Sylvia, how skilled are you at joinery?'

UPSTAIRS there is a similar layout of two rooms, though there is no fireplace up here, and the plaster has come off in even greater patches, letting in mottled light through the woven wattle. The sun casts hard shadows of the rotting window mullions across the rough-grained floor. The door to the smaller room at the end seems, from the curved scrape on the floor, to be jammed half open. Underfoot, the wood plank flooring is dark with age, adze-cut many long years ago, uneven but soft and springy to the tread compared with the packed earth floor downstairs. Bird droppings and nest material lie scattered around.

Alice stands at the top of the ladder staircase and looks around. 'Who lived here, I wonder?'

'Mollie says it's ours.' Sam dodges round her and runs across the room into the small end chamber.

'Do you like Mollie, Sam?' Mollie is a mystery to Alice. She says not a word, either in or out of Isabel's presence. What was it Betsy said? *They say she talks with the children.* Clearly Mollie has spoken with Sam while the rest of the household were at church.

'She's got a funny voice,' Sam says. 'We play games.' Sam dances back towards Alice on the creaking boards and stops in the middle of the room. 'We did lots of these.' He performs a crooked head-over-heels, landing on his side. 'And she says I can go and talk to her in the pot room as long as Isabel doesn't know.'

He clambers to his feet and Alice moves to brush leaves and twigs off his jerkin. 'Back downstairs for us, I think, Sam.' She waits at the top as he makes his way down the ladder, still chattering, 'Mollie showed me where to hide if Isabel … oh!' He is peering out of the cobwebbed window.

'What is it, Sam?'

'It's a lady on a horse, and she's going round the house. That way,' he says, pointing.

'I wonder who it is.' Alice turns. From the window in the gable end, she will be able to see. Sam is mounting the ladder again as she starts across the chamber. The floor is even more springy in the middle of the room than at the edge. A board groans as she treads, the next creaks, shifts underfoot. The impossible is happening, the wood bending. Too late, Alice tries to step back, but with a soft splintering, the floor caves in. She topples sideways, frantically grabbing, but the boards crumble at her touch, and then there is nothing but air and she pitches, hitting the packed earth floor below. Lengths of wood plunge and clatter all around, toppling across her and thudding on the hard floor. The dry rattle of plaster chunks bouncing, breaking and slithering away through the leafy clutter. A shower of dust and flakes filling the air.

Alice lies, fleetingly robbed of her wits. It takes a few seconds to register a sharp pain where she landed on her elbow.

Nearby someone is crying out, frantically shouting her name, and there is another sound, a banging on the door outside. She twists round and can discern little through the rising clouds of tawny dust. The voice calls again, high, urgent, and she looks up through the rust-coloured air to make out a great ragged hole where the upper floor was. That, and Sam's face crumpled with terror peering over the edge, his little fingers curling round the honeycombed rot of a floorboard.

'Alice! Alice!' he calls, over and over. 'Alice!'

'Sam, darling, don't move! Stay very still.' Half the floor has collapsed with her and here she is, hampered by debris, several feet from where he kneels up there on the edge. She pushes a jagged plank aside but as she rises, it catches in her skirt. Any second now, the rest could give way and cast him into the chaos of splintered wood. 'Don't move, Sam, I'm coming to get you.' She can see it in her mind's eye as though it has already happened, herself critical

inches away, the worm-eaten wood exploding in a russet cloud …
On all fours as he is, he will drop head first.

'Stay where you are, sweeting …'

The sickening crunch as his skull smacks on wood. The splintered points piercing his baby skin.

'Stay very still!'

More of that hammering outside, she wishes it would stop. Scrambling up, hampered by teetering wood, trying to keep him calm, trying to keep herself calm, desperate that he should stay still.

'Don't move!'

His little body horribly splayed and still. *Oh, God, take anything but let me catch him!*

'I'm coming—'

She claws her way across wood and rubble, straining to reach up, too slowly, like a bad dream. As a loose board gives and tips her to her knees, the front door is kicked violently from the outside and the whole house shudders. There is a soft tearing, splitting sound and whatever still anchors Sam's floorboard slips its hold, pitching him head first, clutching air.

11

As Sylvia gapes at Jerrard's suggestion that she should help replace floorboards, he goes on, 'So what of your own contribution to these improvements, Sylvia?'

With doom in his heart, Allan watches Sylvia's rapid recovery. With a bright smile, 'I would allow Mollie to share with us,' she says. 'She can live in the end chamber and that would save money for her bed and board here – at least, her bed.'

'Her warm bed by the kitchen fire here, yes indeed,' Jerrard says. 'And here's another thought, Sylvia. You could get her to do all the menial jobs in the lodge in return.'

Sylvia's face takes on a look of surprise. 'I hadn't thought of that, but of course it would be fair exchange.' Allan foresees with new dread a lifetime of making apologies and excuses for his wife's clumsy incursions. But Sylvia has not finished yet. 'I cannot help feeling,' she says, giving Jerrard a look from under her lashes, 'that there must be more enjoyable ways to spend money than paying for tiresome petty repairs. Running a demesne such as High Stoke must be so burdensome, the constant demands on your purse. And here is Allan, ready and willing to use his skills for your benefit. All he needs are the materials. Surely it's worth taking a gamble you cannot lose?'

Allan stares dumbstruck. Jerrard turns narrowed eyes on Sylvia. 'If that's all, I'd like to finish my meal now.' Allan grabs Sylvia's wrist, this time keeping his grip, and pulls her towards the door. Behind them, Jerrard says, 'Understand me, both of you. You've been here long enough, you especially, Allan, to know that there's no spare money even for repairs to this house, and no matter if there were, you will never have the lodge. You will have the room at the end of the kitchen passage and there's an end to it. So go and get married and stop weaving these fancies.'

'Come on, Sylvia,' Allan pleads. Sylvia glares at him. She jerks her arm free, pushes past and sweeps out.

'SAM!' Alice makes a frantic effort to throw herself forward, reaching up desperate hands. He pitches straight at her, knocking her onto her back. Small as he is, the thump of his body forces the breath out of her. Instinctively, she wraps her arms round his head and rolls to cover him as more rotten planks thud all around. Something heavy chops down across her back. She braces herself for the roof trusses, the smothering weight of thatching, to bury them both. Twisting her head round to see, she gasps as a billowing cloud of dust washes in her face, blinding her. Above them, the long creak of wood strained beyond its strength, the splitting and tearing as more boards break and plunge. The dead thump and roll of rubble, lumps of plaster bouncing and breaking, the slide of wood on wood, wreckage settling, the trickle of dust.

And finally silence.

Already Sam is struggling in her clutch but she clings, overwhelmed by a desire to hold him forever like this, to bury her face against his warm, baby-soft skin, exult at the life in him. Even so, with mouth and nostrils clogged, the need to cough is competing with the need to breathe, and trying to breathe makes her cough out what little air is left in her. The choking tightens like a band round her chest. Then scrambling, sliding footsteps, the weight of the beam is lifted, dragged aside, and hands loosen her hold on Sam, lifting him. Someone asks him if he is hurt. The band round her chest bursts and her craving lungs suck in air. Instantly a long wheezing cough convulses her. Gasping and panting, she is aware of a calm soothing voice encouraging Sam away. He should come outside, the voice says, and his mother will join him directly. Half blinded, she peers after the diminishing pair through the powdery cloud. Another gulp and she doubles over, head down, whooping.

She tries to get to her feet, sliding amidst teetering planks and rubble. With watering eyes she watches the hazy shape of a man approach, climbing over bits of wood, kicking debris out of his way.

'You damned clumsy oaf!' she rasps.

'Come, mistress.' He takes her hand.

She snatches it away. 'You could have killed him!' she croaks. 'Shaking the house like that!'

'What in God's name are you doing in here anyway?'

'I don't need your permission,' she scrapes out the words before another coughing fit doubles her up.

'It is not safe here. Come.' She feels her arm taken. Despite trying, she finds she cannot rise, and the arm circles her waist, lifting her to her feet. She continues to whoop, and now he too is coughing. Together they clamber across the wreckage towards the doorway.

In the fresh, sweet air outdoors, she leans against the wall and searches for a kerchief to dab her streaming eyes. Behind her, the man re-enters the lodge to thrust debris away from the doorway.

'Alice, are you all right, Alice?' Sam's hand on her waist, her free hand drawing him to her, ruffling his gritty hair. 'Yes, Sam, I am well – you are not hurt?'

'No,' answers Sam brightly. 'I landed on you, it was like flying.'

She gives a shaky laugh, the dust in her eyes making her blink. 'Don't cry, Alice.'

She hugs him close. He is well, has taken no hurt. Her eyes slowly clear. Sam's face is powdered with plaster and she suspects hers is the same. 'Look at us,' she says. 'When we get home, Henry will mistake us for scarecrows and put us in the fields to frighten the birds away!' They both laugh at that, and Alice can now look around.

Two horses are tethered to a tree some thirty yards away. Making her way towards the lodge is the most beautiful woman Alice has ever beheld. Straight and slender, with gleaming coils of dark hair around forehead and temple, the woman moves as though stepping along the smoothest flagged walk instead of over rough tussocky ground strewn with last year's briars.

'Mistress, what has happened here,' she says, a frown of concern between the brows. Large brown eyes, fringed with dark lashes, are set in an oval face above a straight nose. The generous mouth has just the slightest upturn at the corners. A faint flush of rose sets off the high-set cheekbones. 'Are you hurt?' So, a lady attended by her groom, perhaps. But, clumsy fellow as he was, he meant well.

'I thank you,' Alice croaks, still hoarse. 'Your man came crashing in and—' She turns to indicate her rescuer emerging from the doorway and sees the last person in the world she expects to meet at that moment. Not overly tall, simply dressed in russet breeches and doublet, dark hair catching bronze in the sunlight, and a slight doubling of the chin under a full lower lip. It cannot be. And yet it is. The man who just kicked in the door of her lodge and pulled her out is the same man she saw from her chamber window, talking with Sam the morning after they arrived. She looks again at the horses, and recognises the big-boned bay.

'— and he very kindly freed us,' she weakly finishes. A groom, she decides, would not possess such elegant wear. Is he the lady's secretary, perhaps? Her steward? He props a couple of half-rotten planks against the wall. 'If I can jam … this door … shut again,' he says, jerking it by degrees almost closed, 'I can maybe block it off until the building can be made safe.' He sets the two planks crosswise and packs them in the embrasure, knocking off lumps of worm-eaten wood until each is wedged in place.

With a conscious effort, Alice pulls her gaze back to the woman. She cannot help envying the dark velvet habit shining with hints of blue where the sun catches its folds. The pleated high-crowned hat sits at a slight angle, and a long white ostrich feather drifts in the breeze. Fine Milanese lace at her throat heightens the clear ivory of her face. In stark contrast, Alice is acutely aware of her own torn and unkempt appearance. She puts a hand to her cheek and feels the gritty plaster powdering her face white as a Southwark whore.

Casting around for something to say, she falls back on introducing herself and Sam. Sam performs the angular bending of joints that constitutes his bow. Bits of plaster drop from the neck of his shirt. Alice's curtsey gives her time to think, especially as her skirt catches on a briar and she spends seconds agitatedly releasing it. She realises that her palms are full of splinters.

'Of course, you are Henry's wife,' the lady is saying. 'Forgive me, I forget myself. Olivia Egerton, at your service.' She makes her curtsey, which is, to Alice's further mortification, a study in flowing lines. 'I had your note of thanks,' Olivia says. 'We are delighted you liked the ham. And please allow me to introduce my husband Jack.'

Not a secretary, not a steward, this is her husband, this is Betsy's Young Master Jack. Near neighbour and friend of Henry. Rider of a big-boned bay. Bearer of a ham for High Stoke, befriender of Sam, and the man she has just castigated when he came to her aid. She shrinks within.

'I knew you must be James Edwards' daughter as soon as I saw you,' he says, and Alice, assailed by mortification, can find nothing to say. 'Same hair as your father,' he explains and her mind goes back to her father's visit to London last spring. To his talk of the 'interesting company' he met by chance there. Henry and the elder Tillotson and this man, Jack Egerton. The reference to her hair, however, causes Alice the uneasy realisation that she has forgotten to don a cap. So now, as well as seeing her asprawl on the floor of the lodge, as well as being insulted for coming to their rescue, he must be wondering what sort of a sloven Henry has chosen, who wanders around the countryside without a decently covered head.

'What happened?' Olivia Egerton asks again. It is her husband who answers.

'The floor gave way. I knew it was unsteady but it should have been checked long since. Mistress Jerrard fell through first and the boy fell on top of her just as I got inside. You are sure you are not hurt?' he asks Alice. Standing close to Olivia Egerton with her smooth braids, Alice feels like a wild woman. 'We are not hurt, I thank you, sir. A little jarred but nothing beyond a bruise or two.' She flexes her arm, suppresses a wince at the tenderness around her elbow.

'And the ruin of your clothes.' Olivia remarks.

'They will wash and these are workaday, as you see,' Alice assures her. 'We were taking a walk around the demesne and—'

'I was showing Alice the lodge,' Sam says.

Egerton turns to him. 'Good day, young master, in fact I should say, well met again, should I not?'

'Is that the same horse?' Sam asks, pointing at the bay. 'You said you had more.' Olivia's eyes flick between the two, wide with questions.

'I only ride one at a time,' Egerton explains, straight-faced. 'The others are working horses.' He turns to Alice. 'I am sorry that your first visit here has been so unfortunate.'

'I must thank you, sir, for coming to our rescue,' she says, 'but I shall certainly talk to my husband about it.'

'I shall come and talk to him about it myself,' he answers. 'And incidentally, you have a lump of plaster in your hair.'

Is that a polite smile or, God's teeth, does he think it's funny she is standing here covered in dust and looking a fool? She tosses her head, disdaining to pick out the debris, and then has to anyway, feeling it clinging in her curls. 'I assure you there is no need for you to talk to my husband about it. I shall speak with him when I am home.'

'I fear I must speak to him myself, nevertheless. Indeed, it should never have been allowed to remain accessible in such a dangerous state.' This is becoming acutely discomfiting; Alice feels ready to sink through the floor. Another floor. Olivia Egerton takes up the argument. 'Indeed, we cannot let it rest there, when you or Sam here, could have been seriously hurt. You could have lain without help for goodness knows how long.'

Alice is beginning to despair of getting rid of this well-meaning couple bent on taking her husband to task for his neglect. 'Indeed, I do assure you I shall talk to Henry,' she insists, 'and see that he does something about it. I am sure he meant to, but I expect it slipped his mind. In any event, he did not know I was going to walk out today so he could hardly have warned me.' She stops, seeing the exchange of puzzled glances between husband and wife. 'What is it?'

'Henry is not responsible for this place,' Olivia says.

Alice is perplexed in her turn. 'As part of our demesne—' she begins.

'No, mistress,' Jack Egerton says, 'it is part of Freemans. You are on Freemans land here. The state of this house is my responsibility.'

'Oh!' Alice gasps. 'I thought ... I mean, I did not realise. I believed it to be High Stoke's.' Now it's worse, they are planning to come and complain to Henry that his new wife, a foul-mouthed, unkempt bawd, is also a trespasser. 'I understand why you wish to see Henry. You will no doubt be seeking redress.'

'Redress?' Olivia stares. 'When our negligence has resulted in an accident? It is no credit to us that it was not worse.'

'I am entirely to blame,' her husband continues. 'Indeed you could not have known whose land you were on; the two run side by side for a space. It is natural that you should wish to examine what you believed was yours.'

'You must allow us to bring you both to Freemans,' says Olivia. 'The least we can offer you is somewhere to furbish yourselves, and a little refreshment, before we take you home.' Alice's 'There's really no need,' is polite if weak, her curiosity about these neighbours already banishing lingering embarrassment. Olivia's 'Yes, I insist,' settles it. 'Jack will go to High Stoke now to let them know where you are so that Henry does not worry about your absence. I shall sit your horse, Jack. Yes, never mind the saddle. I shall do very well if you will give me a step up. Mistress Jerrard shall have my mount, and young Master Sam can ride behind her.'

BEFORE Alice and Sam have followed the big-boned bay half a mile, a large building comes into view. To Alice's eye, parts of it are older than High Stoke. It has been much extended over the years, with roofs added here and there seemingly at random. Outbuildings straggle.

'We shall go direct to the stables,' says Olivia, pointing to the huddle behind the main house. 'I can more easily find Robert from there. He is our head man; he directs the outdoor servants. You are not tired, Master Sam?'

'Can I see your horses?' asks Sam by way of reply.

'Of course you shall if your mother allows – Mistress Jerrard?' She has a low-pitched, melodious voice. Alice thinks, I could listen to that voice for a long time. She says, 'Sam enjoyed playing in the stables back at Hill House where I lived before, and already he spends much of his time with the horses at High Stoke.'

'We have five here,' Olivia tells Sam. 'These two for our riding, and the others for general work, or they can be lent when we have visitors. If Robert is about the place, he will show you them. Ah, I see him,' she cries and urges the bay forward to meet a tall, dark-visaged man in open-necked shirt and breeches, sleeves rolled up, emerging from one of the barns carrying tied sheaves of hay. He puts them down and goes to take Olivia's rein to steady her as she dismounts. 'Robert, this is Mistress Jerrard, our neighbour of High Stoke, and her son Sam. They have met with a slight accident and are come here that we may do what we can for their comfort.'

'Indeed, mistress,' says Robert equably, as though accidents are an everyday occurrence for this household. He hitches Olivia's horse to the handle of the barn door. 'Come, young master,' he says to Sam and lifts him easily from behind Alice, who slips to the ground straight after.

'If you are around the stables for a while, Robert, perhaps you will show Master Sam what we do here. He is mightily interested to see our nags.'

'Indeed, Mistress,' Robert says again and takes the two reins in one hand. 'Well then, young Sam, if you would make yourself useful, you can bring one of those bottles of hay there and come with me to the stables.' Sam bends to the sheaf and half carrying, half dragging it in both hands, follows in Robert's wake.

'Your Robert seems happy enough to have Sam with him. I am grateful to him,' Alice says, turning to Olivia.

'Robert has little ones of his own who are probably around somewhere. I expect one of them will actually show Sam around. Oh, do not be alarmed,' she adds, as Alice looks quickly after the retreating figures. 'They are as well experienced as either Jack or I. They've lived around the stables since they could first walk. I expect Sam also knew his way around your stables from his cradle, did he not?' She leads the way into the house at the side, calling, 'Faith?'

'You are to understand, mistress,' says Alice following her, 'that Sam is not my son. He is an orphan in my care.'

'Ah, I wondered why he called you by your name,' says Olivia, and asks no further questions. When a serving woman emerges Olivia bids her prepare two extra places for their guests at midday dinner. 'We shall be back down within half an hour, Faith. I shall attend to Mistress Jerrard's needs myself. Oh, and our second guest is a child – I am sure we have some comfits he would like, do we not?'

By the time Alice has picked out her splinters and applied Olivia's soothing ointment, Olivia has mended her underskirt and lent her a fresh chemise. Her face washed and her hair and skirts brushed, she follows Olivia down to the hall, where Jack Egerton, lately back from leaving his message at High Stoke, glances, and glances again, as though reminding himself that this is the same woman he saw dirt-smeared, unkempt, dusty and red-eyed at the lodge house.

'It was built before Henry Tudor's time, so it is a little older than High Stoke,' he says in answer to her question, as they sit over the dishes which Olivia blithely calls "refreshment". Pigeons' breasts, spinach tart, a mortis of chicken pounded with almonds, a salad of varied leaves and dried fruits, and a trifle, ginger-hot and rich with yellow cream. For Alice, five dishes well-nigh constitute a feast. And the ale here is amber and flavourful.

'Another glass?' Jack asks, and she realises she has been staring at the deep gold of her drink. She shakes her head, this is stronger than an everyday small ale. Already she is aware of the flush of wellbeing it has brought. She says, 'Sam said Mollie told him the lodge was part of our manor.'

'It was. I bought it from Henry only last year, along with a parcel of land this side of the spring line. He needed … he wanted to concentrate his efforts closer to home, I believe.'

'I'm sure that's right,' Alice says, wondering why it needed to be sold. 'It's rather scrubby land round the lodge, though. Will it cultivate?'

'I'm thinking I'll try fruit trees, they should do well, and the sheep can graze under. But first,' he says, rising, 'the lodge must be made safe.' He turns to Olivia. 'By your leave, lady, I shall go now. I must see that the door and the ground floor windows are boarded up with some sound timber.' He nods to the two women and heads for the door. They hear his footsteps retreating and Alice too rises.

'I think Sam and I should be on our way. It was most kind of you to look after us so well.'

'Do not leave just yet, Alice,' Olivia urges her.

'I think it will soon rain, look at that cloud building up yonder.' Alice points. 'We can be home ahead of it if we leave now.'

'We shall send you in the carriage of course,' Olivia counters. 'We shall not let you walk. And young Sam is so interested in our stables, it would be a shame to take him away.'

'I'm sorry he did no justice to your meal before dashing back to Robert,' Alice replies, recalling Sam, minimally brushed, reluctantly coming to table for all of five minutes. 'He will chatter about it all the way home.' Olivia appears about to persuade her further, but footsteps sound in the passage and Jack Egerton walks back in, followed closely by Henry. Alice's heart lights at sight of her husband, she feels the smile sweep over her face as she breathes, 'Henry!' and holding out her hands she steps towards him.

'I am to understand you tried to kill yourself in my old lodge,' he says, his smile matching hers, and slips an arm round her. 'My love, I am grieved to know that you wish to be free of me so soon.'

'He was just riding in hot-foot from getting my message,' says Jack Egerton. 'Brought a horse for you, too.'

'I'd gone to walk the Long Field with Angus. I must have missed Jack by minutes. I've brought Athena as you've lent Cassie to Grace. Looks like a storm's brewing over the town and coming this way.'

'Henry,' says Alice looking up into his face, 'Olivia and Jack were so kind and insisted on bringing us back here and,' she holds out her skirt, 'refurbishing me. I am indebted to you, Olivia,' and turning to Jack, 'and to you, sir, and I hope we may return the compliment some day. Is it not so, Henry?'

'Come to supper,' he says, 'one day soon when the household has settled down to its new mistress.'

'Olivia, I thank you for the offer of your carriage,' Alice says, 'but as Henry has thought to bring me a mount, we shall be on our way directly.'

'Come and see us whenever you wish,' says Olivia warmly.

'Sir,' Alice turns to Jack. 'I owe you an apology for the way I spoke to you in the lodge.' Jack smiles and shakes his head.

'I'm intrigued,' Henry says. 'What did you say to him, Alice?'

'I ... called him an oaf.' Alice feels her face reddening. Henry's laughter joins Jack's and fills the room.

'I get called that and worse in court on a regular basis,' Jack says, and Olivia explains, 'Jack is a justice, Alice.'

'Come, my love.' Henry's hand strokes Alice's hair as he looks down at her. She puts a restraining hand on his arm and turns to the other man. 'Sir, is that so? You are a justice?'

'For my sins, yes.'

'Could you ...? We need to beg Sam, in order to adopt him. Is that something you can arrange?'

'For certain. I shall need details, but if you stay now, you will all three be soaked. I'm in London tomorrow but I'll call by when I next go into Guildford and we can go through it.'

As the three take their leave, Alice on Athena, her working mare from when she lived in Dorset, and Sam up in front of Henry on the grey, Olivia stands next to Jack in the doorway. They wave their goodbyes as the two horses round the end of the barn and disappear from their sight.

'That's a relief,' says Jack, and at Olivia's puzzled look, he adds, 'I thought he was going to bed her right there in front of us.'

'He is surely smitten,' she replies. 'He needs a good woman to steward him, and I don't mean Isabel.'

'I hope Isabel will not be a fly in the ointment.'

'And that other matter?' she asks him. 'I thought you might bring it up when you mentioned him selling us the lodge.'

'The lodge wasn't part of that, just a need for ready cash for repairs. I don't need to mention that other matter, I think. It died with Frederick Tillotson.'

Olivia nods. 'Best not to speak of it.'

12

The sky is darkening faster than they anticipated, the heaped clouds advancing apace. Henry wraps his short cloak round Sam as they feel the first drops, large and sparse, and they spur their horses over the open ground through the dimming landscape. Athena is sluggish and unwilling to hurry. They are only a few hundred yards out from Freemans when they feel the first spits of rain, then larger drops that spread coin-sized on their clothes. Within seconds a shower starts in earnest, quickly filling to a cloudburst that flattens their hair into dark rats' tails clinging to forehead and neck. Through the driving sheets of grey they go, Alice's borrowed chemise rapidly soaking and clinging to her arms. Her skirt flapping against Athena's streaming flank takes the wet through, and the draggled underskirt clings to her thighs. Henry's doublet darkens as the downpour soaks in. His breeches flap as wetly as Alice's skirt, and they wryly regard each other's condition. But even the deluge cannot urge more than a trot out of Athena. Water trickles cold inside Alice's bodice and her cheeks sting from the pins of rain driving in her face. Traversing the copse is no relief; the barely budding trees offer no protection and the bushes either side brush wet against arm and leg.

Henry's short cloak shields Sam from the worst of the downpour, but his hair is dripping by the time they ride into the kitchen court at High Stoke. Joe is nowhere to be seen, and they dismount and lead the horses into the stables. Sam is all for raking out and renewing their straw, but Alice diverts him with a wisp of hay to help her rub down Athena while Henry removes the saddles, fetches water and attends to the grey. Having settled them in their stalls, the three make the short dash into the house.

Numb-fingered, hair dripping in her eyes, Alice fights in vain to untie Henry's short cloak from Sam's shoulders, eventually slipping it over his head and dropping it in a sodden heap on the floor. 'We must get you out of these wet things, Sam.' One rain-darkened little shoe joins the other on the floor, followed by his sodden stockings, and Sam hops on pink-toed feet on the cold stone flags. Mollie appears at the door of the pot room, and immediately starts to retreat.

'Mollie!' Sam cries in delight, hampering Alice's efforts to undo the ties of his shirt. 'Look, we got wet and more wet in the rain. And I saw Robert's horses, and I fed them and—' Sam prattles on about all the things he is bursting to tell Mollie, who has drawn back as far as she can and is peering round the door jamb with anxious eyes.

'Mollie, don't go away,' Alice says. 'Do you take Sam and dry him off. He will need a fresh shirt and dry nether hose and shoes, you'll find them up in his room. There, Sam, go with her and get dried off. Mollie, do you make a fire in his room, please, I don't want him catching cold. And please stay there with him until I come.' Mollie curtsies and nods and curtsies again, bobbing like a little boat in choppy seas as she approaches to take Sam's hand and bear him off. Sam has not stopped chattering all the while about his new friends at Freemans.

Henry has unbuttoned his saturated doublet and it hangs open, the shirt underneath plastered to his chest. He bends to pull off his boots. Alice slips off her squelching shoes and takes them in one hand, holding her drenched skirt away from her legs as she pads across to the kindling box. As she takes handfuls of wood shavings to stuff into the toes, a small gasp escapes her.

'You're hurt,' he says in quick concern, crossing over to her. 'Let me see.'

'It's nothing. I jarred my elbow when I fell, that's all.'

'That's a nasty bruise. I'll send for the apothecary.'

'Not at all, Henry. I've something in my box that will take

it down.'

'Sam seems well. No cuts or grazes.'

She laughs. 'He had a soft landing on me.'

'I should have told you about that place, not to go in there.' He slips an arm round her.

'You weren't to know Sam and I would go adventuring.' She twists round in his hold and her chemise, clinging to her skin in wet veins, drags as it pulls against the linen shirt stuck to his chest. His flattened hair drips on his shoulders and down her bodice. They stand clasped together, laughing at their saturated state, until his face bends towards hers and the laugh stills to a smile, a look, a slow brushing of lips. For long seconds they stand body to body. Her fingers loose his shirt and run along his ribs, finding the furrow of his spine, as his hands follow the contours of her bodice, her hips, and he pulls her hard against him. Her fingertips light on each ridge of bone down his back until he swings her up in his arms and she clings to him, mouthing the wet roughness of his chin, jaw, neck as he bears her out of the kitchen and along the screens passage.

Neither sees Isabel emerge from the still room to gaze along the screens passage as he turns into the hall. The steward stands deathly still, arms clasped in the long V before her, head cocked as the faint padding of stockinged feet crosses the hall. She cannot possibly hear him climb the stone stairs at the far end, but still the pin-point irises stare unblinking under drawn brows. The slam of the main chamber door sets her lids flickering, and the slightest of tremors shivers her body. Deep in her narrowed eyes, black smoulders.

13

Alice stops by the doorway to a small room off the screens passage. It is just large enough to house the table at which Henry sits, and a stand of shelves on which are stored an assortment of boxes, rolls, keys, clay pipes, papers, sealing wax. The surface of the table is scattered with a litter of sheets from small mean notes with crabbed writing to large square-cut sheets covered in flowing hand.

'It's the first time I've seen in here,' she says taking in the scene before her, lit by a single small casement. 'Is this where you do the accounts?'

Henry leans back in his chair with a sigh. Under his hand is a sheet in his writing, figures in columns. 'I wish I could collect rents as easily as I seem to collect bills,' he says, and picks up a sheaf of papers. 'Bills for hay, bills for straw.' One after another he lets them fall. 'For ale, cheese, rush-lights, wax candles … wax?' He picks up the last again. 'What need have we of wax candles? And this – forks! Have we become so fine?' He casts it aside and continues. 'Charcoal, pipe tobacco, a hogshead of what? Oh, more red Gascony wine.'

'Did you need a whole hogshead?' Alice asks, closing the door behind her. 'It seemed to me the last one has nearly run to vinegar.'

'Mayhap.' He pulls her onto his lap and continues shuffling through the pile. 'But there won't be much more Gascony for a while anyway, if we go to war as he wants to.'

'His Majesty?'

'Or Buckingham – sometimes I wonder which one is the king.'

'But how can we afford to go to war when people can barely feed themselves?'

Henry shrugs. 'I don't believe that was ever a reason to keep the peace. Whether or no, it'll not help me settle these bills. Rather the reverse – he'll want to raise even more money.'

'There was talk of a forced loan. Is that still going to happen?'

'I'd not be surprised. Jack says the king won't negotiate with Parliament, he merely orders them around. Oh, Alice.' He links his hands round her waist and nuzzles her neck. 'We'll have to do something now, or that'll be another bill we can't pay.'

Alice feels like asking him what he thinks the steward is doing about it, but suppresses the urge. That way lies disagreement. 'Where does High Stoke's cash come from?' she asks.

'Rents, some. Selling the wool clip, for what that's worth, this isn't the best sheep country. The barley grain goes to the maltster down at the mill wharf; that's our main income.'

'Which you then spend buying ale. Why don't we use some of that malted grain to make our own ale?'

'We do.'

'Where?'

'At the end of the wash-house.'

'Where?'

'That storeroom at the far end.'

'That? That's so crammed with throw-outs there's no room to move, let alone brew ale.'

'Well, I don't know, Alice.' A note of irritation is creeping into his voice. 'Perhaps Isabel decided it wasn't worth it any more. I've told her she must buy in the good stuff, the stout ale, from the Red Lion, but she has a free hand with the everyday ale.'

'This much?' Alice says, waving the brewer's bill. 'I thought the buttery looked very full when Isabel showed it to me but she says everything there has your sanction. Who drinks it all, Henry? There's enough for dozens of servants in there.'

'Well, how would I know? I don't keep a tally like some purse-pinching Banbury Brother!'

'I know, my dear,' she says, running an arm round his neck,

'and I love you for your open-handedness, but you need to know where your cash is being spent.' She pulls out a floridly styled sheet. 'Look at this for instance, pewter candlesticks.'

Gently he takes the sheet from her and screws it in his hand. 'I wanted you to have good candlesticks for the bedchamber, Alice.' His look disarms her.

'Those? Oh, Henry.' She kisses him. 'They are beautiful, but I had no idea you had bought them new just for me. You should not, when we are so stressed.'

There is a short silence between them. 'Of course, there is one way we could pay these at a stroke,' he says.

'Yes? How so?'

He shuffles the pile of sheets together and plumps it down in the middle of the table. 'We could sell Hill House.'

She stares at him. 'Sell my home? No, Henry. Decidedly no.'

'It would solve everything.'

'It would solve nothing.'

'Pay everything off, do repairs, buy new, live without constantly feeling the pinch.'

'Forgive my reminding you that you sold the lodge and a parcel of land to the Egertons not so long ago, yet now you're short of cash again.'

'The roof of the barn was leaking badly. Something had to be done fast.'

She shakes her head. 'I don't understand. A household like this with the land you have, it ought to be thriving.'

'It could, if I had ready cash from Hill House. It would give us a breathing space to—'

'It would merely put off an even worse crisis in a few years' time.'

'— to improve High Stoke's standing.'

'We'd have to spend and spend to maintain that standing.'

He holds up his hands. 'All right, we'll make changes.'

'Yes?' she says, encouraged. 'What changes?'

But now a frown of impatience sours his features. 'If I had the answer, do you think I would be sitting here confronting mounting debts? You're of a practical turn of mind, Alice, but when I make a practical suggestion, you turn me down.'

'Do you wish to know what I think?'

'I wish you to sell Hill House.'

She ignores that. 'Give me leave to direct the household.'

'You do, Alice. You're mistress here.'

'I don't, as you well know. Isabel keeps a tight hold and declines to discuss anything.'

'Then tell her!'

'She doesn't listen, Henry. She wouldn't even let me in here when she showed me the house on Saturday. She pretended she'd mislaid the key.'

'She's only protecting her position.'

'Her position won't exist if High Stoke fails because of bad husbandry.'

He shrugs and sighs. 'Alice, she simply works in a different way from you, that doesn't make her wrong. You must be patient and persuade her to change if that's what you want.'

'Ooohh, Henry!' Alice wriggles off his lap and turns to glare at him. 'Have you listened to a word I've said? Do you have any idea what an uphill struggle that is, with someone who has not the slightest intention of changing?'

'She's been here a long while. Change isn't easy when you're older, Alice.'

'She's not that old. She can't be much older than you.'

'Why can't you be reasonable with her? Give her time, like I said.'

'We have no time. You've just said we have to make changes now, Henry. She cannot rule here! What tasks would she do that I can't do better? Do we even need a steward?'

'You cannot simply dismiss people because you don't like them!'

'I didn't say "dismiss", but can you see her accepting a position as a maidservant again?'

'Now you're being ridiculous.' He pulls a sheaf of bills towards him as though to continue his accounts. Alice leans her hand on them. 'Isabel wants to pretend I don't exist. She knows I know what I'm talking about. For her, my very presence is a threat. No, please listen to me, Henry. For years she has done the job you wanted her to do, no blame to her for that, but the case is altered now. Her ways are not the ways High Stoke must adopt in order to recover. Why doesn't she go home to her father? I can make four, six, ten times what it would cost you to give her a pension. That would be an honourable way out for her.' She rests her hand on his arm, leans forward to meet his eyes. 'Please Henry, at least think about it.'

'Don't you ever stop? Money, money, money!'

'I'm merely trying to—'

'Your father was the same, typical yeoman farmer, forever talking yields!'

'Don't you dare bring my father into this! You hardly knew him!'

'All you people ever talk about is money!'

'All *you* ever talk about is the lack of it, but you're too much of a fine gentleman to do anything about making it!'

He jerks his arm from her hold, hunches his shoulder and goes back to his figures. 'Close the door as you go out.'

For several seconds she stands by him aggrieved, confused at this storm that has blown up out of nowhere. Surely he will turn at any moment. She reaches out to lay a conciliatory hand on his arm. 'Henry don't let's—' but at that moment he leans across the table for the inkwell. Her hand drops to her side. Without a word she turns and leaves the room.

14

The collection of books Alice owns is a bare handful, each one a treasure. Some are her mother's receipt books which have been Alice's for years anyway, but amongst the rest is a book her father bought for her on his visit to London last year.

Called *Delightes for Ladies,* it is a beautifully printed and illustrated work covering all manner of information and advice on cookery, physick, brewing, preserves, perfumery and suchlike. Unlike her mother's books, which were compiled in haphazard scribbled manner as receipts for this and that came to hand, this is ordered in sections, making everything easy to find. And not only does she value it for this, but also because it is one of the few things she possesses with that direct connection to her father. Now both her parents are dead, such possessions as these are an infinitely precious part of their memory.

On discovering the books piled in a coffer earlier this morning, Sam was disappointed to find that the pictures are of things like cooking pots, which are not interesting, he told Alice. No devils, no arrows, no skulls, nothing exciting.

The quarrel with Henry last night has left Alice shaken and unhappy but unrepentant. By this morning she has resolved that if the price of turning round the fortunes of High Stoke House is a scolding from her husband then so be it. This morning they dressed in frozen silence and when she braced herself to ask him if he was coming down to breakfast with her, he replied that he would only do so if she agreed to be reasonable.

Alice fumed. 'And am I to be "reasonable" about Isabel or "reasonable" about selling Hill House? Or both, perhaps?' When he didn't answer, Alice marched down tight-lipped to the kitchen. There, to Maureen the cook's stunned indignation, she took down two dishes which she piled with slices of the Egertons' ham and some medlar cheese from her Hillbury preserves. In the dairy where Mollie had just scalded the floor and was sweeping the steaming water into the drainage channel, Alice helped herself to a child's measure of milk and carried her gleanings up to Sam's room. There, to his great delight, they sat and ate together on his bed.

At some point, Henry went out without saying where or for how long. She tells herself she does not care. But in the emptiness, employment is more than ever necessary. Sam's discovery of the books has decided her to unpack the remaining things she brought from Dorset, clothes, kitchen items, her prized set of Venetian wine glasses, linen. Sam returns with Samuel and Zachariah, his two crudely whittled wooden figures, and follows her around, keen to be useful and at the same time keeping her informed of the scrapes his two toys are getting into. When she takes items to the kitchen, he keeps close by her side as Isabel's eye falls on him. Finally, Alice comes back to the books. The thought of leaving her collection of receipts in the kitchen where Isabel's hostile hand might too easily deface them is not to be thought of. Alice decides to make space on the bookshelves in the winter parlour. Sam announces his retreat upstairs, where she guesses he will find material enough on the rush-strewn floor to challenge Samuel and Zachariah.

The sun pours obliquely through the window, warming the room and making the fire in the hearth unnecessary. This morning there is more than a touch of spring in the weather. She drags a backstool and stands on it to reach the top shelf where, by shuffling a few books together, she makes space sufficient for her needs.

She straightens the spines, jumps down and crosses to the window. Outside, Allan has been working on the herb garden, clearing last year's dead growth and trimming back the little box hedges that have been left to sprawl too long. She set him this task partly to separate him from Joe, whose resentment has simmered ever since the betrothal on Sunday. But also she wants to see how Allan works on his own. She was prepared for the inevitable tussle when Isabel remarked, 'He cannot be spared to dabble with flowers.'

'It's a herb garden, Isabel.'

'He has important work in the fields with the others.'

'I realise that, but what is more important than ensuring we have the herbs we need for meat and medicine?'

'We buy what we need; we always have.'

Not always Alice thinks, or the herb garden would not be there. 'We can produce our own more cheaply. My husband and I wish to save as much money as we can, Isabel.' Two can play the 'my cousin' game, she thinks and watches Isabel's black pin-point eyes bore into her before the steward turns on her heel without a word.

In the back of Alice's mind is the idea that if Allan proves hard-working and responsible, it will not only be good for the demesne, but will mean she might raise his status and offer him some extra recompense to help towards living expenses when he and Sylvia are married. She looks out on the herb garden where one corner looks decidedly improved. The straggly growth is cut back, dry dead leaves cleared, form sheared out of chaos. Weeds and cuttings are piled on some sacking, and tools lie nearby, a rake, a twig broom. As she looks, Allan comes into view and approaches the window. In the warmth of the day he has shed his jerkin and rolled up his shirt sleeves, revealing sinewy forearms already well browned by exposure to sun and weather. He signals towards the front of the house, mouthing the word 'message'.

'Come round to the front door,' Alice says, pointing, and at his questioning look, she indicates, 'I'll meet you there.' She offers the reassurance, guessing that it is likely he hesitates to be seen at the front of the house for fear of an upbraiding from the steward.

Bright sunshine dazzles her as she pulls open the heavy door and she puts up a hand to shade her eyes. Allan is by the door in the garden wall, trying to persuade a child to accompany him, but the child hangs back, clearly unwilling, perhaps frightened, to come nearer. She can be no more than seven or eight years old, dressed in shapeless bits of cloth that look like cut-down hand-downs from generations of needy. Even the most deserving poor wouldn't want what this girl wears. Her feet are bare and the only covering for her arms is a piece of frayed sacking she holds wrapped round her shoulders. Her hair hangs in greasy tails over her round young face. Long exposure to wind and weather has reddened her cheeks, roughened the skin of face and arms. Both hands and feet carry the ingrained filth that comes from lack of washing. She holds a short stout stick in one hand. Allan approaches Alice.

'She brings a message from Master Tillotson, mistress,' Allan says. 'He is a neighbour. He asks if you can spare me for a few hours, not more than a day he thinks, to mend his cart. She does not know the exact fault.'

'I have heard of Master Tillotson,' Alice says. 'Does he live nearby or do you need a horse?'

'He lives over the road, well, up the hill a bit, and then on a bit,' Allan says, and adds by way of explanation, 'If you keep going it's not far from St Martha's.'

Wherever St Martha's is, thinks Alice.

'I can walk it in half an hour. No need to go mounted.'

'You have gone to Master Tillotson's aid before, I think, Allan?'

Allan nods. 'Mostly for his father, Master Frederick, when he was alive. But I've done bits for young Master Jeremy too since he came back to run the farm.'

'How do you find him?' Useful to have another opinion about the ways of this neighbour of hers.

'Always very kind, very glad of help given, and shows himself thankful as his father did before him.' By which she understands that Jeremy rewards Allan directly with some form of gratuity.

'Will you need help there? Should Angus go with you?'

'Angus has got fencing to repair.'

'I mean, will you need help with the cart?'

'Oh, no,' Allan assures her. 'Len's there, Jeremy's man. He tackles most jobs. He just doesn't understand carts.'

'And you do?'

'I was apprentice for a while to a cartwright. Until he died.'

'So you've not yet finished your apprenticeship?'

'Nor ever likely to,' he answers with a wry grin. 'But I know enough about carts.'

'You would be happy to go and mend it?'

'Surely, mistress. I should dearly like to go.' This last said with eagerness. She finds it disheartening, how much he wishes to be away from here, even for a matter of hours, then chides herself for imagining things.

'I think tomorrow morning will be best,' she says. 'Since we do not know the exact nature of the job, you may take all day if necessary.' A thought occurs to her. 'When you return, perhaps you would ask Master Jeremy if it would be convenient for you to load the cart up with some clothes he plans to send us and bring them—'

'Oh, the clothes were brought down yesterday,' Allan says, pointing back at the waiting child. 'She said it was when the cart came back empty to Tillotsons that they went to load some barley for the maltster and the side collapsed.'

Behind him, the child's laugh, innocent, merry, transforms her face. 'Grain were everywhere,' she giggles, 'geese were gobbling it up.'

Geese. The stick in her hand. Alice turns to the small figure. 'You must be Sir—' What's the man's name? The coroner who kept stepping across to Tillotsons after old Master Tillotson died. Mortimer? Markham? '— Sir Malcolm's goose girl, is that right?'

The girl nods, and Allan adds, 'She often walks the geese round by Master Jeremy's. It's only a few minutes' walk, and old Florence there usually gives her something to eat.'

Alice turns back to the child. 'Tell me, what is your name?'

'Hannah.'

'Well, Mistress Hannah, did you catch all your geese?' Hannah nods again and makes herding strokes with the short stick in her hand.

'And where are they today? Are they safe?' Alice asks. She dreads another stray goose around the place, another execution. The "noble knight" will surely become suspicious at the gradual erosion of his flock. If Henry and he are not on good terms, as it seems, that could mean unwelcome trouble if a connection with High Stoke is made. But Hannah points towards the belt of trees across the clearing. 'All on the tether,' she says.

'Did you say Master Tillotson's man delivered the clothes, Hannah?'

'Len said it was the clothes as were too heavy, and he said, *See, I told you so,* and Master Jeremy said to mind his tongue and get grain back in the sacks.' Hannah grins. 'They were trying to scoop it up and geese were trying to get at it.' Clearly the incident was a grand diversion for the child.

'Are you going back that way, Hannah? Can you take a message?' Alice says. 'Please tell Master Jeremy that Allan will go there tomorrow morning.'

Hannah leaves in due course, having been rewarded with a mug of small ale and a slice of meat pie Alice finds in the still room. 'Isabel will not like you taking it,' Maureen warns. And Alice replies, 'I think we can leave Isabel to speak for herself, Maureen.' Somehow she omits to tell Hannah that the meat is from Sir Malcolm's executed goose.

GRACE slides off Cassie's back and leads her into the stables. All is quiet. No Joe. Not that it matters; she has known what to do ever since she first clambered onto the sagging back of a neighbour's nag at the age of eight. Her opportunities for riding have been few over the years, but on each occasion, the unfamiliar quickly becomes familiar. She undoes the girth and hauls off the saddle, easing it onto the bench by the stall, following it with the folded blanket.

In the little plain-stitched pocket tucked under her skirt at her waist, Grace can feel the cloth-wrapped, round white cheese she made yesterday. She wonders, not for the first time, where she will find the courage to offer it to the mistress.

Grace's arrival home brought relief and optimism to her family. For all their efforts, they have not the talents for nursing that she possesses. Grace herself knew only anxiety and sleeplessness for two nights until Monday brought a perceptible change. Her mother's recovery at the hands of the apothecary was a great weight off the whole family's mind. Her father, looking aged and desperate when Grace arrived home, has regained his vigour, and by this morning, they were all satisfied that in a day or two her mother will be herself once more. Grace left with a light heart, and in her relief, she had to resist the impulse to sing on the way. Nothing, she feels, can ever again plunge her into such melancholy as she knew on Saturday.

And then there is Allan. In all, she feels pleased at her strength in not allowing herself to think about Allan for three whole days. She traces again in her mind how she succeeded in not thinking about Allan at church on Sunday, not thinking about him at night as she lay awake next to her sleeping sister, not recalling his smile while she cooked and washed for her family, and this morning several times not allowing herself to imagine him riding alongside her. Three whole days since she saw him, three days since he brought her those beautiful primroses. She allows herself the passing thought that there might be another posy when he knows she is back.

As to Sylvia's warning about Allan's roving eye, the thought occurs to Grace that Sylvia has misread Allan. After all, Grace thinks, look at Joe; Sylvia has no idea of Joe's devotion, never seems to notice him, even though it is as clear as day to Grace. Perhaps Sylvia is not quite as knowing as she likes everyone to think. And what of the fallen dairymaid Mary? Grace imagines hard eyes and black snaking locks, a temptress if ever there was one, casually coupling with some passing rake, and blaming Allan for the resultant child. No, Sylvia means well, wanting to put Grace on her guard, but Sylvia has entirely the wrong idea about Allan. Grace is resolved to trust her own feelings in future and not be swayed by others.

The ambling pace she has allowed the mare on the return means that Cassie is not lathered, so a quick rub-down will suffice. Then she must change these dusty clothes for clean and get to the dairy. She eases the bridle from the mare's head and hangs it on a nail. At that moment a shadow falling across the doorway makes her jump.

'So, you've come back. Value your place after all, do you?' Isabel's voice sets up the familiar churning in Grace's stomach. *Stand up for yourself, her mother said. The softer you are, the harder she will hit. You're sometimes too gentle.* Grace takes a deep breath and finds a smile from somewhere. 'Good morning, Isabel. I came back as soon as I could.'

'Is that so?'

Grace tries to ignore the sceptical tone, the lack of curiosity about her mother's health. 'I can take over the dairying as soon as I have seen to Cassie and changed.' *You're a good dairywoman, her mother said. Remember that. Talk to the mistress, tell her what you can do.*

'Leave that and come now,' Isabel orders and steps into the stable to drive Grace in front of her. As she does so, Isabel's foot kicks a pitchfork leaning against the stall and it falls, its pointed tines narrowly missing Grace's face. Isabel turns an accusing eye on her. 'Stupid girl! That was a dangerous place to put it!'

In the face of sudden accusation, Grace is nonplussed. Isabel stoops to take up the fork. Her eyes light on its twin, curved tines, fix into a fascinated stare.

'Shall I put it out of the way, Isabel?' Grace asks, and gently possesses herself of the long handle. She does not like the look in Isabel's eyes; it sets up a thumping in her chest. She props the pitchfork safely in the corner and when she turns round, Isabel seems to have recovered. In silence, Grace walks ahead across the court and into the kitchen. From the closed aspect of the washhouse, she realises with regret that Betsy is not around. Of course, it is Tuesday, she will be doing the washing at the Egerton's place. Grace would have welcomed Betsy's company, would have liked to talk about her family. Betsy would understand how worried she has been.

'You can wash your hands in the bucket there and get straight on with some work,' Isabel commands, stepping into the kitchen and closing the door. 'You've some catching up to do, miss.' Isabel heads up the screens passage; a door closes.

As Grace leans to the bucket, the door of the still room silently eases open a crack. Through the gap a pair of sliding eyes tracks her every move.

IN her soft house slippers Alice arrives at the end of the screens passage and stands for a moment in the dimness outside the kitchen listening for Isabel's voice. Why has the steward not told her of the arrival of the Tillotson clothes? And where has she stored them? Alice makes a mental note to look through for a set of clothes, a little jerkin or a cloak at the very least, for Hannah. The days are getting warmer but nights are chilly and from what Allan could tell her, Hannah leads a wandering life sleeping mostly in barns or under the stars. It appears that Sir Malcolm does not see fit to reward his goose-girl with a roof over her head. From the way she wolfed the goose pie, coarse pastry and all, it seems he does not give her much to eat, either.

Alice peers into the kitchen. Only Maureen's voice, retreating into the pot room as she berates young Mollie for some sin of omission. About to pass on, Alice stops at sight of Sylvia emerging from the still room. There is a stealth about the way the girl moves across the stone flags and out into the kitchen court. What on earth is she doing? Avoiding some task Maureen has set her? Alice dismisses the thought, time to wonder about that later. At the moment she needs to find Isabel about these clothes. She turns towards the servants' parlour and pokes her head round the door. Some knives lie on the long table alongside a pile of round bread trenchers. Curious, she approaches, only to note with disgust the jaundiced colour. She picks one up and feels its barely edible denseness. Clearly the oven was not properly heated, something else to take up with Isabel, the list becomes ever longer. The disc makes a flat thud as she drops it back.

From the parlour, she makes her way along the dim kitchen corridor. Cool air fans her face from the door of the dairy and as she comes up to it, she sees the door opposite standing open to the dairy court, propped with one of the milk buckets. This side of the house is still in shadow and the breeze drifts fresh from outside. Grace is back, standing by the churn in the doorway, her hand on the paddle, but instead of working it, she is gazing outside, her back to Alice. Something in the girl's intent stillness halts Alice.

A voice, light and teasing, drifts from the dairy court. Sylvia comes into view round the end of the wash-house, and with her, Allan. She is laughing and encouraging him forward. He looks about him, squinting in the sun.

Alice looks at Grace looking at Sylvia and Allan.

The pair come to a halt in the middle of the dairy court. Beyond the shadow cast by the house, the sun shines over the roof straight in Allan's eyes. Sylvia slips slim arms round his neck and backs him up against the wall of the wash-house. She draws his face towards hers, arches her body against his and reaches for his hand, bringing it up to cup her breast, holding it there. The kiss lasts as long as it would take a shot bird to flutter to the ground and flap out the last of its life.

Sylvia takes a step back, tweaking the ties of Allan's shirt. He has a dazed, perplexed look on his face. Sylvia's words drift across the court, 'It's nearly time to eat, why don't you go in through the dairy? It's all right, Isabel's in the accounts room, she won't see you. I'll join you in a moment, Allan dearest. Save me a place by your side.' With a parting smile, she turns and swings away towards the cow byre. Allan shrugs and heads for the dairy. He steps in, his eyes adjusting too late from the strong sunlight.

'Grace! I —'

He glances over his shoulder. Sylvia has disappeared. He swallows and says, 'I didn't know you were back.'

'So I see,' Grace says. Her voice is flat, toneless, the words as though dragged out of her. Alice is transfixed in the gloom of the passage.

He hangs his head. 'I ... I wanted to tell you.'

She picks up the bucket and moves to close the door. 'You don't have to tell me anything, I can see for myself. Now I have work to do. You'd better go.'

'We are—' He stops, looks away down the dairy court while she waits. He seems to gather himself as he turns back to her and takes a deep breath. His head comes up and he raises his eyes to her face. 'Sylvia and me – we are betrothed.' His gaze falls and he hangs his head once more. 'I'm sorry.'

Grace could be a statue. At last, in tones of loathing, 'Plenty of leg and low-cut bodice there – should be enough, even for you.'

'What?'

'Get out!' She has hold of the door and pushes it against him.

'Grace, let me explain—'

'There's nothing you can say that I want to hear. I never want to talk to you again!' He reaches for her hand, but she pulls back. 'Get away from me! You deserve each other!'

15

The heap of clothes behind the cow byre is too large to have been sheltered by the newly sprouting hedge. Yesterday's downpour, as well as splattering the outer fringes with mud, has penetrated more than one layer. Left overnight, the wet has seeped. Sodden indigo sprawls over blue-smudged linen; wringing-wet red spreads rose stains on neighbouring whites. There are skirts, shirts, undershirts, breeches, mufflers, sleeves, bonnets, frontlets, nightwear, footwear, netherwear. And that is just the parts she can see. Len must have cast some sacking over the heap, but it has billowed and flapped back in the breeze, catching on the hedge and leaving most of the pile exposed. The whole lot is of decent quality, if badly worn, moth-eaten and very outdated. Alice regards the ruin, reining in with difficulty the impulse to berate. Isabel, drawn all unwilling from the accounts room, waits expressionless for Alice to speak.

'Did Len come to see you when he brought this lot yesterday, Isabel?'

'I take it you refer to the serving man from Tillotsons?'

'You remember you were with me when Betsy asked me about it on Saturday?'

'There was brief mention, as I recall,' Isabel says.

'He brought this cartload of clothes for Betsy to sort through and offer to those in need around here.'

'Tillotson cast-offs,' Isabel says, pulling a face.

'And what instruction did you give him when he arrived? What did you tell him to do with these things?'

'He was about to leave them in the kitchen court,' Isabel says. 'I told him that was not acceptable.'

'Did you tell him where, then?'

'He suggested bringing them into the house!' Isabel says it as though Len proffered a nest of rats. 'The house, I ask you!'

'Why not? They could have gone in the end room.'

'You ordered that room cleared for Allan and Sylvia,' Isabel reminds her.

'I know, but—' Alice takes a deep breath. 'Never mind. What about the wash-house, didn't you suggest that?'

'Betsy had already left. It was locked.'

'But you have a key!' *Ooh, to shake this woman!*

'Betsy does not like the wash-house to be used when she is absent,' Isabel tells her. There is little Alice feels she can say to that, not knowing the routine well enough, though the fact it was Betsy who had brought up the subject in the first place does not suggest that she would object.

'Why not in the granary, then? Anywhere is better than leaving them to ruin in the rain.'

'And allow those – thieves – to pilfer grain while they pretend to choose clothes for themselves? My cousin would never allow such a thing!'

So, it is "my cousin" again, the subtle wedge, the reminder of Henry's favour, the years they have known each other. Alice fumes. There is no reasoning with this woman. 'Isabel, some of these clothes are now ruined beyond saving through being left out in the rain.' Alice tries to keep her voice even, reasonable.

'I cannot be held responsible for the weather.'

Alice sighs. This is getting nowhere. 'You have the key to the wash-house?' she asks, holding out her hand.

Isabel's hand flies to cover the bunch dangling amongst the generous folds of her silk gown. She hesitates. 'It may be—'

'The key, please, Isabel? Unless you'd like me to leave you to move this heap yourself?'

Slowly Isabel unhooks a key; she holds it in her palm, obliging Alice to reach for it. 'Thank you. Now you may help me get it all under cover. And another thing. Ask Mollie to come and light the fire in the wash-house to help dry these things.'

Isabel glares at her. 'It is wasteful to use wood on unnecessary fires. My cousin dislikes waste.'

Alice very nearly smiles as she replies, 'I too dislike waste, so from tomorrow please ensure that all fires in the house are left unlit, unless my husband or I say. The weather is quite warm enough now.'

By the time Alice brings the first armful round to the kitchen court, Isabel is nowhere to be seen, but Mollie hops past, evidently with orders to assist. Deciding that two work-stained but willing hands are better than two white and very reluctant ones, Alice lets it go. On the way back to the heap, she turns off through the dairy court to exchange a few words of welcome with Grace, enquiries about her mother, and a tentative question as to Grace's wellbeing. Grace's laboured assurance that she is quite well renders it impossible to offer comfort, and Alice is obliged to leave the stony-faced girl to her misery in the solitude of the dairy.

The heap of clothes is considerable. As they work their way through, despite herself Alice finds her humour lightening. She cannot help but smile at the puffy trunk-hose, is that some pre-Spanish-fleet fashion? She regards in disbelief a woman's embroidered doublet with great padded wings pointing up at the shoulders; there is much to be said for the simpler fashions now.

It is hard to tell how many generations of Tillotson clothes have been stored over the years. After several trips the heap outside is subsiding. Mollie, silent as ever, skips to and fro, whether loaded down or returning for more. The wettest items they spread over the sinks or out on the drying bushes. Mercifully the rain did not penetrate more than a layer or two, and by the time they are finished, the rest fills all the spare floor space at one end of the wash-house. Alice props the door ajar with a stone to give air for the fire Mollie is now tending, and stands for a moment looking at the key in her palm. This, she determines, is the first of many she will wrest from Isabel's grip.

16

'What on earth is ailing the household?' Henry asks, jug in hand. He makes pouring gestures towards her. Alice shakes her head; she cannot face yet another breakfast with flavourless small-ale. 'How long do you have, Henry?' One by one, she ticks off her fingers. 'We have a betrothed couple and patently *he* does not wish to be betrothed, and *she* retains a roving eye. We have a dairymaid who is heartsick, a stable boy smouldering with jealousy, and to round it all off, we have a laundress who I suspect is about to leave us.'

'Betsy? Who says?' Now she has his attention.

'She's looking unhappier by the day. She said to me on Saturday she is getting too old for the work she does. I fear she may go and live at Freemans if we're not careful.' Betsy talked with her on her return from Freemans, animated as she spoke of the Egertons and of head man Robert and his young family. 'She was speaking so fondly of them when she came back last night. I doubt Olivia would suggest it, being a close neighbour, but if Betsy asked …' Alice leaves the words dangling.

'By no means can you let her leave.'

'What are we going to do to keep her here, Henry? I feel I can rely on her and I don't want to lose her.'

'You must do whatever you think fit. The women servants are your care, Alice.'

'My care! Try saying that to Isabel. The only point on which she agrees with me so far is that the weather is warm enough to leave all the fires out.' And that is hardly agreement, more an isolated truce wedged between hostilities. 'I ask her what we pay our servants and she avoids the issue. Betsy could do with warm stockings to ward off the cramps – why can't she afford it?'

'How would I know anything about Betsy's stockings? We can't afford to pay her more if that's what you mean, this place doesn't bring in enough.'

Alice sighs. 'Why doesn't it bring in enough, Henry? You have such a deal of land here, it ought to support the people we have *and* show a surplus with ease.'

'We've been through this.' He pushes away his plate and leans back in his chair. 'We clear hardly enough to make ends meet.'

'Where do the peas and beans come from that we make into half-cooked horse-bread to give the servants?' she asks.

'We don't give them horse-bread!'

'When did you last visit their dining parlour, Henry?'

'We don't, do we?' She can see she has shaken him. Horse-bread is the lowest of the low, even worse than the coarse pastry that encases meats and fruits for oven-cooking. Only the very poorest eat such lowly stuff, to the rest it is animal feed. As Alice continues to look at him, he says, 'That's not good.'

'Don't you grow any wheat here?'

'Wheat? No, not here. The land doesn't have enough heart.'

'Are you saying you buy in wheat for breadmaking?'

'There's an established supply to the town from further afield. It's barley we grow here; there's always demand for barley.'

'Yes, I saw a rash of inns and alehouses in town. Do you supply them?'

He shakes his head. 'Not direct. Our grain goes to the maltster near the meal wharf. He'll take whatever I supply, and then he sells on to brewers, or direct to inns to brew their own.'

'The meal wharf, you say? Where do goods go by river from here?'

He smiles. 'I see what you're thinking. It might have looked a large river to you, Alice, compared with your gentle Dorset stream at Hillbury, but forget it, it's not navigable. We can't use it to send grain anywhere. The granaries just happen to be there, the maltster, the brewer. They always have been. Perhaps the Brothers stored their grain there last century before Queen Bess's father dissolved the Friary in the thirties. Bread grain goes for grinding at the watermill anyway.' He sits forward and leans an elbow on the table. 'What are you thinking?'

'I'm thinking that wheat brings in more per bushel than barley. I'm thinking that if we were growing wheat, albeit we cannot ship it from here, it could be carted to wherever it's needed. And we'd have no need to compete for business with the town supply if we were supplying London, would we?'

'Places around London supply the whole city already,' he says.

'But London is growing apace,' she counters. 'Why are you smiling like that?'

'I certainly married a farmer's daughter, didn't I?' he says.

'A yeoman's daughter,' she reminds him, and could bite her tongue out. 'I'm sorry.'

'I too said I was sorry,' he reminds her without rancour. Time and again last night they made their peace with each other, each unable to sustain proud isolation, each needing and offering forgiveness in the curtained darkness. And now her quick tongue putting all that at risk again. She reaches across and rests her hand on his arm and he takes her fingers and keeps hold as he goes on, 'Whatever London might need, you cannot escape the fact that wheat needs soil in good heart. Even putting the sheep on the stubble afterwards isn't enough. It starts off well, then you get lower and lower yields. Barley is more tolerant; that's why we all grow it.'

'Don't you practise up-and-down husbandry, Henry?'

He laughs. 'You sound like George Renwick, forever up to some new idea. He keeps trying to get us to join him in his latest slow-top scheme.'

'Up-and-down is not that new, Henry. And it's not slow-top, it's good sound husbandry. You put a different crop on the land before you grow wheat again. It seems to strengthen the soil.' Chin on hand she regards him. The persuading might go to and fro in this way for some while, she thinks, before she convinces him that it is worth the attempt, but she will keep trying. Once he realises there can be benefits, then there might be changes, and not before time.

'That reminds me,' he says. 'I'm going over to George's place to see the new chestnut mare. He says she'll outdo my grey. Mind you, he would say that.'

'Ask him about up-and-down, Henry.'

'After that I must go into town and see what price I can get for the wool clip this year.'

'You're avoiding me.'

'Oh, I think not.' He reaches out a hand to her bodice. 'It's you women who do the avoiding. Why do you barricade yourself with all this bone and buckram?'

'It's to keep your mind on the task. Ask George about up-and-down, Henry.' As he gives her a doubting look, she adds, 'Do it for me. Even if you don't believe me, it will do no harm to ask, will it?'

IT is a short while after Henry has departed for George Renwick's that Alice heads for the kitchen to attempt a discussion with Isabel about the women-servants' situation. The kitchen is empty, no one in still room or pot room. But more than that, there is no crackle of the kitchen fire. Normally, the kitchen fire would be kept going throughout the day, regardless of the weather. Briefly Alice wonders if the steward will make a habit of over-interpreting, deliberately misunderstanding, as when Alice asked to see the house on her first morning. But her ponderings over what to do about relations with Isabel are cut short as she glimpses the flap of a cloak in the kitchen court. Maureen, basket on arm. Alice catches up with her as she hastens out of the yard.

'Isabel said I may go,' Maureen says, digging into her basket.

'I go every Wednesday and I am not back till afternoon.' Which at least explains the lack of kitchen fire, Alice thinks. Maureen continues, 'Look, here is the list,' thrusting it forward like a proof of innocence.

For Alice scanning it, it is further evidence of poor management. Herbs for cooking, ale, spring cheese ... 'Cheese, Maureen? Do we not have a dairymaid?'

'Ah, but Grace is just a raw country girl. We buy our fine cheese from Mistress Sanderson. When it's not pouring with rain, that is,' she adds pointedly looking up at the threatening grey.

'From Mistress Sanderson?' Alice begins to laugh. 'So Mary makes it, does she, the Mary who used to work here, and was turned off, and she went to work for Mistress Sanderson?'

A sour look settles on Maureen's downturned features. 'If you stop me from going, she'll have sold out and it won't be my fault.'

Alice ignores that. 'Why this order for butts of small ale? There are stacks of butts in the buttery.'

'I've been told to buy the same amount every week,' Maureen answers.

'Even though we don't need it, Maureen?' And when Maureen shrugs and says nothing, Alice goes on, 'Anyway, why do we not make our own?'

Well, Maureen has heard tell that the master's mother used to make it. Now they buy it.

'Can't we make it?' Alice asks.

But for Maureen, it is enough to declare that brewing is not her trade and she cannot be blamed for it. Alice cancels most of the cheese and all the ale, and releases Maureen, who glowers in silence and hurries away. Alice knows herself perfectly capable of making both cheese and ale if necessary. The maltster near the meal wharf, Henry said. Very well, when he comes back from George Renwick's she will persuade him to accompany her to select a few bushels of malted grain. Henry drank ale of her making when he visited her home in Dorset, complimented her on it. She will show this household how small-ale should taste. Meanwhile, cheese.

She finds Grace scrubbing the dairy shelves. The most important thing in the dairy is cleanliness. Without that, all tastes are tainted. This room and everything in it is spotless every time Alice visits. Grace herself is heavy-eyed and subdued.

Talk to her about things that will ease her heart, steer away from her cruel disappointment.

For a few minutes while Grace rinses and salts and wipes the surfaces, Alice speaks with her of her home, of the apothecary's visit, of her mother's recovery. Gradually Alice brings the conversation round to dairying. From the way this dairy is looked after, clearly Grace has learned well at home, so how different is that from the way things are done here? Can she make cheese for instance?

At that Grace hesitates. 'Until I came here I never made the cheese we make here,' she says, and Alice wonders whether Isabel is right after all and Grace is a girl with few skills.

'But I made many types of white meats at home,' Grace goes on. 'Many soft cheeses, the sort we could be making here, now that the kine are out in the fields again.' She hesitates, then takes a deep breath. Her words come out in a wavering rush, and a blush rises and spreads over her face. 'May I be allowed to make cheese, mistress? I only make country cheeses and they might not be good enough for your taste, but I should dearly like to show you what I can do.' Grace moves to the shelf as she speaks and takes a little cloth-wrapped shape from a bowl. Alice watches her unwrap it with trembling fingers, revealing a small white round of cheese.

'You made this?' Alice asks. 'May I?' She takes a spoon, scoops a little and tastes, holding it in her mouth to savour it before swallowing. 'This is good, Grace, mild and soft.'

'It needs a little more time for the flavour to come,' Grace is almost apologising. 'I only made it on Monday.'

'Grace, if you can make cheese like this, what sort of cheese have you not made?'

'The hard cheese we eat in the servants' parlour. I made winter cheese at home, but never that.'

Alice recalls the tired yellow brick at every breakfast. 'Is that all we make here?'

'Isabel said I was not to try any other.'

'So you're using only skimmed milk?'

'Twice skimmed.'

'Twice! And you make cheese with the blue milk that's left?' No wonder it looks so sickly, Alice thinks. It's been skimmed to death. I've known better thrown out for the animals. 'This is just flet-milk cheese.'

'Isabel calls it two-meal cheese.'

Alice bites back the tart comment that Isabel clearly doesn't know what she's talking about. 'Two-meal as I know it,' she says, 'uses skimmed from one milking and whole milk from the next.' As Grace nods her agreement, Alice says, 'So what happens to the whey?'

'We throw it out.'

'We have no pigs to give it to?' And as Grace shakes her head, Alice asks, 'And the cream skimmed off the milk?'

'I churn it into butter.'

'How many kine have we?'

'Seventeen in milk,' Grace tells her.

'But that would make mountains! What do we do with all that butter?'

'What we don't use I salt and store,' Grace says.

'Don't we sell it?'

'I don't think so. Nobody's been to market.'

'What about the buttermilk left over?'

'Throw it out.'

'You don't give it to the poor?'

'Isabel says they are not deserving of it.'

'God-a-mercy!' Alice cannot help exclaiming. 'And you help Sylvia milk these kine.'

'No, I don't help Sylvia.'

'But how does she do so many, then?' A dairymaid would be doing well to milk a dozen, fifteen at best, twice a day.

'I mean, I milk them all.'

'Oh! I thought—' Alice is momentarily at a stand. Didn't Isabel say Sylvia helped with the milking? So Grace milks all seventeen by herself, while Sylvia carries the odd pail in affected fashion to pull the wool over Isabel's eyes. And that means that when Alice thought Mollie was taking a share of the milking in Grace's absence, perhaps Mollie did all the milking on her own. 'Oohhh!' Angrily, Alice shakes her head. Isabel must be disabused as to Sylvia's 'honest industry'.

'Mistress?' Grace asks, her eyes anxious. 'Did I do something wrong?'

'By no means. If anyone is wrong, it is me.' Alice feels her own blame, that she should have made it her business to know from the start, instead of finding out by chance. Nevertheless Grace is proving her value as a well-versed dairywoman and Alice is determined to see her rewarded accordingly. 'So, Grace, here's what we are going to do …'

17

Sam is delighted to have Alice to play with and is making the most of it. With the lull brought about by the lack of cooking activity while Maureen goes to market, Alice has decided to order the household to their various routines and leave them to it. Betsy is sorting the Tillotson clothes and Alice has assigned Sylvia to help her. It will ensure Sylvia does not get up to any more tricks at Grace's expense, Betsy will see to that. Allan left early to go to Tillotsons, and Joe is not needed in the stables for the morning, so she has sent him to help Angus repair some fencing and a sheepfold that Angus mentioned to her. That will keep them busy this morning and Betsy will take midday meal to them in the fields. Henry can stable the grey himself on his return.

The showery morning disinclines Alice from venturing outdoors and she is playing robbers with Sam in the winter parlour. Mollie, released by a reluctant Isabel, has joined them. Alice crawls around on all fours with Sam astride her back wielding a stick gleaned from Allan's cuttings in the herb garden. Mollie plays highway villain, trounced time after time by Sam's courageous swordplay from the back of his trusty mount. As a horse, Alice is not expected to talk, and so, on mute Mollie's behalf, she makes bloodcurdling yells as Mollie hops to the attack. One, twice, half a dozen times, is not enough for Sam. He wants 'More, more!'

After a while, Alice tires and even Mollie looks as if she would like to continue playing dead for a while. Alice rears up, tipping Sam off her back, grasps him and playfully pulls him to the floor. The two of them are rolling and laughing when Alice becomes aware of Mollie scrambling up to stand immobile with downcast eyes. Sam clutches Alice and she looks round. At the door, the steward stands, her arms in the long V with hands clasped, her black pin-point eyes boring into Alice just as they did earlier when Alice explained that she wants Grace to try her cheesemaking skills.

Deliberately, Alice remains lying on the floor, looking up. She puts up a protective hand to cup Sam's head. 'It's all right Sam, it's only Isabel.'

'Master Egerton's man to see you.'

'I'll come straightway.'

Alice hurries into the kitchen where the Egertons' head man waits, hat in hand. 'Robert, what can I do for you?' Stockily built, his black wiry hair and beard both comfortably sprinkled with grey, he projects an air of solid reliability, an impression heightened by big, capable hands and far-seeing grey eyes. 'I fear my husband is gone to Master Renwick's this morning.'

'It was yourself I was sent to see. I bring a message from my mistress.'

'From Olivia? How is she?'

'She is not well, I fear. It is not serious,' he adds at Alice's quick concern. 'She merely asks whether you might have an hour or two to come over and sit with her.'

'Of course, I shall come now.'

'She does not wish to disrupt your day.'

'She does not disrupt anything. I shall be pleased to come. I was with Sam, but Mollie is free to stay with him. What ails your mistress?'

IT is only headache, Olivia explains, sounding apologetic. 'Indeed, it is fading already, but it leaves me so weary.' She gives a wan smile; her face is drained of colour, hollowed out, great shadows circling her eyes.

Alice sits by the bed in a small chamber overlooking the fields at Freemans. From here the land falls away in a gentle slope to a track running right and left. Beyond, the ground rises to a small hill on which cattle graze around a spinney of trees crowning the ridge. Olivia lies propped against pillows, clad in a loose shift of soft wool. She is wax-pale, eyes sunk in dark sockets amidst a look of exhaustion. She looks small and vulnerable, a far cry from the arresting beauty Alice met two days ago.

'Thank you for coming, Alice, it is a great comfort and has stopped me falling into a melancholy.'

'Feverfew does not help?' Alice asks. 'I usually chew the leaves when I have the headache. Or vinegar?'

'No, none of the usual remedies. All I can do is lie down and pull the bed curtains until it goes away. Sometimes it lasts for two days,' she says. 'This time I have been lucky, it only started last night. At times like this, I see bright lights like harsh sunlight, even when my eyes are closed, and round my head it presses like a band of wetted leather tightening as it dries.'

No ordinary headache, this. 'The migraine, then?' As Olivia nods, Alice thinks. 'I have heard of a remedy of betony and … something else, what is it? The leaves of one, the root of the other, I seem to remember.'

'Alice!' Olivia's eyes widen. 'How knowledgeable you are. I am astounded that you trip it off so easily.' A glint of amusement flashes in her eyes as she asks, 'Are you a cunning-woman perhaps?'

Alice laughs. 'No such thing. I helped the local apothecary in our village last year and learned much from him. It's in an old herbal he gave me. I'll turn it out and copy it for you. Who knows, it might be worth trying.'

IN the early afternoon, Alice leaves Freemans to ride back to High Stoke. At Olivia's insistence, head man Robert accompanies her, despite Alice's protestations that it is a short distance, and not even on the highway. Nevertheless she admits to herself that it is pleasant to have the company of the man who so calmly occupied and amused Sam after the accident at the lodge.

The day continues warm, though the ground is still soft from the morning's showers. They pass the lodge where Jack Egerton has completed boarding up the ground floor and the house is now secure against unwitting entry. It will be expensive to rebuild the interior, Alice guesses, perhaps impossible if the rot extends to roof and walls. Beyond the resources of High Stoke, for sure, so perhaps it is as well that Jack bought it from Henry, since he is clearly planning to do something with both house and land.

Through the unkempt copse the trees are still dripping. As they emerge the tufty grass ahead is visibly higher than two days ago. Riding in sauntering fashion, Robert's legs hang down either side of his mount, almost brushing the herbage. The rein rests slack in his hand and alongside him Alice has to hold back Cassie, keen for a canter across the open country.

In due course they breast the rising ground and she catches sight of the now familiar chimneys of home through the sprouting treetops. Ahead, the trodden path leads towards the gap between woodshed and stables. It comes as a pleasing surprise to Alice that already she feels she is coming home. Henry will be back from comparing Master Renwick's new mount – no doubt unfavourably – with his own grey. So they can go to the maltster's this afternoon, perhaps take Sam, he will enjoy the ride. Shortly, her own home-brewed ale will be ready for all the household to enjoy. And before that, within days in fact, she will be able to say to Henry that the soft cheese on their table is made here in the dairy at High Stoke. She has further plans for the cheese, but for the time being, that will remain between her and Grace. And bread, she thinks, decent bread is vital, so perhaps they will also see the miller on their visit to the meal wharf. Already she sees change happening.

And something else she sees. Several hundred paces away to her left a figure makes his way through the trees that flank the road to Guildford. With no track to follow, he pushes slowly along, bearing what seems like a weighty bundle, from the way he staggers side to side. She realises she has drawn Cassie to a halt. Robert moves to take protective hold of her bridle. 'Stay a while, mistress, I'm not sure what's toward.'

'Who is it?' Alice says.

'I don't know what he's up to, poaching or some such perhaps, but I don't like the look of it. I think I should take you to the house and I will come back to see what he's doing.'

'Hold a moment,' Alice says as the figure emerges from the undergrowth. 'Look, he's carrying someone, a woman.' The figure stumbles along on a converging course with theirs, making heavy weather of it, halting to hitch his load. 'It's Allan, Robert,' Alice says. 'You know Allan. Come, he needs our help.' She urges Cassie forward, and Robert releasing her bridle follows close as she breaks into a canter. 'Allan!' she calls, waving to catch his attention, and then notices the rich coppery curls of the figure he carries. 'Oh, my goodness, that's Sylvia, she's swooned.'

Sylvia lies limp in Allan's hold, one arm swinging. Her head has fallen back, chestnut tresses swaying, limbs dangling and unresponsive even when he hitches her again to ease his failing hold. 'Dead weight' comes unbidden into Alice's mind. With Robert following close, she hauls Cassie to a sliding stop yards from Allan, drops from the saddle and covers the ground at a run.

'What happened?' She looks at Sylvia's face, the slightly parted lips, the immaculate skin, pale and bloodless, no swoon this. Sylvia is too still, the slightly open eyes are fixed. Carrying her, Allan is gritting his teeth, his mouth twisted to a stiff grimace with the effort. His face is suffused red from the strain and the cords stand out on his neck. He stops, looking at them, clutching his burden in a trembling grip. The strap of his tool bag hangs where it has slipped to his elbow.

'Robert, can you—?' Alice starts, but Robert is already stepping forward, arms extended. 'I'll take her.' He eases Sylvia's lifeless form from Allan's hold. Allan's arms fall and the tools clatter as the bag hits the ground. He stares down at it, making no effort to take it up, while Robert, with Sylvia's limp form draped in his easy hold, turns in the direction of the house. Robert places himself, without design it seems, between the other two. While Allan stands unmoving, Robert catches Alice's eye and directs his look to Sylvia's head. Blood cakes her hair at the back.

Alice suppresses a gasp, steadies her voice. 'Let us bring her to the house. Can you manage her, Robert?' At his nod she turns to gather the reins of each horse. She realises Robert is trying to maintain a protective stance between herself and Allan but there are greater concerns here. Whatever Allan might have done, he is in no state to offer violence to anyone. He seems like a man in a bad dream, not quite recognising what he is doing here. With a small shake of the head to Robert, she moves to Allan and rests a hand on his shoulder, urging him forward. 'Come Allan.' She reaches down and grasps the strap of the tool bag, holding it out to him. His mouth is working with the struggle to form words.

'I didn't mean it like this,' he murmurs, so low she only just hears it.

'Like what?' He looks at her then, his eyes focusing as though he is only now seeing his surroundings. 'Like what, Allan?'

'What?' He seems unaware of his words. He looks down at her hand holding out the bag of tools. He hoists it as of habit onto his shoulder and turns to follow Robert. Alice follows. Time enough for questions when they are alone and quiet indoors, when he has recovered himself somewhat.

In silence they walk towards the outbuildings and pass into the kitchen court. A muddy puddle has formed beyond the stables where the run-off from the wash-house collects. So Betsy has already started laundering the Tillotson linen. Waving the other two towards the house, Alice leads the horses into the stables. No sign of Joe. It was a fortunate decision to send him with the others to the fields today. She loosens girths and pushes the two mounts into stalls before picking her way to the dryer ground of the sloping kitchen court. Betsy has come to the door of the wash-house, wrung shirt in hand, staring at the convoy passing. She cannot have failed to see the blood-caked hair. Alice steps towards her as Betsy whispers, 'She's hurt?'

Alice looks at the older woman's kindly face creased with concern.

'She is all right, isn't she?' Betsy repeats.

Alice struggles to find the words.

'What happened?' Betsy asks, and Alice thinks of Sylvia's eyes, of the spirit severed from the body.

'Sylvia's dead.'

18

Betsy stands rooted at the door to the wash-house. 'But ... she was here, she was well. Grace and me, we left to take the men their meal and she said no, she'd stay. But, I tell you, she was well.'

'Betsy, I am as amazed as you. We just met Allan carrying her. I promise I shall tell you more as soon as—'

Isabel's outraged tones blare from the kitchen and Betsy almost pushes Alice. 'You'd better go, mistress.'

In the doorway to the screens passage, Isabel points stiff-armed at Robert. 'What does he think he's doing?'

'There's been an accident, Isabel,' Alice says and sees Isabel's eyes widen at sight of the bloodied hair. 'Allan has brought Sylvia home.'

'Accident?' Isabel aims her look at Allan. 'What sort of "accident"? What have you done to her?'

Alice steps between Allan and Isabel, causing the steward to take a pace back. 'Do you give me the key to the chamber at the top of the stairs, please Isabel? Is my husband back?' Alice beckons Robert through towards the hall. 'He's not allowed up there!' Isabel's shocked words echo in the screens passage. Robert stops, glancing towards Alice for guidance.

'The key, please, Isabel,' Alice asks again. 'In fact, both keys if you will.' It is a guess but she feels fairly sure the household will have a second set of keys. 'Is my husband returned?'

'I am not in the habit of monitoring my cousin's goings out and comings in.' Isabel points at Allan. 'And *he* may not come into this part of the house.'

'Allan has a right to come through, he is her betrothed.' Alice waves Allan through. 'And Sam, where is he?' He must not be suffered unwittingly to come upon them and see Sylvia.

'The boy is in disgrace.'

'In disgrace?' For a moment, Alice is distracted. 'Why? What happened? Is Mollie with him?'

'I found the boy wreaking havoc in the wash-house. As you did not stipulate where he is or is not permitted to go, but on the contrary, insisted—'

'Isabel, where—?'

'As the *scullion* was solely responsible for him I felt it incumbent upon myself to take the situation in hand before he defiled the Tillotson *things* for which you hold such a high regard—'

'For God's sake, will you tell me where Sam is!'

'— before I was blamed once again for a situation outside my control!' Isabel finishes. Out of the corner of her eye, Alice sees Robert roll his eyes and hitch Sylvia in his hold.

'No one's blaming you, Isabel. Where is Sam?'

Isabel purses her lips, her arms back in the habitual V, hands clasped. 'I returned them both whence they came.'

'And do I take it from the word "disgrace" that I must needs ask you for the keys to the winter parlour also, Isabel?' *So after all that self-justification, while we stand here with a dead girl on our hands, we finally discover that Sam and Mollie are back in the winter parlour. God's teeth! as Henry would say.* Alice seethes as Isabel meticulously unclasps each key from her ring.

Both pairs of keys unwillingly surrendered to her, Alice leads the sad train through the hall and up the stairs, rounding the corner into the chamber passage. She fits the key in the lock of the first door and with a slight creak of unused hinges, it opens to a shrouded chamber. A curtained bed stands against the wall opposite the fireplace, and the sparse furniture is hidden under sheets. The room is cool, with an unused odour compounded of soot and starched linen. Alice draws back the bed-curtain. A plain coarse sheet covers the bed and Robert gently lays down his burden. Alice lifts a strand of chestnut hair off Sylvia's face, while at the foot of the bed, Allan bends and with shaking hands eases off each of Sylvia's shoes in turn.

'She would not wish to lie in muddied sheets,' he mumbles, holding up a shoe to show its soiled condition.

Alice straightens Sylvia's arms, smoothes the skirt to her ankles. All the while Sylvia's half-open eyes gaze straight and unblinking. For a moment, the three stand looking down at the dead girl. Alice lays a hand on Allan's arm. 'She can lie here in peace, and I shall lock the door so that she shall not be disturbed.' He nods, still gazing down at the beautiful face of the woman whose death has released him.

ALICE is alone. Or rather, she feels alone as she watches Robert turn his horse for home. There is a hush about the kitchen court, all doors closed, even the wash-house, as though no one wants to ask the first question, and yet the hush is heavy with questions. Allan she has settled in the dining parlour. He needs privacy as well as quiet, and she wants to talk alone with him before others get to him. She would have liked to keep Robert by her, his quiet strength would have been welcome, but it is necessary that he return to Freemans as soon as possible. And he has been equal to the moment. A father himself, Robert clearly understands the need to protect the very young from the aftermath of violence. Without a word from her, he has offered to take Sam to stay a night in the company of his children, with the comment that, 'They may all play in our wash-house if they wish,' adding grimly, 'little enough havoc a child may cause in a wash-house.'

When Sam, released along with Mollie from the winter parlour, heard that he was to stay with Robert's children, his delight was only checked by hearing that Alice would not accompany him. 'But I shall come to fetch you very soon, Sam.' And Robert has successfully distracted Sam by promising him a seat up in front on the ride to Freemans. Leaning round Robert, Sam gives her a merry wave that both gladdens and saddens her. Once they are on their way Alice returns to the kitchen where Isabel has remained throughout. It is almost certain that the steward will object to fetch even watered-down small-ale for a servant, so ignoring her stiff hostility, Alice goes to the buttery, takes a jack and draws the bung from the little barrel of hefty October ale.

'That ale is for the master!'

Alice tips the pipkin forward and dark liquid glugs into the jack. She takes a deep breath before she answers, 'It's for Allan, Isabel,' and pushes the barrel upright once more.

'He's killed her, and you're rewarding him with a drink? What are you about?'

Alice slams the bung back. 'Don't you dare make unfounded accusations!' Her hand itches to slap this woman, and something in her face or her tone causes the steward's black-eyed glare to falter. She follows Alice out of the buttery.

'We don't give mere servants the good ale.'

'I've noticed. Only the watered-down slop!'

'I suppose you'll be pleased with yourself when they decide they want fine ale every day and there's a peasants' revolt?'

'I don't have time for this, Isabel.' Alice reaches for the latch.

'You don't have time? Well, perhaps you'll have time when Master Townsend comes to hear of this outrage!'

'Master Townsend?' Alice is momentarily distracted, the name vaguely familiar. 'Who's Master Townsend?'

'Our local justice. He will have to be told. Or do you think yourself above the law?'

'Enough, Isabel!' Isabel hastily backs to the wall as Alice advances, putting her face close to the steward's. 'You are very close to the line of what is acceptable in a servant.' She has picked the word deliberately, and she watches Isabel blink. 'And for your information, Robert is already on his way to inform Master Egerton, who I feel sure you know is also a justice.'

'Master Townsend is of greater rank, he is justice to the assizes.'

'But Sylvia was one of those "mere" servants, so doubtless Master Egerton is equal to the task.'

She leaves Isabel standing and makes her way back to the dining parlour. Allan makes to rise as she re-enters but she waves him to sit.

'I've brought you some ale,' she says, putting the mug on the table. He turns away to stare out of the window at the sheep calmly nibbling their way across the clearing in front of the house. She takes her usual chair where she sits when she and Henry dine, and rests her arms on the cool waxed surface. Under the table, stools stand in two neat rows and one of these Allan has pulled out for himself. On the sideboard across the room, two candlesticks stand ready for use alongside pewter goblets and stacked dishes. All is orderly in a way that seems unbefitting Allan's presence, the story he carries. Beyond the closed door the house is quiet.

She wonders about those words of his, "I didn't mean it like this". Many are the constructions that can be placed on such words. Regret, remorse, responsibility? Perhaps all three?

She slides the mug towards him. 'Take a sip, it will help bring you back to yourself.'

He stirs and pushes it away. 'I will go and sit with Sylvia.'

'Best not, Allan. No one will disturb her, you saw me lock the door.' Guilty or innocent, he is in enough trouble already. He could so easily draw down accusations on himself if he were left alone with her body. 'Allan, do you know what happened?'

He shakes his head. 'I found her like that. She was already dead.'

'You could tell?'

'Her eyes. She looked, but there was no seeing.'

The sliding eyes that would slide no more. 'Where was this?'

'On the track coming back from Master Jeremy's.'

'From Tillotsons?'

'Yes. She was lying by the side of the way.'

'Whereabouts? Near Tillotsons or nearer here?'

'Nearer here. This side of the Long Down.' He explains, 'If you go over the road from here and follow the track up the rise, the Long Down crosses it at the top.'

Alice and Henry rode up there on her first day. The breeze caught them at the top, a surging burst of spring scents, fresh clean against the skin. Four days ago. A lifetime ago. 'There's a chalky scarp,' she recalls. 'If you turn right along it, doesn't it lead down towards the town?'

Allan nods. 'That's it, that's the Long Down.'

'And Sylvia was near there?'

'This side of it. She was lying by the side of the way.'

'When was this?'

'I was coming back home for my dinner.'

'So … around midday?'

'Quite a bit after, I was late.'

'Did you finish the repair to the cart? What was wrong with it?'

'No, I didn't repair it properly. The side of it gave way. It's been going for some time, Master Jeremy said, but he hadn't got round to doing anything about it.'

'So you shored it up?'

'They had some bits of wood and I fashioned new struts and cross pieces.' Distracted for a moment, the craftsman in Allan frowns. 'It was all different woods, not a proper job.'

'Master Tillotson is content with it for the time being?'

Allan makes a wry face. 'He thought it matchless. I told him we've got seasoned beech or ash in the woodshed here, but he said not to trouble, just do the job with what was to hand.'

'So when you had done, you left to return along the track, and you found Sylvia.'

'From a distance, her pale skirts, I thought it was a sheep, they wander the area. But I soon saw it was her.'

'And when you reached her, what did you do?'

'I thought she'd swooned, because she's ... because she wasn't used to walking.'

'Was she still living?'

'I called to her. She didn't answer, didn't move. I bent down and touched her face. Then I saw her eyes were half open, but she wasn't looking at me. She was still warm, right down to her fingers. It was so hard to believe she was dead when she was warm to the touch.'

Alice shivers. Although the sky is still day-blue, the sun has long since gone round and this side of the house is in shadow. 'Are you saying you think it had only just happened, just before you got there?'

'It must have done. I looked around but I didn't see anybody.'

'Where you found her, that must be, what, about a mile from here?'

'Bit less maybe.'

'And you picked her up and brought her back here?'

He looks at Alice as though she is challenging him. 'She belongs here,' he says simply.

'Allan, you say you thought Sylvia might have swooned through walking too far. Was Sylvia not strong?'

'Oh yes, I mean ... no.' He stops. Alice waits. Eventually he struggles on. 'It's a warm day, you see, and she was ... delicate, so I thought ...' His words trail off. He fiddles with the mug on the table, turning it round and back again. A worm of unease twists in Alice's mind, and hard on that, another thought. 'When did you notice the blood on her head, the wound?'

Allan rouses. 'I put my arm under her shoulders to pick her up and I saw it on the ground under her head. Then I saw her hair was bloodied.' He puts a hand to the back of his head. 'A gash—'

The distant crash of a door banging back on its hinges. A man's shout, the words unclear, the import crystal. Allan jumps to his feet, faces the door.

From the kitchen, the bellow again. 'Where is he?' Another door, closer, flung back against the wall, and now in the screens passage the voice yells, 'Hiding! Running scared!'

'What's going on?' Alice also rises. She reaches to pull open the door. Across the passageway, his back to her, Joe marches into the hall bawling, 'Come out, you coward, I'm going to kill you!'

'Joe!' Alice demands. 'What do you think you're doing?' He swings round, dark brows hooding glittering eyes. Sees Alice. And sees behind her.

'Murdering bastard!' He heads straight at her and she flinches back as he powers past, launching himself at Allan. The two fall together into the sideboard. Locked as one they crash to the floor amidst a cascade of pewter. Alan is underneath, a whoosh of air forced from him as Joe lands on his chest. Plates, goblets, candlesticks slide clanging across the floor. Joe draws back his arm, swings a fist. Allan throws up a hand, mouth open, gasping for breath.

'Joe!' Alice shouts.

'First you steal her!' Joe savages his foe. 'Then you kill her!' Allan twists from side to side but Alice sees more than one blow connect.

'Stop this!' she orders them, but grappling on the floor, neither takes the least notice. With the greater force if little art, at this range Joe can hardly miss. At each punch, 'I'll kill you!' he bellows, 'Kill you! Kill you!' Allan beats, tears, pummels, struggling and kicking. A stool falls clattering on its side. Amidst the lashing and punching and ripping, Alice jumps clear of their flailing limbs, shouts again, 'Stop it! Both of you, in God's name, stop!'

With a sudden gulp, Allan regains his breath and begins to shove Joe away. 'Get off, nowt-head!' and with a mighty heave topples him. They roll, each struggling for primacy in a kicking, punching tangle of limbs. A stool goes skidding away. Allan pushes at Joe's chin, forcing his head back. Joe punches him in the belly and Allan grunts, losing his grip. Joe's hand shoots out, grabs a rolling candlestick, raises it high and Alice leaps forward, seizes his arm and hauls. At the same instant Allan jabs two fingers at Joe's eyes. Joe screeches and falls sideways, hands clutching at his face. The candlestick clangs onto the flags.

'Stupid bugger!' Allan growls. His booted foot lashes out, narrowly missing Alice as he kicks himself free and stands. She steps between them, shoving him bodily back. Even as she does so, Alice feels her ankle yanked from under her. She hits the flagged floor, sprawling full-length, her elbow bruised from the fall in the lodge lands on the candlestick. The pain that shoots up her arm freezes her in a coil of agony on the flags. A silent scream washes through her, wave after wave, and she wants to weep with the pain.

An age seems to pass before, infinitely slowly, she draws breath. By degrees she pushes herself into a sitting position, nursing her elbow in her hand and rocking herself to and fro. She opens her eyes. Dead silence has fallen on the room. Above her the two stare down, Joe rubbing at his half-closed eye, Allan apparently unaware that blood wells from a cut on his lip.

Joe is the first to react. 'That was your fault, Wenlock! Look what you made me do!'

'I didn't do anything, hoddy-doddy, you picked a fight!'

'Oh, for God's sake, you two, just help me up, will you?' The after-wash of pain brings out a sick sensation in her throat and with it, exasperation. Either side of her, Allan and Joe bend to help her. As soon as she is on her feet Joe abruptly lets go but Allan keeps a steadying hand. 'You should sit, mistress, you are quite pale.' It surprises Alice how grateful she is to be supported to her chair. Thankfully she sits, still clutching her elbow, and regards the dishevelled, wild-eyed pair before her, the disorder in the room.

'I'll get you some small ale,' Allan says. He takes a step towards the door but Joe is ahead of him. 'Oh, no you don't!' He kicks the door closed, plants his feet apart and blocks Allan's path.

'Get out of my way, yappy-dog!'

'You'll hang for what you've done!' Joe flings out a fist but Allan is ready for it and bats his arm aside, chanting, 'Yappy-dog! Yappy-dog!'

'Don't call me that!' Joe swings again, misses again.

'Yap-yap,' Allan taunts.

'Failed 'prentice!'

'Yap-yap, yap-yap-yap!' Allan ducks and steps aside, easily dodging Joe's ever wilder punches. Then abruptly he makes a grab for Joe's wrist, bending his hand back to an impossible angle. Joe cries out, shoves a hand in Allan's face and the two lock together again, swaying towards the table. Alice jumps up out of the way. 'Stop this, both of you!'

Joe kicks Allan's shin, pushes himself free and aims a punch. Allan dodges but by chance or mischance turns his head straight into Joe's other fist smashing into his nose and cheek. The table scrapes across the flags as Allan reels back against it. Ale slops from the mug. He puts a hand to his face, shaking his head as though to clear it. Joe, eyes wide, begins to smile. And in that instant Allan lunges, grabs a handful of Joe's hair and yanks his head back.

'Allan!'

His head forced almost to his shoulder, Joe still accuses. 'Took her and then didn't want her!' He tries to punch his rival, but at such close quarters, the blows have little impact. 'Smashed her head in!' he spits. Allan presses his advantage. As Joe's knees start to give, he tries one last thrust. 'Grace knows!'

Allan rams his forearm across Joe's neck, driving him back to thump against the door. 'You piece of shit!' He pushes hard, leaning his whole body into the effort. Joe gives a strangled squeal and tries to pull at the arm cutting off his breath.

'Let him go, Allan!' Alice shouts. Still he presses at Joe's throat, and Joe's face turns red, then purple, his eyes bulge and he tugs in frantic desperation as he slowly strangles. Alice grabs Allan's ear and twists hard. His hold breaks and he claps a hand to his head. With the pressure on his neck removed, Joe's knees sag, and he drags great gulps into his starving lungs. Bent over and clutching his bruised throat, his jutting chin still declares his resolve to have the last word, 'Wiped the blood off yet, have you?'

Alice confronts them, jabbing an arm upwards, finger pointing. 'Sylvia lies dead up there and the two of you make havoc in this house! Where is your respect for her? Shame on you both!'

'He killed her—'

'Shut up!' Although the nausea is receding, in its place is a trembling in her limbs, the fine balancing point between fury and tears. She clings to her rage. 'I will not have you make mischief born of your own jealousy, do you hear me? And you, Allan, you should know better than to provoke his anger with your needling words!'

'I was only going to get you some small ale—'

'I don't want that sickly swill!' she snaps. 'I'll have the autumn ale since you don't want it.' She reaches shaking hands to the mug.

The pause in hostilities gives her a breathing space, a few sips of the ale begin to calm her. The two young men stand silent, a room's width apart, eyeing each other in hostile readiness. Only now does it occur to her that the commotion has not brought anyone to the dining parlour. 'Where is everyone?' She thrusts the mug at Joe, pushes him aside and opens the door. At the end of the screens passage a scuttle of servants melts away. 'You!' Alice calls to a man. 'Yes, you,' as he turns. 'Come here. You're Ned, is that right?' One of the silent many Isabel tersely presented to her. A solid-built man, broad of chest, thick of neck, right for the job.

'Yes?' the man says, not moving.

'"Yes, *mistress*".'

'All right, all right,' he mutters. 'Missus.'

'Come here when I tell you!' The man slouches up the screens passage towards her. 'And take your hat off when you speak to me! You work with the cattle, don't you? What are you doing in the house?'

'Er … it seemed … we thought …' The man clutches his battered headgear to his chest. 'They said …'

'Well, since you are here, and clearly idle, I have a task for you. You will stand outside this door and allow no one in or out at all unless I say. Is that clear?'

'What, me?'

'Yes, you. Do you understand?'

'I mean, for how long, missus?'

'Until I say.'

'Well, that's all very well,' Ned expostulates, 'but …' He breaks off, eyes suddenly pleading. 'I have to tell my wife where I …'

The thought of this bull of a man being in terror of his wife threatens to tip Alice into laughter. 'Then tis a pity you did not think of that, instead of standing listening at doors.' She leans into the dining parlour. 'Joe, you come with me. And you, Allan, do you set this room to rights.' As Joe follows her out, he turns and shoots a triumphant smirk at Allan. Alice pulls the door and latches it. She addresses Ned. 'You will not leave this door, nor allow any other to come near or speak with Allan, nor will you say a word to him yourself, at risk of losing your position. You will stay here until I and only I say otherwise. Do I make myself clear?'

Ned sighs. 'Yes,' he mumbles, 'missus.'

Alice leads Joe into the kitchen. Aproned skirts twitch into the dairy, someone shushes in the servants' parlour, boots scrape behind the still room door. Only Mollie appears to be doing any work. She stands on one leg at the kitchen table pounding something in the mortar. Next to her, Maureen uncrosses her ankles and jumps up from her stool. She casts around, grabs a spoon and raps Mollie's knuckles. 'Careless girl!'

Alice continues without pause through the kitchen to the wash-house. The door stands ajar, no one within. Betsy is probably one of those who vanished into the dairy. Linen is soaking in one of the sinks, two baskets nearby are full of wrung-out items. Several heaps of the Tillotson garments lie around. Even at a quick glance Alice can see working clothes, night clothes, women's wear, head-gear. 'In there, and make yourself as comfortable as you may,' she orders Joe.

'In the wash-house?' Joe's drawn brows declare his outrage at being placed in a woman's domain.

'As you see.' In his stinking working clothes she does not want him sitting on the cushioned backstools in the winter parlour, and this is the only other place where she can secure him under lock and key and so separate him from Allan. 'And don't touch the clothes sorted here.' Joe slouches in and she draws out the key she gleaned yesterday from Isabel. He gives her a stunned stare as she fits it in the lock.

'You're locking me in?'

'Of course. You have just attacked a fellow servant. Did you expect me to reward you? You may thank the Lord you have time to reflect on your actions before I ask you to account for them.'

'What if I have to pee?'

'Perhaps you would prefer the necessary-house with the door barred on the outside? You'll be free to relieve yourself as you please but there's less room and more smell. Take your pick.'

Joe punches the wall in front of him and then abruptly plumps down on the edge of a sink, arms folded, staring ahead.

'And if you pee anywhere other than in the drainage channel, I'll see you scrub this place from top to bottom under Betsy's supervision.' Alice snaps the door shut on him and turns the key. For a moment, she remains in the kitchen court, thinking. The curiosity of the servants is hardly blameworthy. She has been harsh on Ned, knowing the rest were listening behind doors and round corners. It was necessary to stamp her authority on a situation fast running to mayhem, but it is only fair that the household should know some of the facts before supposition and rumour take over. She slides the wash-house key into her pocket and starts across to the house. In the kitchen, she loudly declares, 'The rest of you may come out of hiding now. I wish to speak with you all.'

19

Afterwards they disperse quietly enough, slipping away in groups, murmuring amongst themselves as they leave the servants' parlour where she has given them the bare facts of Sylvia's death. She has promised to let them know further tidings as they emerge, but cherishes no illusions that it will hold gossip at bay for long. While she spoke, she noticed Isabel slip into the parlour to stand nearby, not close but close enough for the household to understand that she was there as authority rather than audience. But now that Alice has dismissed the household, Isabel has disappeared again. Perhaps she is still angry that her preferred Justice Townsend has not been called in, but Alice keenly resents the lack of practical assistance the steward could have offered. If not to me, Alice reasons, then surely in recognition of Sylvia, who was her declared favourite. She might have helped at least to damp the surmising amongst servants, the speculation between spouses.

As to spouses, Alice believes she has identified Ned's wife amongst the listening group. A short, frowning woman with a turned down mouth, hands on hips, staring pointedly around, craning her neck as they all left. Well, she must needs wait a little longer for her husband's company.

One small figure is the last to leave. It is the tiny whimper like an injured animal that draws Alice's notice.

'Mollie?'

Mollie stops and bobs a curtsey, nearly losing her balance. Alice goes swiftly to her side. Mollie stands on one foot, the other held free of the ground, concealed under her skirt. 'What is it, Mollie? Come and sit down.' Alice runs her arm round the girl's waist and half-carries her to the bench, kneels in front of her. 'What ails your foot, child?' Mollie's watering eyes dart uneasily between Alice and the door. 'It's all right, you're with me, Mollie, and you will stay with me until I have seen this foot.' Gently she raises Mollie's skirt and draws the ankle towards her, rests the heel in her lap. 'Oh, Mollie, how long has it been like this?' The foot is red and angry, the swollen toes plumped up like a line of little sausages. Even if she owned shoes, Mollie could not possibly wear one on this foot. Alice recalls her hopping hither and thither with the Tillotson clothes, gamely playing villain this morning for Sam's entertainment, standing on one foot as Alice passed through the kitchen with Joe. No wonder, Alice thinks. It must be agony to put her weight on it, poor child.

Betsy clumps back into the servants' parlour. 'Mistress, did you know Joe is in the—'

'Betsy! The very woman I need. Can you stay here with Mollie and support her foot? She must not move. I must treat this and get the poison out.'

'Ooh, nasty,' Betsy says, looking. 'That's a splinter, you know.' And Alice remembers.

'I know where the lodge is,' Sam said. They climbed in through the rotten window, went up the wooden ladder, rolled head over heels on the rotting wooden floor. Sam and shoeless Mollie.

'This happened in the lodge, didn't it, Mollie?' she says and Mollie's face takes on a hunted look. 'It's all right. I know you and Sam went there, but you were not to know it was unsafe, any more than I did, and you know what happened to Sam and me. At all events it has been boarded up now. Did you get the splinter there?' Mollie nods. 'Three days,' Alice says to Betsy and gets up.

She hastens up the little spiral stairs, pushes open her chamber door and kneels down by the bed. Reaching underneath she hooks her fingers round a small chest that she brought from Hillbury and pulls. Inside are medicines and creams and amongst these she will find something to take down the swelling and bring forth the splinter. She draws out bottles and pots, pulling off stoppers here and there, examining or smelling until she finds what she seeks. The rest she returns to the chest and hurries back down to the servants' parlour. Betsy is working on Mollie's foot, peering and repeatedly pulling, while Mollie winces with tears in her eyes.

'Can you get at it?' Alice asks as Betsy pulls and misses and pulls again.

'Can't see such a tiny thing,' Betsy says squinting. 'All I know is I can feel it under the skin. There.' She presses on the ball of Mollie's foot. 'Sorry, dear,' as Mollie flinches.

'Let me see.' Alice sits on the floor in front of Mollie and peers. 'I really need warm water to clean this dirt off so that I can see, but I went and ordered all fires out today.'

'Well why didn't you say?' Betsy scolds. 'You asked me to wash the Tillotson things, didn't you, dear? And how would I starch without a fire to boil it up? There'll still be some warm water. And that reminds me. Why is Joe—?'

'Ah, yes. Joe is to stay there for the time being,' Alice says reaching into her pocket. 'He needs to cool his heels. There's the key. If you can get some warm water we can have this done in no time.'

Betsy pushes herself groaning to her feet and puffs out of the parlour, nearly colliding with someone coming in. 'Ah, Master Jack, we're expecting you,' she says. Mollie rises and tries to curtsey, but Alice presses her back on the bench and turns.

'Close the door, would you, Jack?'

Today he is in doublet and breeches of striped grey fabric, the points of his ties silver, as are his shoe buckles. Along with the hat he carries, his attire has a formal air. He crosses the room to sit on the bench next to Mollie. 'I was just back from London when Robert came to tell me,' he says, running a finger round his neck to ease the starched ruff. 'Alice, this is sore news I hear about your maidservant.'

'Sore news indeed, poor Sylvia.'

'Robert said you saw Allan carrying her and she was already

dead. Is this connected?' He indicates Mollie's foot.

'No, this happened a few days ago but I've only just noticed. It needs to be cleaned and dressed.'

'And Henry, where's he?'

'He went to see Master Renwick's new horse, from there he was going on into town.' Then that faint doubt Isabel planted rises in her mind. 'Jack, was I wrong in asking Robert to summon you? Should I have sent for Master Townsend?'

'Not at all. We're both justices. Either of us can deal with this.'

'Allan is in the dining parlour,' she tells him. 'I'm keeping him there for his own safety.' And as Jack's eyebrows rise, 'Joe took this news very ill and attacked Allan. I had to separate them.'

'I see,' Jack says, rising. 'I shall need to speak with both of them, then. But first Sylvia. Robert said he placed her body upstairs. If you will take me to her, it will help my enquiries if I can see her.'

'I would, but I must treat this infection first or …' She does not finish the sentence. No call to frighten Mollie with the threat of some sawbones tying her to a table and taking her leg off at the knee while she finally finds her voice only to scream out her agony.

The door opens and Betsy trundles in with a bucket of steaming water which she plumps down by Alice. 'There we are, dear, that'll do the job nicely. And a couple of clean cloths. There's the key, it's locked again.'

Alice reaches into her pocket. 'Another thing, Betsy. Will you let Master Egerton into the spare chamber to see Sylvia?'

'And while we are about it,' Jack adds, 'if Betsy is willing, I suggest she attends to Sylvia and leaves her in just her shift. I've sent word to Sir Malcolm so he will be here later with a jury and they will need to inspect the body. You may not have met him. He is—'

'— the coroner, yes I have heard of him. Betsy?' Alice hands her the key.

'Surely, dear. I'll see all's right for Sir Malcolm.'

'But don't wash her,' Jack adds. 'That can come later when Sir Malcolm has seen her.'

'When you come down you'll want to talk with Allan,' Alice says to Jack and gets to her feet. 'I must tell Ned he may let you in.'

'That's all right, I know Ned, I'll tell him,' Jack says.

'I think not,' Alice says. 'I was obliged to put the fear of God into him to stay at his post and he is like to obey my orders to the letter.'

When she returns to the servants' parlour, Mollie is washing her own foot, which with the benefit of warm water is already looking almost clean. It is now much clearer to Alice where the splinter entered. What Betsy thought to be the tip is dirt plugging the open end. The splinter itself is in deep, hardly visible amidst the angry swelling all around. Alice opens the pot of salve. 'This is chickweed lotion, Mollie, it will help draw the splinter out, and it should also calm these hot humours.' She tears strips off one of the cloths, and folds one over and over into a pad. Onto this she smears the pale green salve and applies it to the swelling, binding it to Mollie's foot with the other strip.

'There is to be no more standing for you until this has done its work, Mollie. And I want an apothecary to look at it. So for now you are to rest. I shall arrange for you to be taken up to Sam's room and I'll make up the truckle bed.' Betsy will know where the sheets are kept, she thinks. 'That will make it easier for me to re-dress your foot in the night if necessary,' she explains. The salve could take several hours to draw the splinter, and in any event she wants Mollie under her eye and not in the kitchen where Maureen can rap her knuckles for no reason, or Isabel bully her.

Jack puts his head round the door. 'I've seen Sylvia, thank you Alice. I'm going to talk to Allan now. Constable Hart should be here soon and he should wait outside the dining parlour. Round-faced, merry-looking fellow, does as he's asked. Do you want to be there when I talk to Allan?'

'I will as soon as I have settled Mollie. Don't wait for me. I have told Ned that when you go in there he is released. Will you send him to me, please?' Alice checks the bindings on Mollie's foot and declares herself satisfied as Ned comes to the door, hat in hand. 'I have a job for you Ned, if you please,' she says. 'Do you carry Mollie upstairs.'

Ned points. 'Wot, her?'

'Through the hall and up the main stairs. And see that you treat her tenderly, I shall be right behind you. Come, now.'

Ned's shoulders slump. 'A minute ago I was a sentry,' he grumbles. 'Now this.' He picks up Mollie, none too gently.

'A cheering thought indeed,' Alice says, 'that having wandered by chance into the house you find your natural skills so gainfully used.'

'As body servant to a bloody scullion?'

'Better and better, Ned,' Alice says as she follows him to the stairs. *A pleasant change from being a henpecked husband.*

By the time she returns to the dining parlour, Jack has been some minutes with Allan. The two of them sit at the table, Jack leaning back in a chair, ankles crossed, while Allan occupies a stool, elbows resting on the board. The furniture is ordered, the pewterware back on the sideboard, no sign of the earlier fight.

'He has told me what he has told you, it seems,' Jack says. 'That he was returning from an errand to Jeremy Tillotson and discovered Sylvia lying by the way, realised she was already dead and brought her home. Right?' he asks. Allan nods.

Something nags at Alice's memory. Something that was said, a detail that has slipped down some crack in her mind. Perhaps it will come to her. She takes her chair. 'It would be useful to me to see the place,' she says. 'That way I believe we may more easily piece together what befell her.'

'I shall be going up there myself,' Jack says. 'We should not do it today, I think. Wipley and the jury could arrive at any time and you need to be here for that. He doesn't convene a court, you see, he prefers to do it on the spot.'

'Oh,' she says. She has no knowledge of coroners' courts, would not have asked the question.

Jack points to Allan's lip oozing blood, and the bruise now spreading on his cheek. 'I want to know more of this ill-feeling with Joe. You were about to tell me about Joe and Sylvia, Allan.'

'There was no "Joe and Sylvia",' Allan says. 'She never even noticed him. Angus and me, we call him Yappy-dog because he's forever following her around, offering to run errands, clean her shoes, that sort of thing.'

'For no return favours?' Alice interposes.

Allan shrugs. 'More fool him.' Allan must be ignorant of what Betsy saw, Alice thinks, Joe following Sylvia from the drying bushes, she tying her chemise, the day before she and Allan became betrothed. But perhaps that is best left unsaid. There are various ways to read it, after all.

'And meanwhile you were in love with Sylvia,' Jack says.

'No ... yes.'

'Make up your mind, Allan,' Jack says. 'What's it to be?'

'We were going to be married.'

'Forgive me saying this,' Alice says, 'but when I called you and Sylvia to the hall on Sunday evening you did not look to me like a man in love.'

'Well ...' Allan bridles. 'It was unexpected. I needed time to get used to the idea.'

'So it was not you who proposed, but Sylvia, is that it?' Jack asks.

'Yes ... no ... I mean ...' Allan tails off, sighing.

'Why did you feel it needful to explain yourself to Grace when she returned yesterday, Allan?' Alice asks, and watches his eyes widen in surprise.

Jack asks, 'Grace is ... ?'

'New dairymaid,' Alice explains. 'Allan, I was in the passageway when you came to the dairy.'

Allan stares. 'None of this is Grace's fault!' he blurts.

'No one says it is,' Jack replies. 'Now answer the question. Why did you have to explain yourself?'

'I couldn't leave her to hear it from …' He bites his lip, his look falters.

'To hear it from Sylvia? Why not?'

Allan collects himself, draws himself up. 'Grace. She was fond.'

'Of you?'

'Yes.'

'You mean you let her think you loved her, knowing all the while that you were planning to marry Sylvia?'

'I didn't plan it with Sylvia,' Allan says. 'It just happened suddenly.'

'So one minute you're making love to Grace, the next you decide Sylvia is the woman for you, is that it?'

Allan's head hangs.

'Answer me!' Jack orders him. 'You deceived Grace?'

Allan's 'Yes' is muttered so softly that they only just catch it.

In tones of loathing Jack says, 'If any servant of mine behaved in such a way, he'd have a whipping.' He gets up, opens the door and leans out. 'Ah, Hart, you've arrived. Good man.' He steps back and hauls Allan to his feet, pushing him towards the parish constable. 'Do you take this cheating princox here and keep an eye on him. Bind him to whatever you like but don't let him out of your sight.'

He closes the door and leans back against it, shaking his head. 'I thought better of him. It seems I was wrong.'

'Jack, this is all awry. He must be concealing something. I'm quite sure he never designed to mislead Grace. I've seen them together. More to the point, so has Betsy.'

'Sylvia had a sharp blow to the back of the head, Alice. Enough to make a hole and shatter the surrounding bone. Someone wanted her out of the way,' he says. 'If what you say is so, then Allan might well have wished it. What was she doing up there anyway? Going to meet him?'

'I have no idea, but it cannot have been a prior arrangement. Allan did not know until he got to Tillotsons exactly what the job was. So he couldn't have known how long it would take.'

'But she knew she would find him up there?'

'It was no secret.'

'So did he actually finish the job, or do a hasty repair and finish early?'

'You mean, did he plan to finish early and arrange to meet her secretly? I doubt it from what he told me. It was Jeremy Tillotson's cart. The side of it had collapsed. Allan wanted to repair it properly but Jeremy said to make do from the wood they had there.'

'I can check that with Jeremy. Meanwhile, I need to understand this business of Sylvia's swains. What of Joe? Let's talk to him. Where is he?'

'Let me tell you first what I know of the heated feelings that have swirled around this betrothal.' Briefly she explains the household's surprise, Isabel's opposition, seconded by Betsy and, privately, by herself, Grace's ill-concealed misery, Joe's retreat into scowling silence. 'He was very angry. He burst in here and threatened Allan,' she says, 'so I locked him in the wash-house.'

'In the wash-house?' Jack chuckles. 'That won't improve his humour, if I know Joe.'

'It's true he feels it degrading, but I have nowhere else to secure him and he was quite violent.'

'Well, let us hope the shame of it has cooled his choler.'

20

'I saw him!' Joe declares, and even before Jack, following him into the dining parlour, has closed the door, Joe is in full spate. 'I saw him take her and force himself on her. I saw it, I tell you! And her in a swoon and couldn't help herself. I'll see him dance on a rope for this, Master Egerton!'

Jack latches the parlour door. 'Sit down and calm down, Joe.'

Alice takes up station on the window seat. Having heard Allan's story, she wants to listen and watch as Joe tells his. Although she is aware it is not Jack's duty but that of the coroner and his jury to determine cause of death and guilty party, she wants to know the wider story behind Sylvia's death. She is hoping that the jury will be as assiduous over Sylvia as Isabel said the coroner was over old Master Tillotson. But that is not a matter in which she can have any part, for one thing she does know is that the coroner's jury will be men.

Her best hope, she feels, is to support Jack. Before they went to release Joe from the wash-house, Jack explained that his task is to find the evidence to support the coroner's verdict. Then it will go to court. If the evidence is sufficient, the court will pronounce guilt and pass sentence, but if it does not stand up, the accused will be free to go. This is how justice works. Not quite the same as finding out what happened, she feels. There are factors here that surely anyone interested in the truth should know, and it is a relief that Jack appears to be listening to evidence straight away without waiting for a coroner's conclusion to narrow his search.

Alice has also given Jack a version of the fight between Joe and Allan, carefully leaving out her part in it. She wants no hint of it getting back to Henry, who might take his own measures against either or both young men.

The period of waiting had not improved Joe's temper. When they reached the wash-house, he was leaning against the wall, arms crossed and scowling. 'Why should I move? You've locked me up here like a felon. Mayhap I'll just stay here.'

'If you so wish, Joe, we'll talk to you here,' Alice conceded. 'Of course, that will delay Betsy's work as you see, so when we are done I might set you to help her get it finished before supper.'

With a loud sigh, Joe pushed his shoulders off the wall. Still with folded arms he strode ahead of them into the house. And now here they are in the dining parlour, with Joe launching into this sudden further claim against Allan. Despite Jack's command to calm down, Joe balls his fists and pokes his head in the justice's face. 'I want to see him shake with fright at the gallows! I hope he burns in hell forever!'

Jack's hands come down hard on Joe's shoulders and he plumps onto the stool Allan occupied earlier. 'You mind your mouth in front of your mistress,' Jack orders him, 'or I'll have you in the standing stock, do you understand?' Joe glowers but sits still. Jack leans against the wall and folds his arms. 'Now, tell me about this incident.'

Alice listening from her window seat abruptly recalls a fragment of Joe's charge against Allan during the fight. *Took her and then didn't want her!* So that was what he meant by 'took her'.

'She went in the woodshed, to see him as a friend, to warn him,' Joe insists. 'She didn't know he was going to jump on her. He had his hands all over her—'

'When did this happen?'

'Sunday.'

Jack's eyes open wide. 'Sunday?'

'After we all got back from church,' Joe confirms, 'afore midday.'

'And today is Wednesday, and you have said nothing in all that time? You told no one?'

'She said not to.'

'Where were you, Joe, while it was happening?' Alice asks.

He screws round to her. 'Outside the woodshed door.'

'What were you doing there?'

'I saw her go by the stables, and I knew she would come back after to see me. We were betrothed.'

'What are you talking about? She was betrothed to Allan,' Alice says.

'She was betrothed to me afore that. Secretly.'

'Did you break it off, then?' Jack asks. 'Did Sylvia?'

Joe swings round to him. 'No, course not! He attacked her, so she had to get betrothed to him.'

Alice glances at Jack, whose face remains impassive. 'Go on, Joe,' he urges. 'You were expecting Sylvia to come into the stables. What then?'

'I went over to the woodshed when she didn't come, and I heard them talking, then he grabbed her.'

'Were they arguing?'

'No. Like I said, she went to warn him. About Grace.'

A puzzled frown crosses Jack's face. 'What about Grace?'

'She's been leading him on. She laughed about him to Sylvia and threw away his gifts. He's stupid, Grace only had to look all pure and he thought she was an angel. But she was cruel cold behind his back, sniggering about him, Sylvia said.'

Behind Joe, Alice shakes her head at Jack.

'What was Allan's response when Sylvia told him this news about Grace?' Jack asks.

'He had to believe it when Sylvia proved it.'

'How?'

'Showed him a letter Grace had hidden. From her lover. Grace used it to gain your leave,' Joe says, turning to Alice.

'That's not true,' Alice protests. 'Her mother was ill.'

Joe shakes his head. 'No, she lied. She never went to see her mother. She was meeting *him,* the lover.'

Jack looks enquiring at Alice. Incredulous, she says, 'I spoke with her, comforted her.'

'It was all there in the letter. Allan read it.'

'How did such a letter get into Sylvia's hands,' Jack asks Joe. 'A document like that would hardly be left lying around.'

'Sylvia found it in Grace's things.'

'What was she doing going through Grace's things?' Alice demands. She remembers the sliding eyes, the contrived lovers' scene with Allan in the dairy court.

'She was tidying their chamber, found it in one of Grace's stockings.'

'A convenient find,' Alice says drily. 'How did Allan respond to this news?'

'He started kissing her.'

'Just like that?' Jack asks. 'He agreed Grace had deceived him and kissed Sylvia?'

'Oh, he was very clever,' Joe says. 'Moved closer to her, almost like you wouldn't notice, then suddenly he had his arm round her and they were rolling on the floor.'

'And Sylvia allowed this to happen?'

Joe crosses his arms. 'What's the point in telling you when you don't believe me?'

'I'm asking you, Joe. Asking you whether Sylvia wanted this to happen. If not, what exactly her response was. How did it seem to you?'

'She—'

'You did witness this scene yourself? You aren't just repeating something you were told?'

'I saw it! With my own eyes. She didn't know what was happening. It all happened so sly, like he was creeping up on her.'

'What did you do to stop it, Joe?' Jack asks.

'Well ... nothing.'

'Why not?'

'Well, it … it all happened so fast.'

'You just told me Allan moved closer to Sylvia as though creeping up on her. Are you telling me that you watched the woman you loved, your betrothed as you tell us, being stalked and attacked by another man and you did nothing about it? Look at me, Joe!' Jack orders.

'I told you, it happened so fast! He had his hand on her skirt and was holding her round the waist and then he forced her backwards.'

'And you didn't even call out, or go in and confront him?'

'No,' Joe mumbles, head hanging.

Jack's voice has an edge as he demands, 'Did you enjoy watching it, Joe? Was that it?'

Joe's head comes up fast. 'No! No! I wanted her, I loved her, I wanted to marry her, but I thought …' He stops.

'You thought you might have been mistaken about her feelings and that she might be willing to lie with him?' Alice asks gently. 'Is that why you did not interrupt them, Joe?'

His voice crumples. 'Oh, I wish I'd gone in. I wish I had. She'd be alive now. Untainted.' He buries his face in his hands and heaves a great sob. 'She'd have married me, and I'd have given her everything she wanted.' He gives way to crying in earnest, tears mixing with saliva dropping from his open mouth. Alice wishes herself anywhere but where she is. Joe's tortured groans render her acutely uncomfortable and speechless. Where is any ease for Joe in this tangle? She looks down at her hands in her lap and waits.

It is Jack who breaks the moment. 'Did you tell her you had seen what happened? Did you ask her what she felt about it? At what point did you stop watching the two of them, Joe?'

Joe sits up, wipes a hand across his tear-stained face and sniffs hard. He shrugs.

'You said you saw him ravish her.'

'Well … not exactly … that happened after I left.'

'Where did you go when you left?'

'Back to the stables to wait. She came out of the woodshed a bit later and saw me.'

'How did she look Joe?' Alice asks. 'Was she crying? Running?'

'No.'

'Was her clothing disordered?'

'No, none of that. But when she saw me, she ran in and pulled me into one of the stalls where we couldn't be seen.'

'Did she tell you what had happened with Allan?' Jack interjects.

'No, she asked me what I was doing. I told her I'd seen him attack her.'

'What did she say to that?'

'Said it was just like me to dog her steps.'

'So she was angry with you?'

'I thought she was, but she said no, she meant she could rely on me always being there.'

'Did she? Then what?'

'I asked her why she hadn't fought him. It was because she was swooning with terror of being hurt.'

'Is that what she said?' Jack asks.

Joe is silent.

'Or did you say it?'

'I might have said it.'

'Did she ask you why you had not defended her honour?' Jack asks. And as Joe hesitates and turns to Alice in confusion, she explains, 'Didn't Sylvia have a right to expect you to go in to help her?'

'No, she said she had no claim on me.'

'Why on earth not?'

'Because she was no longer a pure woman.'

'She said that? That she was no longer pure?'

'She didn't have to. I could tell that was what she was thinking. I told her I didn't mind that she was tainted, I still wanted to marry her.'

'Joe,' Jack says, 'how did you resolve it with Sylvia?'

Joe squares up. 'I declared I'd smash his face through the back of his head!'

'Hmm. I'm guessing Sylvia said not to?'

Joe's shoulders droop. 'She said she was going to have to marry him and she didn't want to marry a man with a broken nose.'

A dishonourable urge to laugh threatens Alice's gravity. Jack bows his head and puts up a hand to cover his face. Alice asks, 'What did you say to that, Joe?'

'I told her I wouldn't just break his nose, I'd break every bone in his body, it'd be a fight to the death!'

'And did she welcome your chivalry?'

Joe looks perplexed.

'Your manly offer?'

He sighs. 'No. She begged me not. She said she couldn't bear it if the man who had wronged her was killed by the one she loved most in the world.'

'The one she loved most being yourself?'

'Of course.'

'And you relinquished her – let her go?'

'We both cried and said goodbye forever,' Joe finishes in tragic tones.

Alice sits shrinking and silent, unequal to the drama of Joe's high ideals. Jack raises his head. 'Where were you this forenoon, Joe?'

'Out in the fields.'

'What were you doing?'

'Repairing a sheepfold.'

'All morning?'

Alice rises and moves to a chair at the table where she can more easily see Joe's face. 'Was Angus with you, Joe?' she asks.

'Yes.'

'Where did you take midday meal?'

'I didn't.'

'Didn't Betsy bring you something? She was going to.'

'Didn't see her.'

'Did Angus eat?'

Joe shrugs. 'Dunno.'

'Weren't you with him, Joe?' Alice persists. 'The master wanted you to work together to get it finished.' *And I wanted you to be together to keep you away from Sylvia.*

'We finished the job,' Joe says. 'Then he wandered off.'

Jack intervenes. 'Where?'

'Dunno. Back to the house maybe. Asking where was his meal.'

'And what did you do?'

Joe shrugs. 'Sat a bit.'

'Joe, you returned to the house well after I did,' Alice says. 'That leaves, what, a couple of hours? Just sitting a bit?'

'Well, I ... wandered down towards town.'

'And what did you do there?' Jack asks.

'Not a lot. Wandered a bit.'

'Did you have a drink, meet friends, what did you do, Joe?' Jack insists.

'Nothing.'

'Did you speak with anyone there?' Alice asks.

'No.'

Jack leans forward. 'Perhaps you didn't go to town after all, Joe. Perhaps you came back to the house.'

'No!'

'You're very sure of that.'

'I wish I had! I'd have braved anything for her, but she ...'

'Go on, Joe,' Alice encourages him.

'She told me on Sunday I must leave her to her fate,' he finishes and sighs.

Briskly but not unkindly Jack says, 'Very well Joe, that's all for now, you can go. But stay within the kitchen court area, I may need to speak with you again. And if you see Allan, you don't talk to him and you walk away in the opposite direction, do you hear? If you so much as approach him, I'll have you in my court so fast your feet won't touch the ground.' Shoulders drooping, Joe gets up and shuffles out of the room. Jack closes the door after him and shakes his head. 'He's at a dangerous age for a young man. His heart sits out there on his sleeve for anyone to take a tilt at.'

'How much of that do you believe?' Alice asks him.

He sits down on the stool Joe occupied. 'As much or as little as you, I suspect. I didn't really know Sylvia, but the two young men's versions don't tally by a long way.'

'That letter,' she muses. 'I'm so certain it was nothing to do with Grace.'

'We'll need to find out what we can from Allan about that,' Jack suggests. 'Meanwhile, this is what I ask myself as a Justice. Did the betrothal to Joe exist? If so, his doubts about her sincerity when she dissolved it are a strong motive for him to kill in a rage.'

'Jealousy? Well, perhaps.'

'Next, did the letter even exist?'

'Probably, yes. There had to be something powerful enough to push Allan away from Grace and into Sylvia's arms.'

'And the next question is, how long was it before Allan realised his mistake?'

'At least by yesterday,' Alice tells him. 'Grace returned from a few days away looking after her mother and Allan went shame-faced to confess he and Sylvia were betrothed. But,' she objects, 'that doesn't mean he took out his regret on Sylvia.'

'It might if he felt tricked by Sylvia.' He takes a breath. 'Alice, I can see you find it hard to believe in Allan's guilt, but looking at this with an open mind, either of those two young men had motive and both had the time and the strength to kill her.'

'I'm not suggesting it was Joe,' she says. 'There might have been another person altogether.'

'Quite right. But at this moment, it's the relationship with Allan I should like to explore further. If we have him in again, I might be rough with him, I warn you. Do you wish to stay or let me talk with him alone?'

'I would rather stay if it will not inhibit you,' Alice answers. A knock comes on the door and Jack rises to open it. Betsy stands there. 'May I come in Master Egerton? I've something to tell you and the mistress.'

Master Egerton, not Master Jack, Alice notices. Betsy's face is drawn in a frown, her eyes troubled. As Jack ushers the laundress in and closes the door, Alice rises to join them. 'What is it, Betsy?'

'I took off Sylvia's clothes down to her shift, as you said, Master Egerton, to make her ready before Sir Malcolm sees her. And I discovered something. Something none of us knew.'

'Tell us,' Alice urges.

Betsy bites her lip. 'I've helped many a woman through her childbearing months in my time, some that were happy for it and some that weren't, and a few concealing the fact for as long as they could.'

'Oh, please God, no,' Alice breathes.

'Say it out, Betsy,' Jack says.

'It seems Sylvia was with child, well gone in fact, at least five months I'd say.'

21

Alice watches from the window seat as Allan sits rigid and marooned on the stool in the centre of the room. He looks like a man washed up in a strange place, faced with threats he never envisaged. Jack leans against the wall as before, arms crossed.

'I'll ask you again, Allan, when did you lie with Sylvia – how long were you lying with her until you finally agreed to marry her?'

'I didn't! I keep telling you, I never lay with her!' His fists bunch, and his arms lift and then fall, as though deprived of a table to bang his fists on.

'We hear that on the day you became betrothed to Sylvia you ravished her! What have you to say to that?'

'What?' Allan stares aghast. 'No, of course I didn't. Why would I do that?'

Jack leans forward. 'You were seen, Allan. There was another person at the woodshed who witnessed the whole thing. Saw the two of you—'

'The woodshed?'

'You deny you were in the woodshed with Sylvia?'

'No. Who was it? Who was there?'

'The two of you were discussing Grace, then you kissed Sylvia and either forced her or took her to the ground and had your way with her! How long will you go on denying?'

'No! No! No!' Allan springs up and confronts Jack. 'It's a lie! They're lying!'

Jack turns away and paces the room, running his hand along the smooth surface of the sideboard as though musing. 'Mayhap a night in the lockup will change your mind. Along with the cheats and horn-thumbs. Piss on the floor and your bread thrown through the bars.'

'I never lay with her. Never!' Allan shouts at his back.

'Is that so?' Jack says still not looking at him.

Allan kicks hard at the nearest object. The stool hits the wall and clatters to the floor, a chunk of plaster breaks away. As Alice rises apprehensive, Jack swings round, takes two paces and hooks an elbow round Allan's neck, twists his arm up his back. 'So when you can't get what you want, you get angry, eh?'

'You goaded me,' Allan growls.

'Did Sylvia goad you?'

'No ... aahhh!' as Jack pushes his arm up.

'Did you get angry with her?'

'No, I only—'

'What? What did you only do?'

Allan grimaces as Jack pushes again. 'Put my arm round her.'

'And?'

'Nothing!'

'And?'

'Aahhh! Kissed her.'

'And pushed her to the floor—'

'No! Aghh! Please, Master Egerton, I promise! I kissed her, that's all.'

'You kissed a woman and then out of chivalry offered to marry her. Am I hearing this aright?'

'You're twisting my words.'

Jack releases him. 'Pick up that stool and sit on it and stay there!'

Nursing his arm, Allan gingerly rights the stool. He turns to Alice. 'I'm sorry, mistress, I didn't mean – I'll repair the damage.'

'It's all right, Allan,' Alice says. 'It's all right.' As she too sits down, she can feel the thumping of her heart right down in her fingertips gripping the edge of the seat. She reminds herself that Jack warned her this might be rough. She wonders what level of roughness is tolerable, and at what point her conscience will prick her to intervene. For the moment, she thinks, I will be silent while Allan re-tells his story in this new vein.

Jack is leaning against the wall again. 'So. Why did you kiss Sylvia?'

Allan sighs. 'Her hair had all tumbled down and it smelled so sweet, and she always smelled so sweet …'

'So you thought kissing her would pass the time enjoyably?'

'She'd just told me lies about Grace, only they seemed true … I was lost …' His voice trails off. The low afternoon light reflecting from the clearing outside falls sickly yellow on the planes of his thin face. Jack and Alice wait. 'I thought … I don't know what I thought … I just kissed her. I meant – like – thank you for telling me, but her arm was resting on' – Allan's hand moves to his thigh, fingers facing inwards – 'and working up my leg and …' He balls his fists and bangs them on his knees. 'Arrghhh!'

'You were angry with her?'

'No! I'm angry with myself now. God, what was I thinking? I thought she was being kind.'

'And she wasn't?'

'Not her. She had it all worked out – a cat stalking her prey.'

'Well, you were sitting close enough to her that she was able to lean on your leg. Then what?'

'I had my arm round her waist. And then I lost my head and we were kissing.'

'She was kissing you back?'

'Oh yes.'

'And you pushed her to the ground.'

'No, I swear!'

'What, then?'

'I felt – felt her hand on—' He breaks off, face reddening. 'Can I talk to you alone, Master Egerton?'

'No. Mistress Jerrard is a married woman. She's not about to swoon from maidenly distress.'

Allan sighs and ploughs on. 'I felt her hand inside my breeches. She was grasping ... me.'

'Hardly surprising,' Jack says, 'when you had your own hand up her skirt.'

'No, I never did!'

'Were you planning to stop chastely at the garter, perhaps?'

'I didn't! I didn't put my hand up her skirt. I didn't want her, not like that. I didn't touch her anywhere ... apart from her hair ... and her shoulder.' Another pause. 'And round her waist. I know it sounds foolish but—'

'It surely does,' Jack agrees, 'but let's hear it anyway.'

'I suppose I had it in mind that we would kiss a bit.'

'While she was busy pleasuring you? And when you had had your fill, did you "have it in mind" that this pleasant dalliance might be worth the trouble of marrying her?'

'It wasn't like that,' Allan almost wails the words. 'I pulled away. Whoever said I forced her, it's a lie. She wanted me to lie down with her but I told her I couldn't ... I wasn't ...'

'The moment had passed.' Jack supplies for him.

'The moment was never there,' Allan says bleakly.

'Oh? So sitting cheek to cheek and letting this fragrant woman fondle you while you feel her all over and kiss her – all that was done as a favour to Sylvia for telling you about Grace, is that it?'

Allan is silent. Down the chimney comes the soft cooing of a lone wood pigeon, rhythmically repeating its five mournful notes. *I rue you, beloved; I rue you, beloved.*

'There was a letter,' Jack says. 'Tell us about that.'

'She said she found it in Grace's things, that Grace used it to deceive the mistress into letting her go away.'

'What did the letter say, Allan?' Alice asks. This letter, she is thinking, where did it come from? Grace was given a message, not a letter, and I cannot believe she was concealing.

'It was like a love letter, but it was coarse, not the sort of letter a girl like Grace would value, but I didn't see that at the time. Such things.'

'What sort of things?'

'Oh, well …' Allan glances at Alice, a desperate look, before stumbling on, 'about having her, like they'd been lovers … I was so mad that she and some fellow might have …' He pauses, rocking himself to and fro. 'I can't say that about Grace, I can't,' he finishes.

'And Sylvia encouraged you to believe what was in this letter?'

'She said other things, too. That Grace had been laughing behind my back. I believed that. God, am I a fool or what? Ever since Grace came here I thought the chance of her loving me was too much to hope for. So when I read this letter, it was like, there you are, what did I expect?'

'Who was the letter from?'

'From?'

'Who signed it?'

'I didn't see the – now I come to think of it, it wasn't signed.'

'Might it have been written by Sylvia?'

Emphatically Allan shakes his head. 'Sylvia can't … couldn't write. She could read but she couldn't write.'

'Where is the letter now?' Jack asks.

Allan frowns, as at a new thought. 'I don't know. I didn't leave it in the woodshed.' He stands up, patting his breeches, reaching fingers into first one then the other pocket in his jerkin. 'I don't know.'

'Didn't you keep it?' Jack asks. 'Didn't you plan to confront Grace with it on her return?'

He faces Jack. 'Why would I? I mean, at first I was mad, but then I thought, why did I ever think she would want a failed apprentice like me, and there was an end to it.'

There is a short silence. Alice, bearing in mind Jack's observation that she is unduly partial, wonders whether that simple description of himself as "failed" is Allan's honest assessment, or is he being disingenuous to make them believe him innocent?

Having admitted his disappointment in love, it seems to Alice that Allan relaxes. He sits down on the stool, his heels scraping on the stone floor as he stretches out his legs, crossing his ankles.

'So you decided you'd be better off married to Sylvia?' Jack asks.

'Not really, no. She told me she was with child.'

'Sylvia told you that?'

'Yes.'

'Did she say who the father was?'

'Well, me of course. That's why I had to marry—' Allan stops. His mouth gapes. To Alice it seems as though he shrinks before her. 'Oh, no.' Abruptly he draws up his knees, props his elbows on them and buries his head in his hands.

'So you had lain with her before?' Jack's voice, ice-cold.

A nod.

'You lied when you said you had not?'

Another nod. 'Yes.'

'How many more lies have you told me, Allan?'

Allan's head comes up. 'None. I promise. I only lied because I thought we could keep that out of it. I wish I'd never done it. I don't want Grace to know. It happened before she came here.'

'Grace knowing about it is the least of your problems at present, young man,' Jack tells him. 'When did you first lie with Sylvia?'

'First? It was only ever the once!'

'When?'

'Valentine's Day.'

'You're sure about that?'

'Valentine's Day – we were all at breakfast. The master said the men should have hot spirits against the cold, but Joe sneaked two more shots while Isabel's back was turned. It made him bold and he started saying sweet things to Sylvia. She ignored him so he started needling me. Angus thought it was comical and egged him on. I got up and went out.'

'What was Joe needling you about?'

Allan shrugs. 'I dunno, it's always something. Trying to make me look small in front of Sylvia. As if I cared. I went to chop some wood to get away from them. After a bit Sylvia followed me. We ended up in the granary.'

'You say this happened on Valentine's Day and that was the first time?'

'And the last,' Allan says, emphatically.

Jack stands in front of Allan, considering him. 'I've had enough of you now, Allan Wenlock. You want me to believe that Sylvia was barely two months with child. Let me tell you that we know Sylvia had been carrying for at least five months. That means you lay with her last autumn.'

'What? No!'

'It is well known that you have been to Tillotsons to help out on many occasions and you knew Sylvia before she came here at New Year.'

Allan is shaking his head side to side. 'Five months? Five?'

'There was only old Florence to keep an eye on Sylvia's wellbeing up there. It would not have been hard for someone like you to evade the old woman—'

'No!' Allan insists, 'No!'

'— and take advantage of a girl who was lonely and anxious for company.'

'She never looked twice at me when I went up there. I wasn't good enough for her. She had her sights set higher.'

'On whom?'

'I don't know, old Master Tillotson, I thought.'

'You'll have to do better than that,' Jack tells him. 'Apart from anything else, his health had been failing from last summer. It's hardly likely he would be capable of wooing her when he was approaching his deathbed. So, Allan,' Jack says, 'suddenly when

Sylvia came here, you became desirable to her, is that it? Do you honestly expect me to believe that?'

Allan is silent. Alice feels a twinge of sympathy for him. His tone rings true, although his words are contradictory at best. Once a lie is told, she reflects, who knows where it ends? And once a lie is discovered, who knows what to believe?

Jack steps to the door and summons Constable Hart standing directly outside. 'Edmund, take him outside and wait for me. Perhaps a chilly night in the lockup will jog his memory.'

Alice rises quickly to remonstrate. 'Jack, is this really necessary?'

'It's the truth!' Allan exclaims, as the parish constable urges him to his feet and pulls the door wide.

'Like all the other lies, yes I know.' Jack turns away.

'Tis God's truth!' Allan is almost shouting now. 'I only lay with Sylvia the once!' As he repeats his insistence, Edmund Hart pushes Allan out into the passage. Allan gives a dismayed, 'Oh, no!' and Alice rising quickly, is in time to see Grace, her face stricken, turn on her heel and run down the screens passage.

'THAT I did not intend, and I am sorry for it, Alice,' Jack says. They are sitting once again at the table in the little parlour.

'She must have been waiting outside to offer him some encouragement,' Alice says. 'Poor Grace. Twice disappointed in him.'

'But if betrothal is ever in the air between those two, it is best Grace knows what he is capable of before she commits herself.'

'Jack, is there any way you will change your mind about Allan spending the night in that dreadful lock-up? He is not a wicked person.'

'An uncomfortable night will do him no harm,' Jack replies, 'and it may loosen his tongue. That boy has wasted our time with his denials and I want to be sure about his claim that Valentine's Day was the only time he and Sylvia lay together. If we can accept Betsy's estimate, which I believe we can, Sylvia's condition began in late October or November, so mayhap there is yet another lover.'

'*All our swains commend her,*' Alice quotes. 'She was well named, was Sylvia, though we don't know how many swains she had singing her praises. There's poor Joe, Allan who should have known better, how many other jealous young men? Have you considered Jeremy Tillotson? He came home in the autumn. Or his man Len?'

Jack shakes his head. 'Jeremy Tillotson's fancies show no signs of extending to women. And as for Len, he has twice Allan's years and half his hair. No competition against a comely lad like Allan. Which leaves us with the question of who might have fathered her child?'

'More to the point,' Alice says, 'why did she not speak out when she had been so wronged, insist on marriage? All this was going to come out soon and yet she remained silent and tried to cast Allan as the father instead. And then somebody killed her.'

Jack shakes his head. 'Perhaps we should return to Joe and his calf-love. Joe went missing this afternoon.'

'I cannot believe she ever allowed Joe to seduce her,' Alice says. 'Henry said Sylvia was aiming high when she first came to High Stoke at New Year, that she made a play for Master Renwick.'

'Well, she wasn't on her way to see him today.' Jack points out of the window. 'She went up the hill that way. George Renwick's in that direction,' his arm swinging a quarter turn, 'down towards town. But that's a useful piece of information.'

'Even so, she could hardly declare him the father of her child unless she knew him before she came to work here,' Alice points out.

'I shall certainly follow that up.'

'Perhaps she realised it was going to take too long for Master Renwick to take the bait.'

'And hence her move on Valentine's Day, is that what you're saying?'

'Why not? To secure a husband, any husband, if the worst

came to the worst. She might have been aiming higher all the time.'

He looks surprised, but nods. 'Any one of us. Townsend, Wipley, Henry, me, Sanderson …'

'I'm sorry, Jack, I wasn't meaning to accuse.'

'You didn't, but let's say one of us was the father of Sylvia's child. To put it bluntly there would be no need to kill her because she was going to marry Allan and was therefore no threat.'

'Watching Allan and Grace together must have been a terrible blow to Sylvia,' Alice muses, 'the end of her good name, her hopes for a life of ease. Think of the disgrace she was facing, the banishment. She must have been desperate. I have to admire her courage in concealing it.'

'She wouldn't have secured much ease in marrying Allan.'

'No, but she did ask Henry if Mollie could live with the two of them. Henry reckoned she had it in mind for Mollie to do her fetching and carrying.'

'Well,' Jack rises, 'if you still want to go up to the place where Sylvia was found, I'll call by tomorrow morning. Speaking of Henry, is he around yet? I'd like a word before I go.' He bends to pick up the chunk of plaster that broke off the wall when Allan kicked the stool.

Alice also rises. 'I'll go and see. And if you are set on taking Allan to that dreadful place full of felons, I insist on taking him a meal. I will not have him scrub around in the filth for something to eat.'

Jack gives a thin smile. 'I admit I piled Ossa on Pelion, as Virgil says – it's not quite as bad as I painted it, but I will make a bargain with you. If you will keep him secure overnight, I'll send Hart home and leave Allan in your charge. And by "secure", I mean locked up. Until Sir Malcolm gives his verdict, I have to regard Allan as the most likely perpetrator.'

He turns the lump of plaster round and back in his fingers,

looking at the hole and back at the piece. 'In any event, tomorrow, I want him to show us the place where he found her, so it'll save me a trip into town if he's kept here overnight. Then I shall go on to Jeremy Tillotson to tell him what we know, and assure myself that Allan finished his cart repairs and left there when he said he did.' He positions the lump of plaster, pushing it into place. Apart from a few missing flakes, it is nearly whole. 'There, a bit of lime plaster and that will be good again.'

Until this moment, Alice has persuaded herself that for all his even-handedness Jack is somehow on Allan's side. Now she looks at him afresh. 'Surely you don't doubt his story of finding her?'

'On the face of it, no. But set that against his lies and evasions and there is quite a question there.'

'You think he killed her?'

Jack's face is noncommittal. 'He was in the area at the time, and he regretted his betrothal. We know that for sure, because he tried to conceal his duplicity from Grace. Yes, Alice, he must be first among suspects.'

'But he openly told Grace he was betrothed.'

'But not *why* he was betrothed – that he had lain with Sylvia at least twice, maybe a dozen times for all I know. Yes, I would call that duplicity.'

The circumstances are damning, whatever the truth. 'Very well,' she concedes, 'I'll lock him in the wash-house for the night. But I still don't believe he killed her, and even if he did, I feel sure he had no prior intent.'

'The law hardly recognises that as a defence for murder.'

'No, but … she had a calculating way, did Sylvia. That story about a letter in Grace's possession – I shall prove that a lie, at least.'

'Which may just serve to prove that his motive was all the stronger.'

Another reminder of Allan's probable guilt. Jack's determined open-mindedness is starting to irritate her. 'It seems I have a choice either to exonerate him or look to Grace's good name,' she snaps. 'And at this moment hers is the greater need – a man may retrieve his reputation in time, but a woman once besmirched carries the stain all her life!'

He meets Alice's gaze. 'By all means let us try to get at the truth. See if you can discover that letter. But remember that I have a duty also towards the dead, who cannot speak for themselves.'

Rebuked, Alice glances away, blushing.

'Allan is fortunate in his mistress,' Jack says with moderated voice, and as she looks up, 'because if he is innocent, he'll need a champion like yourself.'

'Jack, if he really is the father of Sylvia's baby, or even if he only believed he was, he did an honourable thing in betrothing himself to her. Surely that counts for something?'

Hand on the latch, Jack says, 'If that's all he did.'

22

Someone of scant patience is beating at the front door. Thrashing it, as though it has caused offence. It resounds in the kitchen where Alice has just re-entered the house after seeing Jack mounted and on his way. The hammering continues. Not Henry, she cannot imagine him employing such violence to gain entrance. She stands in the empty kitchen and sighs. It would have been good to have a few minutes to herself to think. She unlatches the door to the screens passage but stays her hand as she hears the creak of the front door opening, Isabel's honeyed tones. 'Sir Malcolm, we are happy to see you.' Then in a raised shout, 'Girl!'

So it is the coroner, Alice realises. And presumably "girl" is Mollie. But Isabel does not know that Mollie has been taken upstairs to save her from just such a summons. Alice pulls open the door. In her soft house slippers, she approaches the steward, who starts and swings round as Alice says, 'Mollie is not here, Isabel.'

'She never is,' the steward complains. Beyond her, Alice can see the shape of a man on horseback. Both rider and mount are within the shadow of the house. Behind them, the low afternoon light on the clearing outlines the rounded rump of each as the man leans forward in the saddle to peer into the house. In his grasp is a whip. She wonders if he thrashes his horse as hard as he thrashes doors.

'Sir Malcolm, pray enter,' Isabel coos, stepping back, dipping her head and holding out her arm towards the hall. *Why in God's name is she behaving like this?* Almost, Alice expects her to kneel.

'You!' Pointing the whip at Alice. 'See to this horse,' he orders and swings a leg over its neck to dismount. He is a man large in every respect. Thick of neck and solid of body, his trunk-like legs encased to the knee in massive boots, to Alice he seems the size of man to need a carthorse, and at the same time the sort of man utterly to repudiate such an affront to his dignity. Hooded eyes above a straight slit of a mouth look past Alice into the house. It strikes her that the earth-coloured cloth he sports, shot through with fine silk threads, possesses a gleam not unlike fresh dung. He shoulders past Isabel and enters the hall.

'And take this.' He swings the heavy fur-lined cloak off his shoulders and tosses it and the whip in Alice's direction. 'Don't get it muddied!' As he draws off his gauntlets he surveys the hall. 'Where's Jerrard? Still not repaired this draughty old place?'

'Sir Malcolm is pleased to jest,' Isabel twitters.

'My husband is not yet home, sir,' Alice says, and at the word "husband", his glance swings towards her, eyebrows raised. The steward takes advantage of his pause to step between him and Alice. 'Sir Malcolm, be assured we wish to make your visit here as pleasurable as possible.'

From the doorway behind them, Alice says tartly, 'I must assume that Sir Malcolm's pleasure in being here will be tempered by his reason for coming, Isabel.' She starts across the hall. 'And now, sir, if you will follow me, you may be more comfortable in the parlour.'

The coroner steps in her path. The high-crowned hat sitting horizontal on his flat forehead, the straight locks hanging to either side, give his head the appearance of a great cube. His eyes appraise. 'Well, well, where did he find you, then?'

'I was born in Dorset, sir,' Alice answers evenly, 'not far from Sherborne.'

'Never heard of it.' Behind her, Isabel titters. The coroner pokes his head forward. 'So, you're the little country wife. I've heard about you.' He looms over her and to Alice he seems to block the light.

'If you will follow me, Sir Malcolm,' she says, 'I will show you to the winter parlour.' It is some measure of satisfaction to watch the steward's face as she adds, 'Isabel will arrange for your horse to be stabled.' Alice leads the way across the hall, the coroner all the while keeping pace, his boot kicking her skirt, his swinging hand brushing her arm. She pauses to lay his cloak and whip on the table and he leans over her shoulder, opens fleshy fingers and lets fall his gauntlets. His hand brushes her shoulder as he swings back his arm. She continues to the winter parlour, praying that the members of his jury will arrive very soon. 'Pray take your ease, Sir Malcolm,' indicating a backstool. He sweeps a glance round the parlour, pointedly raising his eyebrows at the cold grate. 'No one else here yet?'

'You are the first, Sir Malcolm. A glass of wine while you wait?' It is the best she can think of to flee his presence but it is the coroner himself who provides her escape.

'I shall take a turn outside until they are assembled. Leave the wine in here and tell them to wait. Now, this body. A wench of yours, I gather?'

'Sylvia. She came to us from Tillotsons early this year when—'

'And another of your servants claims he found her dead?'

'Allan Wenlock. He was up at Tillotsons mending—'

'Wenlock. Did he ravish her as well?'

'He did nothing but bring her home. No one's ravished her, Sir Malcolm.'

'I'll decide that.' He holds out his hand. 'The keys?'

'Keys, sir? To what?'

'The outbuildings of course.' The coroner rolls his eyes. 'Don't tell me you stretched her out on the kitchen table?'

'We took Sylvia to the small chamber, the first one you come to round the corner from the top of the stairs.'

He snorts. 'In the house? This is a maidservant we're talking of?' Hands on hips, he bends towards her, speaking very clearly. 'A – maid – servant?'

'Certainly.' She is careful to keep her tongue from a hasty retort. If the dislike between him and Henry is mutual, he could well be needling the wife to get at the husband.

'Well, you do have some strange little country ways, don't you? A maidservant in the guest chamber! What next? The sheep and kine dining at high table? Hah!' His laugh is more like a shout. Immediately he becomes for her less intimidating, simply ill-mannered. 'What will your husband have to say to that, little country wife?' He pokes his cube of a head forward as his eyes narrow. 'Mm?'

Alice swings on her heel. 'When you need the key to the chamber, do you let me know, Sir Malcolm.' As she pulls open the door he leans a hand on it, snapping it shut, towering over her.

'The key.' As she hesitates, he snaps his fingers. 'Come now, the key to the chamber.'

She knows she has no choice, that refusal might give him cause to blame Henry for her lack of compliance. Reluctantly she takes it off the ring. He drops it into his pocket where it clinks against another. 'Now I shall take a turn. Tell them to gather here. Off you trot now, little country wife.'

In the kitchen, Alice closes the door and leans against it, biting down the fury of impotence. In the screens passage she hears low voices and recognises the tones. Isabel, no doubt re-stating her delight at Sir Malcolm's visit. Alice sourly wishes her joy of his company. After a short exchange the door of the accounts room closes and the front door opens and slams shut. For long seconds, Alice counts down her bile, regretting the waste of all the witty rejoinders that rush belatedly to mind. Then the door from the kitchen court swings open and Henry steps in.

'Henry! Thank God you're home!' She crosses the kitchen, reaching towards him.

'Alice? What's wrong, sweeting?' His arms go round her. 'What ails you?' Holds her tight and she clings momentarily to him.

'I'm well, Henry,' she breathes, relief overflowing. 'I'm well. I needed you so. Where have you been?'

His chin on her hair, Henry says, 'I was at George's and I've been into town. Is that Wipley here? Looks like his horse in the stable.'

She takes his arm. 'Walk with me and I'll tell you.'

23

Grace's heart hammers painfully in her chest, thump-bump, thump-bump. *Don't do this,* it says, *you'll be in such trouble if you're caught. Isabel is already distraught at Sylvia's death. If you're caught now you will lose your position. Then what will you do, no work and no testimonial? And this is no small step you're taking. You're stealing.*

Grace stands behind the door of the dairy, forcing down the voice of her conscience. *If you're caught now ...* But she *will* do this. She cannot leave Allan to be dragged off to prison without some show of support. She knows in her core he did not, could not, kill. But what of the other thing, his admission as the constable manhandled him out of the dining parlour? *I only lay with Sylvia the once.* Only? She does not want to think about that. All she is going to do is give him something to eat. She overheard Isabel tell Maureen to make sure he received no food, before Isabel went off to the accounts room. Then Maureen slopped out to the servants' parlour, muttering something about needing a rest – Maureen seems to spend her life needing a rest.

For several minutes Grace hesitates, battling her fears, starting and retreating. She is halfway along the passage to the kitchen when there comes a banging on the front door, and back she scuttles to the dairy. She hears Isabel's fawning greeting to Sir Malcolm. Then to her shock, the mistress emerges from the kitchen and joins Isabel and they all go into the hall. At that Grace nearly loses her nerve completely. She was so convinced that the kitchen was empty. Concocting a pretence that she needs something in the still room has not occurred to Grace. Her mind is filled with the necessity of ensuring Allan does not suffer hunger as well as the loss of his freedom. Grace fidgets in uncertainty. She is supposed to have started the late milking already. Finally Isabel returns to the accounts room, and all goes quiet again, except that Grace's heart is banging harder than ever. She cannot wait any longer. It's now or never. She takes a deep breath, slips out of the dairy and speeds into the kitchen, into the still room.

Once there, it seems so much easier than she imagined. What a coward she is! With shaking hands she lifts the pie from shelf to table, takes a deep breath and cuts a chunk. Now the stolen slice is in her hands, but suddenly the kitchen door opens, snaps closed, and the mistress is breathing hard, muttering angrily, 'Such a man! Oohhh!' Grace stands trapped in the still room, even considers putting the slice back on the plate. But no, she *will* get it to Allan, even at the expense of her position.

Perhaps because it is the mistress and not Isabel, Grace prepares to emerge from the still room and face the storm. She takes a step and is full in the doorway when the back door opens and the mistress with a joyful cry runs to greet the master, welcoming him in tones of relief. There they stand in the middle of the kitchen in close embrace. Completely exposed, Grace freezes and awaits her fate.

But neither notices her. The mistress takes his arm and they turn towards the screens passage, 'Walk with me, and I'll tell you.'

'IT'S all right, Sir Malcolm's gone out to take the air while he waits,' Alice tells him. She hurries him up the screens passage and into the hall. 'Something dreadful, Henry. It's Sylvia, she's dead.'

'Dead? Sylvia?'

'She's upstairs in the spare chamber.'

'Upstairs? I don't understand, Alice. Come.' He draws her across the hall into the winter parlour. As soon as the door is closed, 'Tell me what's happened?'

'I don't know exactly,' she says. 'Allan found her and brought her back.'

'Back from where?'

'He found her as he was coming back from Jeremy Tillotson's.'

'Oh, Lord. He went to mend the cart. I remember you said.'

'The side broke.'

'And he brought her back here?'

'Yes, he carried her back.'

'What happened to her?'

'We don't know. It seems someone struck her a sharp blow on the back of the head.'

'Dear God!' He shakes his head. 'Was he seen?'

'The man who hit her? No, Allan saw no one.'

'You've put her in the spare chamber, you say?'

'Isabel didn't like it.'

'Never mind Isabel. You did the right thing.'

And so much for Sir Malcolm's scorn too, she thinks. 'I've locked the door but Sir Malcolm wanted the key. He's gone out to walk around until the jury arrives. Jack Egerton came over earlier. He's seen Sylvia, he asked Betsy to undress her to her shift, prepare her for the jury. Henry, there's something else you need to know, something none of us knew.'

He looks sharply at her. 'What?'

'Betsy says Sylvia was carrying a child. Several months forward.'

He lets out a long breath. 'Dear God!' he says again.

'Jack thinks Allan lay with her when she was at Tillotsons. Allan went up there many times last year to help out, apparently.'

Emphatically, Henry shakes his head. 'I can't believe she even looked at him then.'

'That's exactly what Allan said.'

'An unfinished apprentice wouldn't hold any interest for her at that time.'

'But Allan has admitted he bedded Sylvia in the granary here in February.'

'What? No!' Henry runs a hand through his hair, an exasperated sigh escaping him. 'The stupid lad.'

'So now Jack is wondering how many other times before that, because apparently Sylvia was at least five months forward.'

'Did Allan know she was with child?'

'Yes, he says they coupled on Valentine's Day but not before that. Jack thinks Allan's lying because he doesn't want to look bad in Grace's eyes.'

'This whole business is going to look bad for him. Sylvia is dead, conveniently found by Allan, who admits he bedded her. You told me this morning he regrets being tied to her – if you and I know that, be sure the whole household knows. How long before Sir Malcolm gets wind of it?'

'Sir Malcolm has already suggested Allan killed and ravished her.'

'She was ravished too?'

'No! Assuredly not. Betsy would have said. I think Sir Malcolm was trying to shock me.'

'Was he offensive to you?'

'I assume that's his normal manner.'

'Steer a wide berth, Alice. He's going to enjoy this, is Wipley.'

'Enjoy?'

'Oh, yes. He'll make this as difficult for us as he can. I suggest you keep out of sight until it's over. I'll take care of the jury – there's someone now.' Footsteps in the hall and the murmur of voices, breaking off as Henry pulls open the door. 'Ah, Fulwell, Stanhope. And Oliver. Come in, please. Thank you, Isabel.' He stands back and they file past, each with a grave greeting or shake of the head.

The man called Fulwell commiserates, 'A sad business, poor girl.'

'So late in the day to be summoned, Jerrard.' This from Stanhope, a man of mature years and fretful mien. 'I sup early; was just on my way home. Tomorrow would have been more convenient.'

'Sorry to have to intrude, Henry, but you know how it is.' The man Henry calls Oliver is a thin-faced man of middle age, well but quietly dressed in fine woollen doublet and calf-length breeches of a forest green striped weave. He looks to Alice like a prosperous merchant.

They all exchange courtesies with her. To Oliver, Henry says, 'Perhaps you met when Alice called on your wife and daughters on Monday?'

So this is Master Sanderson. As he bows over Alice's hand, 'I did not have that pleasure,' he says. And he goes on to give messages of condolence from his womenfolk, who fluttered round Sylvia throughout that visit, chattering about the cloak to be made. And Alice thinks, that's why Sylvia decided against a gown, her condition would have been discovered.

Within minutes, another juryman enters, tall, stout and clad all in black, relieved by the white of wispy hair, of lawn at neck and wrist, and bone buckles to his shoes. 'Middleton,' Henry greets him, and turning to Alice, introduces her to the local apothecary.

'Sir, well met indeed,' she says, and noting his raised eyebrows, goes on, 'Though you are here as a jury member, may I crave a few minutes of your time later?'

'You are unwell, mistress?'

'Not I, sir. One of my maidservants has contracted an infection.' And at Henry's question, she explains about the festering splinter in Mollie's foot.

Middleton frowns. 'Since we are not yet all gathered, I think it will be well that I see the young woman without delay,' he says. 'Have you cleansed the part?' Alice leads him out of the winter parlour, explaining the salve she used. He is keen to return to the stables, 'I believe I have the infusion you will need,' and once he has secured it from his saddle pack, she leads him up the little back spiral stairs, crossing to Sam's chamber at the end of the passage.

Lying on the truckle bed, Mollie gazes up as Alice precedes Middleton into the room. She makes a grab for Alice's hand. 'Naught to be frightened of,' Alice assures her. 'Master Middleton is an apothecary. He is going to make your foot better.' Middleton is quick and efficient, inspecting and pressing, careful to cause as little pain as possible. Gradually, Mollie's clutch on Alice's hand relaxes.

He straightens. 'Hmm. Figwort, as I thought,' he says, 'for its cleansing properties.' He hands her a small phial. 'And when the swelling subsides you may find it has drawn the splinter out as well.' As soon as he has advised her on dosage, he leaves to return to the winter parlour, 'for if I am not mistaken the others will soon be gathered and I must join them. Sir Malcolm does not like to be kept waiting.'

ONCE he is gone, Alice re-bandages Mollie's foot and draws the blanket back over her. With further urging that she should try to sleep as the best way to get better, Alice quietly pulls the door closed and heads for the main stairs to the hall, her footsteps in her soft house slippers barely sounding on the boards. The rushes strewn there a few days ago have been removed and not replaced, though she now regrets this measure of hers to reduce workload. The muting effect of rushes under booted feet would have been a mark of respect when the jury comes up to examine Sylvia's body.

It is as she is turning towards the head of the stairs that she hears the sound. Like a footstep. She stops. Not Mollie, nearer than that. She looks round, no one in the passage. Downstairs more members of Sir Malcolm's jury clump across the hall, greeting those who have already arrived, and their voices fade as the winter parlour door closes. Again that sound nearby. It seems to come from the room where the body lies. Alice creeps back round the corner and stares at the door. It cannot be Sylvia.

She was already dead; I could tell by her eyes.

A creak of bed ropes. No, it is not possible, Betsy has laid her out, Betsy can be relied on to know. But of course Sylvia's body was still warm ... have they all made a terrible mistake? Is it possible she is still living? With a broken head and those unseeing eyes?

Sylvia had a sharp blow ... splintered the bone.

But something is alive in that room. Alice's hand moves towards her pocket where the second key to the chamber lies. The footstep again. If she unlocks the door, if she looks, she will know forever what secret is in there. Now a different sound, faint but distinct, like a rasping across rough linen. If not Sylvia, then who? Then *what?*

Tainted Sylvia is damned, scolding Vicar Fitzsimmons would say. Well, he would, but in truth is she already prey to some skeletal horror squatting over her? Are its sharp, slavering teeth already tearing at her flesh, its claw-like fingers pulling aside her shift, hooking out her vitals, searching for the soul God has abandoned? Hollow eyes, a gaping gargoyle mouth trailing bloody innards? Once seen, there will be no way back, no un-knowing, no peace of ignorance for Alice. The thing will crouch in the shadows of her mind, a profanity forever staining her thoughts.

Calm this nonsense! she rebukes herself. *Such weak-minded fears! You are alive. Hell's horrors cannot threaten you as long as you remain strong.*

She draws the key from her pocket and looks at it, looks at the door. As she hesitates, a gasp and a muffled curse, sounds that are very much of this world. The incubus born of her heated imagination dissolves into the image of an exasperated middle-aged Englishman. Someone, not some thing, is in there, secretively doing – what? Within the chamber, a boot scrapes on the floor treading cautiously. Step by careful step she backs away from the door. Whoever it is, he is being as furtive as she to avoid detection. It takes Alice seconds to tiptoe the few steps to the main chamber. With infinite care she raises the latch, edges the door open just enough to slide through and pushes it almost closed, her ear straining at the gap.

For long seconds there is only silence. Then a slight squeal of hinges, a pause, and silence but for the remote murmur of many voices from the winter parlour. The graze of metal on metal and the sound of a key turning. Alice minutely, minutely, draws open the chamber door, silently thanking Isabel's affection for Henry that these hinges have been hushed with grease. She puts her eye to the crack.

The bulky figure shadowed against the end window removes the key from the lock, straightens and pockets it in a doublet of some dark cloth sheened with a fine silk thread that lends it the gleam of fresh dung. What on earth was Sir Malcolm Wipley doing in that chamber? He stands a moment, his back to her, pulling a kerchief from his pocket, spitting on it, rubbing at his hand, his fingers. Satisfied, he returns the kerchief. Then, not openly or confidently, but furtively, he steals round the corner and heads for the stairs.

Silently Alice latches the door and leans against the wall, struggling to comprehend what she has just witnessed. How can this be happening? In her house! She presses fingers to her temples, wills herself to think back. The conversation, the questions, the key – yes, he secured everything he wanted. On an impulse, she speeds to the window, stands at its very edge looking down to see, unseen. Outside, afternoon shadows stretch away from the grazing sheep and their lambs, making long-limbed copies of their every movement. Except for them the clearing is empty and still. So it remains for the space of a minute, then the front door slams. No one has arrived and no one leaves. Already Isabel will be surging from the accounts room, sprinkling compliments as she accompanies him towards the winter parlour, believing him just returned from taking the air while waiting for his jury.

Alice flies for the locked door, drawing the second key from her ring, shoving it in the lock. No need for secrecy now. She pushes open the door and stands a moment, taking in the chamber she last saw a few hours ago. The curtained bed and beyond, Sylvia's gown and cap lying across the coffer where Betsy will have placed them, alongside on the floor Allan's bag of tools. On the bed, the lifeless figure of the beautiful girl in her shift, the linen falling over the swell of her unborn child. On the shift, smears of mud. And there's a surprise, Alice thinks, that Sylvia might don a soiled shift, or fail to change it after a mishap. Or was it muddied on her way up to the Long Down? But the smear is not at the hem where her shoe could have marked it. Alice takes hold of the shift to look closer. On the sheet underneath are more traces of mud, traces that do not tally with marks on the shift. The sheet was clean when they laid Sylvia on it. How can this be?

Wondering, she looks around. What was he doing in here? With what intent?

A scuff of mud on the floor at the foot of the bed catches her eye, and from there she is drawn to the coffer where Sylvia's shoes lie, still mired from her walk up to the Long Down. She reaches and takes one up. Where it was caked around the soles, now it is smeared along the leather where fingers scooped off the mud. She steps back to the bed, regarding the soiled shift. Carefully she draws the hem above the ankles, up to the knees, finding there what she dreaded to see. So that's what the coroner wanted – an easy culprit, an accusation of, at best, interference. At worst …?

Alice stands a moment, fighting down disgust, outrage. Impossible to leave things as they are, but she cannot do this alone, she needs help. There is only one person she can ask. But first to delay the coroner's jury. She leaves the chamber, quickly locking it behind her, and hares across the passage. Down the back spiral stairs she leaps, two, three at a time, sliding and steadying herself between the curved walls. Soars into the kitchen, into the buttery, grabs a pewter jug and yanks the bung out of the barrel of

Gascony. Red slops onto the floor, sloshes into the jug. An accusing voice from the servants' parlour, 'Who's that?' and the scrape of pattens on the stone floor. Behind her the cook pokes a sour face round the door. 'Steward doesn't allow—'

'Maureen, fetch all the pewter goblets you can. All those up on the shelf and any more we have. Bring them to the winter parlour. A dozen, fifteen.' She doesn't even know if Maureen can count. 'As many as you can carry. For your life, Maureen, be quick!' As an afterthought, she adds, 'This is for your master!' Maureen's loyalty to Isabel suggests she will resist helping Alice but will comply if it is for Henry. Alice dances with impatience by the barrel, willing the wine to gush faster. At last, she can re-bung the barrel and grab a handful of goblets while Maureen fusses around collecting more.

'That's enough! Follow me!' Alice commands and almost runs up the screens passage to the hall. There she slows, pins a smile of subservient hospitality on her face and approaches the winter parlour. Behind her Maureen slops along, complaining, 'This isn't my job, serving.'

Alice enters the parlour. The coroner is already advancing, the men of the jury, now swelled to a fat dozen, preparing to follow him. Alice stands in the doorway effectively denying passage and hopes she sounds docile enough. 'Sir Malcolm, I have been most remiss. I offered you wine earlier and my husband will hardly pardon me if I fail to honour that pledge. Forgive my tardy ways, I beg of you.' Fervently she hopes it is the sort of wifely humility Sir Malcolm expects. Glancing up she sees the group of slightly bemused faces gazing at this unlooked-for bounty, and begins to pour. 'Henry, husband, you will join me, will you not, in offering this greeting to our neighbours gathered here?'

This is the test, the crux. If this fails, if Henry does not follow her lead, then all her worst fears for Allan's fate will be realised. And yet Henry and she have no secret language such as a long-married couple would read in each other's very gestures and expressions.

Something connects. There, in his eyes, in the minutely lifted eyebrow, the mask of grave hospitality he adopts. 'Gentlemen, my wife appears indeed an untutored girl, but she is new to the married state and I pray your indulgence. I beg you will all take a cup of wine for your comfort at this unhappy time.' There are murmurs of appreciation, several looking to the coroner.

'We follow where you lead, Sir Malcolm,' says the little man Stanhope who complained to Henry earlier about the lateness of the hour. Not too late to stop for wine. Alice proffers a brimming goblet and holds her breath, in terror that she has overstated. But no, the coroner is enjoying his pre-eminence. He stands there, looking right and left at the respectable townsmen of Guildford politely hanging on his decision. After a moment, with a gracious nod he accepts. Alice fills more cups, holding them out to whoever will accept. She thrusts the jug at Maureen, effacing herself with a fluttering, 'Ah, methinks another jug,' and pulls the door closed behind her. Untutored girl? The galling thing is, of those faces closest to her, none seemed to find the expression amiss.

Alice grasps her skirts and runs. Across the hall, down the screens passage, through the empty kitchen, pulling wide the door to the court. 'Betsy? Betsy!' But of course Betsy will not be in the wash-house, because Allan is locked in there for the night. Oh, where is Betsy? She races back through the kitchen, flies along the dairy passage and slides to a cushioned halt against the laundress peering out of the dairy.

'Whoa! What's to do, dear?'

'Betsy! Thank God! We have only minutes at best,' Alice says in a low, urgent voice. 'I need you. Is Grace in there?' She pokes her head into the dairy.

'No, dear, she's milking. What's this all about?'

'God send she stays there. I need your help,' Alice breathes. 'Do you find me one of Sylvia's shifts, Betsy. She had more than one, I guess?'

'Five, can you believe?'

'Fetch one. And a sheet. Harden linen, not fine. I'll bring water. Meet me upstairs. Go!'

Alice speeds, skirts flying, out of the dairy through the dairy court and round the end of the wash-house, digging a hand in her pocket for the right key. She fits it in the lock and jerks the door open to see Allan up on his feet, staring.

'Help me, Allan, and I promise you this will help you. Pour me some of that water into … into …' Her eyes scan to find what she needs, '… this.' She lugs one of Betsy's wooden buckets towards the cauldron Allan is lifting. Thankfully, Allan does not question, merely pours, and as he passes her the bucket she puts her hand to his face. 'Bless you, Allan, and though I must lock you in again, I promise I will do my utmost to prove your innocence in this business.'

Holding the bucket close to her chest she carries it out and re-locks the door. It is tempting to take the short route back through the kitchen, but an irate clank of the pewter jug banged down on the buttery shelf brings her up short. She must not be seen, especially by Maureen, who would wonder aloud to the company in the parlour what the mistress thinks she is doing carting around buckets of water. Two-handed to keep the slopping to a minimum, Alice hastens round the end of the wash-house and re-enters through the dairy. In the dim dairy passage, she listens for a moment. No slap, slap of Maureen's pattens, no clip of heels portending Isabel. Alice crosses the passage, hitches her skirt over her arm and makes her laborious way up the spiral backstairs. Betsy stands at the door of the little chamber, linen sheet over her arm, puzzlement on her face. 'I'll just go upstairs for another shift,' she says. 'They'll be in her coffer.'

'No matter, I'll run up in a moment.' Alice joins her at the door and gently lowers the bucket to the floor. She feels in her pocket for the second key, fits it in the lock.

'What are you doing, dear?' Betsy demands. 'Master Jack doesn't want her washed.'

'I know,' Alice says grimly and opens up. She shepherds Betsy inside and closes the door. At the foot of the bed, Sylvia's slim feet poke out from the hem of the shift, her arms lie straight at her sides, her glorious chestnut curls flow over the sheet.

'Dear God and all the saints!' Betsy is gazing transfixed at the mud on Sylvia's shift. 'What's this?'

Alice puts down the bucket. 'That wasn't there when you left her, was it?'

At the second attempt, 'How can this be? What devilry is at work here?'

'No devilry. This is human agency.'

'It was clean. Her shift was clean,' Betsy insists. She takes hold of the fabric and lifts. 'Her legs are muddied!' Betsy pushes the fabric right up to Sylvia's waist and Alice sees what she could not bring herself to check a few minutes ago. Betsy turns angry eyes on Alice. 'Who did this? She was untouched when I checked how far she was with child. You must tell the coroner of this. Tell Sir Malcolm.'

'He has no need to be told.' Alice says.

'Yes, dear, you must.'

'He has no need to be told.' Alice says again and watches the thoughts flitting over the creased face, the turmoil there. It seems an age before Betsy finally meets her look. 'No!'

'Yes. I heard him, then I saw him leaving this room. He had muddied his hand doing it. When he came out he used his kerchief to wipe his fingers clean.'

'Mother of God!' Betsy breathes. 'How could he do such a thing?' She takes up Sylvia's unresponsive hand, holding it between her two. 'The poor child.' She turns to Alice. 'I don't understand why.'

'He suggested when he arrived that Allan abused Sylvia and

then killed her. This is his way of concocting evidence against Allan.' She leans and takes up one of Sylvia's shoes. 'See? Her shoes were muddied when Allan brought her back. I saw them. In fact, Allan took them off her feet because he said she would not like to lie in muddied shoes. But Sir Malcolm used these to smear her and her shift, to suggest a rough attack on the Long Down.'

The laundress asks, 'Why would he want to accuse Allan? The boy is no killer.'

'Good question. You know Sir Malcolm better than I do.'

'To show how diligent he is, I suppose.' Betsy's voice hardens. 'But it's a terrible wrong to accuse an innocent boy. I hope Sir Malcolm pays for this.'

'I hope so too,' Alice says, 'and having his intentions frustrated today will be his first payment. Help me move her off the bed and we'll wash this off her.' She steps to Sylvia's head and between them they gather up the inert figure and lay her gently on the floor. They work the shift up, drawing it from under the legs and Alice pulls the bucket slightly slopping.

'That's all right, dear, I'll do this,' Betsy says, and Alice is silently grateful that it is one who knew Sylvia well who now cleans her body. 'You ought to check Allan's bag,' Betsy advises, 'just to see if Sir Malcolm has interfered with the tools.'

She's right. Nothing should be assumed now where the coroner is concerned. Alice leans and flaps open the toolbag. Mallet, files, wide chisel, small saw, drawknife, gouge, auger, other tools, some she does not know. She checks steel and tooth and blade but all are innocently clean, even of wood shavings or sawdust – sign of a careful craftsman, though equally it might be sign of a careful killer. Well, nothing to be done about that. Alice goes to the bed and hauls the sheet off the coverlet it was protecting, drops it on the floor. She reaches for the fresh sheet as Betsy wrings out a handful of Sylvia's shift and gently dabs clean the skin of the dead girl. 'Why?' Betsy demands. 'Why risk his reputation?'

'Sir Malcolm?' Alice catches at the fresh sheet and flaps out the folds. 'I suppose it excites him to get away with it. Perhaps he found that worth the risk. And what would the jury do if they saw muddy marks on her? For sure they would blame Allan. Would they even look any further? They all seemed to be hanging on Sir Malcolm's words when I gave them wine a few minutes ago. The coroner disposes of his case quickly and they can all go home to their supper.'

Betsy holds the soiled shift up to Alice. 'Show this to Master Jack. It's proof it happened *after* he saw her.'

Pulling and straightening the sheet, Alice shakes her head. 'We cannot use it, Betsy. The minute we admit we have been in this chamber, our case falls flat, for who knows what we might have done to corrupt the evidence? Master Egerton did not examine her minutely, did he?'

'No, he mainly wanted to see her head injury. And she was still dressed then. He said to tell him if I saw anything else he should know. I'd hardly have missed it.'

Satisfied that she has settled the sheet, Alice leans to the bucket. Water slops as she hauls it across to the traces of boot print on the floor. 'We must hasten. I've delayed them with wine but one at least of the jury is impatient to get home. Can you find another of Sylvia's shifts now?'

'I doubt there's time,' Betsy says. 'I'll do this. You get one of your own shifts.'

There is no time to argue, and she's right, this will be quicker. Alice gets to her feet. At the door she pauses, listening. The voices from the winter parlour are still muted but perhaps a little louder than before. The soothing effect of a cup of wine on men mindful that they are here to view death, to pass judgment on cause and perpetrator.

In the main chamber, Alice drags partlets, caps, chemises from her coffer, scattering linen until she finds the shift she wants, a plain one, not dissimilar to the one Wipley despoiled. He will note the change, but cannot say anything. She speeds back into the little chamber. Betsy has been quick. Already she has wiped the floor of all mud traces and is drying the boards with the discarded sheet.

They settle the fresh shift over Sylvia's head. Betsy gently guides the arms into its sleeves, wrists now stiffening into rigor, and draws the linen down over the body. The sight of her tenderness gladdens Alice's heart that it is Betsy's help she has enlisted. Such care is the least they can offer Sylvia who, whatever she did in life, did not deserve this besmirching in death. Together they bend to take Sylvia's shoulders and legs, lifting her back onto the bed.

The door is slightly ajar, and with a shock Alice realises the voices are suddenly clearer. 'Betsy, hurry!' They lay Sylvia on the bed and Alice hastily spreads the hair around again. 'Throw me that wet shift, quick!' Betsy reaches down and tosses it to her. And while Betsy settles the girl's limbs and tweaks the replacement shift, Alice dabs at the wound on the back of Sylvia's head. The dampness is enough to soften some of the drying blood and she rests Sylvia's head down, lifting it again to check that the linen is taking the red stain as though it is the sheet Sylvia has lain on for a few hours. Betsy has picked up the bucket and is heading for the door. Sheet and soiled shift under her arm, Alice follows her, glancing back for a check. She can hear voices clearly now; already they are out in the hall.

Where the bucket stood, a ring of wet on the floor. Alice dives for it, whispering, 'Quick, into my chamber, Betsy!' She rubs frantically with the sheet. That will have to do! Speeds after Betsy. The tool bag! The flap is still open. A quantity of shod feet clumping on the stairs. Turn back.

Sir Malcolm's tones. 'A moment, gentlemen.' She rounds the bed, flaps the bag closed. His voice, slick with deceit, calling down to Henry, 'The first chamber at the top, did you say, Jerrard?'

As if you didn't know. She leaps for the door. Above the general murmur, Henry's voice from the hall, directing. As she pulls the door closed, the squeak of the hinge is a screech to her ears. Wipley again, some sham comment about being unsure of his way as he steps from stone stair to wood floor. Lock the door, fingers shaking. He is mere steps from the corner as she jerks out the key, nearly dropping it in her haste. So close, so close. Flying for the main chamber, Betsy holding the door as she whips through, the two of them latching it silently, leaning against it. And then, unable to move, her skirt caught in the door in their joint haste. How much of it is showing outside? She tugs at it, feels a staying hand on her arm, sees Betsy's warning shake of the head. The shuffle of booted feet outside the door and her heart hammering like a gong. Wipley's voice, 'What's this?' and her mind sucked dry of answers as she waits for them to push into her chamber and demand to know what she is doing lurking behind the door with a bloodied sheet and a soiled shift in her hands.

'Hah!' Wipley again, that hard laugh. 'Wrong key, I see. Here's the right one.' Hinges squeak and they troop in to look at Sylvia. The voices become subdued as someone closes the door, while a few short paces away, Alice and Betsy lean foreheads together and silently let out their breath.

24

Henry pushes a book back on the shelf and turns as Alice hurries into the winter parlour. 'Alice! Where have you been? I delayed them as long as I could but Stanhope was fussing about getting home.'

'It's all right, Henry, dearest husband,' Alice encloses him in her arms. 'You did all that was required of you, and with no warning and no idea of what I was about. Thank you for your trust, your quick thought.' She stands on tiptoe and kisses him.

'I'm sorry about *untutored girl,* Alice.'

'No matter. It fits Sir Malcolm's opinion of me as a raw country wife and it persuaded him to accept that wine, which gave me the time I needed.'

'To do what? What's going on, Alice?'

'First, take this, Henry. It's the second chamber key.' She presses it into his hand. 'Put it in your pocket, he may ask for it. Remember, I gave it to you as soon as you arrived home. It's been in your possession—'

'Jerrard!' Wipley's voice from upstairs. Alice and Henry look at each other. She whips to the window seat and sits with folded hands as Henry slips the key into his pocket. He pulls open the door and stands ready while a low murmuring and the clatter of feet heralds Sir Malcolm and his jury gathering in the hall. The coroner approaches, his tread heavy on the flags. He enters the parlour speaking over his shoulder, 'Very well gentlemen, you may leave. I have no further need of you.' As Henry steps into the hall, Sir Malcolm catches sight of Alice and comes to a frowning halt. With narrowed stare, he eyes the picture of wifely obedience before him.

Blandly, Alice regards him. 'I trust the wine was to your taste,

Sir Malcolm?' In the hall, Henry is making thanks to the men for their trouble, bidding them farewell. A muscle jumps in the coroner's face, briefly pulling the slit mouth into a travesty of a smile. Will he say anything? Can he?

'Somebody has washed the body.'

Alice holds herself very still. 'Sir?' Have they missed something between them, she and Betsy?

'Who did it?'

Surely they tidied everything, right down to the bucket marks on the floor. 'Why do you believe she has been washed?'

'Who's been in there?'

Clearly he is prepared to fly close to the flame. Well, she thinks, I too can fly close. 'I have.'

'So it was you!'

'I went in there with Allan, and Robert, the head man from Freemans.'

'What was he doing here?'

'Robert was escorting me back from Freemans when our man Allan Wenlock arrived, carrying Sylvia. Robert carried Sylvia upstairs. We were all three together. They watched me lock the room after. Betsy undressed Sylvia to her shift later, at Master Egerton's request, to ready her for your jury.' The truth, if only part of it.

'Then Wenlock washed away the signs after he ravished her, before he brought her home.'

'Sir Malcolm, there has been no suggestion that Sylvia was ravished. And there is no stream atop the hill where he found her.'

The coroner is clearly casting around to justify his theory. 'He could have used her skirts.'

'Then by all means examine her skirts. They will be in the chamber,' Alice says.

Henry reappears in the doorway, grim-faced. 'They're saying you hold Allan Wenlock responsible. How can this be, Wipley?'

'Constable Hart says Wenlock found her and brought her

back. Sanderson says the wench was betrothed to this Wenlock. It speaks for itself.'

'What does?' Henry insists.

'He didn't want to marry her, only bed her. So he took his pleasure and then killed her.'

'Betsy found no evidence of that when she prepared Sylvia.' Alice is adamant.

Ignoring her, the coroner says to Henry, 'The evidence has been washed from the body.' Still he persists in trying to suggest that an attack preceded Sylvia's death.

'Betsy would have spoken out if she had found evidence of abuse,' Alice persists. 'She would be incapable of remaining silent on such a point.'

'The wench was big with child.'

'That would hardly have been the result of such recent relations as you surmise.' Alice flashes back before she thinks.

'Do not play games with me, young woman!'

'Sir, Betsy told Master Egerton and myself of Sylvia's condition. Betsy has experience in matters of bringing women to childbed, so her conclusion is drawn not merely from what she saw when she unlaced Sylvia, but also—'

The coroner turns to Henry. 'Who is this Betsy?'

'She's our laundress.'

'Ah, of course, a washerwoman would be highly knowledgeable in such matters.' Wipley's voice is heavy with sarcasm.

Alice interposes. 'The only way Sylvia could have been touched in the manner you suggest was after Betsy prepared her. But Betsy locked the room and brought the key straight to me.' But in trying to block the move to incriminate Allan, Alice has also blocked any counter-move against the coroner for creating false evidence.

The coroner eyes her under hooded lids. 'There is always a second key to a room, Mistress Jerrard.'

'Ah, indeed.' Henry reaches into his pocket and holds it out. 'I secured this on my return home as soon as my wife told me what had happened.'

Alice looks straight at the coroner. 'While you were taking your exercise, sir.'

A hint of misgiving flickers in the coroner's eyes, and Henry looks from one to the other, a puzzled frown creasing his forehead. He asks, 'How did the jury come to this decision about Allan's guilt, Wipley?'

'They all agree with me. It is the only conclusion.'

'All?'

Wipley's mouth works. 'Sanderson and Middleton think to confound them. Middleton puffs himself up with notions of anatomy to place confusions in the way.'

'In the way of what?'

'The fact that Wenlock took the wench shortly before he killed her, and cleaned her up before he brought her back. They say, *Where is the evidence?* I ask you! He's not going to leave evidence lying around, is he?'

'Master Middleton strikes me as an informed man,' Alice offers. 'I think the opinion of an apothecary is relevant to—'

'Yes, well, what a woman thinks is of little matter. The jury is overwhelmingly of my conclusion. Egerton will be instructed to investigate for evidence of Wenlock's guilt.'

'And that is your conclusion?'

'Clearly she was a cheap bawd, steeped in her own sin.'

'That's very harsh—' Alice starts to say.

'Wenlock killed her to be rid of the bastard he had spawned.'

'The boy merely found her!' Henry objects. 'He had nothing to do with her death.'

'You know that, do you?'

'Wipley, there is nothing to suggest—'

'He must be taken now. Where is Constable Hart?'

'He left at the same time as Master Egerton,' Alice says.

'Sloped off did they, the pair of them?'

'Allan is detained in our wash-house at the request of Master Egerton, pending your decision,' Alice explains.

The coroner sniffs. 'Then he will be taken by the sheriff's man tomorrow. Tonight he is to remain locked up here. I deem Isabel shall hold the key. Or rather, keys, she will know how many there are.' He fixes Alice with a hooded look as he adds, 'Isabel can be trusted.'

ALLAN stands in the wash-house miserably aware of Isabel's hot blast of satisfaction as she relocks the door, imprisoning him at the coroner's bidding. He can hardly avoid hearing her rancorous, 'There!' as she turns the key in the lock, her triumphant, 'The sheriff's men will be the next men you see.'

He was sorely tempted to push her aside when she unlocked the door to announce that she and not "that woman" would hold the keys, that she would ensure he was delivered up to the law in the morning. The temptation was severe; he could so easily have overpowered her in her rash vindictiveness. All he wanted was to scramble round to the dairy court and burst in on Grace. He had no plan in his head but to apologise, beg her forgiveness, explain what he did, what he did not do, see her reassured, knowing her trust in him was not misplaced.

But her trust in him *was* misplaced. He plumps down on the edge of a sink. He and Sylvia took their lust of each other in the granary, and Grace knows it. And he abandoned her and betrothed himself to Sylvia. Bleakly he regards his prospects. He reminds himself that they have not long known each other. Grace has had no time to know him, to know his heart. Who on earth, as he admitted to Master Egerton, would cast the slightest glance at a failed apprentice, a mere unskilled labourer without prospects of improving himself? What can he offer a girl like Grace? He has no funds set aside for completing his apprenticeship, no patron prepared to invest the requisite amount, no hope of betterment. Only, if he lives, a lifetime of finding the next labouring job, living in a hovel at a rent he can barely afford, let alone finding a home suitable to bring a wife into. Why would a bright, clever dairymaid give a second look at someone like him? He was foolish ever to think of her, to allow himself to imagine a future with her, to indulge in the delight of loving her, let alone having her love him in return.

In that sudden visit for water, the mistress told him she believed him innocent. It was balm to his soul, but all the water in the world cannot wash away the fact that it is Grace whose trust he destroyed. All Grace knows is that he has damned himself in her eyes. No wonder she turned from him without a word and went back to the dairy. All because of a resentful, passing whim on his part, to salve his stupid injured pride at Joe's Valentine's Day taunts. He will pay for it lifelong. And lifelong might not be long, for jail and a trial and the hangman's rope is all he can look forward to.

He no longer abhors Sylvia. A part of him still resents the artful way she coaxed him into betrothal, but the fact of her death demands his forbearance, insists he and not she was blameworthy, he and not she must carry the censure, the guilt, the condemnation.

He is jerked from the lashing of his conscience by a shadow across the window. A figure stands in the dairy court, the sunlight beyond her outlining the rounded shoulders, the gentle curve of her neck, her face in its neat cap, creating a honey-gold halo of escaped tendrils. Surely not? Can it be … ?

'Allan?'

He leaps up from the sink, heart soaring like the swifts that swoop and dive amongst the outbuildings. He strains out between the wood mullions for a touch of her. 'Grace!' but she hastily backs out of reach. He pulls himself together, withdraws his arms and clutches the mullions instead, all the while devouring the sight of her he thought never to see again. Prisoner and prison visitor. She has actually come to him!

'Grace, I'm sorry. I'm so sorry. It was nothing. It meant nothing. Not like—'

'Don't say that!'

'She was nothing to me. Please believe me.'

'You lay with her, and regarded her as nothing?'

'No, I didn't mean that.' This is all going wrong. 'I meant ... what I feel for you is so different.'

'How can you say that? How can you compare the two of us? She must have meant something, yet now you revile her?'

He tries to find the words. 'She wasn't ... I didn't ...'

'I brought you this,' she says. 'You'll be hungry,' and pushes a cheesecloth-wrapped bundle between the mullions. 'It's a piece of pie.'

In grasping the wrappings, he tries to take hold of her hand but she is ahead of him, rapidly withdrawing, and only his fingers' ends have brushed her fingers' ends, and she has turned and he strains to keep her in view as she crosses the court and disappears into the dairy and the door closes.

25

Someone is screaming. A woman. Screaming over and over.

Alice pushes herself upright in bed, eyes barely open. Pitched high, one hard on another, scream after scream fills the air with shrill compulsion. Somewhere downstairs. In a haze of dream shreds she blindly pushes away the coverlet, fiddling in the dawn light to pull aside the bed curtains and slide her feet to the floor.

'Alice?' Henry's voice blurred with sleep. 'Who's that screeching?'

'I hardly know. One of the maidservants.' She spies her shift on the floor, briefly wonders how it got there. Ah yes, she discarded it, preferring instead to lie tucked into his body, skin to skin, her back warmed against his chest, his arm over her. They had both needed that comfort last night. No more, just that.

Across the bed Henry is pushing himself onto an elbow. He blinks at her as she pulls the shift down over her head, her hands struggling to find the armholes. 'Wait, Alice. Don't go down alone,' he says, drawing back his bed curtain, swinging his legs out of bed.

'Just listen to it.' The unremitting cacophony seems to her ears to stem less from terror than from a determination to cry havoc. 'Naught to be afeared of in that.' Nonetheless, whatever the cause, she needs to be there to calm the household, discover the source of such anguish.

'I'm coming with you,' he says, pulling on his nightshirt. 'Let me get my gown.'

Already she is unlatching the door, crossing to the little spiral stair, her toes recoiling at the cold stone of the steps. All the while the screams pulse, louder and louder as she scurries down. She jumps the last two treads and speeds along the passage into the kitchen.

Flat on the floor, arms flailing, heels drumming, screaming and screaming, lies Maureen. Mollie kneels by her, trying to stroke Maureen's face, a gesture both sympathising and calming, but at every touch Maureen strikes away her hand. Repeatedly she fills and re-fills her lungs.

'Ahhh! Ahhh!'

Walls of noise. Alice approaches the stricken woman and bends over her. 'Maureen, what is it? Maureen!'

'Ahhh! Ahhh!' Maureen continues, throwing her head from side to side.

'Tell me, Maureen!'

Maureen opens her eyes, screws them shut again. 'Ahhh! A witch! Ahhh!'

It is hurting Alice's ears. 'For God's sake, stop screaming!' she shouts. 'Where is this witch?'

But Maureen, after a further glance up, screws her eyes shut. Her arms quiver, her heels drum and she lets out a further series of shrill screams.

Alice straightens, looks around. On the table next to a beaker, an ale jug. She grasps the handle and casts its contents in Maureen's face. The screams stop dead and Maureen glares up at her. Mollie stares, hand to mouth, eyes dancing, as she takes the jug from Alice's outstretched hand. Alice kneels down by Maureen and takes her arm. 'What is it? Tell me what's amiss, Maureen?'

'He's a witch! I knew it all along.' Maureen pushes herself into a sitting position. Her shift under the bodice has taken a soaking along with her face and cap. Maureen licks at the dark drops around her mouth, and in another part of her mind Alice registers that it is the best ale Maureen pours for herself before the household are up.

Henry bursts into the kitchen. 'God's teeth, who was making that racket?'

Alice reaches back a stilling hand and turns once again to the cook. 'A witch, you say, Maureen? Who's a witch?'

Maureen wipes a hand across her forehead and licks her fingers. 'That Allan.'

'Allan? Nonsense!' Henry declares. 'What are you talking about?'

Maureen shoots Alice a defiant stare. 'Allan! That you locked in the wash-house. *Locked!* Well he's gone, and no way out except the chimney, so that proves it!'

'Of course he hasn't gone! Get Isabel.' Henry flings the door wide and strides across the kitchen court. Alice rises, making reassuring signals to Grace hovering at the door to go back to the dairy. Alice catches up with Henry as he rattles the latch of the wash-house door, still locked. 'Allan? Allan, are you awake, man?'

Alice bangs on the wood. 'Allan!'

'The window,' Henry says. It is on the opposite side, and together they round the end of the wash-house and come into the dairy court. Henry takes hold of the wood mullions and peers between, looking one way and another. 'She's right. He's gone.' He straightens, reaching an arm to draw her to the window. 'The blanket you gave him last night is there, see?' She peers between the bars. It is dim within, this being the one window, but sure enough, only the clothes Betsy was sorting lie in their separate heaps, the blanket Alice pushed through the bars to Allan last night has been discarded across one of the sinks.

A thought occurs to her. An impossible thought, and yet a cheering one if true. 'Do you think Isabel released him after all, Henry?' If so, misguided as it was, it was that spark of human kindness Alice has sought in the steward since first meeting her.

Henry shakes his head. 'Can't see it myself. She's too enamoured of Sir Malcolm to go so expressly against his command. He made her responsible for the keys. But I mean to ask her all the same. Come.' Together they retrace their steps to the kitchen just as Isabel arrives clad in a loose-gown over her shift. But where

Alice is barefoot, her hair flowing over her shoulders in tangles of kinked curls, Isabel has been careful to brush her black hair, to tie a day-cap over her head and to don house slippers. She orders Mollie to bring fresh ale.

'Mollie will do no such thing, Isabel,' Alice says. 'She should not even be on her feet. Mollie, back upstairs this instant.' And while Mollie hobbles towards the spiral stairs, Henry goes straight to the point. 'Isabel, do you still have the keys to the wash-house?'

'Indeed cousin. They have not been out of my sight since Sir Malcolm entrusted them to me.' There is a metallic clink as Isabel draws out a lace tied round her neck. 'You see?'

'Well, someone has released him. He's gone.'

'How can he be gone?' Without the harsh black casing of her gown, Isabel appears somehow frailer, Alice thinks, almost likeable in her evident confusion.

'We mean to discover,' Henry says. 'I have to ask you this, Isabel. Have you unlocked the wash-house at any time since Sir Malcolm gave you those keys last night?'

'And let that killer loose? You know what they say? That he ravished her and then smashed her head in?'

Alice rolls her eyes. She takes the jug and heads for the buttery. Henry addresses Isabel. 'Knowing Allan as we all do, I could hardly blame you had you taken compassion on him.'

'I would as soon cut off my hand!'

'Very well, Isabel,' Henry sighs. 'You'd better open up and we'll check inside.'

'Sir Malcolm ordered that—'

'Isabel,' Alice calls, filling the jug from the small-ale barrel, 'unless he's hiding under those heaps of clothes, Allan's not in there.' She pushes the bung back and carries the full jug to the table at the same moment that Joe comes in from the kitchen court, pulling on a shirt that hangs out over hastily donned breeches.

'Joe,' Henry signals to him. 'Allan seems to have escaped. We're going to check. You and I will stand by the wash-house door as Isabel opens it in case this is a ruse. Allan may be in there and try to escape.'

'Not while I live, master.' Grim pleasure floods Joe's voice at being offered the opportunity to restrain Allan.

But he is destined to be disappointed.

'TOLD you so!' Maureen crows. 'I always said there was something strange about Allan. A witch he is, escaped up the chimney and now we'll never see him again.'

No one takes any notice. Alice's brief hope of Isabel's heart softening has melted in the face of the steward's fury at Allan's escape. But where is he? How has he escaped? Impossible thoughts revolve that perhaps he did indeed climb up inside the chimney, but they are vying with the certainty that such chimneys can only be scaled by urchins.

Is it possible to remove the door hinges? Certainly he could not reach the lock, which is an old type, fitted on the outside; the keyhole does not go right through the wood, so even if he had a key he could not let himself out. And he could not possibly squeeze between the mullions which are spaced expressly to keep out intruders. When she asked a yawning Betsy about other key holders, there was only denial.

Henry has ridden into town to inform the sheriff's men. Better to do that, he and Alice have decided, than wait until the men arrive to take Allan to gaol, only to discover they are on a fool's errand. And what on earth is she to say to Jack Egerton when he arrives to accompany her to where Allan found Sylvia's body? He trusted her to keep Allan locked up overnight. The thought dogged her as she dressed hastily and returned to the kitchen, thanking God that Sam is at Freemans and did not hear Maureen's screams. Maureen has declared her inability to cook for the time being. More likely, Alice thinks, she resents the absence of Mollie to light the fire for her. So Maureen sits at the table, every now and then placing a hand to her chest and drawing a shuddering breath. Joe slouches on a stool, leaning an elbow on the table and drawing wet circles in the ale Alice spilled when she snatched up the jug to empty it over the cook.

'Joe, have you saddled up Cassie for me?' Alice asks. 'Master Egerton will be here soon.'

Joe grunts and continues to draw circles. 'Doesn't take a minute.'

Alice feels disinclined to insist. After the events of yesterday followed by an hour last evening persuading Henry not to call out Sir Malcolm for his sickening but unverifiable abuse of Sylvia's body – 'We cannot afford a slander case on top of everything else,' she reminded him –Alice dropped into an exhausted sleep. Now woken so rudely, she feels sluggish and low.

With an effort she rouses herself. If she has bad news to give Jack about Allan, at least she has good news about Grace. It was a simple matter to visit the dairy to bid Grace a good morning, to raise again the subject of spring cheeses and to suggest that Grace avail herself of Alice's receipt book in the winter parlour. She felt a twinge of guilt at such a deceitful means of extracting Grace's admission that she cannot read. On its own, that could easily be a lie, but the blush that spread over her face was proof enough of innocence. There was no lover's letter written to Grace. So who wrote it? And how did Sylvia get hold of it?

In the silence, Maureen drones. 'It's all because of the witch mark over the hearth in the wash-house.'

'There isn't one,' Joe says.

'Exactly! See what it's led to?'

Alice pours a cup of ale and pushes it towards the cook. 'Have something to drink, Maureen. Perhaps it will refresh you. How did you know he had escaped?'

'Went to check, see he hadn't thrown things all over the place in the night. And there he was gone.'

Went to gloat over his misfortune more like, Alice thinks sourly.

Joe pulls the jug towards himself and pours. 'It's warlock, not witch.'

'You don't want to drink that stuff,' Maureen warns him. 'Could have put his sorcery in it for all we know.' She pushes her cup away.

'So what's this about witch marks then?' Joe says. He swirls the ale in his cup and raises it to his lips, but hesitates and puts it down again.

'I'm always saying it but does anybody listen?' Hand to her ribs, Maureen heaves another sigh.

'Huh! I've never heard you say anything about witch marks,' Joe says.

'Maureen,' Alice says, 'I feel sure Allan is not a witch, or warlock, or whatever, and the ale is not poisoned. Look.' She picks up Maureen's cup and drinks. The small ale is as poor as ever, but certainly not foul. 'See?'

'You wait,' warns Maureen.

'Anyway,' Joe goes on, 'a witch mark only stops them coming *down* the chimney.'

'If it'd been upside down he couldn't have escaped up it. They should have made an upside-down witch mark.' Maureen says. 'I could have told them that.'

'Doesn't work like that,' Joe argues.

'You don't know.'

'There isn't a witch mark in the wash-house, anyway,' Joe repeats.

'There you are, then.' Maureen sits back, a satisfied smile on her face.

'Why didn't you say, if you know so much?' Joe asks.

'Didn't ask me, did they?'

Alice suppresses a sigh and prays Jack will arrive soon.

'I reckon it's Grace who's the witch,' Joe says. 'Grace let him out. She's playing with him.'

'Joe,' Alice warns. 'Go and saddle Cassie for me.'

Joe draws a head in the ale spill. 'Just another notch to her bow, that's all he is.' He adds a pair of horns.

'Joe, get back to the stables now!'

'Up or down,' Maureen continues to no one in particular, 'it's all the same with witches.'

'Watch Grace, Maureen,' Joe says. 'She'll turn the milk sour, then clear off when your back's turned. Writing letters to her—'

'Stop it!' Alice sweeps her hand across the horned head, wiping it out. 'Stop this slander and go and saddle Cassie! If you utter one more word, I'll lock you in the necessary-house!'

'All right, all right, I'm going.' Joe pushes himself to his feet. He gets as far as the door before he mutters, 'You see if I'm not right.'

26

The spring breeze catches at them as they breast the hill. Strands of escaped hair tickle her face and for several seconds Alice tries to tuck them back whilst at the same time reining in a dancing Cassie. Jack waits. The exchanges between them have ebbed since he arrived and learned of Allan's escape.

'When she gets the wind under her she becomes skittish,' Alice babbles as the mare prances and backs. Jack says nothing. 'She didn't have a run yesterday so she's spoiling for a gallop, you see?' Alice is aware of rattling on in a pointless attempt to keep his suspicion of her at bay. She is weighed down with remorse that she has broken her word to secure Allan overnight. She is not sure whether being deprived of control over the wash-house keys is a help or a hindrance here. Clearly Jack gives no more credence than she to stories of witches, for he walked out of the kitchen in the middle of the cook's maunderings, but it leaves a question of who aided Allan's escape. After the confidences of yesterday when Jack appeared to welcome or at least tolerate Alice's presence as he questioned Allan and Joe, Alice feels the more keenly isolated today. Her company, she suspects, is no longer either welcome or helpful. Rather, it seems an embarrassment he could do without.

He dismounts and takes firm hold of Cassie's bridle, allowing Alice to slide to the ground. 'He found her near where the white lane crosses this track, you said? Which side, right or left?'

'Allan didn't say,' she answers. 'Just that the track turns to skirt the trees and you can almost see the roofs of the town from there.'

'A little further on, then. But best if we start looking from here. I'll take this side if you'll check the bank along there.' Jack ties the horses' reins to a low branch and starts to search through the line of beech trees edging the track.

Without knowing quite what she is looking for – some copper-coloured hairs, signs of a struggle? – Alice walks slowly along, scanning the margins of the track and searching amongst bushes for anything that looks out of place amid the familiar chaos of nature. The ground is dry and hard packed, a mix of chalk and flint. Bright new clumps of grass grow here and there, and the first sproutings of scabious are pushing upwards; in the summer they will display their glorious blue pin-cushion flowers. At present the undergrowth is low and she moves ahead, scanning to right and left. But no conveniently snapped-off twigs, no giveaway footprints present themselves, and already they are not far from the point where their track crosses the white lane running the length of the Long Down. She turns and as she does so, a dozen paces away Jack stoops over something on the ground. She crosses the track to see what it is. There amongst the chalk and flint and sprouting grass, a single splash of dark red, oval shaped, the size of a small dish.

All her life Alice has known the spilled blood of animals from the annual autumn slaughter. And yet this sight appals her, for this is no necessary part of a yearly cull. This was a life that was brought to a sudden and unnatural end. A life that had a future, a life that held another life, so a double death in a single blow. Alice kneels down, touching a finger to the patch. The chalky earth is rough but no longer wet. Within the spread of the stain is a shallow depression, about the size a small animal might make in its casual scratching. Like the rest of the patch, it has received and absorbed, taking the stain more thoroughly here, probably through having held blood longer by acting as a cup.

'So this is where it happened,' she says simply.

He nodded. 'I can see no other trace of blood around here. She was not moved.'

Assailed by sudden distress, Alice says, 'I hope it was quick.'

Jack rises and scans the track this way and that. He falls to thinking, his chin resting on the slight double chin below, his lower lip protruding in concentration, but whatever his thoughts, he does not share them with her.

Again the feeling that something does not fit comes to Alice, as it did when she first talked with Allan yesterday. 'Ah!'

Jack looks round, eyebrows raised. 'What?'

'A thought,' she says. 'She was hit on the back of the head, so her attacker must have been behind her. Was she running away?'

'If she was?'

'We seem to be assuming she was on her way that way, to Tillotsons,' she points, 'but what if she was coming back? We may perhaps find signs of an earlier struggle further on from here.'

'Or perhaps she simply turned her head away, knowing a blow was coming.'

'It was just a thought,' Alice says.

'Mmm.'

Alice takes a deep breath. 'Jack if you suspect us, I wish you to say it to my face. At least then we can defend ourselves.'

He regards her. 'I think you are hiding something, Alice.'

The accusation is so unexpected that for a moment Alice can only stare. How does he know? But of course he does not. Wipley's repulsive sullying of Sylvia's body in the small chamber, lying so heavily on her mind, is entirely unknown to Jack. No, Jack is fishing, he only suspects concealment because of Allan's disappearance, because of the coroner's verdict, for which he, Jack is now bound to seek evidence.

'How can you look for evidence of ravishment when there was no ravishment?' she says at last.

'Who says I am looking for evidence of ravishment?'

'That was the jury's conclusion.'

'Alice, if it gives you any comfort, Master Middleton came to see me last night. He told me what was said amongst the jury.'

'It was not unanimous.'

'There were other opinions,' he concedes. 'Master Middleton amongst them. But in the end, it is the majority decision that directs my actions.'

'But you don't believe it either!' When he does not answer, she persists, 'Do you?'

'I try to keep an open mind.'

'You've known Betsy all your life. Betsy would have told you if she had found any signs of ravishment, wouldn't she? She came and told us about Sylvia's condition.' Did the other jury members really think Allan was guilty? Alice wonders. Perhaps it is convenient to assume his guilt in the absence of evidence to the contrary. Or more likely, the influence of the coroner in local affairs is sufficient to convince most that his preferred conclusion is the politic one to adopt.

Jack does not answer her question. Instead he says, 'Sir Malcolm gave Isabel both the keys to the wash-house?'

The breeze has loosened more strands of her kinked curls, blowing them across her face. 'He did,' she says as she puts up a hand to tuck them away. 'He made it clear he did not trust either myself or Henry and went to see Isabel in the accounts room.' How cock-a-hoop Isabel was afterwards. 'I know he gave her them because she came out almost waving them in my face. When she appeared this morning they were on a lace round her neck. She would never have released him. The last thing she wants is Allan's escape. She favoured Sylvia, and she is convinced of his guilt.'

Jack nods slowly. 'That's fairly spoken.' Perhaps he is wanting to see if she will accuse someone else of freeing Allan. But Alice has not fallen into the trap, so can she hope that it has restored some of his confidence in her honesty?

He takes a deep breath and looks around. 'Let us keep searching either side for a distance.' Slowly they continue, heads down, eyes scanning track and undergrowth. Alice pays close attention once more for the slightest sign of a footprint but it is a futile task, chalky ground always dries quickly. Jack wanders back amongst the trees, checking the low-level new growth. Gradually they move along. On Alice's side, not so much as a twig has been snapped, not a clump of grass crushed, to offer any clue to what Sylvia was doing in this place or who else was here before Allan found her.

Some fifty paces from where the drovers lane, called the white lane, crosses the track Alice stops and looks, trying to see if the roofs of the town are indeed visible from here. And there, in straggly undergrowth not a dozen paces away, a scrap of white, a string trailing to the ground. She gives a shout to Jack and points as she breaks into a run. It could have been dropped or thrown, and has not been there long, for as she bends to take it up, she can see that the string on the ground is unsoiled. She picks at it carefully to release it from the bush. The cloth is lawn, good rather than fine, yet its threads are delicate enough to have caught against the twiggy scrub. Jack comes alongside as she rises with it in her hands.

'A pocket,' she says, 'but the string is torn off one side.' The frayed end dangles, its other end tied in a bow to its fellow, as it would have been tied round the waist. She turns it over; a three-petalled flower has been stitched on its front. 'This was Sylvia's,' she says.

'May I?' He takes it into his hands to examine it, turns it over and back, slips fingers into the opening and looks. 'Can you be certain it's hers? It looks like any woman's pocket to me.'

'I recognize the work. I saw several like this in the wash basket on Sunday. Betsy told me it belonged to Sylvia. She thought the old maidservant at Master Tillotson's had stitched it. What was her name?'

'Florence.'

'Florence. But the seam is ripped, probably when the string was torn off, see, and her kerchief has gone. Surely she was not killed for her kerchief?'

He makes a face. 'I've known it happen, an accident of casual robbery. Assuming she carried a kerchief.'

'Oh, yes. Betsy says she is ... was ... always neat at every point.'

'And we have to consider another possibility.' He pauses, 'I am sorry, Alice, this will distress you to hear it, but there may be another reason for the kerchief not being here.'

'Which is?'

'Master Middleton says Sir Malcolm thinks Allan ravished Sylvia and cleaned away the traces.'

'No, that's not true!' she blurts.

'No?' He waits, looking at her. 'You're very certain.' When she remains silent, 'What do you know, Alice?' he asks.

'Nothing! I simply ...' She trails off, recalling yet again the shameful assault on Sylvia's body, to incriminate an innocent man. But as she said to Betsy, the minute they entered the small chamber, they incriminated themselves. She shakes her head. 'I don't have anything to tell you, I'm sorry.' Tell a powerful figure of the gross abuse of a corpse by his powerful colleague in law? To keep Allan from false accusation, she got rid of the evidence, and without evidence, anything she says is slander. How would that help Allan? It would rebound like a musket ball, the new wife jealous for her husband, devising preposterous lies against the man he dislikes. It would do nothing but afford ammunition for Sir Malcolm's personal feud against Henry.

'There is nothing I can tell you,' she repeats. Which makes her yet another one taking the politic rather than the honest course.

She watches his face harden as he regards her. 'Then I cannot help you,' he says simply, and turns away.

She calls after him, 'Tell me at least who is suspect in your view!' She watches him stop and turn.

The wind has ruffled his hair as it has hers, and dishevelled tails hang down either side of his face. 'Any who wished her ill. Any who cannot show where they were at a given time.'

'Betsy and Grace went to the fields to take Angus and Joe their midday meal. Henry was with Master Renwick, then went on into town. Isabel was around the house, I know, because she found Sam playing in the wash-house and disapproved.' She does not even mention Mollie; there is no possibility Mollie is suspect.

'Whoever attacked Sylvia carried an implement hard and sharp enough to crack a skull open. You don't carry such weapons by chance.'

'I see no signs of a struggle there,' she says looking around. They walk back towards the track, eyes down, searching without success.

Conversationally, he says, 'Allan said you brought his tool bag in.'

'Yes, I left it in the chamber,' she tells him. 'There was no blood on any of the tools, if that's what you're thinking.'

He pounces on her words. 'So you felt it necessary to check?'

'I—' She bites off the words, *"I checked when Betsy and I were in there."* She says instead, 'I wanted to be able to verify his innocence.'

'You wouldn't have removed anything from that bag, would you?'

'Why would I do that? What sort of thing?'

He looks straight and hard at her. 'A mortice chisel? He'd need one for making joints. A tool with a slim, square tip? Very sharp?' As she stands speechless, he turns and walks back towards the tethered horses, leaving her staring after him, remembering.

Amongst the tools in Allan's bag, there was only a wide chisel. Wouldn't a man who works with wood carry a mortice chisel?

ALICE has not accompanied Jack to Tillotsons, he did not press her. It was a formal farewell, wary on both sides, before she turned Cassie for home. Her thanks to Jeremy for the gift of old garments, she reflects ruefully, will instead be by written note and she must await another opportunity to make his acquaintance.

'And Master Egerton may think what he pleases about how Allan escaped,' she says to Cassie as the mare ambles back down the long slope. 'We'll leave him to get on with his investigation and perhaps we'll be left in peace.'

Or perhaps not. She has underestimated how speedily the forces of justice can move when prompted. At High Stoke she is met by a kitchen court full of horses and a sheriff's officer who informs her that he has sanction for a search of the house and demesne in pursuit of the fugitive. Already his hard-mouthed, bull-necked bailiffs are tramping in through the kitchen, brandishing pikes and trailing sweat and gaol-stink in their wake. One of them appears briefly at an upstairs window and Alice flies into the house, takes the spiral stairs two at a time and pushes past a man standing idle sentinel in the doorway of Sam's chamber. There she elbows aside two others and stands with her arm round a trembling Mollie whose truckle bed one of them has just upended.

'Good God, man, what do you think you're doing?' she demands, 'You can see there is no one fitting his description here!'

Apart from a terse, 'Step aside, mistress, or we will move you bodily,' they ignore her, even when she pleads with them as they cast Sam's garments from his coffer in an orgy of vandalism before moving on to the main chamber to do the same. To her relief they ignore, or miss, the box of simples under her bed. Everything else they toss across the floor, logs, fire irons, clothes, pillows, the new candlesticks. They exchange grins as they work.

She takes up post before the room where Sylvia lies and demands the officer's presence, and the search there is quiet and orderly under his eye. And she stands in the winter parlour as they push their pikes up the chimney, but with only the rug-covered table to provide other concealment, they soon abandon the search there. She defends stillroom and dairy likewise but is powerless to do more than watch them ransack the outbuildings, turn over everything in the woodshed to old Angus' silent fury, and in the stables, drive their pikes into the straw and trample the hay in the loft. Finally in the wash-house they proceed to toss the sorted heaps of Tillotson clothes across the floor. Then Betsy storms across the kitchen court.

'Saul Brakespear!'

The men stop dead. Alice watches one of them strut out. A well set up fellow and clearly aware of it. 'Betsy? I thought you were at Freemans.'

'So you thought you'd pillage the place while my back's turned,' Betsy counters, hands on wide hips. Before the man can form a protest, Betsy points at his crookedly laced jerkin, 'Still can't dress yourself, I see, any better than when you were in long frocks. What're you up to here?'

Brakespear shifts uneasily. 'Give you greetings, Betsy, as ever.'

'Greetings? You've given me nothing but curses since I discovered you behind the old friary with a certain person's wife, and threatened to tell her husband.' He strides over to Betsy as Alice reaches her side. Betsy adds in a low voice, 'The husband who is not a dozen miles from us this minute.'

The others in the wash-house are now gathered at the door, necks craning. Brakespear leans towards the laundress, whispering fiercely, 'You said you wouldn't tell.'

'If you acted rightly,' Betsy responds. 'I don't see much that's right here.'

'I have my orders,' he says through gritted teeth.

'Right is right, wrong is wrong,' she says. 'Let's call the husband over, shall we?' And she leans round the bailiff, beckoning to the others in the wash-house.

'All right! All right!' Brakespear turns to his fellows. 'We're finished here, we're leaving.' After some discussion they go in search of the sheriff's officer.

Betsy and Alice watch their departure. 'Don't ask,' Betsy says, before Alice can frame the question. 'I said I wouldn't tell and I hold to that.'

'I'm grateful for your knowledge, Betsy,' Alice says. 'I feared the soiled sheet was in there. What if they'd found that?'

'You think I'd leave a sheet to dry out and stain for evermore?' Betsy is all indignation. 'I had that and the shift soaking in a bucket behind the stables before coroner left. They're on the drying bushes with the rest of yesterday's linen. And now I'm going to the Sandersons in town. I'll be back later.' Betsy plods away without a backward glance.

Alice re-enters the house and wanders through the chaos. The door to the accounts room stands open, the floor awash with papers, amidst which Isabel stands wild-eyed, clutching her hair.

'Oh, Isabel,' Alice gasps, 'in here too?' She bends to take up a sheaf of torn bills under her foot. 'What need had they to do this?'

'As if you didn't know!'

'What?'

'Look at it!' Eyes flashing, the cords in her neck standing out, the steward explodes. 'Look – at – it!' She advances on Alice, waving her arms in unfettered rage. 'This is all your fault!'

Alice rises, dropping the papers.

'You have brought nothing but evil on this house!' She pokes her head forward, stabbing a finger. 'You refused to hand him over to the constable and this is the result!' Face in Alice's face, spit flying from her lips, Isabel shouts, 'This is what happens when women like you take the law into their own hands, twist it to evade justice for their favourites!'

'Isabel! What—?'

'Curse you!' With clawed fingers she seizes Alice by the shoulders. 'Curse you and yours to hell!' She shoves her backwards out of the accounts room, slamming the door. Caught off balance, Alice can only listen to table legs scraping across the floor, wood juddering against wood, as the steward takes frenzied steps to deny further access.

Upstairs, Mollie has been setting Sam's room to rights since the men left. She gives Alice a little anxious smile and an unsteady, bobbing curtsey.

'Mollie!' Alice peers. 'Your foot. Did they hurt you?' The splinter came out and the swelling was almost gone this morning, but if those shouldering ruffians have injured her … 'Let me see.' But Mollie shakes her head, she has other things on her mind. From Sam's bed, carefully laid side by side, she picks up some pieces of stick and cradles them to her chest.

'What's that, Mollie? What have you got there?'

Mollie approaches, eyes big with apprehension, opening her hands to show. There on her palms lie the stamped-on remains of Samuel and Zachariah, Sam's two toys that he brought with him from Dorset.

27

'I just got back,' Henry explains. 'Mollie virtually dragged me up here.'

'Sam is entirely innocent in all this.' Still trembling from Isabel's attack and now this destruction of Sam's toys, Alice wants to weep. 'He has done nothing and yet they destroy the only things he has that remind him of Dorset.'

Henry's arm tightens round her shoulder. 'He has you, Alice, and that is more important.'

'He loved those figures. He was forever playing with them.' Sam's bed creaks slightly under their joint weight as Henry leans to rest his chin on her kinked, unruly hair, and she is comforted by his nearness.

'What have I brought you to, Alice?' Henry asks. 'Marrying you, I meant to give you a better life, more secure, happier, but look at this house. I should have been here when they came.'

'Don't say that, you are not to blame for what the bailiffs did.'

'I should have foreseen it,' he says. 'When I got to Alford's house, he said he—'

'Alford?'

'Edward Alford, the sheriff. I told him Allan had escaped and he said he would have to search the house and demesne.'

'We knew he would want to do that. But why in this cruel way?'

'He sent for his officer and gave him the order. I told Alford I would rather he and not his man had the charge of our keys, but he said he couldn't, he's been summoned to London, he was on the point of leaving.'

'You think he didn't wish it known he ordered this havoc?'

'Not that. Alford's not of that stamp, he's an honest man.

But as I left with Alford's officer, I saw Wipley downstairs so I had to tell him what's happened. My guess is, after I left, Wipley convinced the officer that High Stoke is a guilty household and they had free rein to treat us accordingly.'

She looks up at him, at the frown of concern on his face. 'Everywhere I turn, Henry, it is Wipley who dogs our steps. Why does he hate you so?'

'Who knows?' He pauses to consider. 'Old money is one reason, though that sounds laughable given our current means. What I'm saying is, the Jerrards have been here for generations.'

'But so have others, surely?'

'He constantly goes on about my lack of money to keep this place in good repair. It seems to be his only solace for …' He stops.

'For what?'

He shrugs. 'Who knows?' he says again.

'We've each made an enemy of Sir Malcolm,' she says. 'He knows I saw him coming out of the small chamber. That will multiply his hate. But also his fear, remember that.'

'He was in the Red Lion yesterday,' Henry tells her. 'I went into town after seeing George Renwick's chestnut mare. Wipley was going upstairs as I arrived.'

'Going upstairs? You mean whoring?'

'I'll wager he wouldn't want his dear friend Townsend to find out. Wipley cultivates an air of spotlessness when Townsend is by.'

'Surely Master Townsend knows Wipley takes a whore sometimes?' she says.

Henry smiles. 'I think Townsend would just about manage to connive at one whore, but this was two together.'

'Be careful, Henry. Did he see you?'

'I don't suppose so. The crowd was spilling out of the cock pit and making a press in the passage. A fight or something. I was trapped near the stairs and that's when I saw him. He couldn't push the women up fast enough.'

There is a short silence between them.

'I went down to the mill wharf after,' he says suddenly.

'The mill wharf?' she asks, all at sea.

'You know,' he says, 'I've been thinking much about this place, Alice. I have left things to run themselves, let them slide. No, it's true,' he goes on, as Alice opens her mouth. 'I have neglected the whole demesne. Talking with George Renwick yesterday made me realise that.'

'With Master Renwick? Why?'

'He said you had the right of it with up-and-down husbandry. He wants to make your acquaintance.'

Alice smiles and sits up. 'We're going to make spring cheese, Henry.' And as he regards her in puzzlement, she adds, 'I had a long talk with Grace. She knows how but Isabel won't let her.'

'Ah. Isabel. What about making some small ale too?'

And then it connects. 'Of course, the mill wharf,' she says. 'You were ordering malted grain. Does this mean I have a free hand, Henry?' She feels as if she has been fighting for this forever, though it is only a matter of days.

'You have a free hand. You should have had it from the start. It's about time we had something decent to drink. You could make some for George too, I told him about the brew you made in Dorset.'

'Oh,' she says sitting up, 'so I am to be ale-wife to the community am I? I'll have you know, sir, I shall be no such thing!'

'That's better,' Henry says. 'I prefer it when you're in fighting humour.' She punches his ribs and they laugh softly in each other's arms, an unspoken awareness between them that yards away Sylvia lies dead.

28

Alice has set the main chamber straight, returning the logs to their basket, righting the fire irons and the candlesticks, collecting up linen trampled by muddy boots and restoring the rest to the coffers. Downstairs, the dining parlour looks as it did after the fight between Joe and Allan and she spends several minutes re-stacking the pewterware on the sideboard and straightening the furniture. The door to the accounts room is still shut and she does not test it. Perhaps Isabel has already tidied up and left, or perhaps she is recovering from her hurt at the state of her beloved room and will reappear in her own time. What Isabel cannot know is that a great deal has happened in that short exchange between Alice and Henry. A shift has occurred that will spread its ripples through the whole household. In securing her husband's interest in her knowledge and skills Alice has at last ensured his support for running the household her way. She smiles to herself, clearly much benefit can come from a man's interest in his beer.

She goes to drop off the trodden linen in the wash-house. Henry is out in the kitchen court. He stands in converse with a muscled, weathered-looking man in shirtsleeves by a cart. Both are intent on the sacks it contains. The man gestures as he talks, repeatedly dipping his hand in a sack and releasing a dirty white gravel through his fingers. Henry listens and nods. It is not until Alice comes out of the wash-house, that he turns, squinting against the sun.

'Ah, Alice!' He beckons. 'Come and see what he's brought. This is Will Harvey,' and the carter touches fat fingers to his worn, wide-brimmed hat.

'Give you good day,' she says, crossing to join them. As she nears, a stench somewhere between rotten fish and decomposed vegetation assails her nostrils. Involuntarily she draws back, wrinkling her nose, and waving a hand before her face. 'What is that?'

Henry laughs, 'I told you, Will, it stinks worse than rotted flax.'

'Yes, well, it smells a bit but you soon don't notice.'

'What is it?' Alice asks again. Cautiously she steps closer and looks.

The carter runs more of the substance through his fingers. 'Crag,' he announces, as though all is now perfectly plain.

'Crag,' she repeats. 'Yes?'

'He says it'll make the crops grow,' Henry explains.

'Master Renwick says it'll make the crops grow,' Will Harvey corrects him. 'Come on, missus, take a closer look.' Again he dips large fingers into the sack and again the smell of rot. Leaning away, Alice stretches and picks up a handful of the whitish fragments. They are dry and gritty and make a rustling sound as they run through her fingers.

Henry explains. 'This load's from Colchester, George says. It's broken-up seashells. They spread it once a year in the Three Counties and it keeps the land in good heart.'

'Good heart for what?' Alice asks.

'Prevents it being exhausted by too-frequent cropping,' Henry says. 'A couple of men could do it here easily.'

Alice points to the cart. 'Miraculous stuff indeed if five sacks can feed all our fields.'

'This is just a sample. We'd need a lot more than this.'

'How many would we need?'

'How many did you have on the cart when you came to Master Renwick's yesterday, Will?'

'Fifty, and if you'd stayed you could have helped unload,' Will reproves him.

Henry turns to Alice. 'George is keen for me to try these few sacks here. I'm thinking about it.'

'The Three Counties, you say? You didn't go all the way to Essex for it, did you?' Alice asks the carter.

'Nah,' Will Harvey says. 'Got it near Billingsgate on my last trip to London.'

'A fellow brings oysters to the city,' Henry explains. 'George met him when he was up there awhile back and they got talking. When the oysters are used, the shells go to get broken up. Probably a few dead oysters in there too. Spread it on the ground and you get more bushels to the acre.'

'Then I'd like one of those sacks for my potager, Henry,' she says.

'Your what?'

'Vegetable garden to you.'

'Vegetable garden? Where's that, then?'

'There,' she says, pointing behind the stables, beyond the drying bushes.

He leans to see. 'There's nothing there.'

'There will be. A bit of digging's all that's needed. Master Harvey, Joe is in the fields or I would ask him to unload a sack for me.'

'Where d'you want it?' Will asks.

'Do you take it into the stables there. How much a bushel?'

'We'll take all five, Will,' Henry tells him, 'and then come into the house for a mug of ale.'

'And my money?'

'When you've unloaded.' He turns to Alice. 'I'm going to change out of these town clothes and then I'll get started on your vegetable garden.'

As Henry enters the house, 'I was just saying to your man,' Will says, backing the cart towards the stables, 'pity about your maidservant. Uncommon pretty she was. Gurt on, you old lump.' He shoves at the shoulder of the horse, a great, shaggy-footed giant of a beast. 'Get back, get back. That's it, wo, wo, wo!' The horse stops and stands patiently. 'Maureen reckons she was killed by a witch, you know, but then along came Master Jerrard and told her to hold her tongue.'

'So I should think,' Alice says, noting with disgust the cook's persistent bent for sensation. And noting with satisfaction Henry's tough new manner.

'You're not from these parts, are you?' Will leans comfortably against the horse's flank.

'I'm from Dorset. Lived there all my life.'

'That's a long way, Dorset?' Will prompts.

But Alice is not in a humour for comfortable gossip yet. 'You called here yesterday?'

'O' course, I come every Wednesday, don't I?' Will sniffs and reaches behind him for the ears of the first sack. 'Hundreds of miles away, Dorset, isn't that right?'

'When did you get here yesterday, what time?'

Will lifts his hat and scratches his head. 'I dunno, late forenoon, early afternoon, it's usually around then.' He hefts the sack onto his shoulders and she follows as he lumbers into the stables. 'How about down here?' he suggests.

'Not there, I don't want to mix it with the charcoal. Here.' She indicates the next empty bay. 'Try to think, Will, it's important. Is there anything that anyone said, anything that suggested what the time was?'

The carter swings the sack to the ground. 'How do I know? People don't go round saying, "Tis one o' the clock, neighbour", do they?' He knees the sack into place and heads for the door.

'Did you see anyone?'

'Nah. Only Betsy. I drove into the yard here and there was—'

'You saw Betsy?'

'And the new girl, the one I brought the message for last week.' He points across the fields. 'Going that way, but they didn't see me. They were carrying baskets.'

'Ah. Then it was very close to midday because Betsy took the men their midday meal in the fields.'

'Like I said. Late forenoon.' Will shakes his head. 'I dunno, all this fuss.'

'So you drove into the yard. What then?'

He takes hold of a second sack and heaves it onto his shoulders. 'I wished I hadn't, I tell you. There was this boy, and Isabel was dragging him inside.'

'The fair-haired boy? About four or five?' Alice asks, following close.

'That's the one. Watch yourself, missus, this one's slipping. He was screaming and the little dumb girl come runnin' out, trying to pull him away and got hit for her pains, and I thought to myself, Will Harvey, tis time to be gone.'

Sam and Mollie, in disgrace. 'What were you delivering, Will?'

'Nothing. I came to see if Isabel had anything to send.'

'You talked with Isabel, then?'

The carter pulls a face. 'Not on your life! I left as fast as I could.' He drops the second sack against the first. 'Ooof! These are the devil of a weight.' He drags out a large red kerchief and mops his brow as they leave the stables. 'It's hot work today, even warmer than yesterday. A man could do with a drink.'

'As my husband said,' Alice replies, 'as soon as you've unloaded I shall be pleased to draw you some ale.'

At the cart, he props his bottom against the wheel and folds his arms. 'So you've got family in foreign places, have you?'

'None of your business if I have, Will. And for your information, Dorset is not foreign, it's part of the King's realm. Tell me, did you see anyone else about while you were in the yard?'

Thwarted of the chance either for ale or for gossip, Will straightens and reaches for the third sack. 'Only Sylvia, but that was after I left.'

'Sylvia? When? Leave that sack. When did you see Sylvia,

Will?'

'She caught up with me just outside the yard and asked me for a lift. Look, missus, your man wants this delivered, so by your leave I'll do that.'

Alice stands back as he hauls the sack and plods towards the stables.

'You gave her a lift? How far?'

'As far as the road. Well, that's what she wanted at first. Soon changed her tune once she was up on the cart, reckoned I should take her to the Long Down.'

'The Long Down?'

'At the top of the hill. There's a white lane crosses the track.'

'Yes, I know it. And did you?'

He swings the sack to the ground and works it against its fellow. 'I'm not so green, missus. I said she could come as far as the road but I wasn't taking a loaded cart all the way up there.'

'So what did she say?'

'Told me I'd regret it because she was going to be a lady. Full of it, she was,' Will Harvey says. 'But that was Sylvia. You know, was a time she was up at Tillotsons, she thought she was going to catch old Master Frederick. Ha, ha!'

He heads out of the stables, heaves himself into the cart and drags the last two sacks into place where he can reach them. 'Like I said to Master Renwick later, she was going on about "all that demeaning work" and how there was "lots of money", all pledged, more'n I'd ever see in my lifetime, stuff like that. And she patted her pocket, like this.' Will drops his head on one side and bats his eyelids as he taps his ample middle and simpers, '"Tis all here, Master Harvey".'

He suddenly lunges, 'Oh, no you don't!' and grasps one of the sacks as it slumps and the top falls open. He straightens it and scoops up bits of gritty shell.

'So you made a grab for her pocket?'

'Only when – no, I never!'

'Only when what?'

'Nothing. I took her up as far as the road.'

'You simply said, "Oh, very well, Sylvia, I'll give you a lift for nothing as you're going to be a rich lady."'

Sullenly, the carter says, 'It was just playful, that's all. Like you do.'

Alice leaves the silence hanging.

'I didn't touch her!' he insists.

'The string of her pocket was torn off one side.'

Will scowls. 'That was her fault. When we got to the road, I said she could give me some of that money for my trouble.'

'She had a purse in her pocket?'

'Nah.' Will shakes his head. 'Dunno what it was but she said she didn't have the money yet. So I said I'd settle for a kiss. But she went 'Huh!' like that, declared she didn't want a lift anyway because the smell was making her feel sick. And then she went to get down.'

Leaning against the door of the stable, Alice waits. Eventually the carter goes on. 'I just gave a little tug on her pocket-string. It was a jest, no more. She had hold of the pocket as she jumped down and the string broke. And she said, "Look what you've done." And I said, "Where's my kiss, then?" And she just walked away up the hill. That was all.'

'And you followed her.'

'How do you think one horse, even this gurt lump, could drag a cartload of crag up that hill? Of course I didn't follow her! I went to do my delivery. Like I'm trying to do now, and get on my way,' he finishes pointedly, and hefts another sack onto his shoulders.

'Will, I believe you,' Alice says, 'but you understand, this was an untimely death, and I'm anxious to find out how it happened. So anything you can tell me might help.' She moves aside for him to pass into the stables.

'Yes, well, I liked her, for all her airs,' the carter grudgingly admits. 'I'll tell you something. Master Renwick looked mighty red-faced when I said about Sylvia and her riches.'

'Indeed?'

Will drops the sack and knees it against its fellow. 'Mind you, it could've bin because he was thinking about hauling fifty sacks of crag. Big man like him, not used to real work. But red he went, all of a sudden-like.'

'What are you saying, Will?'

'Between you and me,' Will says, leaning close, 'I think he was sweet on her. There were rumours earlier in the year, you know. Now, where's my drink, missus?'

'Where's my fifth sack?'

JACK Egerton rides into the kitchen court as Alice returns from seeing Will away, duly watered and recompensed. She greets him with reserve. 'Master Egerton?'

'No news of Allan yet?'

'The sheriff's men have searched the house and everywhere here. They're going round the demesne.'

'I saw Jeremy Tillotson, and his man Len,' he says.

She waits.

'They verified that Allan did what he said he had done.'

'As I thought.'

'And left when he said he did.'

'… but?'

'No buts. Jeremy asked me to return this, which Allan left behind.' From his saddle bag he draws out a slim implement and hands it to her. It is a chisel, of the sort a worker in wood might use.

Overjoyed, she looks up at him. 'The mortice chisel? So all his tools are accounted for. You see? He didn't do it!'

'Do not rely too heavily on this,' he advises her. 'There is still no evidence that anyone else was in the area at that time. As to the tool that killed Sylvia, it could as easily have been the sharp edge of a flint.'

'There was not a scrap of blood on him.'

'An innocent man has no call to run, Alice.'

'He does if he has no hope of justice!' She bites her tongue at her own discourtesy but cannot find the words to correct it.

He is silent for a few seconds, his lower lip jutting as he thinks. Then, 'You were right about it being Sylvia's pocket. I talked to old Florence. Sylvia got her to stitch it when she worked there.'

'I know how the pocket string was torn,' she tells him. 'Will Harvey the carter just called by. He saw Sylvia leaving here just after Betsy and Grace left for the fields at midday. He gave Sylvia a lift as far as the road. The string tore from her pocket as she got down. He didn't take her up the hill, he couldn't, he was carrying a full load of heavy sacks for Master Renwick's fields.' She points past the cow byre. 'Will just left that way, into town.'

'Good.' Egerton's renewed interest shows in his look. 'Then he can tell me what he has told you.'

'There's still nothing to prove Allan's guilt,' she reminds him. 'Nothing puts him on the scene at the time, beyond his own honest admission. There could have been any number of men there before Allan found her.'

Egerton does not answer. He screws round in the saddle. 'Is that the grey I see in the stable? Is Henry around now? I'd like to have a word.'

'He's upstairs changing,' Alice says. 'He'll be down soon.'

'While we're waiting, when are you going to tell me what you know?'

The key to the chamber, the mud smears like grasping fingers all up her legs ... does Jack Egerton have any idea what sort of a man the coroner is? Does he even care? she wonders. *But I have to tell him something.*

Aloud, she says, 'I can tell you this. When Henry arrived in town yesterday, he saw Sir Malcolm Wipley pushing two bawds upstairs in the Red Lion.' Even as she speaks she wonders why she said it at all, how feeble it sounds. There is no Lady Wipley, apparently, so would his fellow men be that surprised at Wipley taking a whore? And surely he is not the first man to engage two together?

'What time was this?'

'Henry left Master Renwick's for town as Will Harvey arrived there.'

'So, midday Will was here. He goes up to the road where Sylvia gets down, then on to Renwick's. We'll allow a few minutes for courtesies and ten minutes for Henry to get into town. So at around a quarter to one, Sir Malcolm Wipley was seen to take his leisure with two of the Red Lion ladies.'

'That would have been about the time Allan found Sylvia, I suppose.'

Egerton half-smiles. 'It would, wouldn't it? You have told me a great deal; I am glad to know it.'

In dismay, Alice realises how much she has been hoping that by some roundabout means the coroner will be found out for his abuse of Sylvia's body, how certain she has been that he has something to do with her death. Instead, all she has done is to cause Henry to give his worst enemy an alibi. Not only Henry, but also the two whores, can prove where Wipley was when Sylvia was murdered. Wipley didn't kill her, and on top of that, Egerton is evidently pleased that his colleague in law is off the hook.

29

Time after time Alice watches Henry stab his spade into the ground, drive it in with his boot and toss great clods of grass and earth to one side. He has not stopped since they marked out with sticks and twine the space that is to be the vegetable garden. It is beginning to look like a small ploughed field. Lagging behind him now, she pushes her fork into the turned soil and stoops to shake out the straggling growth to be burned later. Her hands full of earth and weeds, she looks along the dug line at her husband. 'Henry, won't you tell me what vexes you?'

'Nothing,' he says and continues digging. 'Don't fret yourself, Alice.'

'You've been like this all afternoon.'

There is silence but for the rhythmic slicing of his spade. She straightens, throws aside the weeds and goes to stand in front of him. 'What use is a wife who looks the other way and lets her husband fret?'

He drives his spade into the earth, breathes out hard. 'What use is a husband who lets his wife work the land like any labourer?' He grasps her wrist and turns up her palm. 'Look! You're ruining your hands.'

'And you're blistering yours.'

'I'm making you a drudge, Alice.'

'No.' She indicates the plot. 'You and I are building our life. And I'm proud of it. This is not what's troubling you. Please, Henry, tell me what is.'

His hands are caked with earth, so he hooks an elbow round her neck and draws her to him, rests his chin on her kinked curls spreading in tangled disorder around her face. 'You heard what Jack said. My story doesn't tally with what Wipley told him.'

'I thought Master Egerton believed me when I told him that you had seen Wipley with the two whores. Then he challenges you with Wipley's story of riding on Guildown with his men. Is Guildown near the Long Down?'

'No, other side of town. We came over it when we arrived on Friday.'

'Why couldn't Master Egerton have told me where Wipley said he was?' she asks.

'Perhaps he wanted to see my reaction.'

'He knows we're hiding something. He thinks it's to do with Allan's escape.'

He releases her and takes up his spade once more. 'Add that to Wipley's different story and who is Jack going to believe?'

'But Wipley's lying!'

'How does Jack know that, when Wipley's men are backing him up?' He lifts a spadeful and turns it.

'The two whores can confirm.'

'No one is going to listen to two whores against Wipley and his men.'

'Surely Master Egerton can see through that?' She dusts off her hands and goes to fetch her fork. 'What about the innkeeper? He must have seen Wipley.'

'Melbury will see what he's told to see because Wipley has a powerful friend in Townsend, and it's Justice Townsend who controls the Red Lion's licence. Still,' Henry gives a grim smile, 'I'd like to watch Townsend getting to hear of Wipley's sordid capers. That would set the cat amongst the pigeons.'

Working alongside Henry now, Alice says, 'If he condemns whoring, why are he and Wipley such great friends? What's Justice Townsend like?'

Henry leans on his spade and counts off his fingers. 'Rigorously principled, upright, unyielding, honest, grave ... oh, and sober, in every sense.'

'I wonder he has any friends at all, let alone a man like Wipley.' She strikes ineffectually at a large clod of earth.

'Not the easiest of men,' Henry agrees, resuming his task. 'But Townsend rose on his own merit. His father was in the cloth trade, worked for Archbishop Abbot's father here in Guildford. So Townsend and His Grace were boys together.'

'I didn't know the Archbishop was a Guildford man.' Alice continues her assault on the lump of earth. It rolls a short way, but does not break up.

'Was and still is. He built that new place at the top of the High Street, the hospital for the poor.'

'The old-fashioned-looking building with the two towers? I thought that must have been built last century.' She hits and kicks at the clod. It remains obstinately whole.

'It was opened two or three years ago,' Henry tells her. 'His Grace is a man of tradition. Modern buildings are too flimsy for his notions.' He pauses in his digging to ease his back. 'Ooh, nearly done. All the great and good of Guildford were there. You should have seen Wipley edging as close to His Grace as possible, to be seen in the right company.' He lifts his spade and pushes it one-handed into the lump of earth she has been belabouring. Obediently the clod falls apart.

'How did Townsend become such good friends with someone like Wipley?' she asks him.

'Townsend has rather too much respect for a title, even a bought knighthood like Wipley's. Hereabouts if you're titled you can count on the favour of Townsend, honest man and friend of the Archbishop. That confers rock-solid respectability.'

'But does Master Townsend mislike you in the way that Wipley does?'

'Not at all,' Henry says. 'We get along when we meet, though I don't know him that well.' He leans, looking down the line he has just dug. 'Straight as a ploughed furrow. What are we going to plant here, then?'

Alice shades her eyes against the sinking afternoon sun. 'I'll tell you as we ride over to collect Sam.'

JUSTICE Jack Egerton dismounts in the courtyard behind the Red Lion and looks around. A scrawny urchin squatting at the stable door rises, straightening his jerkin. It nearly meets his breeches but a strip of skin remains, the rib visible under the flesh. He slops forward, legs sticking out like straws from his ill-fitting boots. 'Give him a rub down and some hay and you'll get the other half when I return,' Egerton says, passing a coin. The boy takes a wary glance around but no one is paying attention to a menial collared for a task. When mounts are collected, that is when the eyes search for money changing hands; the rest of his tip he will have a fight to keep. In a single smooth movement the boy raises a foot and slips his prize down between leather and ankle before turning without a word to lead the bay towards the stables.

Egerton stands a moment taking stock of his surroundings. He entered this courtyard from the High Street down the short passage between the buildings, though he might equally have come up from Lower Back Lane at the opposite end, along the trodden path between cultivated strips. Here in the courtyard, the stables and hayloft flank one side, adjacent to the back of the inn. The narrow passage through to the High Street separates the inn from its brew house. This and the adjoining malt house, its brick chimney built out at the end, form that side of the court. On the fourth side is a ring of benches enclosed by a circle of willow hurdles. It is referred to as the horse-ring but most of the town knows it for a cock pit.

The taproom of the Red Lion is one Egerton visits occasionally. The beer is quite good, but there are other hostelries in town with better, and which are not liable to disruption by excited rowdies disputing the performance of this or that hapless bird in the latest cockfight. He turns and enters the inn, passing the shadowy stairwell where a damsel sits splay-legged on the stairs, another ensconced a few steps up in the corner of the turn, eyes half closed, drawing on a small clay pipe.

'Make yer swell with pride, y'r honour?'

Egerton pauses. 'Give you good day, Francine. I see the whipping that Justice Townsend ordered has not mended your ways.'

Both women laugh, a harsh cackling. 'Not never likely to, neither,' Francine says, 'lemon-faced old kill-joy he is. But I'd suck you into a swoon any day, you know.'

'A generous offer, but not today, I fear, Francine.'

'That's what you always say.' The woman settles the pipe back in a gap between yellowed teeth. 'Your loss.'

Egerton moves on and makes his way to the barrels. The tapster lounges, arms folded, before a sparse roomful of regulars.

'Master Melbury within?' Egerton asks him.

'E's pokin' the fire for the maltin' floor,' the man says a shade too easily.

'More likely he's poking one of his own whores,' Egerton replies. 'Go and tell him I want to see him.'

The tapster looks furtive. 'E's busy, not to be disturbed.'

'And that if he does not come straightway I shall go upstairs and open every chamber door until I find him.'

The tapster pushes his shoulders off the wall and slouches towards the kitchen whence much cursing and banging of pots declare the incendiary activities of Mistress Melbury. From past visits Egerton knows there is a second flight of stairs from the kitchen.

A couple of dusty, many-paned windows light the High Street end of the taproom and Egerton selects a table by one of them where the sun struggles through. From here he has a fair view of the interior, and he sits where he can lean back against the wall and look round. The taproom is dingy, not only from the blackened beams running front to back, but also from the smoke-browned plaster of ceiling and walls. Two lines of spaced, rough-cut oak pillars betray where the inn has been extended back aeons ago from its original square room facing the High Street. It is now nearly three times as long as it is wide and becomes progressively dimmer towards the back. In winter, unless a customer pays for a rushlight on his table, only the fire affords any glow.

At the far end of the inn the landlord appears on the lowest stair, pausing to drive Francine and her companion up out of sight. He wears a stout leather apron, and as he approaches through the taproom he ostentatiously wipes his hands and brow with a dirty cloth. 'Tis hot work on the malting floor. Good day to you, Master Egerton.'

'Strange place you've moved the malthouse to, Melbury,' Egerton says. 'Last time I looked it was outside. And yet you came down the stairs.'

Melbury's laugh is prolonged and hearty. 'What a noticing man you are, Master Egerton. I was just, er ... just ...' He holds up the cloth. '... getting a kerchief.'

'Were you indeed? Well, it's not your dainty habits that concern me at present, Melbury. Sit down there where I can see you. Tell me, Sir Malcolm Wipley was here yesterday, was he not?'

The landlord pulls out a stool and perches while he considers his response. 'Sir Malcolm. Let me think.' His eyes shift warily. 'No, not yesterday.'

'Had a drink, did he? Autumn ale? Watered it down with the everyday, didn't you?'

'Is that what he's been saying?' Melbury bristles in self-defence. 'He had Old Leo's best, the four-year old! I served it myself, so he's no cause for ill satisfaction!'

'So he was here?'

'Devil take it!' Melbury sighs over the trap he has so easily fallen into. 'All right, he was here. No harm in that.'

'And took two of the house whores upstairs.'

'Master Egerton!' Melbury's face is a study in indignation. 'We no longer run a house here, as you well know. No man says we do!'

'No man says so, because those who aren't customers can't claim it, and those who are, never will!'

'There's naught of that goes on here, master.'

'I had an offer as I came in.'

'A maidservant's jest. I keep a clean ale-house as you know.'

'No you don't, Melbury. At this moment, I can smell cheap gillyflower water and it's coming from right across this table. Would you like me to line up all your bawds to smell which wears cheap gillyflower water?'

Melbury puts out calming hands. 'No, no, don't be doing that, sir.' His face clearly sketches his conflict of emotions. 'I was only taking the new maidservant to task. These girls, you know—'

'I don't know, and I don't want to. When did Wipley arrive?'

Melbury considers. 'A good while after midday, a bit before most of the crowd. Is this about that girl that was murdered on the Long Down?'

'What did he do?'

Melbury shrugs as if the answer is obvious. 'Had a drink, as I said. Look, Master Egerton.' He rises. 'I'm sorry to be rushing off but I've malt to turn. Don't want it scorching, do we?'

Egerton leans back against the plaster and looks up at the innkeeper. 'Except that any barley on the malting floor needs no turning because that chimney's got no fire in it. So sit down, Melbury, and tell me what I need to know.'

The landlord's shoulders sag and he perches on the edge of his seat, uneasily glancing round at the room now starting to fill up. ''Tis not good for me to be seen talking overlong with a Justice.'

'Then answer my questions and we'll keep it as short as may be,' Egerton replies. 'Wipley had a drink. Then what?'

'He left, of course.'

'Stop lying to me, Melbury.'

'I'm not!'

'He was seen going upstairs.'

'Oh Gawd!' Melbury leans forward, frantically whispering, 'Sir, if it got back to Justice Townsend that I had ratted on his friend Wipley, he'd take away my licence. Tis my livelihood!'

Egerton folds his arms and ponders aloud. 'Perhaps I should ask Mistress Melbury if she wears gillyflower water with too little of cloves in it.'

The landlord squirms. 'Sir Malcolm said not to blab.'

'Who would you rather face? Townsend or your wife?'

'Oh, my Lord.' Melbury mops his now genuinely sweating forehead. 'It was like this, he was having his drink and he called me over. Snaps his fingers and points to where I'm to stand in that way he has that makes your teeth stand on end. So I goes over and he says, like, *Who's in*. And I says there's only Red Peg or little Amy.'

'Red Peg I know, she regularly graces my courtroom. I assume little Amy is the new, er … maidservant?'

'That's right. Well, when I told the girls it was him, Red Peg weren't best pleased. But when I said he wanted both of them together, I had to threaten to turn them off to make them go with him.'

'When did Wipley go upstairs?'

The landlord scoffs. 'Oh, he went straight up as soon as I'd fetched the ladies.'

'So, say, half past midday or a bit after?'

'Nearer one.'

'And how long was he up there?'

'Well how do I know? I don't up-end the hour-glass.'

'Weren't you here?'

'I was busy!'

'Downstairs or up?'

Melbury's mouth stretches in a mirthless smile. 'Such a jesting man you are, Master Egerton.'

'Did you see Master Jerrard come in?'

'Master Jerrard? No. But he was here.' Melbury points. 'Sat over there in the corner. Making notes on a little tablet. Had some Leo's Best too. *And* showed his appreciation,' Melbury finishes, rubbing thumb and finger together, 'which is more'n some.'

'How long was he here?'

'Well, I saw him well into the afternoon—' Melbury stops and looks hard at Egerton. 'Oh, no.' He waves a fat finger to and fro. 'He was down here all the time, he didn't go upstairs.'

'But you weren't around all the time, you said. How would you know?'

'I'd know. Tapster keeps an eye. Anyway, very happy with his little wife, is Master Jerrard.'

'Unlike some,' Egerton says.

'Yes, well.' Melbury winces at a burst of pot-banging from the kitchen. 'I saw Mistress Jerrard at church on Sunday. That hair burstin' out under her cap. Those violet eyes. He would be happy, wouldn't he?'

'You escorted Wipley upstairs?'

Melbury shakes his head. 'I told the ladies to wait on the stairs. Then I went to his table to tell him they were ready.'

'He went straight up?'

'I'll say. Tried to look all unhurried but he couldn't get to the stairs fast enough.'

'Which stairs?' Egerton asks.

'Those.' The landlord points at the passage from the stable court.

'You're lying. You sent him up the private stairs from the kitchen because he was taking two bawds instead of one and didn't want to be seen.'

'On my life, no! The wife would've spit-roasted me for supper, seeing that!'

'You're not telling me Mistress Melbury is ignorant of the goings-on here.'

'Course not. What I'm saying is, my wife thinks of profit. She knows a man will come down for food after, or he'll want a smoke and a drink, see? But two women – they sap a man's humours, make him good for nothing but sleep. So it takes up chamber space. Him, he told the women to stay in case he needed them again. Getting his money's worth.' Melbury puts the flat of his hands on the table and makes to rise. 'Anyway, Master Egerton, if that's all …?'

'I suppose you are telling the truth, Melbury?'

Melbury gives a ghastly smile. 'Always happy to help the law.'

'Well, thanks to you, Sir Malcolm is now safe from any unfortunate misapprehension of a legal nature.'

'Eh?' The landlord looks blank. 'Dunno what that means. Suppose you're looking after your own. You lot always do.'

'You have helped prove that he was nowhere near the poor girl on the Long Down.'

Melbury's lip curls. 'Bastard. If I'd thought, I'd have sworn on my life he was never here. So if that's all you came for—'

'No. There is another matter altogether, Melbury.'

'Now what? I've got work to do, you know.'

'Not until I'm finished with you. Sit down.'

The landlord sighs.

'The cock pit.'

Melbury rolls his eyes. 'It's not illegal.'

'I didn't say it was. But knifing is, so what's this Constable Hart tells me about a fight yesterday?'

'Oh, that.'

'What am I to think of a landlord who cannot control his own cock pit crowd?'

'Didn't see a thing,' Melbury declares. 'I only heard about it when they poured in here and tapster came for me to open up the buttery for a new barrel.'

'Where were you, then?'

'In the malthouse. Yes I was!' He glares as Egerton's eyebrows rise. 'And the fire was going, ask anyone who was here.'

'This fellow who pulled a blade?'

'Harmless brawling.' On safer ground, Melbury dismisses the matter with a wave of the hand. 'Some young blood trying his strength. Accused Nol Simpson of cheating him or some such.'

'Wouldn't be the first time,' Egerton says. 'Simpson's been up before me more times than I care to remember on charges of that sort. So this time he's victim with a slash across his face, eh? This young blood, then. How about giving me a name, Melbury?'

The landlord spreads his hands. 'Would that I could, Master Egerton.'

'Pity,' Egerton says, rising. 'I'll just pay my respects to your wife on my way out, then.'

'All right! All right!' the landlord says. 'Joe from High Stoke.'

30

She has just poured the first warm milk from her pails into settling bowls ranged along the dairy shelf. There the separation will take place overnight, the cream rising to the top ready to be skimmed off for … which cheese is she to make tomorrow? Think, Grace! Morning Milk cheese, was it? It's hard to concentrate. Where is Allan? How did he escape? When will she see him again? Not that she wants to see him at all. She pours fair water into each pail, swills it around and sloshes it into the drainage channel. She doesn't even want to think about him.

But an imp of mischief has settled in her head like a court fool nudging with inconvenient truths. *So this is you not thinking of him, is it?*

She is done with him.

Hmm.

He looked so miserable when he told her of his betrothal.

Remind me, what was it you said? the imp asks. *Plenty of leg and low-cut bodice. Ooh, I detect the sulphurous whiff of jealousy.*

She should at least have hidden her feelings, made a heroic effort and wished him and Sylvia well, instead of losing her temper and giving herself away.

And what else did you do? Ah yes, slammed the door in his face.

Of course he had to marry Sylvia. It is no secret to Grace that Sylvia was with child. The two girls shared that end of the attic. Grace was always up before Sylvia woke, and in the warmth of the roof space, Sylvia frequently pushed away the bedclothes in her sleep. At first Grace thought Sylvia was eating more than her share and growing stout. It was the betrothal that revealed to Grace the necessity for Sylvia to find a husband or face dismissal and ruin. And it was overhearing Allan's admission to Master Egerton, *I lay with Sylvia,* that finally brought the pieces of the picture together. Allan and Sylvia loved each other all the time and she was carrying his child.

For the twentieth time, Grace's former hopes wither and she sighs for the loss of her open-hearted trust, chides herself into unwilling acceptance of his pretended affection. The imp whispers, chuckling, of her foolish heart, her girlish vanity. *You really think he found you desirable? You? Compared with Sylvia? He was amusing himself,* the imp insists. *You know it.*

But he was so forlorn there behind the bars of the wash-house. His eyes, those beautiful soft brown eyes so sad. She desperately wished she could unlock the door and set him free, no matter if she never saw him again. Then he spoke of Sylvia meaning nothing to him and all her anger burst out that he could so easily discard a pure woman whose virtue he had taken. Stealing food for him changed to a shabby act, the joy of bringing it to him crumbled to dust, and she turned her back on him.

Admit it, you thought to reconcile. The imp snorts. *You thought he would say the right words and things would go back to the way they were. Back to your silly dreams of lying in sunny glades. Well, it wasn't you he wanted in a sunny glade, was it? And now he's gone. Somebody let him out, somebody with more wit than you.*

A tear forms and slips down her cheek and her heart aches in her chest. If only he would just walk into the dairy, like the other day. She would control her feelings, listen to him, make peace with him. If only …

Outside on the cobbles of the dairy court, the slap of feet.

Who … ?

ALICE looks across at Sam seated in front of Henry on the grey. Riding back from Freemans, it is an open run over grassland and Henry is drawing Sam's attention to a kestrel hovering above the sloping fields away towards the river. With arms folded tight across his chest, Sam looks the other way. He was overjoyed when she and Henry arrived at head man Robert's house on the Egertons' demesne, until he realised it meant taking leave of his new friends. Despite pledges on both sides to meet again, Sam is out of humour, knowing that returning home in the evening means bed follows very soon. With his head so full of his new friends, Alice knows she will be hard pressed to lull him to sleep. But whatever his humour now, it is good, she thinks, that Sam has so easily slipped into friendship with Robert's children. She hopes the uneasiness with Jack Egerton will not put a block in the way of that. If she can simply come and go freely to Robert and his wife, the Egertons need not know, though it is with a twinge of regret that she considers the loss of that budding friendship with Olivia Egerton. Now both Alice and Henry are under suspicion for Allan's unexplained escape. And still there is no clue as to who killed Sylvia or why.

'Look who's coming,' Henry calls across, rousing Alice from her musing. And there to her dismay not a hundred paces off, Jack Egerton on his bay approaching at a walking pace. 'He must have called at High Stoke,' Henry says, 'or he'd be going home on the road.'

There is no avoiding him. They draw even and pull to a halt. Sam squirms in Henry's hold and Henry lowers him to the ground. 'Don't go far.' Sam wanders a little way and crouches in the long grass, his attention taken by some insect.

'I was just talking to Joe,' Jack says. 'I think we may be a little further through the maze.'

'What does Joe know?' Alice asks.

'He went into town yesterday just as he said. He did speak to someone but I understand now why he denied it.'

'Who? Why?'

'He went to remonstrate with a man named Nol Simpson for cheating him out of the price of several drinks in return for a "foolproof" method of winning Sylvia. He knew Simpson would be at the cock pit so Joe watched several fights while he worked up the courage to have it out with him.'

'Poor Joe.' Alice's sympathies are roused by this uncouth young man cozened by a swindler and rejected by a beautiful woman. 'It must be hard for him to admit he made a poor choice.'

'And has been made a laughing stock. Simpson brushed him off and fists started flying. Simpson drew a knife but Joe got it off him and cut him across the cheek. The cock pit crowd pulled Simpson into the taproom and Joe thought he'd better make himself scarce.'

Henry says. 'What was Simpson's foolproof method?'

'To write a letter that would melt Sylvia's heart and cause her to fall into Joe's arms. Apparently Sylvia mistook some of the words and the effect was that the letter read as familiar and insulting.'

Henry looks at Alice. 'So Sylvia was never betrothed to him, despite what he claimed.'

'On the contrary,' Jack says, 'she did agree to marry him, but it was to be kept a secret.'

'Because she was with child,' Henry says.

'Joe didn't know that.'

Henry frowns. 'Then why keep it a secret?'

'Because she saw her chance,' Alice says, her mind's eye clearing. 'Her chance of winning Allan instead.'

'Exactly,' Jack says.

Henry looks from one to the other. 'How does that work?'

'She uses the letter to convince Allan that it is a letter Grace received,' Alice explains. 'She points out the crude wording, implying that it came from a lover and that Grace deceived us all and was playing with Allan's affections. And Allan in his anger and disappointment with Grace betrothes himself to Sylvia.' She turns to Jack. 'When he told us he was lost, he spoke truth indeed.'

'Joe heard bits of the conversation between them,' Jack explains, 'and my notion is that being so wishful that Sylvia was in love with himself, he remained blind to what was really happening and convinced himself that Allan took advantage of Sylvia.'

Henry says. 'Allan was taken in by a clever woman.'

'Allan was fickle and unreliable throughout!' Alice fires up. 'Grace has had her character blackened, her love thrown in her face and her trust in Allan shaken to its roots, but has she said a word against either him or Sylvia? Wherever Allan is at this moment, I hope he is thinking on these things!'

There is a little silence, broken at last by Jack. 'I think you have the right of it, Alice. And something else you have the right of. Sir Malcolm Wipley did indeed engage two whores at the Red Lion.'

'Oh!' Alice feels the sudden heat wash into her face and wishes she had never made her ill-thought revelation. 'If his pleasures follow that bent, he is quite at liberty—'

'And given that Henry saw Sir Malcolm going upstairs,' Jack continues, 'which the innkeeper confirms was around one o'clock, and since Allan found Sylvia on the track shortly before one o'clock, that puts not only Sir Malcolm but also Henry in the clear.'

Alice's mouth drops open. She looks at Henry, who appears equally stunned, then back at Jack. 'But how could you think Henry would—?'

Henry lays his hand on her arm. He turns to Jack. 'I still say Allan is innocent and will be proven so.'

'I'm keeping an open mind. When Will Harvey delivered the crag he says George Renwick coloured at mention of Sylvia.'

'Yes, he did. Mention of Sylvia always made him blush. But that means nothing. You know how it is with George, Jack. Gets tongue-tied where beautiful women are concerned. He's the same with Olivia, isn't he?'

'That's true,' Jack concedes. 'Well, I'll leave you to get on home.' He addresses himself to Sam, now returning. 'Master Sam,

Robert says the children were delighted when you came back with him yesterday.'

'Master Robert told us a story when we went to bed,' Sam says. 'It was a good one.'

'He's a rare storyteller, is Robert,' Jack agrees, and Alice slides down from Cassie to go to Sam.

'He was going to tell us one tonight as well, but you wouldn't let me stay,' Sam accuses her.

'Oh, Sam, I'm sorry, sweeting, but I'm sure I can think of another one to tell you tonight.'

'And Sylvia was going to tell me a story in the wash-house,' Sam complains, 'but then she didn't.'

'The wash-house?'

'It's not fair,' he says. 'I found a paper with writing and she took it away. She promised to tell me a story for it, but she didn't.'

'When was this, Sam?'

'After you went to see Mistress Egerton.'

Over Sam's head the three exchange looks. Yesterday. The day Sylvia died. The last hour of Sylvia's life. Slowly, Alice kneels down by Sam. She reaches to smooth away the hair falling in his eyes. Very carefully, she asks, 'Tell me what you did after I left with Master Robert. You were with Mollie in the winter parlour. Then what?'

'We played some more. Then I was hungry and we went to get something to eat, but Isabel said Mollie had to go and help her.'

For a second or two, anger flares, disrupting Alice's thoughts. None of this entered Isabel's self-righteous account of Sam causing havoc in the wash-house. She steadies her breath. 'So what happened then, Sam?'

'I went in the wash-house and I played with the clothes.'

'Betsy wasn't there?'

'No, I saw Betsy through the window, she was talking to Grace by the dairy.'

'Did Betsy have a basket?'

Sam nods. 'Just a little one, and Grace had one too. It had a big black bottle sticking out.' Sam funnels his hands like the neck of a leather flask.

'So Betsy and Grace were about to leave for the fields taking midday meal to Joe and Angus,' she says, to verify the time for the other two. 'Tell me about the clothes you played with, Sam.' And for Jack's benefit, she adds, 'The old clothes that came from Tillotsons.'

'There was a round hat thing.'

'A bonnet? With a little brim about this wide?' She indicates the length of her little finger.

'Yes,' he says. Alice noticed it too, a soft wool cap on one of the heaps. A young man's size but too big for Sam, and moth-eaten, good for nothing but playing with. Sam goes on, 'And a big coat with fur all down.'

'The scholar's gown?' Possibly Jeremy's father's, she saw that also. Too good to cut up or give away. Jeremy must be given it back. 'Dark red, like plums?'

'Yes, and it had pockets, and I looked in the pockets and I found the paper.'

'How many sheets of paper, Sam?'

'Only one. Sylvia took it.'

'Ah yes, Sylvia was in the wash-house helping Betsy sort the clothes. What did she do with it?'

'Nothing. She was sitting on a sink, and I asked her about the story and she just said, "Later, later."'

'Poor Sam.' Alice puts her arms round Sam and draws him to her, gathering legend and parable to form a fresh narrative in her head even as she kisses him. 'Never mind, sweeting. I have a story for you. You wait till you hear the tale of the badger who lost his stripes!' Sam hugs her in anticipation, and Alice glances up at the other two. In that short exchange, much has become clear.

Sylvia loitered in the wash-house when Betsy and Grace took midday meal to the men in the fields. Sylvia would have known to remain concealed in case Isabel saw her and gave her work to do. Sam wandered in and started playing with the clothes. Seeing him discover a note in a gown, Sylvia became curious to read it, and the contents so buoyed her up with notions of great wealth that even in her condition, the distance and the climb up the hill to Tillotsons did not deter her. The appearance of Isabel in search of Sam was Sylvia's opportunity. Intending unauthorised flight, she stayed hidden. As soon she could, she set out, the paper in her pocket. The carter's arrival was an unlooked-for bonus. Predictably, she tried to sway him to take her up the hill. But then who else did she meet and tell about the paper, after she left the carter and before Allan found her? Someone who wanted it so badly that they killed her to get it. And here, through the scholar's gown, is yet another piece in the puzzle, with the link not to Allan but to Tillotsons.

Henry is frowning, gazing at Jack, who is staring down, musing, lower lip jutting. After a few seconds Jack rouses, turning the bay for home. 'I should be on my way. Give you good evening, Master Sam. I hope we'll see you again before long.' Jack nods to them and turns the bay's head for Freemans. When he is out of hearing, 'What's he up to? Why isn't he going to Tillotsons?' Alice asks. 'Surely that is where he will find the answer.'

Still frowning, Henry stares after Jack. 'I've no idea.'

31

They are nearing the ruined lodge, scene of Alice and Sam's adventure just days ago. The door that Jack Egerton was jamming with rotted timber after getting Sam and Alice out is now blocked with boards nailed firmly in place against ill-advised entry. The downstairs windows are boarded likewise. The rotted window upstairs, one of its two mullions gone, gazes out lop-sided at the countryside.

They have just paused to look when Betsy bursts from the trees crowning the rise ahead. She rocks precariously from side to side as she runs full tilt down the slope. 'Master Jerrard! Mistress!' she pants.

Henry spurs the grey forward. 'What is it Betsy, what's the matter?' But Betsy's run is already carrying her past him, her arms windmilling in the effort not to tumble headlong. She cannons into Cassie, who shies and backs as Betsy grasps at the saddle and comes to rest, breathing hard. 'You have to … I don't know what … Isabel won't …' she gasps. Exertion has forced the blood into her face and neck, and under her headcloth, damp strands of grey hair stick to her forehead.

Alice jumps down, putting out an arm to steady her. 'Come and sit, Betsy. You're in no condition to talk yet.' Betsy leans heavily against her as they cross the once-cultivated patch in front of the ruined lodge. The boarded-up door provides support as Betsy sinks down on the doorstone. Alice sits beside her and waits while the laundress, fanning herself with her apron, gradually steadies her breath. A dozen paces away, Henry gently thwarts Sam's efforts to dismount and run to the women.

Eventually Betsy draws the heel of her hand across her forehead, wipes it on her skirt. In a low voice, she says, 'I came as fast as I could. Isabel didn't want me to, said it's not necessary.'

'What isn't necessary?' Alice asks her. *More trouble with Isabel?*

'She wouldn't send Joe or even Angus, and Maureen was crowing and saying she was right all the time and the milk would be sour—'

'Betsy, please! What's happened?'

'Grace. It's Grace. She's disappeared.'

'Grace?' Alice cries. 'Disappeared? What—?'

Betsy clamps her hand on Alice's mouth. 'Shhh! The little one'll hear!' She takes her hand away. 'Somebody's taken Grace.'

No! Almost Alice can hear a voice crying out. Behind her, the house creaks in its infirmity and the thought flits through her head that soon it will all come crashing down. She demands, 'Who's taken her? When?'

'I don't know, dear. I went to see her like I do every day. I'd told her I would as soon as I got back from Mistress Sanderson and she said she'd be milking and I was to be sure to go and find her. But she wasn't milking, although the cows were gathered by the gate, and they're not milked.'

'Did you look in the dairy?'

'Not in the dairy.' Betsy shakes her head. 'Just some milk in a couple of settling bowls and her pails on the shelf, like she'd started and then broken off.'

'In her chamber? Is she sick? The necessary-house?'

At each question Betsy shakes her head. 'No, no, nowhere. I called and searched through the whole house.'

'The outbuildings? Granary? Who was the last to see her?'

'Joe said he saw her go into the field to do the milking. Then nobody's seen her since.'

JACK Egerton rounds the house to the sunlit terrace overlooking the garden at Freemans. 'I guessed you'd be here,' he says. He sits down on the low wall next to Olivia. His wife regards him closely, rests a hand on his leg. 'Not a good day?'

That contact. He is always glad of the times he comes home and Olivia is there to talk to. Today he has need to unburden himself and she will always listen while he works out his concerns, his uncertainties. 'There's something they're hiding,' he tells her. 'I only saw Alice this morning and she was evasive; as though she thinks I'm siding with Wipley because I detained Allan. Henry was in town. I saw him later but he wasn't giving anything away, either.'

'About what?'

'Allan's escaped, how did that happen? They're not saying. I don't know whether to be angry or glad.' He gives a wry laugh, laying his hand over hers. 'Wipley's making the most of it, of course.'

'You didn't believe Allan guilty when you came home last night.'

'Nor do I today. The lad's not capable of it.' He stares into the dazzle of the sinking sun. 'But until I can place someone else on the Long Down at that time, he has to remain a suspect. I checked Wipley's alibi – he's so insistent to accuse Allan, he makes himself suspect. Turns out he was at the Red Lion, not riding on Guildown as he claimed. But he only lied because he was whoring and didn't want to admit it. I'm afraid he's accounted for, not only by Melbury but by Henry himself who saw him when he went in there yesterday.'

'So you're no further forward?'

'No further forward. And you remember that old issue? I've just discovered it's probably about to be resurrected. I'm thinking now we should have told Alice when she was here with Sam. She might have been more open with me this morning if I had.'

'But why is it raising its head now, after all this time? I thought we agreed it was over after Frederick Tillotson died.'

'We did, but Sylvia found something in a pocket of his gown and I think it's that paper.'

'Are you saying she was murdered for it?'

'Could well be. She had it yesterday and Will Harvey the carter tells me she was boasting about it to him, so that's at least one person she told. It wasn't on her body, and we found her empty pocket on the Long Down.'

'If Wipley's men were not riding with him on Guildown, where were they?' Olivia asks. 'What if Sylvia came across one of them up there? She would know them, being neighbours when she worked at Tillotsons.'

'Good point,' he says. 'If one of them silenced her and that paper has got into Wipley's hands, there's bad trouble coming for High Stoke. I must check the alibis of all his men.'

Olivia leans, concern on her face. 'More importantly, Henry and Alice need to know, Jack. As soon as possible.'

'There's nothing Wipley can do tonight, but yes, you're right. I'll ride over first thing in the morning.'

BORED and fidgety, Allan waits in his hiding place, itching to be doing something, he doesn't know what, and he wonders for the tenth time why he agreed to be released from the wash-house, why he promised to remain hidden and wait here in the ruined lodge with a flask of ale and a hunk of cheese, why he ever believed that his innocence will be quickly proven and he can return to High Stoke exonerated.

But he did so agree, and while he struggles to control his impatience, he becomes aware of horses approaching his lair along the track from Freemans, heading for High Stoke. From his hiding place at the rotted upstairs window he lifts a cautious eye and espies the master and mistress bringing Sam home. And then, from up the slope, Betsy erupts towards them, her panic-fuelled words a jumble of desperation, and the mistress sliding down to steady the laundress.

And the word 'Grace'.

He strains to overhear Betsy's breathless story of Grace gone missing, told in little more than a whisper so that young Sam will not hear, and knows at last he has the excuse he needs. Excuse? Compulsion. His promise to stay put no longer counts. He is going to leave here as soon as they are out of sight. There is no decision as such; Grace needs him and he is going to find her.

Once the little party has disappeared over the rise towards High Stoke, Allan checks all around from his viewpoint at the window. The ladder he climbed last night to get into the boarded-up lodge is no longer to hand, of course. Angus carried it back and will have propped it carefully in the woodshed once more. Last night Allan stood on a rung of the ladder and broke off one of the rotted wood mullions to get into this hiding place, but getting out is a different matter. He peers down. Below, the overgrown grassy area beyond the doorstone. Between himself and the ground no great fall; the ceilings of the lodge are low. He works his way backwards out of the window and lets himself down to hang onto the rotting sill by his arms, his hands. He kicks himself away and lands in the soft growth. Then he is up and running, an easy long-limbed lope towards High Stoke, making sure to keep out of sight of the party of four in front. Within minutes, he is ducking into the belt of trees circling the front of the house, working round towards the road. As the trees give way to the road, lush spring growth gives him sufficient cover to crawl forward and check both ways. Satisfied that he cannot be seen, he settles down to wait. Full well he knows there might be sheriff's men on the lookout hiding amongst the trees. Already dusk is advancing, but he stays put, mastering the urge to move, while he scans constantly amongst the spring growth for the slightest leaf tremble in the still air. If he is caught now he is no help to Grace; it is vital he remains at large.

The sun once set draws the light away with it. One or two stars wink in the darkening sky. When it is dim enough but he can still see, he carefully crawls forward through the trees two hundred paces to the next bend in the road, stopping every few seconds to check his surroundings and scan the undergrowth across the road. Painstakingly he crawls back, and repeats the exercise the other way, all the while checking around. Nothing. No sound, no movement. He takes his decision, chooses the best location where there is good cover on the other side and makes a dash across the road, diving into the vegetation, ready for a warning shout, running boots. Not a sound. He is past the worst danger. From here it is an easy progress to make his way to the track that leads up to the Long Down. If Grace has been lured away, he reasons, it might well be to the same place near the White Lane where he found Sylvia. He has nothing else to go on, and it is a starting point, at least. If she isn't there, he will search in ever widening circles until he finds her.

32

A breeze has got up. It soughs amongst the trees that crowd around the walls, sending a murmuring moan through the dark places of the house. Draughts spurt under doors and shadows dance on the wall to her fluttering candle. Since dusk the air has turned sharply chill. It is a false spring, a trap for the unwary, and above the neckline of her chemise, icy fingers stroke her skin. She tiptoes for the second time this night into the little end chamber, steps past Mollie wakeful in her truckle bed and holds the candle over Sam's sleeping form. The coverlet has slipped away and she draws it up over his shoulders, bending to kiss his baby cheek flushed in sleep. It brings to mind all those other occasions last winter when she did the same in Hillbury, when her presence brought calm and comfort to Sam in his disturbed nights. At that time, it was having Sam safe under her roof that gave her an anchorage in her own chaotic world.

But that period taught her how easily life changes, and though her world is no longer chaotic, it is far from simple. For the twentieth time this night she knows the guilt that lurks between the desire to care for Sam and the urge to be with Henry out there somewhere, searching for a lost girl.

All of them wanted to help. Betsy insisted on joining Angus to search the dene that skirts Master Renwick's land. Ned took a lantern and set off alone. Maureen tagged along with Joe, heading out towards Merrow, though from the gleam in her eye Alice suspects that the cook is driven more by the thrill of witchery in the woods than by any charitable desire to find Grace.

Even Isabel offered, once Henry was home and organising the search. Alice, preparing Sam's supper at the kitchen table, watched Isabel's approach to Henry, the smiling entreaty, and Henry's equally smiling but firm refusal. When Isabel persisted, Henry gently took her arm and led her into the still room where a brief, low-voiced conversation took place. When they emerged a few minutes later, Isabel's head was bowed in apparent compliance. But as Henry turned from the steward to take Alice in a brief parting embrace, Isabel's glittering black eyes met hers. It was momentary only, gone as soon as seen. By the time Henry reached to pick up his lantern, Isabel was already straightening a mug on a shelf as she passed on her way out of the kitchen. Alice has seen no more of Isabel since then.

Mollie clearly wished to join the search, but seemed not surprised at being denied. 'I need you here, Mollie,' Alice said to her. Mollie's foot was well enough healed to support her and the kine must be milked, no matter what. Between them they completed the task begun by Grace. Once the milk was in settling bowls, Alice showed Mollie how the cheeses were turned, their cloths changed and their rinds wiped. A quick and interested learner is Mollie, and Alice intends to nurture this particular seedling.

But Mollie's presence is necessary tonight not only for the dairy work. With Isabel remaining in the house, Alice wants that truckle bed in Sam's room occupied, both to give Mollie a second night's rest free of bullying, and just as importantly, that she might be a sleeping companion for Sam. Isabel's initial refusal to start the search for Grace, her earlier outburst in the accounts room, and that malevolent look, argue a state of humours in grave imbalance. A sense of shadowy disquiet nudges Alice every time she pictures that spitting storm of bile.

From the truckle bed, Mollie's eyes meet hers, as though Alice's thought has spirited through the air.

'If Sam wakes and is frightened,' Alice whispers, 'he will be glad to know you are close.'

Mollie and Sam, she thinks, it is strange how these two have come together. There is a language between them that they share with no adult. She pulls the door to as she leaves the chamber, and with no idea of how long the search will take, she goes to her chamber and unlaces. A warm loose-gown over her shift will be more comfortable while she waits for news. Within a few minutes she is making her way down the little spiral back stairs and into the kitchen, anxious for an idea of Isabel's whereabouts. She checks the accounts room, which is locked, no light showing under the door. There is no candle in the kitchen, pot room, buttery or still room. She walks along to the servants' parlour, goes the other way to the dairy, to the end room, all dark. After Henry's departure, the steward must have gone to bed.

In the winter parlour, the fire has died down to the point where it sheds less light than her candle and Alice shivers. Since she could be facing a long wait, and any returners will need warmth, the fire must needs be healthy when they come. From a basket by the hearth she draws sprays of rosemary gleaned from the herb garden after Allan finished his pruning and clearing. Once touched to the embers, the oil in the cuttings quickly feeds the faint glow into licking flames. Carefully she feeds more pieces, then small logs. The flames leaping high briefly roar up the chimney, heating and scenting the air and sending flickering shadows dancing across wall and bookshelf. In front of the hearth lies a cushion she took earlier from the window seat. She plumps it and sits down, curling her legs underneath her. A few stout pieces of wood stacked by the hearth soon add heart to the fire, and she sits back to wait. Just like any lady-in-waiting in an ante-room, she thinks ruefully. And that's what I am, waiting for events to happen around me. Another twinge of conscience nips as she tries to suppress the thought that if she had known, she would have left Sam with Robert and his wife. She sighs and prepares to keep vigil for as long as it takes.

Outside the breeze is a vague bluster, its vigour tempered on this side of the house by the high wall of the herb garden. After a while, tiring of constantly shifting position to stay awake, Alice pulls up a backstool, crooks her arm on it, pillows her head and dozes. Every now and then the fire falls in on itself, jerking her awake. Each time her candle has burned a little lower and her arm has gone numb. Each time, she pokes away the ash, feeds sticks and logs and changes position. The evening wears on. The breeze backs and fills, setting the casement rattling. No one returns to the house. Fed by the darkness, the emptiness, her mind conjures fantastical creatures. Despite herself, she imagines Grace falling prey to some menace of the night. Each time she wakes the wind is higher, now buffeting the windows, and later there is rain. But each time even the loose panes rattling in their leads cannot long keep her eyes open.

ON all fours, breathing hard but hampered by the stitch in his side, Allan fights to subdue his shallow gasps. In his frantic dash, sweat has erupted, his hair is stuck to forehead and temples and he blinks away the salt sting running into his eyes. He can feel the trickling down his back, the hammering against his heaving ribs. He cocks a wary ear for the sheriff's men he so nearly ran into.

He simply must stop for a rest. Despite his bodily distress he is acutely conscious of the dark shape he presents against the chalk track and pulls himself on hands and knees to burrow a hiding place in the low tangle of growth close by. There he pauses, ears at stretch for the sounds of pursuit. Seconds turn into minutes and the stabbing pain at every breath starts to subside. Nothing moves. At last he lets himself sink down onto his back and lies there gazing up. On this side of the pale track stand the shadowy trees, their swelling buds starting to fatten on the winter skeletons of branch and twig, black against a lesser black. No moon, and the stars long since clouded over. On his upturned face he feels the first spits of rain.

A lucky escape that, and no credit to his caution. There he was, assuming they would watch the road when all the time they were waiting for him, several mounted men beside the track, as he loped all unknowing towards them. It was only the clack of hoof striking flint that warned him to leap into the undergrowth and dash headlong, swiping bushes aside, tripping and recovering on the tussocky ground, all the while plotting a wide detour through the scrub. Not wide enough, for they detected him. With a triumphant shout of 'After him!', stealth was abandoned and they surged through the trees in pursuit.

But the darkness was Allan's friend; their racket was their undoing. They could no longer hear the swish of his flight through the underbrush, the stamp of his fleeing feet. By the time another voice, now distant, commanded silence, Allan was far enough away to risk a dash across a clearing, leaping into dense bushes on the far side, crawling head down through last year's unkempt twigginess. The vegetation hampering his progress was a blessing of sorts, it was too dense to take a horse through at anything more than a pushing walk.

After a while the growth thinned and he stood up, listening. He had made a good distance on them and there was no possibility they could sight him, but he sensed he was not safe yet. He fetched a wide circle back to the track, where he raced uphill faster than he had ever run in his life. He ran and he ran until his legs turned to jelly, his run became a stagger and he fell to his knees.

Now here he is, night fallen, the rain coming in earnest. Sprouting branches wave overhead and are no protection. He stands up and moves cautiously into the cover of a trunk. The burgeoning undergrowth has already soaked his hose and shoes, he has no hat, and the rain is sliding down his face. It mixes with the sweat of his desperate dash and he tastes it salt on his lip. A chilly breeze has sprung up. At this moment he is glad of it. As his breath steadies, he revels in its soothing coolness. The shower is all around him, but the woodland is innocent of the sounds of pursuit. They must have taken another direction, and thankfully they have no dogs to scent him.

He is on the Long Down at the crossroads where the track from the road meets the white lane that leads towards town. On the town side, sheep graze the grass short, keeping it devoid of cover. With the sight he has built up in the dark, he can make out their humps here and there, occasionally moving a few steps. He stands close to the trunk, ears pricked like a wild animal, for several minutes. Silence. Nobody. Rabbits scatter as he crosses the track and nearby sheep retreat. He moves down the short-cropped slope on this side, keeping to the edge of the trees to avoid betraying his movement against the clearing. Stepping cautiously in the rain and the dark, he has gone a few hundred paces when he sees ahead another sheep, this one lying down. It does not move as he approaches. Not a sheep? Curious, he stoops to feel and his hand falls on linen skirts, he makes out a leg, a flung arm, pale and plump, in a plain, pushed-up sleeve, long wet tendrils of hair, the back of her head.

'Grace!' He would know her form anywhere. He falls to his knees, heart and mind absorbed with relief and joy, oblivious to the rain and wind and the night world around him, 'Dearest Grace, I've found you!'

Gently he turns and lifts her limp body into his arms. He hugs her close, laying his cheek to her cheek. 'I do so love you.'

She hangs there unresponsive, and with horror he realises she is cold, lifeless.

'Gotcha!' A rough hand grasps him by the scruff and hauls. Another punches him in the face, sending him backwards still holding onto Grace, and then they are all around him, kicking and punching and he is desperately wrapping himself round Grace, trying to protect her from the storm of boots and fists and then another punch jerks his head back and he knows no more.

33

Alice jolts awake to the sound of a downpour beating against the window. Before her, the fire sucks air, driving the flames up in a sudden roar. The draught of it chills her back and her candle blows out, its smoke streaming sideways. She glances round at the rattling windows. Nothing but flame-glistening raindrops sliding down the black panes. The firelight chops at the darkness, sending black and orange shadows skittering across the lime-washed walls. The books on their shelves flicker.

And deathly still in the doorway stands Isabel.

Alice jumps to her feet. The steward's eyes are two huge holes in the white oval of her face. Her black hair flows unconfined, straggling to her waist. Against the darkness of the hall, she appears spectre-like, clad as she is in a white shift fastened high at the neck, the plain, straight sleeves concealing her arms, her wrists, half her hands. From scant tucks at the throat the white lawn hangs straight to the floor. No part of her body disturbs the fall of fabric from shoulder to hem. She might be a wraith, her face and fingers all the flesh there is.

Her throat suddenly dry, Alice has an effort to swallow before she can speak. Despite herself, her voice rasps, wavering and weak. 'What do you want?' For want something Isabel must. This nocturnal creature carries no candle. Something has driven her to creep through the house along passages and across stone flags in the utter dark.

'What do you want?' Alice repeats, this time her voice comes firmer, stronger.

'You think you have secured him. It won't last.'

'What won't last? Secured who?'

'He was destined for me long before you caught him in

your coils.'

'What?' Alice laughs, such a contemptible claim deserves nothing more. 'So this is what it's all about.' She reaches fingers to her kinked curls. 'The only coils I caught him in are my hair.'

This time there is no wild gesturing from the steward, no shouting, only a stillness, a rigidity about her as she speaks in an ardent whisper. 'He brought me here to court me!'

'He brought you here to give you respectable employment!'

'Huh!' Isabel's lips stretch humourlessly. 'That was the story they gave out. It was me he desired.'

'He had ample time to form his intention.'

Isabel's eyes narrow. 'Then you slithered in and snared him.'

'Four years you've been here. Four years, Isabel! And I never even knew him until last year.'

'You drew him in, victim to your deceits.'

'Isabel! Think what you're saying! Does my husband look like a victim?'

'When you're gone, it will be me he returns to.'

'Understand this. I'm his wife and I'm not leaving.'

'Just a little country wife,' Isabel sneers, borrowing the coroner's dismissive phrase, 'and yet you have my cousin so entwined that he is forced to make you his right hand. Against his better judgment.'

So that exchange in the still room encompassed not only Henry's disappointment in Isabel's inaction, but also his decision that the steward would in future take her orders from Alice.

'I doubt he said it was against his better judgment, Isabel.'

'He told me how much he regrets this banishment.'

'Of course he regrets it, you are his cousin. He has known you many years. And withal, what do you mean by banishment?' Whatever Henry said, and he would have used only gentle courtesy towards his cousin, Isabel has convinced herself Henry does not believe in the rightness of what he said to her.

'He shuns me because you have come between us.'

'Oh, go to! He never said that!' A stab of unease that Henry did not give her a hint of that conversation with Isabel, and yet a certainty that driving out the steward is something he would never do. But not knowing exactly what he said, Alice is wrong-footed. Nothing for it but to admit her ignorance. 'I don't think he was intending to speak with you in that hurried way, Isabel. But I suppose your unwillingness to start a search for Grace forced the situation.'

'You see?' Isabel shrugs her arms. 'You "think", you "suppose". He cannot discuss these matters with you. If that is not proof—'

'What arrangement did he make for you, Isabel?'

'It is you who will be banished in the end.'

'God's teeth, woman! When will you understand I'm here to stay? Get used to it or get you gone! I warn you, Isabel, I – listen!'

'It matters not what he was obliged to pretend. I shall prevail—'

'Listen!'

Both women fall silent – through the darkness of the hall a fist hammers on the front door. Hammers again. 'They've found Grace!' Alice exclaims. 'Go and open the door! Go!' Alice turns to re-light her candle. She thrusts a small faggot into the fire and for a few seconds holds its flame to the wick. The candle flares and steadies. Voices shout and the hammering comes again as she hurries through the hall. But no scrape of the bar being lifted away, no soothing words from the steward. Isabel is not by the front door, nor is she in the screens passage. Alice holds her candle high but not the smallest suggestion of white glimmers. Isabel might never have been. Did I dream that, she wonders. Isabel was wraith-like but surely she was real?

More hammering and Alice hastens to remove the bar, struggles with bolts. She heaves open the heavy door to be met with the cold shock of a wet gust. Dimly she makes out a huddled group of men, one holding a lantern that casts grotesque shadows up their faces. The man in front she knows, that great cube of a head is unmistakable. Two others crowd either side of him, hair plastered, jerkins glistening wet, and a fourth man's face is just visible behind. The coroner, face rucked in irate folds, pushes past her, wide-brimmed hat dripping, cloak running wet.

'Where is your husband, madam?' he demands, striding into the hall, swinging round to confront her.

'He is from home, sir. He is searching for one of our maidservants who—'

'He may halt his search then, I have her.'

'You? How is this?' For a moment Alice is at a loss. 'Is she well? Where is she?'

He pulls off his hat and pushes back his soaked locks. His cloak drips. His lower legs have taken a drenching. So he has been out in this for some time. 'You have been searching as well, Sir Malcolm?' This is a neighbourliness she would not have expected, but how did he know?

He shakes his hat to and fro, the drops spattering a line across the floor. His wrath is heavily tinged with self-righteousness as he demands, 'If you and your husband had not interfered, the wench might be alive now.'

'Might be –?' God send Sir Malcolm does not mean it, is overstating for his own purposes.

'You!' he calls. 'Bring her. And you,' to another, 'shut the confounded door.'

Alice turns as the two men in the doorway step aside to give passage to the last, a large fellow, powerfully built. The lantern light makes skeletal shadows of his sunken cheeks, his deep-set eyes. His chest is heaving, breath rasping in his throat, but it is the figure he carries who draws all her attention, a limp, draggled figure, arm swinging, head lolling, honey-gold hair dark and dripping, chemise and skirt clinging.

Is this indeed real or am I summoning another fantasy? This is surely a dream, as the skirmish with Isabel was a dream.

Sir Malcolm's man passes her, she is sure she can hear the whistle of his breath. Grace's shoe brushes Alice's gown, leaving a mud smear. Alice gazes at it. Even that might not be real, except that when she touches it, her finger comes away soiled and gritty. Grace, who had so much to live for, such skills to use and enjoy, such a future, with or without Allan, such a close and loving family. It is inconceivable that Grace is gone. 'Not possible,' she whispers. 'This cannot be.'

'Same as the other,' the coroner adds, and although his words might have been expressly chosen to deny hope, Alice still wants to see for herself. 'Lay her there on the hall table,' she tells the man. He places the limp form gently enough on the table and stands back with a shivering indrawn breath that instantly brings forth a bubbling cough. She leans forward to lift Grace's head, only to feel her arm grasped. 'Don't touch her!' the coroner tells her.

'I only want to see the back of her head. You say it's the same injury as Sylvia's.'

'Dead like the other, not injured like the other,' the coroner corrects her. 'Look.' He pushes Grace's head to one side. There is no blood, no break.

'Her face. Look at her face,' the shivering man rasps. His shaking hand smoothes back the hair from Grace's forehead. There on the temple a massive bruise the shade of thunder clouds, dappled red where the skin is broken, a wide graze scoring her cheek.

'Who did this?' Alice asks the coroner.

'Your favourite,' he tells her. 'The one you released. Oh no, you didn't, did you? The one who "escaped" from Egerton's idea of a lock-up. We caught him red-handed carrying the body off to hide it.'

'Allan? Where is he?'

The man with the lantern guffaws. 'Oh, they've got him tethered. Detained at the sheriff's pleasure, he is. And feeling bloody terrible.'

'What have you done to him?'

'*Bloody* terrible,' the man repeats, and his fellow joins in the guffaw, stopping abruptly as the man who carried Grace cuffs him hard. 'Shut up, you dog,' he grates, 'you're in the presence of death.' He takes a step towards the other, which is enough. With chattering teeth he stands back, rubbing his arms in his soaked jerkin.

'All of you,' the coroner says to the three men, 'go and wait in the kitchen. That way. One of you bring me an ale.'

'You let them beat Allan?' Alice asks him.

'He's a murderer and a vagabond. You let him escape and now he's paying the price.'

Alice stares at him. She wants to believe in Allan, but this is shaking her resolve, even as she answers back, 'We'll see about that.' She leans to study Grace, to look for that tiny pulsing sign of life in the neck, reaches out a hand.

'Don't touch her, I said!' The coroner grasping her hand, pulling her away. 'Nobody touches this body until my jury have seen it.'

'What if she's still alive? Witless but alive? She will need care!' She tries to pull away but he holds fast.

'She's dead. Even your murdering servant agreed she's dead.' He hauls Alice none too gently into the winter parlour and snaps the door closed. 'You saw her face. Battered. Her clothes muddied where he kicked her. You stay in here. I don't want you interfering with another body.'

Alice gasps at his nerve. 'How dare you! Sylvia's condition when your jury saw her was identical to her condition when Allan brought her home!'

He glares but doesn't answer. Instead he turns, still holding onto her wrist as she twists and pulls to free herself. He seats himself on the backstool, tosses the cushion she was using onto the hearthstone and props his booted heels on it. 'Now you listen to me. If you so much as leave this parlour, I'll bring in a verdict of accessory to murder.'

'You can't; you say she's already dead.'

'I can if the body is tampered with.'

'I only wanted to see for myself if—'

'I am the coroner. If I say there has been meddling, there has been meddling, and there will be consequences. Your husband is responsible for you and he will feel the full force of the law for your actions.' He thrusts her away. 'Now sit down there.'

Alice has no idea if he has the powers he claims but it is the sort of law that she can believe exists. She sits. Guilt hounds her that she, the mistress of this household, has failed in her duty of care, affording the perpetrator of these atrocious acts the freedom to return to the attack. How is she going to face Grace's parents? This close-knit family to whom the elder daughter is so vital that her father summons her when his wife is ill. A daughter who worked at learning her mother's skills to the point where she could go out into the world and earn her own living. How is she going to tell them Grace is dead?

Sir Malcolm reaches to pick up the book she was reading. He holds it at arm's length, leaning his head back and squinting. '"Of the – something – of Learning",' he declaims. 'Very Jack-a-dull-boy. Print gets smaller and smaller these days. Francis who?'

'Bacon.' This could last for hours, depending on Wipley's humour.

'Bacon, eh?'

'Lord Chancellor to the late king, if you recall, sir.'

'I know. Is he still around? Thought he was sentenced years ago,' the coroner says.

'He was pardoned, Sir Malcolm.'

'I know that too. It was a jest.' She wonders if he habitually wins arguments by claiming that he knew all along. The book was her father's. She took it down during a spell when she could not sleep, waiting for the searchers to return. Woke later with it closed around her fingers. She wonders, *is that a commendation or a condemnation?*

The coroner riffles through the pages. 'So Jerrard truly reads this stuff, does he?' She senses the vanity of correcting his assumption that only a man would read such a book. He gets up and tosses it on the window seat. 'Now, I wouldn't have thought he knew his Bacon from his ham.' He laughs his short, hard laugh, his stomach pulsing in and out. 'Little country wife is not amused, I see.'

A scorching smell draws her attention; on the hearth, the cushion he used is too close to the flames. She leans and pulls it out of harm's way.

'When's this ale coming? I could do with something to eat,' he says. Alice says nothing, she doesn't want him here that long, but he continues. 'You'd better come with me to the kitchen.'

They find the three men before the kitchen fire, now built up to a good blaze. Their jerkins and breeches steam where they stand facing the heat. One of them assures Sir Malcolm the poker to warm his ale will be hot enough directly. The man who carried Grace is shivering with ague. Being made to go out in the rain will not have helped.

The coroner points Alice to the still room. 'Find me something in there.' His ale duly heated, he takes up the mug. 'I'm going back to the parlour. Take a mug of ale each, just one, mind you, I don't want a pack of drunken sots.' Evidently he is happy to offer High Stoke's ale to his men, but not to join them by the kitchen fire. Not good enough company for Sir Malcolm Wipley, Coroner. 'One of you,' he says, 'make sure you accompany her back. Don't let her near the body.'

Once he is gone, Alice listens to the banter between Sir Malcolm's men while she looks along the shelves. These men who beat Allan, enjoying her ale. 'Why did you attack my servant? Three of you against one man?'

'We didn't,' the man with ague croaks, sitting down on a stool. 'That was the sheriff's men. We'd just linked up with them when they sighted him.'

'We helped them a bit, that's all,' the man who carried the lantern says, grinning.

'*You* did,' the man on the stool says. There seems little love lost between the two.

The third man appears fascinated by the bricks stacked on the hearth. 'What's these for, then?'

'Give 'em here,' the other says. 'Don't you know a hot-brick when you see one?'

'Wassat, then?'

He points at his seated fellow holding out shaking hands to the flames. 'To heat up this here corpse, you lobcock.'

She can't help feeling a little sorry for the sick man at least. A thought occurs to her. 'There is the last of a game pie here,' she says, drawing it off the shelf. 'Why don't I share it out amongst you?' It is in some measure poetic, she reflects, that the coroner and his men should be offered the coroner's goose. She cuts slices, watches them wolf it down almost as hungrily as the coroner's goose-girl did. 'So how did you come to be out looking for my dairymaid?'

'The message Isabel sent,' says one through a mouthful of pastry.

The shivering man rouses. 'She didn't send, she came herself,' he grates. 'Didn't you send her?' he asks Alice.

'No doubt my husband did.' So that's where Isabel went earlier this evening. The thoughts chase each other as she slides the last piece of pie onto a plate. Did Isabel see a chance to ingratiate herself with the coroner once more? To take a measure of revenge on Henry? Was she aiming at a role for herself in the coroner's household? Is that why she didn't open the front door, afraid that one of the men might give the game away?

Back in the winter parlour, Sir Malcolm struts around the room, jaws champing on his pie. Alice picks up Francis Bacon's book and places it back on the bookshelf. The coroner approaches and stands behind her, screwing up his eyes to scan the titles. 'You know, I find the best volumes are always on the top shelf.' Looking up, he leans towards her. 'Now, there's a title, for instance, "Delightful Ladies".'

When she does not respond, the coroner tries again. 'So, husband forbids little country wife to read it, does he? What delights does it hold, I wonder, that he must needs place it out of reach?'

He steps round her, his hose brushing her leg; somehow this man is always half a pace too close. His eyes narrow as he glances down, and Alice hunches her shoulder. She would normally only see friends or household when wearing a loose gown and no bodice, the coroner was the last man she expected. Does he always play the lizard with women, she wonders, or only with those who oppose him? Almost, she has pity for the shallowness of the man. What misfortune of creation made him this mean-spirited creature? What fortunes of life raised him to a position where his power is not a responsibility but a weapon to be used at his will?

Perhaps her disgust shows on her face, for he continues, 'I see I have shocked you. Is little country wife about to throw up horrified hands? Come now, madam, while your husband is from home, let us take a peep into his pillow delights? Mm?'

He reaches up, pulls the volume from the shelf, all the while looking at her, waiting for her to blush, her glance to fall, modesty outraged, confusion manifest, and his dominance thus confirmed. She sighs and gives him back look for look. 'I fear you will be disappointed, sir. The title is "Delightes *for* Ladies", the sort of delights a woman is more likely to appreciate.' Deliberately she holds his stare as she goes on, 'Such as the correct manner of skewering a cock on a spit.'

His gaze falters, he looks down at the volume in his hand, opens it, flips through. There are pictures of women in the kitchen, still room, dairy, sick chamber.

'Do you not know a household book when you see one, Sir Malcolm?'

'You, madam, take liberties.' He pretends to read.

Alice folds her arms. 'And you don't?' Too late she bites her lip; she did not mean to refer again to his abuse of Sylvia's corpse, the words are out before she thinks.

'Ah, so sober little country wife *is* shocked.' He draws out a loose sheet, some note she has written and placed between the leaves for safekeeping. She has a habit of doing that, copying receipts, noting quantities, jotting ideas for flavourings. 'What business is it of yours what I do?' he demands.

'What business?' Alice pushes on. 'What if it became the business of one whose good opinion you court? Justice Townsend for instance?'

Wipley snorts, still making a show of interest in the book. 'You don't know much, do you?' He licks his finger to flip the page. 'There's no proof, no proof at all.'

'You were seen coming out,' she says.

'Not by Townsend, he never goes near the Red Lion.'

Alice momentarily falters. The Red Lion? What has that to do with Sylvia? But of course, though his offence against Sylvia looms large for Alice, it barely figures in Sir Malcolm's thoughts. It is not Sylvia he is thinking of but the two women at the Red Lion.

At her silence, Wipley glances up from the book. 'Oh-ho, did you hope one of the cock pit crowd would go tattling to Townsend? I suppose Egerton's been spreading stories about witnesses, has he? Let me tell you, he's just fishing. They were too busy pressing in for their drink. I was back round the turn of the stairs so fast they never saw me. So no one who counts saw me leave. There's not an honest man amongst that mean sort anyway, none would believe such cheats.'

'I doubt they cheat any worse than yourself, Sir Malcolm.'

From his wordless stare she knows she has surprised him more than she expected. Much more, for his grip on the book loosens at that moment. He grabs as it slips, but things fall. They go sliding, floating, fluttering to the floor. Instinctively she bends to retrieve, even as they skim away across the flags, jottings, receipts, some flat, some folded, a pressed sprig, a scrap of linen, a half-worked bookmark, little notes. One in particular catches her eye because she does not recognise it. 'What's this?' she murmurs, taking it up. It is a small twice-folded sheet, grey and coarse, of the sort they give you when you call for writing materials at a tavern. Momentarily distracted, Alice opens it up. Incredulous, her eyes fly across the words, even as Sir Malcolm's hand shoots out and snatches the paper from her grasp.

'Sir Malcolm!'

But she saw.

The ink having bled into the paper made the letters hard to decipher. It is not a receipt, it is something altogether different. She has heard of these, although she has never seen one. It is a short few lines, hastily dashed off, the writer clearly under some irritation.

> *I pledge ... dwelling ... all that demesne ... to Malcolm Wipley, ... Poyle by Guildford ...*
>
> *... October y xxii yr ... James Stuart, Rex ...*

'Sir Malcolm, please give me that back.'

He passes her the book instead. The sheet he keeps tight hold of. Carefully, as though he fears dropping it, he smoothes it out close to his chest and looks, his face slowly transforming. She can tell he is not reading it, rather his eyes are feasting on it as though sating an appetite long starved. He has seen this before, knows what it is. Almost, the shadows on his cube-like head soften, he smiles. Sir Malcolm Wipley, Coroner, 'bought' Knight, man of power, has come into a considerable property.

'Not yours, madam,' he says as he folds the sheet and tucks it into the breast of his doublet.

'It came out of my book.'

'Yes, but how did it get there?'

'How would I know? I put all sorts of things in there.'

'But not that.'

'… No.'

Clearly, he did not know it was there in the book, any more than she. Nevertheless he knew it existed, he was quick to recognise that sheet amongst the scatter of papers on the floor. 'So Sylvia did find it,' he muses. 'Little liar. She always denied.'

Strange how Sylvia suddenly transforms from 'the wench' of yesterday, to a woman with a name, and evidently with some history of dealings with the coroner. 'You told Sylvia to look for it?' she asks.

'Of course I told her to. I knew Tillotson must have concealed it somewhere.'

'And what was to be her reward?' Sylvia talked to the carter of great riches.

'Oh, she had her reward. Several times over.' His voice is suppressed laughter, triumphant, boasting, and a thought creeps chill down Alice's back. Something Betsy said. The coroner kept going back after Master Tillotson's death. Sylvia was maidservant at Tillotsons. 'You fathered Sylvia's child.'

He shrugs. 'The silly callet. She thought I was going to raise her state. Marry a serving wench? Me?' He falls to musing again, as though Alice is not there. 'When did she find it, I wonder? Why didn't she bring it to me before?'

'Why should she, when you took her and then rejected her?'

295

But he is not listening, he has returned to the backstool and is propping his heels on the hearth. He cannot resist drawing out the paper again, taking another look. Alice's eyes bore into him. This loathsome man contemptuously drew Sylvia into his scheming, into his bed. Poor, foolish Sylvia. She was going to be a lady, she said to Will Harvey. Lady Wipley. She was on her way that final day, not to Tillotsons, but to that nearby dwelling, to find Wipley, to close the bargain at long last. Marriage with the man who had discarded her, in return for a piece of paper carrying the pledge of a gentleman's property. Whose? Tillotsons? It is a tiny satisfaction to Alice to let him think Sylvia found and hid it all this time, to let him think that for a space Sylvia outwitted him.

While Alice stands jostled by thoughts, the door opens and one of Wipley's men puts his head round. 'Ready to go when you are, Sir Malcolm,' the man says.

The coroner is already re-folding the paper, pushing it inside his doublet. 'Then get my horse,' he growls and reaches for his cloak. The man disappears and Sir Malcolm shouts after him, 'If the saddle's wet you'll pay for it with a flaying!' He swings the cloak over his shoulders, pulls his hat onto his large head and strides from the parlour. She follows him through the hall where he stops to warn her, 'Touch that body and you know what will happen.' His man with the lantern falls into step, assuring him his mount is ready. At the front door, the sick man stands, still shivering. The brisk breeze gusts in as he opens the door. She fidgets with impatience as the three walk out into the night where the last man holds the coroner's horse and the rain has dwindled to sparse needles darting through the lantern's glow.

Not waiting to see them mounted, Alice pushes the door closed and bars it. *Touch that body and you know what will happen.* Well, does Sir Malcolm imagine she will not even pay her respects? Alice hastens across the hall to the still form outlined in the glow from the parlour, takes the cold, lifeless hand. 'Grace. I'm so sorry.

After all you've been through, how could I let this happen to you? Who did this?' Her other hand moves to cup the rounded cheek, a gesture of affection, apology. 'I should have been more …' One finger is resting on the neck. She stares. Moves her hand, fingertips searching, pressing the skin. 'Grace?'

Hating herself for the intrusion, driven by compulsion, Alice loosens the bodice lacing and presses her hand under the heart. 'Grace?'

Two thumps on the kitchen door are followed by Ned's call, 'Master? Mistress? You there?'

Alice makes her way blindly through hall and passage to unbar the kitchen door. She pulls Ned inside. 'The very man I need!' she says. 'Come, Ned. Bring your lantern.'

''Tis mortal cold out there.' He doffs his rain-soaked hat and kersey cloak and stamps his feet. The mugs left by the coroner's men are still on the table. 'You got some ale, missus?'

'Later,' Alice says. 'Follow me.' She leads the way to the hall. Behind her, Ned grumbles, 'Bin out all night, no thanks, no food.'

'Do you pick up Grace and bring her into the winter parlour.' Alice tells him.

He peers. 'Lord's sake, she looks dead to me. Is she dead?'

'We must get her warmed up quickly.'

'It's like midwinter out there,' Ned complains. 'You'd think—'

'Ned!' Alice interrupts. 'The winter parlour? Now?'

Ned sighs, hoists Grace with ease. Before the hearth Alice throws down all the cushions she can find, roughly arranging them on the floor. On top she casts the rug from the table. 'Lay her down here. That's right. Now take my candle and go into the kitchen. You will find some hot-bricks by the fire. Bring them.'

Alice grasps his lantern and sprints upstairs to Sam's room. Mollie has crept into his bed, he is nestled in her encircling arm. Both are fast asleep. Alice steps carefully to the coffer at the foot of Sam's bed and from it takes two blankets and makes her way back downstairs. She kneels by Grace's form and covers her with both. Then she sets about building up the fire. It still has a good heat in it and needs only a few of the rosemary cuttings to shoot into flame once more. Alice takes Grace's cold hand and rubs it vigorously between her own. 'Come on, Grace. Please.'

Ned returns with three hot bricks wrapped in cloths and puts them down on the hearth. With rough sympathy, he says, 'I just hope you're not wasting your time, missus.' He holds his hands to the blaze.

'Chafe her hand,' Alice orders him. 'There's still warmth in her.' She goes to slip off Grace's shoes and stares as she sees one ankle is swollen to twice its normal size, the foot bulging. It is with difficulty she can prise off the shoe. The flesh, she rejoices, is hot to the touch. *You have to be alive with an ankle that hot.* 'She fell.'

Alice places the warmest brick on Grace's stomach and unwraps the other two to reheat on the fire. *There's no blood, no injury I can see, other than this sprain and this bruise and the muddy graze down your face. But if you were running hard and fell headlong ... who were you running from?*

'He must have caught her quite a blow to bruise her face like that,' Ned says, as though reading her thoughts.

'Keep chafing!' Alice commands. 'Can't you see? If he'd hit her there, she'd have fallen backwards. Not grazed her—' She stops. 'Of course! What a fool I've been! Why didn't I see it?'

'Still looks like a corpse to me,' Ned insists.

'Shut up!' Alice glares at him. 'There's no corpse here till I say there's a corpse.'

He rolls his eyes. 'Have it your own way.'

She needs to remove Grace's soaked clothing but can't do that with Ned here. 'Listen,' she says, 'in the buttery is the ale barrel. Take a full jack for yourself and warm up by the kitchen fire.'

With a muttered, 'At last!' Ned clumps away through the hall.

With Ned gone to enjoy his drink, Alice shuts the parlour

door. Alone with the limp figure, she unties and unlaces and pulls until Grace's sodden clothes lie discarded in a draggled heap. One of the blankets she uses to pummel Grace's body, her limbs, to warm the blood in the same way she was able to warm the blood in Betsy's leg when she was attacked by cramp. All the while she encourages and coaxes but elicits no response from the blue lips. She feels the side of Grace's neck again. That pulse is still there. The only reason she knows about this is from the apothecary in her Dorset village last year. *If you can feel that,* he told her, *the mind is alive even if the body appears dead.* Grace's skin feels warmer, she thinks, though it might only be the fire. Away from the fire, the draught is as chill as the night.

She casts one of the blankets over Grace, tucking it close round her. The bricks she re-heats in rotation, wrapping each in its strip of cloth. One she places to Grace's heart. When the humours are cold and wet it is a sure sign of melancholy. Given the past few days' events, Grace's heart is in want of warmth, and now this additional misfortune of lying in the rain on a chill spring night. She places another brick to Grace's uninjured foot. It is strange, she muses, but warming the extremities somehow warms the whole body. The last wrapped brick she places on the stomach, the other vital focus of the humours, and wraps Grace's hands round it. Finally she casts the remaining blanket over the top, tucking it well in.

She can do no more. Now to wait. And think. She has much thinking to do.

IN the still darkness, she has lost all sense of the night passing and has no idea how long before day will dawn. It seems a lifetime since the coroner left. The rain has stopped, even the breeze no longer sighs in the chimney or blows disconcerting draughts to flicker her candle and dart shadows across the walls of the screens passage. The house is quiet, without even the night-time creaking she has already come to know, like an old lady easing her joints when she thinks no one is looking. In that silent space of time, the world has changed for Alice. Her mind free to wander where it will in the darkness has shown her truths she is loath to accept.

When did Sylvia realise that the coroner was not going to marry her, was only using her to find the pledge at Tillotsons? Was it when Sir Malcolm rid himself of her by arranging for fawning Isabel to engage her? It certainly seems to have been then that Sylvia set about creating the fiction that Allan was her child's father. Used Allan's weakness for a pretty face, luring him into the barn on Valentine's Day. But then Grace arrived, turning Sylvia's plans to dust.

It was only when Sam innocently found the pledge that Sylvia saw her chance to retrieve her fortunes. If she went to the coroner's house at Poyle she might have the wit to play her cards well enough to secure him. *All that demeaning work,* Will Harvey the carter thought Sylvia said. No, it was "all that demesne". Sylvia dazzled by visions of marriage and land, her state raised, no need to work. Henry refused her the lodge but once she had this paper, what did she care? The coroner's standing would be enhanced by this new property, and Sylvia, Lady Wipley, could live her life of ease. But fortune, or rather, misfortune intervened.

Someone knew what she was about, that person waylaid and attacked her. They took the paper and carried it with them until they found a hiding place for it. In Alice's book, thinking it would be the last place anyone would look. There have been many men in the winter parlour since Sylvia was carried home. An entire coroner's jury. Which of them lingered by the shelves, pretending an interest in the books? When were they going to retrieve it? Whatever plan they had was set at naught when the coroner chose to take down that book whose title, misread, appealed to his rank fancies. As a result, he is to be the richer by an entire property which perhaps was never intended to be handed over.

Sylvia paid for that paper with her life. And it was not Sir Malcolm who took it from her.

34

Henry arrives home last of the searchers. She hears his tread pause in the hall and knows he has seen her candlelight under the door of the parlour. Half of her, yesterday's half, wants to run to him. Today's half keeps her sitting by the fire as he pushes open the door.

'Alice?' His face is as grey as a cold dawn. The former half longs to wrap her arms round him. Yesterday's Alice would happily ignore the mud on face and clothes where he must have fallen, would pull him into a kiss born of all the constrained anxiety of recent days. But this is another Alice, another day, a day for questions, for truth-telling, a day for hard heads and hard hearts.

'They found her,' she breathes. 'Sir Malcolm and his men brought her back here.'

'I know,' he says, and his voice is weary, drained. 'I met one of the sheriff's men. He told me Allan killed her, but I simply don't believe—'

'It's not true.'

'That's what I thought too, but they were out searching with Wipley's men when they caught him in the act.'

She shakes her head. 'No.'

'This is my fault.'

'No! They caught Allan with her, that's a very different thing. They thought she was dead so they beat him and they've thrown him in gaol because they want to believe him guilty. Or perhaps simply because he led them a merry dance—'

'Thought?' he says. 'Thought?'

'She's alive, Henry. Grace is alive!'

He stares at her, mouth working. At last, he manages, 'But they were in no doubt! What happened?'

'I don't know for sure, she hit herself a great blow on the head. When they brought her back, they were so insistent she was dead, and Sir Malcolm wouldn't let me touch her, said if I did, you would be held responsible, accessory to murder. It wasn't until they left I could check. She was out of her wits, very chilled, and I warmed her with bricks and eventually she came to herself.'

'Thank God! She wasn't attacked, then?'

'No one attacked her. She remembers running from the Long Down and taking a heavy fall. But she cannot remember anything else.'

'What was she doing on the Long Down?'

'That's what she cannot remember. She's in bed now, exhausted and sleeping. Betsy came home soon after and is with her. Everyone else is back.'

He puts a hand to his face and draws a deep shuddering breath. 'Thank the Lord.' He looks at Alice. 'You've not had any sleep, you look exhausted too. Come, let's take what's left of the night.'

'We have things to talk about, Henry.' She is looking into the fire, reluctant to face him.

'Can't it wait?'

'Things that only you can tell me.' She forces herself to look in his face. 'Things you have been keeping from me.'

He spreads his hands but does not approach the fire. 'What things? What have I kept from you?'

'When Sir Malcolm brought Grace back here, he took refreshment while his men dried out in the kitchen.'

'I'd like to think he appreciated it but I doubt it.'

She doesn't want to look at him so she picks up the poker and pushes it into the fire, riddling away the ash. 'He decided to while away his time at the bookshelves.'

'He's welcome. Some of those books could do with being taken down and read occasionally. What's this about Alice?' He is puzzled now, alert that something unexpected is coming.

'He chose to take down my household book,' she says.

'I didn't know you had any books.' His voice registers only baffled enquiry.

'Just a few. I put them there earlier in the week.' And now she looks him in the face. 'On the top shelf. Where I saw you replacing a book when you came home on Wednesday afternoon.' Now she has his whole attention. 'In the book was the paper Sam found in Master Tillotson's gown …' She picks up a scrap of fabric by her side, shakes it out. Good rather than fine linen, neatly hemmed, and there in the corner a worked three-petalled flower. '… and Sylvia's kerchief.'

And something more, a red-brown smear across the fabric.

The colour that was returning has drained from his face, it is as though the flesh itself has shrunk and she is momentarily reminded of Isabel's gaunt, skeletal look earlier in the night. Although not blood relatives, both are tall and spare, both hollow-eyed when under severe strain. Until this moment Alice has clung to the hope that her conclusions have been in some way flawed, that the explanation will turn out to be altogether different. But his knowing silence and the blanching of his face confirms it all.

'You concealed it from me, Henry. All along, you knew what she found, what it meant. How could you keep quiet, especially to me? How could you so deceive me?'

Carefully he sits down on one of the cushions beside her. 'I didn't lie to you, Alice.' He reaches for her hand.

'Don't touch me! Why did you hide it from me?'

'I was going to get rid of it. I was going to burn it but there were no fires, not even in the kitchen. You saw what it said?'

'I saw part of it. Some land pledged to Sir Malcolm.'

'The land is not rightfully his. But I don't know how Sylvia came to know of the existence of the pledge.'

'I can tell you that. After Master Tillotson's death Sir Malcolm instructed her to search for it, on promise of marrying her if she found it. And bedded her on the strength of it and got her with child.'

'He told you that?'

'I put it to him and he boasted of it. Which explains why he smeared mud on her dead body.'

'For his own pleasure, I suspect,' he says in disgust.

'That too, I suppose, as much as to put the thought in the minds of the jury that Allan ravished and killed her on the Long Down. But he does not know that she found the paper yesterday. Which means Master Egerton has not informed him that Sylvia was expecting to be rich.'

'Did you think Jack would?'

'He seemed to lean towards sympathy with Sir Malcolm. Yesterday when Sam said that the paper had been in Master Tillotson's gown pocket, Jack did not go straight to Tillotsons, remember? You were as puzzled as I, Henry.'

'I still am.'

'Maybe he knows more than he's telling, but I don't think that means he is against us. At all events, I thought about that pledge, wondered who wrote it. I never knew Master Tillotson of course, but hearing how well respected he was, it seemed to me there must be some monstrous secret that could compel such a man to sign away his land, or that having done so he would then renege on his word of honour.'

'Frederick? No! You mustn't think—'

'Then it occurred to me that perhaps it was written by his son. That Jeremy had somehow got into a situation with Sir Malcolm that obliged him to pledge his future inheritance. That would explain how the pledge got into his father's pocket – that he confessed to his father, who took charge of it.'

'Alice, no—'

'But that is not possible – the pledge was written a year ago last October and it is known that Jeremy had been living in the North for a couple of years before his father's death. He could not have written that pledge.'

'No, Jeremy would never do such a thing.'

'All along, Henry, you have been keen to protect people who have come under scrutiny. First there was Allan. But given the nature of the pledge, he could not be the writer as he has no land. Then as soon as Master Renwick is mentioned you declare he is not involved with Sylvia, only a blushing admirer. In any event, he could not have written the pledge or he would have got rid of Will Harvey at the first mention of Sylvia and her riches, and gone in search of her.'

'Well of course he didn't. George Renwick? It's unthinkable.'

'Now the Tillotsons, father and son, and here you are once again eliminating them from suspicion.'

'Of course. Listen, let me tell you—'

'And there is only one—'

'Listen!'

'One person left who could have written that pledge, Henry!'

'Yes, all right, it was me!'

'You pledged High Stoke!'

'Yes, I pledged High Stoke! I wrote that paper! It was me!'

Now that she has his admission, she hardly knows what to do with it. She has thought about this ever since the coroner and his men left, chewed over the things that have been said these past two days. It is the inexplicable nature of what Henry did, and why he did it, that baffle her. Her husband, the man she chose, has done this thing. It is with disgust, as much for herself as for him, for having allied herself to this man, that she adds, 'You married me knowing this. You brought me here knowing this. And you want me to sell Hill House so that you can buy back High Stoke.'

'No!' He leans and grips her shoulders, his fingers digging in as she squirms against his hold. 'No, Alice, never! I wanted you to sell Hill House because this is our home and money needs to be spent on it.'

'Why spend money on a property you don't own?'

'I *do* own it, it was always mine! That pledge is false and Wipley knows it!'

'But you admit you wrote it?'

He lets go of her shoulders. 'I need to tell you what happened. I hoped not to have to. If I had been able to burn it, none of this would have happened.' He hesitates. 'It's where to start …'

'Let's start with yesterday,' she says. 'You told me you saw Sir Malcolm engaging two whores at the Red Lion.'

'I did. I saw him going upstairs. What of it?'

'He wasn't going upstairs, he was coming down, and was panicked by the cock pit crowd that you were caught in. Although he pretends to disdain them, he feared being seen. He bolted back round the turn, pushing the women before him out of sight.'

'It looked to me as though he had just arrived.'

'But you knew that you did not reach the Red Lion around one o'clock when Jack thinks you did, Henry. You knew that was not possible because you had made a long detour from George Renwick's. You never went straight into town from there, but you let me believe it, didn't you?'

Clearly he wants to contest what she is accusing him of, but cannot find the words, and she keeps going because if she stops now, this will fester between them for the rest of their lives. 'Henry, you are the one person who knew what Sylvia had in her possession and where she was heading. When Will the carter arrived at George Renwick's with the story of Sylvia and her riches, you realised what she had found. You knew she was on her way to do a deal with Sir Malcolm and you knew you had to stop her. So you made an excuse to George about going into town and instead you rode up to the Long Down and caught up with Sylvia.'

'Yes.'

'She must have made good time up the hill because she was at the top by the time you got there.'

'She started to run when she realised I was coming up the track. As I caught up with her, she was panting for breath. I told her she didn't understand what she was carrying and to hand it back. She tried to argue it was a personal letter and nothing to do with me. Then suddenly she collapsed.' He looks her in the eye as he says, 'God forgive me, I thought it was another game she was playing. I didn't touch her. I didn't kill Sylvia.'

'I know,' she says.

'You do? How?'

'I realised when I saw the bruise on Grace's forehead. Ned thought someone had hit her in the face but in that case she would have fallen backwards, not grazed her face. Similarly if you had hit Sylvia on the back of the head to cause that injury, she would have fallen on her face. She fell on her back, there were no signs of a struggle, no other mark on her. That's how Allan came upon her, and when I went out there with Jack, we found the place where she lay. She had not been moved. I remember there was a little depression in the ground where blood had collected. You knew she was dead didn't you, Henry?'

It is a while before he answers her. He sighs. 'I told her to get up and go home and I'd say no more about it. When she didn't move I bent down to look.'

'And lifted her head, and saw a blooded stone? A piece of flint sticking out of the ground?'

'I couldn't believe it, that she was alive and arguing one minute, trying to tell me it was her letter and then she went down. It was horrible, a sharp flint, all covered in blood. In a fit of ... I don't know what ... I prised it out and flung it away. It seemed to me she had tried a silly ploy and paid for it with her life, poor girl. I couldn't grasp the suddenness of it.'

'What were you thinking of, Henry? She had just hurried up that hill. And she was with child.'

'I didn't know that at the time.'

'That was no game, it was a swoon. She was tight-laced, chased and stopped by you, deprived of her hopes of comfort, security, riches.'

'When you put it like that, yes.'

'Why didn't you go straight to Jack Egerton and tell him?'

'You've changed your tune. Yesterday you had him rejoicing at eliminating Wipley from suspicion.'

'I don't believe he would ignore an honest open confession. Surely if you took the flint to him and confessed, you would have a fair hearing?'

'I went looking for the flint but there's so much undergrowth round there, I never found it. I took the pledge and wrapped the kerchief round it, I didn't know I had made that smear on it. I put them in my pocket and took the lane by Poyle into town. I thought much about what to do when I reached the Red Lion. I even jotted down possible courses I could take, none of them to any purpose,' he finishes bleakly.

'You left Sylvia lying there. How could you do that?'

'I knew straight away the one thing I couldn't do was tell anyone what happened.'

'Why not?'

'And have Wipley jump at the chance of deciding I killed her? One of his dearest wishes is to get his revenge on me for denying him High Stoke. Any connection between me and Sylvia out on the Long Down was going to look suspicious.'

'But you left Sylvia out there for someone else to find, Henry.'

'At that moment all I could think was to get as far away as possible. I am sorry, Alice, with all my heart, but I wasn't thinking as I should.'

'Go to Jack anyway. When it is light, go over to Freemans and tell him what you have told me.'

'There is something else I need to tell you.'

'Not more, Henry?' she protests.

'Not bad things,' he reassures her. 'At least … I want to tell you about the night I wrote that pledge.'

He reaches and throws a log, then another, onto the heart of the fire and settles down next to her on the cushions. Perhaps he senses that she is no longer avoiding him. Listening to his admission of weakness she is only too aware of her own mistakes – those that fell in the desperate winter just passed at Hillbury, mistakes that risked her reputation and nearly cost her life. Henry knows what happened, yet never a word of admonition has he uttered, though many a man would have used that right.

'Whatever it is,' she says, 'we'll find a way through this tangle.'

'Last autumn twelvemonth,' he starts, 'at the Red Lion it was. You may find this hard to believe, but I was playing dice with Sir Malcolm Wipley. I know,' as she opens her mouth to protest. 'I've never liked the man but we were not enemies and I occasionally played him. We had both drunk more than usual, there was a group of us celebrating with Oliver Sanderson. I remember he had secured a very good deal with a maltster supplying taverns around the Charing Cross in London. Eventually everyone went home but Wipley challenged me to continue. He had been needling me all evening, in jesting fashion as any friend might, except that it was a running sore in any converse I had with him. I thought to take a small revenge so I agreed.'

'What was he needling you about?'

'The draughts in the hall here, leaky roof, rotten wood, the lodge falling to pieces, suchlike things. He would offer me a knock-down price, well below what it's worth, just to get at me. He knows full well High Stoke's not for sale.'

'So you agreed to play at dice.'

'More often than not I won against him. He tends to overplay and lose his advantage, so knowing this I thought I would see how the game went and quit after I had lightened his purse.'

'I didn't even know you diced, Henry. I'd much rather you didn't.'

'I don't, not any more.'

'You lost High Stoke on a throw of dice?'

'What happened was, we got into play and just when I was winning a little he would make a good throw and win it all back. It seemed it was not my night for winning. This happened several times and instead of calling a halt I stupidly raised the stakes.'

'And so it went on, higher and higher?'

'I was too angry to think straight by then. I let the stakes go higher and higher and the sums became too serious to quit. I pledged the pewter, the better furniture, then the grey.'

Yes, she thinks, I can well imagine that with a gamester for a husband this will happen again sooner or later. 'What in heaven's name were you thinking of, Henry?'

He shrugs. 'I seemed to be outside myself. It was like watching an ant scurrying here and there.'

'You wrote that pledge to hand over the whole of High Stoke and the land. Didn't you feel anything as you wrote it, Henry, knowing you were signing away everything you owned?'

'It wasn't like that. He had won the grey, he knew that would hurt, and before I could win it back again he changed the game. Offered the grey and his chestnut against High Stoke—'

'What! I can't believe you took him up?'

'— if he won two out of three throws.'

'Is that possible?'

'Vanishingly possible. I refused him but he persisted and I thought at last he was overplaying. So I agreed. I resolved I would win back the grey and his chestnut and call it quits.'

'But he won.'

'If you can call it that. He cheated, as he had been doing all along. Only, I didn't see it.'

'Then he could have taken possession immediately. Why

didn't he?'

'Unknown to both of us, old Frederick Tillotson was sitting in the shadows studying the game, waiting his moment. When those two throws came up, Wipley was crowing his triumph, treating me as though I was the cheat, and all I could think was how you only truly value a thing after you've lost it. Then Tillotson challenged. Wipley was switching the dice when it suited him, throwing his own dice and then switching back again.'

'Fulham dice.' She has heard this expression, but for her it is a ploy that tricksters use on raw youths, not something that would ever touch her life.

'Exactly, loaded to land with the same side uppermost every time. He was switching the dice every now and then, and I didn't see.'

'How could you not see? You were at the same table!'

'At the Red Lion, they use pig fat rush lights. You know what they're like, you can hardly see anything by them. Very well for gaming amongst friends, but Wipley must have been waiting his opportunity. That evening was his chance. When I suggested a move to the Swan where they have brighter rush lights, Wipley just turned it aside and we carried on playing.'

'Then how could Master Tillotson see?'

'Tillotson had his suspicions already, so he was alert for innocent-looking movements that give the game away. He possessed himself of dice and pledge, cursed me roundly for a fool, and told Wipley that if he ever heard of him cheating again, both pledge and dice would be shown to Townsend. Believe me, old Tillotson cut a stern enough figure that even Wipley was silenced.'

'You dice away your property, and by sheer good fortune you get it back again immediately.' She snaps her fingers. 'As easily as that! So where are the dice? As long as you have them, Wipley cannot use the pledge.'

'I don't know. I checked the gown, they're not there,' he says.

'They must be! We'll go through every pocket in every garment in the wash-house until we find them.'

'I've been through all of them,' he says. 'Twice. I have to assume that either Tillotson destroyed the dice or Wipley found them when he went to Tillotsons after Frederick's death.'

'Or Sylvia found them for him,' Alice says sourly. 'Hardly surprising he didn't boast of that. Or perhaps Master Tillotson destroyed such infernal things.' Bleakly she wonders, what is the future for this house she called beautiful when first she saw it only a week ago? The house that has somehow wrapped itself around her, has already become home to her. 'So what now, Henry?'

'We must face the possibility that High Stoke is lost to us, Alice.'

She realises she has devised plans for this house and the demesne, the restoration of its fortunes, and with it the raising of the whole household. All that, gone. Lost by deceit and trickery and, if she's honest, her husband's rash stupidity. So that was why Wipley nearly dropped her book when she accused him of being a cheat. He thought she knew. 'Master Tillotson was right,' she says, her anger spilling over into accusation. 'How could you be such a fool, Henry? A man of your years! You're no better than a greenhorn at a Michaelmas fair!'

'I made a mistake, that's all. A mistake!'

'That's all? When is the next game to be? Will you pledge my own Hill House? Perhaps you did that while you were at the Red Lion yesterday?'

'God a' mercy, Alice! I've not diced since that October night and I've no intention of ever starting again!'

The enormity of the things he has done hangs before her, deriding her hasty decision to marry him. 'You left a dead girl where she lay.'

'I never meant ... I thought it was only my presence there that would give Wipley the chance to accuse me of murder.'

'You never meant it?' Her anger with him, is it also a shield against her anger with herself? 'You let another pick her up, and with her, that accusation of murder!'

'I didn't know he would need a scapegoat for Sylvia's being with child. I thought he would view it as the accident it was. That's why I had to get Allan out.'

'You what? You set Allan free?' This new revelation, dropped heedlessly into their exchange, makes her lightheaded with confusion. 'You didn't think to tell me, Henry?'

'I didn't want to involve you, Alice.'

'I am involved! I made a promise to Jack Egerton! When will you stop taking matters into your own hands, disregarding others to suit yourself?' She springs up, paces to the window and stands staring out at blackness, struggling to choke down her anger.

Across the room, 'I'm sorry, do you hear? I didn't know you'd want to have your say.'

It has started to rain again, pattering on the window, the dark drops making veins on the glass as they slide down. She thinks, Be fair, he doesn't know you any more than you know him. She turns. 'So how did you release him from the wash-house? Isabel had both keys. They were on that cord round her neck.'

'Angus and I did it in the night.'

'Don't tell me there's a third key?'

'We didn't use keys. I sawed through one of the mullions in the window and he squeezed out.'

'The window is whole,' she says. 'We went and looked through, you and I.'

Henry is shaking his head. 'I was holding the loose strut. Angus had pushed earth around top and base to hide the cuts but it was none too steady.'

'Where did he go? How was he to live?'

'Angus got one of our ladders from the woodshed and we carried it to the lodge, put it up against the rotted window. We hid

Allan in there, gave him food and a blanket.'

'The upper floor? I suppose if the Sheriff's men searched that far they disregarded it because the ground floor is boarded up. Chancy, Henry, it could have collapsed.'

'Less chancy than letting him be taken to gaol. We'd never have got him out of there.'

'All this you concealed from me. Will you always treat me as if I am of no account in this household?'

'I didn't want to burden you, Alice.'

'I'm not a child, I'm your wife! I am the mistress of High Stoke! I have had to fight for the right to be its mistress, am I to fight you for everything, my whole life through? Am I to discover your doings from others rather than from you, my husband?'

'I thought you would turn away from me.'

'I am the more like to turn away if you constantly cut me out of your confidence!' Hold fast, she tells herself. Take a deep breath, calm down. She returns to the fire and sits. In a moderated tone, she says, 'In all essential things, Henry, I need to know that you confide in me.'

'No matter what I have done?'

'Believe me, it is so much worse to find out by other means.' Unthinking, she leans forward and rests her hand on his. He raises his other hand to cup her face. 'I am sorry, Alice, more sorry than I can say.'

He leans forward as though to kiss her, but she shifts minutely backwards.

'Do you hate me?' he asks.

All the voices of fair play harangue her to deny it, reminding her of her own faults and weaknesses. Hate him? No, of course she does not hate him. By the same token she has lost that closeness with him. 'If I am to be honest with you, Henry, I have to tell you that I am only now realising what I did in marrying you. I was aware I did not know you well, but I thought I knew enough, that everything would fall into place as we got to know each other. Only now do I realise what it means to marry someone you don't know. If I am disappointed, I have no one but myself to blame.'

'That's almost worse,' he says. 'That I disappoint you.'

'I saw an open, generous-hearted man, a man who listened to me, who did not try to control what I did, or dictate what I thought, as so many would. A man of courage, I will never forget what you did for me that day at Hill House. That was the man I married. Now I'm seeing another side of you, a side that has consistently refused to accept your own accountability. The side of you that turned your back on Sylvia.'

'It's hardly fair to condemn me for one mistake,' he protests.

'Not just one mistake. For years, you have turned your back on your cousin's inept handling of the household, her pitiful thrift. She walks around in silk, she lets Maureen drink the best ale while the rest of the servants drink small ale that's so poor it's practically pond water, did you know that? Perhaps between them they also finished up the White Gascony that so unaccountably disappeared. You have been wilfully blind to all this. As a result you have allowed your people to be neglected, abused and ill-fed. You have avoided caring for this house and keeping it in good repair. You helped me yesterday with the vegetable garden but how long will that last? On the face of it, Henry, you don't deserve High Stoke. What I want to know is whether you can change this habit of abandoning your duty of care. You tell me, what sort of man is Henry Jerrard?'

There is a long pause. The conflict between awareness and denial is clear in his face. 'I was giving Isabel an opportunity. She said she was ready to steward the house.' He shakes his head. 'I've just realised how foolish that sounds.'

'You should have checked that she was indeed ready.'

'I know, I know.' There is a silence between them. She is loath to break it while he is thinking, weighing himself in his own balance. He sighs. 'I'm seeing a side of myself I never knew before.'

And? she thinks. There's more due than that.

'I can't promise never to make a mistake again,' he says.

It draws a short laugh from her. 'I wouldn't believe you if you did. But I want to know what you *can* promise me, Henry.'

'I can promise you that you are mistress of High Stoke, your word will be observed and none shall gainsay. I said that to Isabel last night, and told her if she cannot accept it we will give her a pension and she must leave. If you are ever in difficulties and want my help, I will help you.'

His assurance of solidarity heartens her. 'And likewise if you are in difficulties, I will help you, Henry. This is not a one-sided undertaking.' Nothing about sharing and confiding, but perhaps it will take time for that to become a habit of thought. This is a start, and there is no point in hounding him further at the moment.

In the silence of tentative companionship that has fallen between them, they sit gazing into the embers, while the walls creak around them. These walls, she realises, have witnessed so much this past week. Me arranging my books on the shelves. Sam, Mollie and me rolling on the floor in play. A coroner's jury preparing for their grim duty, and Henry's quick understanding over my offer of wine to the jury. My waiting vigil last night and the spectral Isabel threatening. The triumphant look on the coroner's face as he held the damning pledge. Henry and me finding and facing the truth.

In the darkness outside a fresh shower patters against the window panes.

'Jack Egerton,' she says. 'I misjudged him. I thought he was untrustworthy when it came to Sir Malcolm, but nothing he has done can be construed as prejudicial towards us. He broke Sir Malcolm's lie about riding on Guildown, and he believed he was clearing you from suspicion in placing you both at the Red Lion. He has been uneasy about me because he senses I am hiding something from him and he is right. I should have gone to him for help, told him how I knew Sir Malcolm violated Sylvia's dead body, but I feared he would side with Wipley, use it against us. So I too am guilty of concealment.'

'Dearest Alice,' he says, taking her hand.

'Jack left Allan here in our care, and for that he has borne Sir Malcolm's censure for poor judgment. Many justices would have taken their brief to prove Allan guilty and looked no further, but Jack said he was keeping an open mind and he has done so. Go to Jack,' she says. 'Tell him everything, Henry. About that night at the Red Lion, about the pledge, about Sylvia.'

He sits back. 'There must be another way.'

'In fact, Henry, I'll come with you. I shall tell him everything I know about Sir Malcolm, how he corrupted Sylvia, his broken promise to her.'

'But this is different, Alice. It's not simply mending a friendship. He may not believe Sylvia swooned and broke her head as she fell. There is no stone to prove it, remember. He may be obliged to charge me with murder.'

'We'll insist on searching for the stone, we will find it if we look hard enough. When we do, we can fit it in that place where Sylvia's head lay and that will prove it.'

'Well ...'

'You should go to Jack Egerton, tell him the whole story, Henry. He will help you as best he can. And it will release Allan from prison. It proves him to be innocent of the first offence, and the second cannot stand anyway, as Grace is alive and she knows no one struck her.'

'True.' He considers for a long moment. 'So be it,' he says at last. 'I'll go as soon as it's light.'

35

Henry is breaking up the remains of the fire and Alice is returning the cushions to the window seat, when there comes a tap on the door and Betsy puts her head round. She wears a nightcap and has thrown a blanket over her shift, but she is shivering even so. 'Master, mistress, I'm glad to find you. You'll want to know this,' she says, edging into the room. 'Grace woke up. She's remembered what took her to the Long Down.'

'Yes?' they both say together. And Alice adds, 'Come to the fire, Betsy, there's still warmth in it. What has Grace said?'

'It was another goose,' Betsy explains, approaching. 'It wandered in like the last one, one of Sir Malcolm's. Grace is a soft-hearted girl, you see, and didn't want Joe to behead it like the last one. So she decided she would not tell anyone, she would take it back to young Hannah, that's Sir Malcolm's goose girl.'

'I know Hannah,' Alice says. 'She was here on Tuesday.'

'I've told Grace she's a silly girl, anything might have happened to her on her own out there, so late in the day. Howbeit, she found Hannah on the Long Down and returned the goose. Now, this is the interesting part. They were talking about Allan because Hannah knows Allan and she told Grace she saw him coming back from Tillotsons and she saw him find Sylvia. She thought Sylvia had fallen asleep – well, she's just a child – and she saw Allan pick her up and carry her down the hill.'

'Then she's a witness,' Henry says, and turns to Alice. 'Jack will need to know about this.'

'Grace was so full of the news, she ran full tilt back down the hill, but in the dusk she put her foot in a rabbit hole and it brought her down. When she came to her wits, it was dark, she couldn't walk, and she was so chilled she was in fear of her life. Next thing she remembers is lying by the fire here and you changing her hot bricks.'

'So she lay out there for hours,' Alice gasps. 'I'm sending for Apothecary Middleton when the house is up.'

'I thought you'd like to know straight away,' Betsy says and pulls the blanket round her ample shoulders in readiness to leave.

'You did the right thing, Betsy,' Henry says. 'We'll get Allan released as soon as possible, and I expect he'll want to see Grace.'

'But will she want to see him?' Alice asks.

'She says not, mistress,' Betsy says. 'Declares like any fine lady that she hasn't the slightest wish to see him. But I told her that she's forgetting Allan risked his life and freedom to find her and would have carried her home. That made her think.'

'Betsy, you're up to something,' Henry says.

'Me?' Betsy shrugs. 'I'm just a simple laundress.'

With Betsy gone, Alice turns once again to Henry. 'Come,' she says. 'You're worn out.' Together they leave the winter parlour and she follows him through the hall. And now that he is away from the fire, she can see he is shivering, his teeth chattering. She feels the back of his jerkin. 'Henry, your clothes are still wet.' She takes the candle and hurries him up the stairs into their chamber. Off come the muddied boots and coarse stockings, the rough linen jerkin and breeches he wore to dig her a vegetable garden twelve hours ago, now smirched with mud where several times he lost his footing searching for Grace in the dark. She pushes back the coverlet and he sits slumped on the side of the bed while she draws the embroidered curtains round. His shirt clings damp to his back. 'God's teeth, but I'm cold! I confess I could do with a hot brick and an hour of forgetfulness,' he says.

'And I shall give you both.' She pulls at the ties of her loose gown and shrugs it off. Her shift follows, slipped over her shoulders to fall around her feet.

'You need to sleep too,' he protests.

In answer, she loosens his shirt ties and pulls it up and over his head, peels it from his unresisting arms and drops it on the floor. She blows out the candle.

'Alice, I have failed you—'

'Shh … we are both far from perfect. Let us forgive each other, Henry. Let us resolve to do better in future, and take such comfort now as we may.'

The rain has stopped. At the window, starlight thins the darkness as she presses him back against the pillow. She climbs onto the smooth linen and stretches out alongside, feeling her own vital life warm against the chill of his skin. She reaches to draw the last bed curtain and pulls the coverlet over them both. Lightly she kisses his lips. The sharp smell of the open air is on him still, or perhaps it is the taste of rain. Breathing him, savouring him, she kisses his mouth, his jaw, his throat, over and over. He lies quiet, his shivering gradually stilled, lightly combing his hands through her hair.

Neither falls asleep. Within the curtained space, she senses a tautness in him to equal her own. For now, everything has been said, the decisions made. All they can do is brace themselves for a vital day ahead, a day that will bring resolution one way or another. She reaches for his hand at the same moment he moves to clasp hers, and they lie wakeful while a rain-washed sunrise draws sharpening shadows of the stitched tree-of-life over their twined forms.

36

The household has stirred to a sluggish start. Heavy-eyed from shortage of sleep after the search, the men have left for the fields for their hour's work before breakfast. There is no sign of Isabel. She is not in her bed, Alice has checked, creeping quietly up the maidservants' stairs to avoid waking Betsy and Grace. Isabel's bed is neat and made, but she could have slept there and risen early, or she could have slid amongst the shadowed places of the house all night. Alice no longer doubts that Isabel challenged her in the winter parlour last night. That was no nocturnal phantasm conjured out of her own anxieties.

Henry has always had his own key to the Accounts room. 'Not there either,' he tells her as they meet in the kitchen, and unease stalks Alice's thoughts. She has instructed Mollie to keep Sam with her in case Isabel suddenly re-appears in that strange humour. And if Isabel does not come back soon, she thinks, we will have to start another search. For these reasons, and in their short-handed state, she has decided with regret not to accompany Henry to Freemans. Maureen she sends grumbling to start the milking. Cooking and cleaning can wait but the kine cannot.

'Why me? Why not Betsy?'

'Because Betsy has been up with Grace all night,' Alice tells her. 'So please do not wake her. I have told Mollie the same. She will get the kitchen fire going, and I shall cook breakfast.' I might have saved my breath, she reflects, watching the cook's resentful back as she slops towards the dairy; Maureen shows no willingness to listen.

The night's rain still drips from tree and tile as Alice and Henry pick their way across the puddled kitchen court to the stables. The court is shadowed by the house, though the early sun catches gold on the wet coping stones of the stable roof. Beyond, grey clouds bulge like dirty pillows heaped in the sky. More rain later. Joe, grateful to have been let off the hook with no more than a stern warning from Justice Egerton for his attack on Nol Simpson at the cockfight, is for the time being in penitent humour. On hearing that Henry is to ride over to Freemans, Joe has saddled the grey without being asked, and is gone to join Angus in the fields.

Alice and Henry exchange few words. She is sharply aware of the gravity of the next few hours; his expression is closed, a man preparing to face what lies ahead. She stands close by him in the stables. Cassie is unusually jumpy today, as though she senses trouble in the air. Alice murmurs calming words and stretches out a hand to her, but the gesture goes only part-way to quiet the mare. She needs a good run, and Alice is in two minds whether to go with Henry after all.

'In truth, I would rather talk with Jack on my own,' he tells her, drawing her into his embrace. 'If I am to confess to these things it is easier man to man.' He forces a laugh. 'He can curse me the more freely if there is not a woman present.'

'I will not be in the room while you talk with Jack, Henry. I will wait with Olivia. Yes,' she says, and knows this feels right. She turns from him and reaches for Cassie's blanket. 'Let me saddle Cassie and I will come with you.' But even as she twitches the blanket off the low stone wall dividing the stalls, he reaches and draws her back to him.

'It's not that I don't want you with me, Alice, but Jack and I have known each other all our lives. I can trust him to do what is right, and I can live with whatever decision he makes. Truly, Alice, I prefer to do it this way.'

Reluctantly she nods. If this is his wish, she will respect it.

'If he feels he must take me to the gaol,' he adds, 'we will ride past here and I will find you.'

'I believe he will be fair,' she says. She has a sudden vision of a blackness engulfing the stables, and for a brief second it is as though he is receding from her. She wraps her arms round him but paradoxically that seems to make it worse, as though her presence is the obstacle. 'Come back safe to me.'

'I am glad you are here to come home to, Alice.'

Cassie is pulling on her tethering rope, tossing her head. Her nerviness alarms Alice. 'Henry, you will come back to me, won't you? Something lurks ... I don't know,' she finishes, overcome by dark imaginings.

'I will always come back to you,' he reassures her. 'I belong here with you.' And he bends his face to kiss her long and deep. She wants to both sink into the kiss and flee from it, and tears of confusion slide down her face. Across the court the click of the latch as the kitchen door is opened.

'When this is all over,' he says, resting his chin on her capless kinked curls, 'I will build up High Stoke again, there will be no more talk of selling Hill House, I will work to make this house pay for itself.'

'We,' she reminds him. 'We shall both—'

'No!' Suddenly he grips her hard, lifts, throws her sideways. Even as her feet leave the ground, something flies past her.

'Henry!'

She clutches air, her head hits stone and she crumples onto straw. Henry? Around the edge of her fading awareness a wail of horror ripples.

37

Alice opens her eyes to a half-light similar to their curtained bed. She looks up at the four posts and wonders why they resemble Cassie's legs. Even the canopy slung above is just like Cassie's underside. She reaches up and the mattress rustles beneath her, someone must have changed the feather one for straw. Even the pillow is straw. Well, money is tight at High Stoke, they both know that, and you have to make savings where you can in such times. Someone has got rid of those old bed curtains, who would want them, falling to bits as they were?

The posts of the bed move and one of them kicks her in the shoulder, sending a sharp pain across her back. The illusion of her chamber shatters as Cassie dances perilously close, neighing in agitation, and Alice looks round at the stall where she lies. Straw rustles and Cassie's hooves stamp and sidestep, black-brown and disturbingly large this close. For a moment she stops, then dances again, one shoe ringing against a flint in the hard-packed floor. Head thumping, Alice gradually makes sense of her surroundings, scuffling noises reach her from beyond the stall, though from where she lies she cannot see what is happening.

'It's all right, Cassie, it's all right, girl,' Alice murmurs. Her voice calms the frightened animal, but her head sings as she pushes herself unsteadily to her knees. She whispers more words of comfort to quiet the mare, while she crawls from underneath. Then she sees Henry.

He is lying on the ground where they were standing together. His legs are bending and flexing as he struggles one-handed to push himself upright. His other hand clutches at his ribs. Between his fingers blood leaks. In a dread that threatens to paralyse her, Alice crawls on hands and knees to her husband. His mouth forms a smile as he looks up at her, but he is deathly pale.

Time halts meaningless as she sees the life pumping between his ribs. She yanks at his shirt. Blood spatters her face as she rips it from neck to waist to expose the gash under his heart. Puts her fingers to the hole but the blood simply leaks round. Wads his shirt, stuffing it over the wound, and it stays the flow for a few seconds before it becomes saturated and the blood escapes again. Another wad and temporary reprieve, then the flow once more. Her gown is of thicker linen and she bunches the skirt, plugging the hole hard until her fingers ache but always the blood wells up and round. He stirs. 'I'm hurting you,' she gasps, 'I'm sorry.'

'It's all right,' he whispers. 'I can't feel ….'

'I can't stop it.' She turns to shout for help. Remembers only Mollie will hear. And Sam is with Mollie. He is sure to come running. Henry? Or Sam? The impossible choice. The cry is stillborn.

'… so tired,' Henry sighs.

To Alice, staunching with her skirt, the point of no return already has her husband in its undertow. She talks endlessly to keep him aware, telling him comforting, reassuring lies that all will be well. She repeatedly makes fresh wads, while she watches the linen grow red, his face grow white. She strokes his cheek and it seems to soothe him; he turns his head into her hand, murmuring blood-smeared words through shallow, gasping breaths. 'Is … is …'

'Is what, Henry? What can I do, my dear?'

'Is … Isabel,' he breathes. 'The pitchfork. She is run mad.'

But surely not mad enough to harm Henry? The man she would marry if she could? 'She loves you. She would never hurt you, Henry.'

'Not me.' Weakly his head shakes. 'Not me.'

And the truth all at once stark. 'She came for me?' That was what flew past as Henry threw her aside. 'Oh, Henry, you took her attack yourself.'

'What else … ?' Breathing is becoming hard for him. Head

back, he opens his mouth as though he would gulp air but only manages shallow gasps. It sets him coughing bubbles of blood. His elbow crooks, his hand pushing feebly against the ground. Reading his wish, she hauls at his shoulders and sits him up. Wherever they touch each other, smears of red bear witness. He sags against her with a sigh, it might be of contentment, and she locks her arm round his shoulder to keep him upright. It makes no difference to the flow from his chest but his breathing is a little easier. One-handed she applies a fresh wad of skirt.

Somewhere beyond the warm red slick spreading down his breeches and soaking into the earth, beyond the smell of blood and straw, beyond the raftered gloom of the stables, trotting hooves approach. They slow to a halt, then a booted footfall. Someone calls, a voice she recognises.

'In here!' she shouts. 'The stables!'

The footsteps approach, the door is thrust back, light floods in and dry straw rustles across hard-packed earth. 'Mother of God!'

Henry's eyes flicker open. A shadow crosses behind her and a figure bends down by her side.

'Oliver,' Henry says. He might be greeting a guest, except that his voice is deathly tired. He even crooks a leg as though to rise.

'Stay put, Henry,' the other says. His hand gently but firmly on Henry's shoulder stays him. 'Let me see, mistress.' Oliver Sanderson, merchant of Guildford, father of three daughters who fluttered round Sylvia, member of the coroner's jury two days ago, a lifetime ago. He crouches down to look. She lifts the wad of linen, the flood pumps. There is a quick indrawn breath, a look exchanged, and mercifully no questions.

'Please help,' she says. 'Please. The apothecary.'

'Bit of a mess,' Henry whispers.

'Always a lot of blood, these chest wounds,' Oliver Sanderson responds in a firmly cheering voice. 'It's not that bad.'

'Fat lot you know,' Henry breathes, his eyes closing again.

Alice shifts her hold to a dry section of skirt, pressing it against the wound.

'I'm going for Middleton,' Sanderson says. 'He'll patch you up in no time. I'll be back before you know it.'

'Make haste,' she mouths.

Sanderson nods rising, a squeeze of her shoulder, a tight smile. Solid reliability. He passes behind her, she hears his running footsteps. Then the scrape of hooves as a horse is pulled sharply round, and the thud of a canter rapidly forced to a gallop that she can feel through the ground like a drumbeat, gradually receding, fading, until it is quiet once more in the stables.

Now Henry's eyelids waver and he mouths words that are between the two of them only; she tries to bolster but he reaches shaking fingers to her lips. In shallow gasps from a mind awash but not yet drowned, Henry is leaving his legacy. Words for her alone, with many a pause as the bright blood bubbles from his mouth, words drawn from their short time together, words of remembering, words of regret, words to sustain her. His eyes seem to sink into their darkening sockets, all the while gazing at her as though he would burn her image onto his mind. And she, with pauses to wipe his mouth clear, kisses those eyes, those lips, returns recollection, forgiveness, comfort. And during one of those pauses, resting in her hold, his eyes still on her face, he has gone.

38

Sticky and red. Whatever she touches comes away sticky and red. There is hardly any part of her that is not soaked in his gore. She hooked up her skirt when it was saturated, to get at her linen shift below, and for a while that held back the flow. Staunched but did not stop it. Like a river overflowing, the blood kept coming. She can hardly believe the volume of blood a human body can hold. It has soaked all the ground around him, and around her where she still kneels by him. Such a short while ago he was making love to her, his fingers causing her ecstasies as they brushed feather-like over her flesh, these fingers that now lie still and curled. These legs were wrapped round her, holding her to him, and she was pressed against his warm chest listening to the beat of the heart that is now stilled. The great gaping hole that pumped so much blood has finally stopped leaking. Now it is a small, neat round. It appears hardly large enough to have allowed such a copious flow.

Carefully she lays him down and sits up, running her sleeve across her eyes. Her head aches so much she is only dimly aware she has smeared more blood. She wonders why Oliver Sanderson came to High Stoke, there was no mention of a visit. Sanderson, the man whose maidservant Mary was going to make cloaks for Sylvia and Allan. A quiet man dressed in sober fashion, a man of calm good sense, a man riding hotfoot to summon the apothecary and his healing skills. Not that any skills can help now.

Henry's grey is restive, showing the white of its eye. Alice wipes her hands on a wisp of straw, to little purpose as the straw does not soak up but smears afresh. She pushes herself to her feet, the sodden shift under her skirt clinging cold to her shins as she goes to calm the frightened animal. It is ready for riding, of course, though the straps have not been tightened, and it will have to stay that way until Joe returns, the horse is too agitated for her to remove the saddle. As she approaches, the grey panics, throwing up its head, pulling on the headrope as it tries to rear. Of course, it is the smell of blood on her, she is just making things worse. If she goes nearer she risks being crushed against the side of the stall or trampled under its hooves. The best thing is to retreat and let the animal calm down in its own time. Alice edges away from the excited grey, and at this moment a voice at the stable door calls:

'Boy?'

In steps an elderly man, peering in the gloom. 'Boy!' he calls again, then stops, his eyes growing round as he catches sight of the body, the blood, the woman by the horse, her skirts soaked red. 'God save us all! What have you done, madam?' And before she can think, he has backed out of the stables, pulling the door closed. She hears him shouting, 'This way! Quickly!' He sounds panicked but also excited, and within seconds there is the growing clatter and splash of many hooves, and again he calls, 'Come quickly!'

Who are these people coming to High Stoke? Why? Who summoned them? The sound of several horses filing into the kitchen court, harness jangling. Booted feet thumping as riders dismount. Men calling, question and counter-question. At any second they will push in here at the bidding of that wretched little man who is calling to them again. Alice kneels down by Henry, placing herself between him and the door. She cannot bear that people she does not know should approach and cast their eyes down on him lying alone. She hauls his dead weight, head and shoulders, onto her lap and takes his unresponsive hand in hers. She waits, attentive to the scuff of boots, the murmuring of men.

The man she cannot place declares, 'Foul murder within, sirs!' and that hushes them. She wonders at his affected tones, the capacity to relish renown as the harbinger of dread news. Straw rustles as the stable door is pushed wide. In the cruel light the full extent of the blood spread is revealed to her.

'Here, see?' says the man, and screwing round she watches him beckon as though welcoming an honoured guest, a figure in dark cloth shot through with gold thread giving it the appearance of fresh dung. Has the coroner had the gall to come with witnesses to claim High Stoke publicly? She pulls Henry closer as though by doing so she can protect him.

Sir Malcolm Wipley approaches, his eyes adjusting from daylight to stable light. But whatever foul play he pictured, clearly this was not it. He stops dead, his astonishment at the sight before him as great as hers at seeing him here. Behind him the others are fanning out, a dozen at least, all men, craning their necks. A collective gasp swells to a babble, and here and there one at the back tries to push for a better view, but those in front will not lightly circumvent the coroner. It seems as much as Sir Malcolm can do to take a pace forward, then another, to verify for himself who lies there. They follow him in a tight vanguard but he commands them back with a staying hand, as though he fears their forward pressure will push him too close for comfort. They are all looking down, but where the men around him bob and peer, variously shocked and appalled, the coroner's amazement quickly fades to a stony stillness, concealing whatever he is thinking.

'He is dead,' Alice says, and the coroner gives her a long look but says nothing. She pushes back the kinked curls that have fallen over her face and can feel the stickiness matting her hair. 'My husband is dead.' In its stall the grey tosses its mane and whinnies, pulling against the tethering rope. Bloody marks smear its flank where she tried to lay calming hands. In the nearer stall Cassie stamps, unnerved by the crowd.

'It is as well I came in here, you see, Sir Malcolm,' says the elderly man. 'I caught her in the act.'

'Isabel did this,' Alice tells them.

'So,' the coroner says, 'I came to view one body and now there are two.' And now Alice understands why all these men are here, why Oliver Sanderson arrived. The coroner, believing Grace dead, has summoned his jury. Now she can place the excited little man, the one who found it inconvenient that Sylvia's death delayed his supper on Wednesday. Stanhope, that's his name, and he pipes up again, 'She was by the grey when I discovered her, Sir Malcolm. She was trying to escape! You have some explaining to do, madam,' he accuses.

Alice ignores him, too weary of spirit to refute his wild assumption. All she wants is to be left alone with Henry, to say her goodbye privately. During those last moments with him she could not quite admit to herself that the time was fast approaching when he would no longer be with her. Her husband of just ten days; the man she never thanked for his kindness, his understanding of her situation when he met her in Dorset. Who became a friend before he became a husband. Who saved her life and gave his own. Whose last words to her were that she should not mourn him but find the happiness he would not be able to give her himself. And then suddenly he was gone and she cannot place the moment, is unsure if she said enough to assure him of her love, to ease his mind before he slipped away.

'Please just leave us,' she says, rocking Henry in her arms. At this moment she feels the need of Charles Rutland, her vicar and tutor during her growing years in Dorset, for his experience of life, the comfort of his wisdom. But Charles Rutland is several days' ride away and she discounts the local man, Vicar Fitzsimmons. The last person she needs is the one who gave that hectoring sermon last Sunday. She moves her hand to gently close Henry's eyes and rests her cheek against his forehead. 'Just leave us.'

'You see, she destroys the evidence,' Stanhope declares.

'What evidence?' one of the jury asks.

Stanhope explains, 'The image of the murderer is reflected in a dead man's eyes.'

Alice was unaware of this, but surely she would have seen Isabel's image? She can recollect nothing but Henry's fixed gaze. 'Isabel,' she says again. 'Where is she? You have to find Isabel.'

Stanhope addresses the coroner. 'You saw her close his eyes, did you not, Sir Malcolm?'

'I did,' the coroner agrees. If anything, his expression has settled into satisfaction, as though a score is settled. 'Not that it makes any difference. There is evidence enough here to burn her ten times over.'

'Not me.' It is an effort to rouse herself to speak. 'Please listen to me. Isabel did this. My husband told me before he died—'

'Everyone into the house,' the coroner orders. 'We'll view the body properly later. Armstrong? You'll do. Bring her.' He turns on his heel. A stout-legged individual detaches himself from the rest and comes towards her.

'No, not now, not yet!' Alice protests. 'Please!' He takes her by the arms, not violently but decisively. She squirms from his touch. 'Let me stay with him, just for a little while?' she begs.

But he is brooking no opposition and proceeds to lift her. 'Come Mistress Jerrard.' He is neither cruel nor sympathetic, merely carrying out an order.

She still has hold of Henry. 'Then let me at least lay him down gently,' she pleads, and he yields his hold enough to allow her this respect to a dead man. She smoothes Henry's hair from his face and bends to kiss him but already Armstrong is pulling her away, raising her to her feet.

'Henry?' she calls as Armstrong propels her towards the door where the others have already gone. 'I shall come back, Henry,' as though he can hear. Just saying the words threatens to choke her. Her head still aching from the blow against the stall, she promises, 'I shall come back and sit with you, I give you my word.'

Outside the jurymen have already moved through the press of

horses in the yard, and the last of them are entering the kitchen. The ground is churned to mud and a couple of late arrivals slither to a halt, looking in stunned silence at the blood-soaked woman in Armstrong's escort. His hold on her is firm but not hostile, he even steers a course avoiding the muddiest patches of ground. And all she can think of is Henry's smile, his kindness, his fulfilment of that promise to take Sam up on the grey.

Sam! Mollie was in the kitchen preparing breakfast. Sam will be there too, will see Alice and rush towards her heedless. She pulls back. 'No, I can't go in there!' At her movement, some of the jury turn to look. Armstrong grips her close, as though foreseeing an attempt to escape. 'My son,' she pleads. 'He's in the house. He's very young. He mustn't see this – all this blood on me. Please!'

One of the jurymen steps forward. Slight and pasty-faced, in plain breeches and a sleeveless jerkin over his shirt, he makes a sign to Armstrong, *Give me a moment,* and looks around the kitchen, peers into the still room, walks away out of her sight. After a few moments he is back. 'There is no boy here, or in hall or screens passage, mistress.'

'A girl? A maidservant looking after him?'

'No one,' he assures her. Armstrong nudges her forward. Mollie, she recalls, grasped her hand in alarm when Alice brought the apothecary to examine her foot. The noisy booted arrival of the jurymen will have terrified her; she must have retreated with Sam to his chamber. *Stay there, Mollie, stay there.*

Amongst murmurs of speculation and discussion in the kitchen, Armstrong brings her in. Heads turn and a brief lull ensues. This is the woman many of them saw only two days ago, offering wine before they viewed Sylvia's body. Then, they accepted her as an inept new wife. It does not take much imagination on Alice's part to realise how they must see her now, a woman spattered with blood from bodice to hem, her hands and cuffs red, smears on her face and hair, the woman who has just tried to resist the hold on her. The jurymen step back and Armstrong leads her towards Sir Malcolm.

'Stand there where I can see you.' The coroner perches on the kitchen table. A few of the men, following his lead, seat themselves on the stools. Armstrong releases his hold on Alice but remains alongside. The men look at her, then at each other and one or two shake their heads. Collective condemnation without a word spoken.

'Where are the servants?' the coroner demands of her. 'Where's Isabel?'

'That's what I'm asking *you*. I didn't do this. She must have fled after she—'

'Well, the others then? Surely you have women to bring ale to all these men who have taken the trouble to rise so early?' Outrage at his demand threatens to overcome her. She lowers her eyes to conceal what she cannot yet control. 'Well?' he insists as she makes no answer.

She takes a deep breath. 'We are shorthanded,' she replies. He can wait for news that Grace is alive. If he knows she is on the top floor he is likely to send one of these men to fetch her. To serve him ale. 'They are out at various duties.'

'Sir Malcolm,' one of the men objects. 'We have no need of ale.' It is the man who forestalled Armstrong until he had checked Sam was not to be seen. From his plain but well-cut clothes, Alice reckons him probably a tailor. He looks uncomfortable drawing the attention of the whole company, possibly a man with just enough substance to be eligible for a coroner's jury. 'We should transact this dread business and go our ways. A search for this Isabel, to start with.' His fellow jurors give him no support, but equally no one gainsays him and he continues, 'Indeed, I could fetch old Florence from Tillotsons, she's a sympathetic soul, she's just the one to comfort Mistress Jerrard—'

'You are not looking at the facts,' the coroner cuts across him.

'You assume this woman is innocent. Consider what Stanhope saw. He foiled her escape attempt.'

'But she couldn't have mounted the grey in that humour,' another man objects. 'The brute would be lethal in an enclosed space.'

'She wouldn't know that,' the coroner says.

They are talking about her as though she is not there, and she breaks into the growing clamour. 'The grey could smell blood,' she tells them. 'Master Stanhope saw me trying to calm it.'

The coroner holds up a hand and they fall silent. 'Jerrard is dead. I say his wife here stabbed him in the chest.'

'I did not kill my husband!' Alice declares. 'It was Isabel. He told me she tried to attack me and in defending me he—'

'Hearsay,' he interrupts. 'As evidence, it's inadmissible. There are no others around,' he continues, 'and as you see, gentlemen, she is covered in his blood. There can be no doubt of your conclusion.'

'Where is the weapon, Sir Malcolm?' one asks. 'Should we not search for a knife?'

'She will have thrown it away by now,' Sir Malcolm says. 'The weapon is not important.'

'I can tell you what weapon was used,' Armstrong says. 'I've seen enough such injuries in my time farming to know. That was no knife wound. It was made by a pitchfork tine.'

'How can you be so sure?' one of the jurymen asks. 'A knife, a tine, the one can go as deep as the other.'

'I saw it closer than any of you,' Armstrong declares. 'It was a round wound, a puncture, not a slit. Somebody attacked Jerrard with a pitchfork.'

The two of them standing in close embrace, that habit Henry had of propping his chin on her head; that's how he saw it coming. In that instant he threw her aside. A split second earlier and they would both still be alive; a split second later and it would be she who was dead.

'It's what I'm trying to tell you,' Alice insists. 'Isabel wanted to kill *me*.'

'Isabel this, Isabel that.' Sir Malcolm jabs a finger at her. 'You don't like her, do you? I saw that two days ago.'

'I have tried to accommodate her,' Alice tells him, 'but she resists me at every turn.'

'Ah, so you were the one with the pitchfork, attacking Isabel.'

'No, she—'

'Typical woman,' the coroner says addressing the men. 'Aims at one target and hits another.' There is an uneasy ripple of laughter, quickly suppressed. Alice tries again.

'My husband threw me aside to protect me from Isabel and took the pitchfork between his ribs.'

'A likely story,' Sir Malcolm scoffs. 'Isabel fighting with Jerrard, overcoming a man his size? So where's the pitchfork, madam?'

'She must have …' She can hardly say the words, 'pulled it out.' Nausea grips her at a vision of the curved tine. She, meanwhile, lying under Cassie's legs, momentarily witless.

Stanhope raises his hand like a schoolboy dying to tell what he knows. 'I can tell you where the pitchfork is, Sir Malcolm.'

'Well?'

'Follow me, Sir Malcolm,' Stanhope says, visibly swelling with self-importance.

'Keep her secured,' the coroner orders Armstrong, who takes her arms once more and marches her out of the kitchen behind the rest. There is a relentless constancy about his hold that tells her he will maintain it if so required until the bailiffs arrive to take her to the town gaol. She wonders what the gaol is like, whether it really is as Jack described it, piss on the floor and food thrown through the bars. *Don't think about it. That way lies weakness.*

Outside, the kitchen court is empty of horses. Hoof prints abound in the churned mud but the jury's mounts have wandered away past the woodshed and are cropping the grass by the track. The clouds have fulfilled their grey promise and it is raining again.

Stanhope slides and nearly falls on the slippery ground. The others follow, treading cautiously. Her arms pinioned, Alice cannot hold up her skirt and feels it drag in the mud. They follow Stanhope across the court to the wash-house where he stands, chest puffed, one arm stretched out, as though awaiting a trumpet fanfare.

Jammed against the wash-house door is the pitchfork Joe uses to shift hay. One of the tines is red for a finger's length from its tip. Alice doubles over, gagging. *The point sank in all that way. Henry saw it coming and threw her aside, took it in his own chest. Last night she accused Henry of not facing his responsibilities. The point must have been agony when Isabel drove it in, worse when she wrenched it out.* Alice feels the tears well and slide down her face.

Clustered around the wash-house door, the jurymen's surprised questions come thick and fast.

'Is this it?'

'Must be, look at the blood on it.'

'What's it doing here? Love of God, it's jammed fast.'

'Why jam the door shut?'

And a joking rejoinder, 'To keep the washerwoman in her place?' Subdued chuckles break out. *How can they stand there laughing while my husband lies dead?*

One of them frees the fork; the joker edges the wash-house door open and with exaggerated caution peers in. 'No washerwoman, only her clothes.' It raises isolated sniggers.

'Looks like she's escaped through that broken window.' A few jostle to look.

'That's the pitchfork I told you of,' Alice insists. 'Isabel killed my husband with it. She was trying to kill me.'

'A likely story, she's worked here for years, we all know her,' Sir Malcolm says. 'A pattern of modesty and discretion.' *How well he thinks of Isabel now. Yet when she fawned on him, he ignored her.*

'We couldn't find her this morning,' Alice goes on. 'She must have been in the stable already, lying in wait—'

'Whereas we do not know you. Suddenly we find you've snapped up Jerrard and here you are, setting the household by the ears. Sending a maidservant off on her own to be murdered by her seducer. Then you pretend to lock the seducer in that wash-house.'

'Sir Malcolm,' she objects, 'you yourself gave Isabel the keys—'

'So he escapes and off he goes to kill another maidservant.'

'Grace is not—'

'You come from outside this area, don't you? Somewhere no one has ever heard of. What does that say, I wonder?'

'Nothing, Sir Malcolm! Except that you are as strange to me as I am to you, but I do not accuse you of murder!'

'An outsider in our midst, playing with words to challenge the law.' She is conscious of the jury looking silently on. There is no Oliver Sanderson to plead with the voice of reason, no Apothecary Middleton to give an informed medical opinion. The tailor has subsided into silence. Whatever the jury are thinking, to a man they are going along with the coroner. He has undermined her by isolating her in their eyes. She can feel the weight of their opinion like a wall. The new wife, the outsider.

Her head aches more than ever but she ploughs on. 'You brought Grace home, perhaps that makes you guilty of murder, Sir Malcolm?'

'Have a care whom you slander, madam!'

'And Allan is not guilty either! He stands accused of murder for no better reason than bringing Sylvia home!'

'He was determined to escape marrying the wench.'

'He was not the father of her child!'

'Next you'll be saying I am!' he challenges. It is a sharp stroke on his part, perilous, but he is a risk-taker as she knows. One who would creep through another's house and falsify the evidence around a dead girl in order to implicate an innocent man. One who would risk his very reputation by using loaded dice to cheat another of his birthright. One who knows his power, who can gauge his adversary, as he gauged Henry, as he has gauged her. Sir Malcolm's relations with Sylvia he has admitted – boasted – but only in private, no witnesses. If she challenges him on that, Alice will only fix a nail in her own coffin. The jury have heard the coroner's scepticism and now they have seen the accused woman lose every point by which she tries to evade justice.

The rain has soaked through her hair and is dripping from its ends, spotting her chemise watery red. The men, protected by their hats and cloaks, do not seem to notice, or don't care. Impotent anger ignites a shivering that she cannot control.

'Henry Jerrard has been murdered,' announces the coroner. 'And his wife is his killer. We are agreed?' A few shrugs but mostly nodding heads. This can't be happening! Alice sweeps a furious look round the group of jurymen.

'Are you going to allow this! Allow him to pass judgement when you haven't even viewed my husband's body as he promised you? Without even listening to me?' They look at each other, look at the coroner. No one meets her eye.

'Remember, gentlemen,' the coroner sweeps on, 'we're here to make a decision, not to get proof, nor to be swayed by a lying murderess. Townsend will gather all the proof needed.'

Alice glares at the jurymen. 'Why are you here?' she demands. 'All you do is stand around like so many sheep!'

Sir Malcolm jabs a finger at her. 'Hold your tongue, woman! You, Stanhope, do you ride into town and tell the Sheriff's officer to bring bailiffs to arrest this woman. Then go to Justice Townsend's house and tell him he has an investigation to carry out.'

'Sir Malcolm, he will be at his prayers these two hours yet.'

'Then you had better prepare yourself for a long wait.' Stanhope slithers across the kitchen court to fetch his mount from the group by the woodshed, an act that rapidly embarrasses him as the other horses jostle him. He becomes agitated, waving his arms and shouting at the horses, which further hampers his efforts to reach his cob. The group stands in the rain watching this new entertainment. Finally with much scrabbling and cursing he is mounted. Red-faced he doffs his hat to the coroner and turns the horse's head for town.

They are gathering to move back into the house when the sound of hooves swells and a rider trots into view through the press of horses. Apothecary Middleton addresses the coroner. 'My apologies, Sir Malcolm, I was called to a mother in childbed at Clandon.' The sight of Alice, blood-spattered, seizes his attention. 'Mistress Jerrard, you are hurt!' Sliding from his mount, he reaches for his bag. 'What has happened?'

'Didn't Master Sanderson tell you?' she asks him.

'Oliver? No, what has Oliver to do with this?'

'He came upon me while … he rode to find you. My husband, in the stables.'

Middleton turns on his heel and heads for the stable. The coroner calls after him, 'Nothing you can do, Middleton,' but they all crowd into the stable anyway.

Unexpectedly, Armstrong says to her, 'Would you rather not go in?'

'I want to be there,' she says. 'Please.' He guides her in and causes the men to part until she can see.

The apothecary is kneeling by Henry, looking for signs of life. Surely, Henry has moved a little since she laid him down? She watches, holding her breath as Middleton places a hand over the heart, lifts an eyelid. He draws out a square of polished metal and holds it in front of Henry's lips, waits an age to her feverish counting, checks it. Holds it to Henry's mouth again. He must have a reason for re-checking. Is that some faint breath misting the mirror's surface? She wants to say, Feel his neck. That will tell you. It told me Grace was still alive. Even the faintest echo of the heart means life. Means hope.

As though the thought has transferred, Middleton rests his fingertips on Henry's neck. Waits, moves his fingers a fraction. Yes? Waits again. Then he rises and quietly returns the mirror to his bag. 'Mistress Jerrard, I am so sorry that this has come upon you.'

It was a fool's hope.

'If there is any means by which I or my wife can help, I beg you will say.'

'Save your breath, Middleton, she's just murdered him.' Sir Malcolm says.

'Oh, for heaven's sake!' Alice whispers, despairing.

The apothecary frowns. 'Will someone please explain to me how I was called overnight to form a jury, where this man is dead but a matter of minutes?'

'It's the dairymaid we were called to see,' one says. 'Now it's Jerrard as well.'

'Two?' Middleton breathes. 'And the witnesses?'

'The boy who killed the maidservant Sylvia was recaptured last night next to another maidservant's body,' Sir Malcolm says. 'And you can see by the blood on her,' indicating Alice, 'that the prisoner here had just murdered Jerrard when we arrived. No need of witnesses.'

'I didn't, I tell you! I didn't! You won't listen to me! Why are you so determined to accuse without reason?'

Middleton turns to the coroner. 'You asked me to be of your jury, Sir Malcolm. It seems to me in this matter of Henry Jerrard you may have reached a conclusion with uncalled-for haste. Where are your witnesses, I say again? Why does Mistress Jerrard feel her testimony is ignored? Perhaps you should listen to all views before you pronounce.'

'You weren't here, Middleton,' the coroner says and his voice has an edge of triumph as he adds, 'She was caught red-handed. Literally, as you see. Armstrong confirms she used the stable pitchfork, you can see it for yourself out in the yard.'

'I didn't, you stupid man!' Alice cries. 'Isabel did! Why won't you look for Isabel? If you won't listen to me, surely you will allow Apothecary Middleton a hearing?'

'And now slander as well,' the coroner says. 'Gentlemen, this *fishwife* with her foul language hardly deserves our notice.' There is a general nodding of heads but the apothecary is not satisfied.

'Look at me, Sir Malcolm, gentlemen. There is blood here on my knee where I knelt, on my cuffs, my hands. Am I guilty of murder?'

'You need not be so specific, Middleton.' The coroner turns his back but the apothecary perseveres.

'This is not justice, Sir Malcolm, what is your reasoning? Mistress Jerrard protests her innocence and yet it appears you have not even listened to what she has to say.'

'She has offered a pack of lies with just enough of truth to trap a weak understanding. And I thank you for your musings, Middleton, but I have jurymen enough without you. We are agreed she's guilty. Townsend will gather the evidence to prove it. Now, gentlemen,' the coroner addresses the rest, 'I suggest we repair to the house. We have another body to inspect, the reason I assembled you. Bring her, Armstrong,' he says. He turns, thrusting through the jurymen, closely followed by the apothecary whispering angrily in his ear and glancing back at Alice. Her shoulders droop. *You waste your time, Master Middleton, he's deaf to entreaty.* She feels Armstrong's firm grip again as he propels her forward and they follow the straggling line of the rest variously trotting and sliding on the treacherous ground.

They pass through the kitchen and in the hall she stands mute as the coroner looks around, opens the door into the winter parlour and peers. 'Where is the wench's body, madam? I warned you on pain of prosecution not to touch the body. Where have you put her?'

'Not upstairs in the small chamber,' she flashes back. 'I cannot tell what might happen to another body in there.' One or two puzzled looks are exchanged but no one asks her meaning. She would like to tell all these respectable men what their coroner did in the small chamber before the jury trooped in to view Sylvia's body. But it would be the word of an accused woman against that of Sir Malcolm with whom they have already sided. Another nail for her coffin.

Sir Malcolm ignores her taunt. 'Where is the body?' he repeats.

'There is no body. You were in error, sir. Perhaps you should have taken Master Middleton on your search last night. He could have told you she had knocked herself senseless in a fall, became chilled in the rain, and needed warmth and a dry bed to recover.' Alice turns her back on him and addresses the apothecary. 'Master Middleton, would you do me the kindness of stepping up to the maidservants' chambers in the attics, to verify for yourself and these gentlemen that my dairymaid Grace is alive and recovering?'

'Gladly, Mistress Jerrard,' he says.

'Though she cannot yet walk,' she adds, to ensure Grace is not summoned to serve ale. He bows briefly before turning to leave the hall, his small show of respect warming her heart.

'Please do not wake Betsy,' she calls.

'You see?' Sir Malcolm says. 'The prisoner doesn't want the servants to know what she has done.'

Alice gathers the shreds of her patience. 'Betsy was out late last night searching for Grace,' she explains. 'And then watched over her while she recovered. Betsy has earned her rest.'

With the apothecary gone, Alice looks round the group of men now murmuring amongst themselves. The tailor has placed himself, as though in solidarity, just two paces away from her. He gives her a quick, encouraging smile. As if to crush even that small comfort, Sir Malcolm moves to regain his ascendancy. 'Even if the dairymaid is alive, it does not alter the case,' he declares.

'This murder of your man is a far more serious affair, madam.' Sir Malcolm takes his seat in the chair at the head of the table, the chair Henry occupied when he and she dined the day they arrived, Isabel herself serving him the oysters she knew he loved, keeping his glass charged, standing at his shoulder and doing her best to ignore Alice. Where is Isabel now? What will the anguish of her act do to her mind?

'Many a long year since we've had a burning in the town,' the coroner muses.

Before they take me to gaol, I must get a message to Olivia about Sam.

'I imagine it will draw quite a crowd.' No one answers the coroner, they all seem to be looking down at their feet or out of the window.

Alice forces her thoughts away from agonising death by fire, strives to concentrate on Sam's future. *First his mother and sister, now Henry and me. He won't understand. I promised him I would always be there.*

The coroner tries again. 'They burned the last one on the castle green, didn't they?'

Poor Sam. If Olivia will send word to Dorset, there are those who will look after him when I am gone.

At last, someone says, 'Castle's privately owned now. I doubt he'd want a burning on his land.' Silence falls once again on the hall.

Perhaps I can persuade Olivia to send Mollie as well, Sam is fond of her and it will cushion the blow.

One or two look up as they hear the apothecary returning along the screens passage. From the doorway he announces, 'Mistress Jerrard has the right of it.'

'The prisoner,' the coroner corrects him.

Middleton continues. 'As Mistress Jerrard said, the dairymaid Grace is well, albeit with a bruised face and a badly turned ankle, both of which require only time to heal.'

A dozen heads turn enquiring looks on the coroner, who shrugs and makes the best of it. 'A good thing we found that villain before he harmed her further,' he says.

'And she is anxious to confirm,' continues the apothecary, 'that she was not attacked but fell at a rabbit hole.' Alice sends him a grateful look across the room. But the apothecary has further news. 'In fact, the dairymaid had just met a goose-girl,' he goes on. In growing alarm Alice listens as he innocently implicates the child Hannah who is dependent on the coroner for her paltry scratched living. 'The girl told her that on Wednesday she saw the maidservant Sylvia lying by the way, *before* the boy Allan discovered her.'

'She says so, does she?' the coroner says with narrowed eyes.

From his place near Alice, the tailor nervously ventures, 'From what has been said here, that suggests to me that the boy Allan is not guilty of murder, since the one is alive unmolested and the other was already dead when he found her.' Alice is beginning to like this man who has the courage to challenge the coroner. The nods he receives encourage him to continue. 'I believe, Sir Malcolm, as soon as the goose-girl has laid her Information, we must review our verdict and release the boy.'

'Except that this will be my goose-girl you speak of,' Sir Malcolm says, shaking his head, the picture of kindly disillusion. 'Alas, she likes to see herself as an object of general interest. She habitually makes up stories from scraps she picks up, in which she figures as a person of importance. I have caught her out before in her lying.' Alice can see, as though it is happening before her, the threats that will be made to silence Hannah.

'I still think we should talk to her,' the tailor says looking around, but the brief support has melted away, most of the others will not meet his eye.

'Oh, never worry, I shall talk with her,' Sir Malcolm assures him. 'I shall have the truth from her.'

No Information will be laid. Hannah will be compelled by whatever means will secure her compliance. With the best of intentions, Apothecary Middleton has just signed Allan's death warrant. Though Allan is cleared of wrongdoing towards Grace, the charge of Sylvia's murder will stick.

'Ah, at last!' the coroner says, his attention drawn across the hall. 'Bring ale and mugs, girl, these men are thirsty.'

Alice strains to see over the heads of the men blocking her view. One of them moves, and there in the doorway stands Mollie.

39

Mollie is soaked to the skin. Her hair hangs in glistening rats' tails and her sodden shift sticks to her arms, the patched skirts clinging. Her mouth works but no sound comes out.

'Ale and mugs! Go!' the coroner orders. Still Mollie stands there, and her lack of response starts to look like defiance. The eyes of those present dart between coroner and scullion. It must be common knowledge that when the coroner barks, it is politic to jump, yet here is one who is not jumping. An air of expectancy spreads in the hall, and with it, the sense that the coroner's authority is being challenged.

'Oh God,' he says throwing up his hands. 'She's simple as well as dumb. Fetch Isabel, girl. She'll know what to do.'

'Is... Isa... bb... bel—'

Alice has never heard this voice before. It is laboured, unpractised, the breath quickly running out at each syllable. 'Mollie?'

'Is – a – bel,' Sir Malcolm mouths, syllable by syllable, as though speaking to a simpleton. 'Fetch her. Now!' He makes shooing motions.

'Isab ... bel – is n...not ...'

'Jesu, it's enough to try the patience of a saint,' he sighs. 'Get rid of her, someone.' He flicks a hand in Mollie's direction. The jury stand as though rooted. A hushed wariness has fallen on them.

'Mollie! Where is Sam?' Alice calls.

Mollie opens her mouth, but 'Get rid of her, I say!' the coroner bawls.

'Sir Malcolm, can you not see?' says the tailor.

'See what, man? I see a disobedient menial and a lot of louts standing around as though you're all afraid of her.' He rises and proceeds to advance on Mollie still standing in the doorway.

'Sir Malcolm, no!' the tailor pleads, grasping the coroner's arm. 'You must not!'

The coroner scowls at the hand on his sleeve. 'You dare detain me, sir?'

'Sir, we all know this girl is dumb,' the tailor explains, 'yet she speaks. You should not approach her.'

Murmurs of agreement accompany this advice. 'Surely she has been visited by the Holy Spirit!' one says, and nods of agreement ripple round the jury. A collective awareness of the gift of tongues causes a general retreat from Mollie's vicinity. Despite Sir Malcolm's outrage, no one moves to do his bidding. It is not a case of disobeying the coroner. A higher authority is present. No man is going to lay hands on one touched by God.

And now, behind Mollie in the doorway, Jack Egerton, drawing the eyes of all present.

'You! What are you doing here?' the coroner asks, echoing Alice's baffled thought. 'I sent for Townsend, not you.' His tones are irritable, and yet Alice can also hear relief. The arrival of Justice Egerton has eased the coroner's position, drawn attention away from his breached authority.

'I was summoned by this young woman,' Egerton says, indicating Mollie.

'Summoned?' the coroner scoffs, throwing himself back in Henry's chair. 'By that one?'

'Mollie, where is Sam? Please, where is Sam?' Alice cries.

'He is safe,' Jack answers her. 'He is with Olivia, and he will remain with us until you are ready to collect him.'

'Oh, thank God,' Alice says, accepting though not understanding, and feels her mouth tremble with the struggle to utter the next words. 'Henry's dead, Jack.'

'I know, my dear,' Jack says gently. 'Wipley, would you care to tell me what's going on?' They part for him as he crosses the hall to the coroner. Seated as he is, Sir Malcolm is obliged to look up to address him.

'She's murdered Jerrard. We caught her in the act.'

'I think not.'

'You're the one who's always talking about proof, Egerton.' The coroner points at Alice. 'Look at her, she's drenched in it!'

'You have witnesses?'

'I don't need witnesses for an open-and-shut case. I have already pronounced.'

Jack indicates Mollie. 'I mean witnesses such as this young woman, who saw all that happened,' he continues. 'She will be laying an Information with me as soon as we can sit down together with quill and paper.'

'Not another one.' The coroner rolls his eyes.

One of the jury explains. 'There's a goose girl who's been making up stories about seeing the serving wench dead before the boy Wenlock "found" her. Now this one.'

Sir Malcolm adds, 'Look at her, her brain's addled, she's dumb.'

'And yet everyone in this hall has just heard her speak,' Jack says. 'Mollie, will you tell these gentlemen what you told me?'

Mollie's eyes grow round, her mouth opens. They wait, seconds pass, nothing comes out. 'Master Egerton should go to her,' Alice urges Sir Malcolm. 'He should stand by her and she will take courage from it.'

'And he can prompt her what to say,' the coroner says nastily as Jack returns to the doorway.

'I object to that, sir!' Middleton protests.

At Mollie's side, Jack takes her hand. 'You see your mistress there, Mollie? She needs you to tell these gentlemen the truth. Tell them what you saw.'

Now Mollie is looking up into Jack's face. He waits quietly, as Mollie takes a breath, then another, and swallows hard. At last the mangled words start to come. 'I saw … Isab … Isabel.

The p…pitch…fork. She tried to … s…s…stab the … m…mistress, but … the master … threw her. The f…fork … went in … she … …' Mollie, her eyes still fixed on Jack's face, opens and closes her mouth, opens it again, but no sound comes out, and the tears stand in her eyes.

'Take it slowly, Mollie,' Jack encourages. 'Say just what you said to me before.' There is tense silence in the hall as they wait.

Mollie nods and swallows, takes another breath. 'It went in … his chest. Isabel … she pulled …he fell. She went to … to kill … the m…mistress … I fought … p…pushed her … the wash-house.'

'So *she* jammed the wash-house door,' says one of the jury members to his fellows on either side.

'Yes, and Isabel's escaped through the window,' says another, and a ripple of speculation runs between them. They are immediately hushed by the rest but the interruption proves too much for Mollie. Though they wait, no further words come.

Jack addresses Sir Malcolm. 'I think you have the essence of it there, Wipley. Isabel attacked with murderous intent, and in defending his wife, Henry took the fork full in the chest.'

'No woman could wield a pitchfork with such force,' the coroner says.

'A moment ago you had Mistress Jerrard well capable of such an act,' Armstrong reminds him.

'Perhaps the prisoner grazed his rib with it, enough to bring him down.' He points at Alice. 'Jerrard threw her off and Isabel went to his rescue. That's what this wench here saw and misunderstood. You've only to see all the blood on the prisoner to know that she finished off the job just before we arrived.'

'I see,' Jack Egerton says. 'So Mistress Jerrard was thrown aside, and while Mollie and Isabel grappled with the pitchfork, Mistress Jerrard finished off the job with what?'

'A knife?' The coroner tries to retrieve his position. 'She could easily fetch a knife from the kitchen.'

'There was only one strike,' Middleton points out, 'and that was from the tine of the pitchfork.'

The coroner casts a malevolent look at Jack. 'Before you came in, Egerton, this was a clear-cut case. The prisoner was on the scene, she is covered in blood, and when she heard us coming Stanhope caught her leaping for a horse to escape. My entire jury is perfectly satisfied she killed Henry Jerrard. Now you start raising issues of finicking detail, and between you and Middleton here, you have confounded their minds.'

Armstrong turns, feet planted wide. 'I for one am not confounded.' The jerkin strains across his broad shoulders as he folds his arms and fixes his eyes on the coroner. 'I already said, the wound was round, as you would get from a fork with curved round tines. It was not a knife wound.' There is no deference in his voice, he is stating a fact.

Sir Malcolm stares back but says nothing. Others now challenge, and more add their voices as they watch the balance of opinion tip, demanding a reversal of his pronouncement. After a few seconds his glance falls. It is over. And since Justice Egerton has supplied the key witness, they want Egerton as the investigating justice. Curtly, the coroner instructs him to look into Henry Jerrard's death, with a view to charging Isabel when she is found. The jury breaks into small, chattering groups. Armstrong has not resumed his hold on Alice since he relinquished it when Mollie spoke. Now he moves away to link up with others of the jury.

Alice crosses to Mollie standing by the door, takes her hands. Mollie's face is shadowed with guilt.

'You did right to take Sam away,' Alice tells her, 'and you must not blame yourself for this. Isabel was run mad yesterday in the accounts room and I didn't properly understand. I saw her again in the middle of the night and I should have taken heed. This was not your fault, it was Isabel's only.' She releases Mollie's hands. 'Now, surely you must be hungry for your breakfast. Do you find something in the still room and take it up to the women's bedchambers. Take enough for Grace and Betsy too.'

The hall is emptying. Alice looks around for the tailor but he must have slipped away, she would like to have thanked him for his support in the face of opposition. Middleton approaches Alice to apologise for his haste in taking his leave, 'But I have several patients I must see.' Of course, she understands that, she says, and tries to express her gratitude. She watches his stout, black-clad figure head down the screens passage. His job is to treat the living, not concern himself with the dead.

Only Jack and Sir Malcolm remain in the hall. With the threat lifted, Alice crosses the hall to the settle by the hearth. She droops onto it, sinking her face in her hands, overcome with a vision of Henry's eyes in that fixed stare. Her head is still thumping and nausea threatens again as the floor goes round and round.

'Well, Egerton, now that you have interfered with my arrangements,' Sir Malcolm is saying with ungracious emphasis, 'I must needs go into town to ensure Stanhope does not haul Townsend untimely from his prayers. And I suppose I must hope he has not already ordered the bailiffs out.'

Jack says. 'If you will give me a moment I shall accompany you.'

'I can't wait more than a minute or two,' the coroner tells him, his heavy boots resounding on the flags as he walks away.

She feels the movement as Jack seats himself at the other end of the settle. She raises her head. The world steadies. She knows she must give Jack the bare facts before Sir Malcolm paints his poisonous slant on events.

'Henry was coming to see you,' she says. 'He had much to tell you. The paper that Sam found in Master Tillotson's gown pocket. Henry took it from Sylvia, but he did not kill her. That truly was an accident.' Briefly she fills in the details of Sylvia's flight, of Henry overtaking her, wresting the paper from her, of Sylvia's swoon that killed her as her head hit the sharp flint, of Henry's flight. She tells him how Henry hid the paper in a book, how the coroner by chance found it. She tells him what is promised in the pledge, by which Sir Malcolm Wipley will soon be the new owner of High Stoke and Jack's neighbour. Jack nods, grim-faced, taking this in.

'Are you coming, Egerton?' Sir Malcolm shouts from the screens passage.

'A moment only,' Jack calls.

She asks him, 'You knew Henry gambled?'

'I have not heard of him gaming for a year or more.'

'Sir Malcolm cheated with Fulham dice,' she whispers. 'I suppose he has found and destroyed them long since, they were not in Master Tillotson's gown, and without them I am powerless to hold onto High Stoke.'

He nods slowly, his face thoughtful, that lower lip jutting, then seems to gather himself. 'Will you give me time to think about this?' he asks. 'I believe we may be able to negotiate something. Will you allow me to help you?'

Alice, in some indeterminate way wanting to fight, finds the idea of negotiation disappointing. Does he honestly think the coroner smugly holding all the cards is going to negotiate? But what else is there? She nods reluctant agreement.

At the doorway, the coroner slaps his gloves repeatedly against his thigh. 'I'm waiting!'

Jack calls, 'I am with you directly.' As they rise she grasps his sleeve and whispers, 'Jack, Sir Malcolm's goose girl, Hannah. You must find her before he gets to her. She saw Allan find Sylvia but Wipley will intimidate her to prevent her laying her Information. He has called her a liar but do not believe it!'

'My dear Alice,' Jack says, equally low-voiced, 'why do you think I'm accompanying him into town? I shall ensure Wipley goes straight to the sheriff's office and I shall divert up to Poyle to find Hannah. Be easy. Allan will be released. I am sorry to leave you but—'

'You must go,' she says, crossing the hall alongside him. 'I am not alone, Jack, I have my household.' But not Henry, she thinks. Not Henry.

'Olivia is on her way,' he tells her. 'She was rising when I left and told me to tell you she will be here as soon as may be.' And with that he re-joins the coroner and they take their leave.

Alice stands at the kitchen door as they mount up and turn their horses for town. The jingle of harness persists after they have splashed out of view, fading until all is quiet. She takes a deep breath and crosses the kitchen court to make good her last promise to Henry.

40

The first stumbling blocks are over, the worst is behind her. That is what Alice tells herself. Nothing can ever touch that terrible day for horror, and now, nearly two weeks later, in a strange reversal, it is as though she feels nothing. She wakes each morning and gets through the day. It gives her no time for sitting, no time for thinking, and she is glad of it. She does all her thinking at night, and it is the same every night. What has happened to Isabel? No one has seen the steward since that day. Where is she? In the darkness Alice's heart jolts every time the house creaks, or one of the women servants crosses the attic chamber upstairs.

Alice wants nothing more than to be busy, and there are all those around her who need her there to give direction. It is clear to her that the household are suffering much from the violent change in their lives. Grief takes them in different ways.

Maureen has been sullen and silent since she returned grumbling from the milking and came up short at the sight of Alice emerging blood-spattered from the stables, followed by Angus and Joe carrying Henry's body on a hurdle. Alice tried to soften Maureen's shock by explaining Isabel's crazed attack, but it is as though Maureen, as Isabel before her, blames Alice for bringing disaster on them all. Alice wonders if Maureen would even admit if she knows where Isabel is.

Joe is angrier than ever. For all his truculence, Alice sees now that Joe worshipped Henry, looked up to him as a model of manly conduct. He cannot forgive himself for not staying in the stables to see Henry mounted.

'I could have foiled it,' he keeps saying. 'I could have stopped her.'

Alice has tried giving him more responsibility, some repair jobs around the house, and hopes it will help. Often, she too catches herself thinking … *If only.*

If only I had realised. Isabel was plainly outside herself in the accounts room after the bailiffs' visit. She was clearly unsound, wandering through the house in the dark that night. If only. And Alice wonders when Isabel will next creep to her door in the dark. She gives repeated instructions about securing the house at night, then waits until everyone has gone to bed, and goes and checks anyway.

Angus's face has taken on a look of permanent perplexity. A man of few words and little experience, his life from boyhood has been with the Jerrards of High Stoke, first with Henry's parents, then with Henry.

'I thought it would be for ever,' he said to Alice when she went to sit with him in the woodshed. 'For ever.'

So did I, she thinks, and she has no answer for him.

When she wakes in the dark she goes round the house again, checking all the windows and doors. Two, three, four times a night.

Grace hardly knew Henry. He was the rarely seen head of the house, and for her, life without a man at the helm is barely sustainable. She wants to make her contribution to help Alice in this precarious state, and has started producing more of her soft cheese, which she sells with the excess butter at market in the high street. Alice has utterly failed to convince her that it is such acts of quiet, practical help that strengthen High Stoke's little community. And Alice needs to feel there is strength in some measure at High Stoke; she has an enduring sense of powerlessness against the threat of Isabel. Where is she? What is she plotting? How long before she comes back?

Allan was released through Jack's prompting earlier than he might otherwise have been, and he appears to suffer mixed feelings. Relief at the lifting of a death threat, a stunned incomprehension of Isabel's frenzied attack, bewilderment at Grace's coldness towards him.

Alice has suggested that he accepts Grace's avoidance. 'Give her time. Take comfort that she does not reject you outright,' Alice tells him. 'Your behaviour has been far less than it should, and Grace cannot be rushed into accepting you.' Part of Alice wishes the two of them were reconciled and married. Then Allan would be sleeping in that end room in the house, ready to call. To her fear that Isabel might break into the house, has been added the terror that Isabel might enter the house to hide unseen by day and spread havoc and murder by night.

Ned came up from his strip to offer condolences, though his wife spoiled it by interrupting to ask for a piece of land next to their cottage.

Vicar Fitzsimmons tried her patience sorely when she and Olivia went to see him. He would be honoured to conduct Master Jerrard's funeral, he said in unctuous tones, but when Alice requested that Sylvia be allowed to lie in a side-chapel until her family could collect her, he made it clear he would have naught to do with The Whore. Biting down her fury, Alice asked what happened to forgiveness, and it was only Olivia's smoothing that prevented a rift. Olivia traced Sylvia's family through old Florence at Tillotsons. They collected their 'shining star' as her mother tearfully described her to Alice, and Alice is glad she arranged the winding-sheet round Sylvia in her coffin so that her condition was disguised. In a sad little procession of parents and brothers, Sylvia's family took her back to Kingston, some twenty miles distant and outside Vicar Fitzsimmons' narrow influence, to give her a Christian burial.

Jack and Constable Hart searched the area on the Long Down and found the flint that Henry had thrown, Sylvia's blood dried on it. They restored it to its depression in the ground and summoned the coroner to this proof of Sylvia's accidental death. It might not be strictly the law, but Alice feels it is justice.

Sam is back with Alice. There have been tears and Alice is minded to keep a close eye on his wellbeing, he has already lost too many family members in his young life. Alice is more than ever keen to formally adopt him and Olivia has undertaken to revive the subject with Jack. Without prompting, Mollie has assumed the role of Sam's nurse. With Sam she still displays elements of childhood, and the two find escape together. But Mollie's tussle with Isabel, the sight of Henry felled with a pitchfork, her flight with Sam to Freemans, and the utterance she forced from herself, all these have taken their toll on her bright innocence and Alice catches her sometimes in troubled thought. Though Mollie occasionally emits a word or two, she has never again strung sentences together as she did that day, to confound the coroner's hasty verdict and release Alice from a charge of murder.

Twice in that one day, Alice keeps thinking, Mollie saved my life.

She resists with difficulty the urge to bring Sam into her chamber at night. Her heart thumps as she imagines Isabel lurking in the chamber passage. Alice wrestles this way and that with the question whether Sam will be safer sleeping with her, or staying with Mollie in his own chamber. And whether the act of leaving Mollie to sleep with Sam will be a danger to Mollie herself.

Olivia is at High Stoke most of the time, staying overnight, and occasionally riding back by day to check on the welfare of the Freemans household. 'It will be very well for Jack to be without me for a while,' she assures Alice when she demurs, pricked by conscience. 'He goes off and leaves me for journeys he makes on the King's business. He may learn now what that is like for me, and to appreciate me the more.' And Jack has been at High Stoke several times for no particular reason that Alice can see, other than to have the company of his wife, thus proving Olivia right.

Olivia tells Alice that when Betsy visits Freemans, she grieves as though she has lost a son. In a way she has, having watched

Henry grow from babyhood through boyhood to man.

'Betsy won't talk to me,' Alice says to Olivia, not without a touch of envy. 'She turns away as soon as she can. So how can I talk to her?'

Olivia says, 'Perhaps one day you and Betsy will share your memories of Henry, it will help you both.'

But at present, she casts off thoughts of Henry as soon as they arise. What she cannot cast off is the mass of lead that seems to crouch in her stomach, robbing her of appetite, weighing her down and opening a gaping hole in her very centre. At night she curls her knees to her chin to find relief, but the lead-weight remains. She dreams blood-drenched nightmares in which she is wading waist-deep through red stickiness, pursued by nameless horrors. She wakes bathed in sweat, and with a lurking sense of something in the dark waiting to spring. She keeps a basin of water in her chamber and splashes her face, but it offers scant refreshment. To escape herself she leaves her bed and wanders through the house, checking rooms, cupboards, windows, doors until the sky is greying.

And Isabel is still out there.

Then one night Alice creeps back to her chamber after another unresolved vigil, to see a form shadowed against the pre-dawn light at the window.

'Isabel!'

'No, Alice, it's me.'

'Olivia! What is it? Can you not sleep?'

'I was going to ask you the same,' Olivia replies. 'And last night, and the night before, and I know not how many nights before that.'

Alice considers passing it off, she is getting quite good at it with various neighbours who have called, some of whom, she is sure, only wish to shiver in delighted horror over the murder of Henry Jerrard. But Olivia is not of that sort, and by chance or intent has chosen her moment well. Alice is cold and bewildered, and sleeplessness has weakened her resolve. She feels her eyes water as she leans against the big bed and sighs. 'You are at peace with yourself, Olivia. I am nothing but a mass of black humours.'

'These are crushing times for you, Alice. You must expect your humours to be polluted. They will find their balance again, trust me.'

'I keep thinking,' Alice says, 'we believe in our modern life everything is ordered as it should be. But it's not.' She feels a tear fall, her voice rises. 'Isabel could come back. I could be run over by a cart. Sam …' Her voice breaks apart.

'It's not going to happen, Alice.'

'I can't protect him. I don't know if she will come for me or for him. I can't protect him every minute of the day, I can't—' She is crying in earnest, great heaving sobs dragged from her. 'Should I keep him close? Should I send him away? I don't know what to do, Olivia.' With the sleeve of her night shift she wipes her eyes.

'Isabel won't come back,' Olivia says.

'You can't know that!' Alice cries. 'She's mad! Who knows what she will do?' She fights to catch her breath but the tears have taken hold, trickling warm down her face, and in a confusion of senses she thinks of blood, and the way the warm blood poured unstoppable from Henry's chest as he lay dying. She can feel it running down her face. 'It won't stop,' she wails.

'What won't stop?'

'See?' she says. Now the blood is trickling into her mouth, she can taste it like iron. 'See?'

'It's too dark, I can't see what you mean.'

'The blood. Look. The blood.' Faintly in the grey, dark splashes show on her sleeve.

'Alice, you're making no sense—'

'Always there, lurking, and I should have looked.'

'What's there?'

'I'm never ready, Olivia, and one day I won't be ready when she comes for Sam, and I don't know how to stop her!'

And no matter how much she dabs at it, the blood continues to come. She feels Olivia's arms go about her, and she tries to push herself clear, warning, 'Blood. Look, it's blood, it's everywhere!'

But Olivia holds on to her, all the while soothing and reassuring until Alice leans against her friend and the force engulfs her like a deluge after drought, pressing down, crushing her. She sobs until she can barely breathe, heaving great gasps and sobbing afresh, and in her mind is the idea of a great black cauldron, its sides cracking and the void within swelling and growing, casting its wide pall, smothering everything in its darkness …

Alice comes back to herself, sitting on the floor slumped against Olivia, shakily drawing breath, eyes tight and puffy, hair stuck to her face, hands wet and sticky and the taste of blood on her lips, in her throat.

'It was a nosebleed,' Olivia assures her, dabbing at Alice's face. 'Just a nosebleed. It started while you were crying. There, it's stopped now. Sit quietly a moment.' In the dim dawn Olivia lights the candles in the pewter sticks that Henry bought for Alice, finds her way to the basin of water. She returns with a wrung-out towel and Alice is grateful to press the cool wetness against her forehead, bathe her eyes, her face, wipe away the traces. She takes a deep breath.

'Better?' Olivia asks.

Alice nods.

'And now I have something to tell you that will ease your mind,' Olivia says at last. 'Jack is coming over this morning. He sent me word last night. I didn't like to wake you but I see now I should have done. Constable Hart says that a body has been found.'

The body, Olivia tells her, is that of a woman of middling age, gaunt, with black hair, in a black silk gown, pulled from the river near the grain wharf. She had tied a bag full of stones round her neck, knotting it many times. The body had sunk, but was now risen again. Alice knows how dead flesh will corrupt, swelling up with putrefaction, floating back to the surface. 'The dead return,' she says. 'In this case, it does ease my mind, I am relieved to know.'

Was it madness, or sanity, Alice wonders, that drove Isabel to plan against her irresistible fight for life in the water? The river meanders wide there, apparently, and Constable Hart reported that the woman would have had to wade well out to reach deep enough water. This was no accidental slip, no cry for help. Isabel ensured she would lose the fight for life.

41

With the threat at last lifted, and with Jack and Olivia's help, Alice starts to piece together what happened after Isabel's outburst in the winter parlour that night. Probably, they conclude, when Henry came home and he and Alice sat getting to the truth about the pledge, Isabel was listening from the darkness of the hall. Perhaps her twisted thinking told her that Alice was putting Henry in harm's way by persuading him to confess to Jack. In her impassioned state of mind she probably believed that getting rid of Alice would persuade Henry to confess his love for herself. Certainly Isabel was already lying in wait in the stables next morning.

'Mollie gave me more of the story than she was able to give Wipley's jury,' Jack says. 'She said she came across from the kitchen, something about collecting charcoal to cook breakfast?'

'We keep the charcoal in a corner of the stables,' Alice tells him.

'Mollie saw Henry fall and Isabel pull out the pitchfork. You were lying in the straw by then and Mollie thought Isabel was going to attack you.'

'Poor child,' Alice murmurs. 'I would give much to lift that haunting from her.'

'Clearly with no thought for her own safety,' Jack goes on, 'Mollie grappled with Isabel, wrested the pitchfork from her and forced her into the wash-house, jamming the door with the pitchfork. Goodness knows how such a skinny child was able to do that.'

'Mollie has been worked hard, is my guess,' Alice says, 'whereas Isabel chose to avoid exertion. Still, it was a courageous act. Mollie was not to know that the window mullion was loose. I don't suppose it took Isabel long to discover it.'

'Then Sam appeared at the kitchen door,' Jack goes on. 'There was no time to go back and check on Henry or yourself. Mollie knew she had to prevent Sam entering the stables. With great presence of mind she pretended she had locked a pirate in the wash-house, and that she and Sam should escape to Freemans and raise the alarm.'

'That took strength of a very special kind.' Alice does not voice her thought that by Henry's act of sawing through the mullion, Isabel was saved from trial and an agonising death at the stake for killing her master. Isabel, as Jack confirms, determined her own end, and any threat to Sam is lifted by her act of self-destruction.

Later, clearing out the accounts room, Alice finds a collection of letters from a Roland Mullen in Devonshire. 'Isabel, dear daughter,' they start, and more than one contains advice to 'think not that he entertains projects of which he does not speak', by which Alice realises that Roland understood Isabel's heart and tried to divert her from its dangerous course. Alice sits down to write the most difficult letter of her life. To tell a man that two of his kin are dead is bad enough, she cannot find it in her to tell him that both deaths were by his daughter's hand.

Her mind dwells on Isabel's twisted humours, and she is filled with anguish at the remorse she imagines dogged Isabel's thoughts in her journey from wash-house to watery death. Obstructive, patronising, bigoted and cruel as she was, Isabel was also a woman in love, even if that love was of the most mistaken kind.

In the end Alice writes vaguely to Roland of 'tragic accident' to spare him the discovery that his daughter's grave is beyond the pale of consecrated ground. 'Did I do right,' she asks Olivia, 'to withhold it from him?'

'I can only say I'd have done the same,' Olivia tells her.

'I wish I could feel that is the last of it.'

'You know, Alice, there will come a time when all this is

more distant.'

'You make it sound as though I shall forget Henry.'

'I don't say forget,' Olivia replies, 'only accept that he has been called away, and you have a life to build.'

42

They are like strangers. Ever since Allan was released, and Grace, her ankle healed, was able to return to the dairy, she has kept out of his way. Each morning she is out and milking earlier than before. Mollie is now helping her, and the two girls stick together. Back indoors, if Allan comes into the dairy court, Grace slips out into the kitchen passage. At mealtimes, Grace makes sure she sits at the end of the bench, with Mollie next to her. Wherever Allan sits, Grace keeps her glance lowered and will not meet his eye.

Betsy watches the dance of avoidance, tightens her lips and waits.

After a while, Allan stops trying to catch Grace's eye. Once he is no longer appearing to take any notice, Betsy remarks on Grace's brief glimpses in his direction as he eats his meal staring stolidly ahead or at his plate. And still they do not talk. Well, Betsy thinks, and what's to be done about this star-crossed pair? She feels like knocking their heads together. Have they no idea how short life is?

She calls in Allan one day to measure the wash-house window. 'It needs a new mullion, as you should know,' she tells him.

'Easily done,' he says.

'You'll need to come inside to fit it,' she says.

'I can just as well fit it from the outside,' he tells her.

'No, I want to see you do it,' Betsy insists. 'So one day when I'm here.'

Allan shrugs. 'Just as you like, Betsy. One of your wash days, then.'

'I'll let you know when,' Betsy says.

ALICE has received a note from Sir Malcolm Wipley, announcing the morning when he will call. Not asking if it suits her convenience, but that is no surprise to her, it is not Sir Malcolm's way to consider the convenience of those he scorns.

THE Tillotson clothes are nearly all distributed now. Alice has selected three pairs of stockings for Betsy to keep. A few items remain in the wash-house awaiting repair or alteration, Betsy tells Grace, a new shift for Mollie for a start. 'But I'm no needlewoman and I know you do some fine work, dear.'

'I could help you once I've done the dairying,' Grace offers, 'in the afternoons before the second milking.'

'Yes, I was thinking it would have to be one afternoon,' Betsy replies. 'I'll let you know which afternoon will be best.'

And now here is Grace perched on a sink, head bowed over her needle and thread, while Betsy wrings out garments, taking rather longer than usual to do it, and looking out of the door every few minutes.

At last she picks up her basket. 'Well, I must be off to the drying bushes,' she tells Grace. 'I'll be back soon.'

Grace nods, not looking up. Betsy goes to the door just as Allan crosses the kitchen court with the new mullion. 'Here it is, Betsy. All right to fix it now?' Behind her, Betsy hears the scuffle as Grace jumps to her feet in panic.

'You go ahead and fix it, lad,' Betsy says, letting him into the wash-house. She leans in as Allan stops dead and the two stare at each other. 'And you've both some fixing to do before I get back. So go to it and see that you do.' She pushes the door closed.

43

The day has come. The day for Sir Malcolm to claim High Stoke. Jack has just arrived, to fulfil his promise to assist in the negotiations. With him is Robert, who is to accompany Olivia back to Freemans. Olivia sits her mount ready to depart. As ever, she is a picture of grace, her tucked hat tilted over one eye and a short, starched ruff at her neck. Over her riding habit she is cloaked against the chill. Overhead, clouds threaten and the breeze carries spits of rain, but Olivia's hair seems not so much disordered as gently waved. By contrast, Alice's kinked hair has kinked even more than usual in the damp air. Despite her cap, tendrils skip to and fro, getting in her eyes.

In the kitchen court, Joe lifts Sam up in front of Robert, before walking round to the front of the house where he will attend Sir Malcolm's horse when he arrives. For Sam, it is a day at Freemans with Robert's children, and he is both excited at the prospect and apprehensive at leaving Alice.

'You will be back here before you know it, Sam,' she tells him. 'Just think, I shall have all day to cook you a wonderful supper. What would you like?'

'Proper white bread,' says Sam. 'No brown bits.' That will certainly keep her busy, bolting the flour through a cloth to separate it from the bran before she even starts mixing in the yeast. 'And a big fish, too.'

'Where am I going to get a big fish, you rascal?' she asks him.

'We have plenty of young carp in our stewpond,' Olivia offers. 'We'll bring some when we come back. They won't take long to cook in butter.'

'We're certainly not short of butter,' Alice says drily, recalling the shelves of sealed pots produced at Isabel's command.

'And Jumbles with lots of sugar,' Sam adds.

'Have you any idea of the cost of sugar, young man?'

'I like sugar,' he insists.

'Then sugar you shall have. This once.' *It may be the last meal I cook here, so I shall make it something special.* 'Now, off with you.' She reaches up to give Sam a parting kiss before approaching Olivia, who leans down from the saddle for Alice's murmured, 'Do you really have a lot of carp?'

'We seem to have a glut this year. How many do you need?'

'I should like to sit down to supper with everyone this evening. In the hall. Everyone from High Stoke, and all of you from Freemans, Robert and Cicely, the children, Faith. It may be the only chance I ever get to thank you all.'

Olivia smiles and whispers, 'I shall bring them all back this evening. Household and carp.' She tilts her head towards Sam chattering non-stop to Robert. 'We shall celebrate your new motherhood, at least. And Alice, even if the worst should happen today, you and Sam have a home at Freemans while you need it.'

'Bless you, Olivia. What would I do without friends like you and Jack?' But beyond her gratitude for Sam's safe-keeping, Alice knows there are those at High Stoke who cannot be left to the uncertain mercies of Sir Malcolm Wipley as their new master. Mollie for sure. Grace and Allan? Well, perhaps not. In some inexplicable way, it seems those two have made up their differences; a glow of happiness follows each around wherever they go.

'I feel sure all will be well,' Olivia says pulling Alice back to the present. 'Sir Malcolm cannot but listen to reason.' Alice doubts that. *Sir Malcolm did not listen to reason when he condemned Allan,* she thinks, *nor when he passed his verdict on me. Why would he listen to reason now, when he holds all the cards?* But she smiles back at her friend, who can believe that such a man as Sir Malcolm Wipley will act with constraint.

Olivia urges her horse forward, Robert falls in behind and

they retreat along the track through the breezy meadowland. Jack stands watching, and after a minute Olivia turns and blows him a kiss and he smiles and raises a hand. How happy they are, Alice reflects and a brief ache clutches her heart. I will not be maudlin, she chides herself. I will not.

She turns to Jack and they cross the court together to enter the kitchen. 'Thank you for being here, Jack. I have no idea when Sir Malcolm will arrive. Come through to the hall.'

'We can deal with Sam's adoption first, if you like,' he says. 'I have the paper here,' drawing it out of his doublet and unfolding it.

'I would prefer to deal with it afterwards,' she says, leading the way into the hall. 'I want to give my whole mind to the matter and I cannot do that while I am on tenterhooks over the fate of High Stoke.' She closes the door and goes to the window. Out there, Joe sits on the grass of the clearing, waiting for the coroner.

'That will be best, I'm sure,' Jack says. He folds the document and slips it back between the buttons of his doublet. Alice paces to the table, paces back to the window, drums her fingers on the shelf of the court cupboard.

'Alice,' Jack says, 'there is something I should tell you about that dice game, something I have held back, but it is part of the reason I am here.'

She thinks, please don't tell me that Henry's story is false, that there was no cheating, that he truly lost High Stoke in fair play. 'If it is about Henry,' she says,' if it is not good, I am not sure I can—'

'The dice,' he interrupts her. 'It's about the dice.'

'Oh, them.' She shrugs. 'Henry said they were Fulham dice but we never found them.'

'It's true, they were loaded to land a particular way every time.'

She stares at him. 'How do you know?'

'I have them here,' he tells her, pulling his hand from his pocket. He opens his palm, tips it, and rolls two dice onto the table.

She hurries across the hall. There on the table, two innocent cubes of wood. Picks up the one showing six. The dots are burned into the surface with a red-hot poker or something finer, perhaps an awl. They resemble tiny sightless eyes. The edges and corners are darkened from much handling. It looks so ordinary. She rolls it and again it lands with the six uppermost. She takes it up, tipping it in her hand, feels the slight, dragging weight on the opposite side and peers closely at the single dot. In the middle of the singed eye is a metallic iris and she presses a fingertip against it, feeling the coldness at its centre. She casts and it rolls a short way, stopping abruptly beside its fellow. Six again. 'A little ball of lead, is that right?' she asks. 'Why do they call it Fulham?'

'There's a lead works there. Down by the river.'

She picks up the other and rolls it likewise. It stops with the two uppermost. 'That's not loaded, then,' she says.

'Roll it again,' Jack advises, and she rolls, and again it comes up two, rolls again, two again. On the opposite face, the centre dot of the five has a cold iris.

'Aren't they supposed to come up six?' she asks.

'Too obvious,' Jack tells her. 'Wherever you have a central dot you can bury the lead – one, three or five. So you can always be sure of throwing a six, a four or a two, depending which dice you're using. With two dice in play at a time, Wipley will have wagered on throwing a total of six or eight, which means he will have had a third dice on him.'

'Why not wager on ten?' she asks. 'That's a six and a four, using the loaded one and three.'

Jack shakes his head. 'You can't wager ten in Hazard.'

'Oh. It's a rule?'

'It's a rule.'

This is the proof I need, she realises, proof that the man cheated. 'When did you find them? Henry said old Master Tillotson intervened and took away both pledge and dice. Are you sure these are the ones?'

'Oh yes, these are the ones. Tillotson came to see me the next day. He was concerned about the risk of what he held, in case they got into the wrong hands. He kept the pledge and asked me to hold these dice.'

'I wish he had destroyed both,' she says with passion. 'Then none of this would have happened.'

'I wanted that too,' Jack says. 'But Tillotson had warned Wipley that if ever he reverted to cheating, this evidence would be placed in the hands of Justice Townsend.' He makes a wry face. 'Neither of us considered the possibility of Tillotson's seizure.'

If Master Tillotson had not died, she thinks, Sylvia would be alive today; the sheriff's men would not have ransacked High Stoke, Isabel's madness would not have been fuelled; some compromise might have been worked out with her, Henry might still be alive.

If, if, if …

'Well,' she says, 'we now have a weapon, thanks to you, Jack.' And as she says this, there is the sound of hooves outside. 'I believe he is come.' She is already moving to the screens passage to save her front door another of Sir Malcolm's thrashings.

Behind her, Jack warns, 'Do not be too confident about this, Alice.'

'It's proof,' she counters. 'He used them to cheat Henry. Master Tillotson witnessed it and took both pledge and dice.' She pulls at the front door. 'Now we can present Sir Malcolm with his own dice and he must back down.' We are where we are, she thinks. Henry was cheated, and Sylvia was violated, and I shall make Sir Malcolm pay for it. Deep within, she feels the fire of retribution flare. Alice Jerrard, Avenging Angel.

The coroner is already dismounting, glancing up at the housefront. Joe takes the horse's head, while behind them the coroner's manservant swings a leg over his mount's neck and slides to the ground. Alice recognises the man who did not know what a hot brick is, who guffawed along with his fellow about giving Allan a beating. Despite layers of wrappings his face looks pinched in the chill air. She is maliciously glad of it.

'Sir Malcolm has brought his second, I see,' Jack murmurs.

'And we both know what that means,' Alice says. 'So that he has a witness to all I say. It's all right, Jack. No matter how this turns out, my object today is to adopt Sam. I shall not put that in jeopardy by getting myself arrested for slander.'

Sir Malcolm stands a moment until she meets his eye, then he turns his gaze and reverts to his scan of the house front, unhurriedly taking in its features from end to end in a measuring way, rhythmically slapping one gauntlet against his thigh, a smile on his face. Sourly, Alice regards the rich crimson of Sir Malcolm's fine woollen doublet and breeches, striped with thin lines of gleaming black silk and resplendent with pearl-like buttons. From where she stands, the shade looks near-black and puts her in mind of the sediment that first day in Henry's glass of wine. At last, his survey completed and his point made, he turns to the door.

'Madam.' His bow is perfunctory, the slightest pause in his progress.

'Sir.' She curtseys and follows him into the hall. 'Master Egerton is here today as my advisor.'

The coroner's man closes the front door and brings up the rear and Alice ushers them all to the winter parlour. The blaze there offers welcome warmth and Sir Malcolm moves deftly to take up position by the backstool nearest the hearth, placing himself such that no one else can occupy it without dislodging him. It is the same backstool he occupied on that night visit, though this time Alice has ensured there are no cushions within reach to be muddied under his heels and scorched by the flames. Today, however, he cultivates a polished air. Even his face shines as though he has been buffed for the occasion. He remains standing, as if to indicate that he is refined enough to await Alice's invitation to sit. He looks around him, weighing up his surroundings. She feels his covetousness like a hot blast. Not so refined that he can decently mask his expectations.

Although she has not gone into detail, Alice has told the household that there may be a change of ownership. They think she is considering selling and have asked no questions, believing they know why. She has seen this in their faces, in the way they do not mention Henry.

She has dreaded this meeting. How to appeal to a man whose acts of philanthropy depend on a comparable benefit, who is wilfully blind to reason, has cheated his way to his claim of ownership, harbours ambitions to rise in power and status, and who disliked and resented Henry. With no plea to oblige Sir Malcolm to change his mind, she has felt all the powerlessness of the dispossessed. Every time she has tried to prepare for it, her mind has fogged, her arguments have melted like salt in water.

Until now. With the evidence Jack holds, her mind has cleared. She does not have to open negotiations. Leave that to Sir Malcolm. Let him state his case, his requirements, she will choose her moment, then she will strike. She invites Jack and Sir Malcolm to sit, while the coroner's man closes the door and leans his back against it. Alice takes a stool for herself and folds her hands. There is a pause, and Sir Malcolm looks puzzled.

'Where's Jerrard's attorney, Egerton?'

Once again, the deliberate exclusion. Alice cuts in, 'My attorney, sir? Why should I want an attorney?'

He looks across at Jack, making a face as if sharing his contempt for women. Unfortunately for him, Jack does not respond and the coroner is forced to reply to her. 'Let us resolve this quickly, madam. The attorney's not for you, you have no claim. My business is with those who would administer the demesne. Hence the attorney. Therefore, I ask again, where is the attorney?'

'Perhaps I can help here,' Jack says.

'No, Egerton. It's the attorney I want to see.'

'Very possibly, but allowing for your former mistaken view of Mistress Jerrard's involvement in her husband's murder, it might be taken amiss in some quarters if Mistress Jerrard is seen to lose this property to you without being permitted to scrutinise your claim. By transacting the business before myself and your man here, the legality of your claim can be demonstrated to all.'

'She can sit there and listen, but she has no claim.'

'Then let us establish that first,' Jack says.

The coroner's eyes narrow as he regards Jack, but apparently he cannot counter the argument. He shrugs and leans back in his chair, crossing one trunk-like thigh over the other. 'For form's sake, then.'

'So, Mistress Jerrard,' Jack turns to her. 'You claim High Stoke on the strength of your marriage to Henry, is that right? And you can produce evidence of your marriage?'

'I can, in the parish rolls of Hillbury in Dorset, from Vicar Rutland who performed the ceremony, and most of the inhabitants there, who witnessed it a matter of weeks ago.'

'And as the sole beneficiary of his Will?'

'Indeed.' The Will was made the day after they arrived here, the day he took Sam up on the grey and went to see his attorney in town.

'And your claim, Sir Malcolm?'

The coroner reaches into his doublet and draws out the sheet of paper he snatched from Alice's hand that night. He unfolds it and leans away as Jack holds out his hand. 'Keep your distance, I hold onto this.'

And there it is again, in all its tortured scrawl.

> *I pledge my dwelling place and all that demesne to Malcolm Wipley, Knight, of Poyle by Guildford, in y County of Surry*
>
> *Signed this XXVIII day of October y XXII yr of James Stuart, Rex*

And there, dashed off at the foot of the sheet, the name.

'You must know your late husband's hand, madam,' he says to her.

'It is like and yet unlike,' she says. 'But yes, his signature at least I recognise.'

'Egerton?'

'I agree with Mistress Jerrard,' Jack says, 'The signature is his.'

'So there you have it,' Sir Malcolm says. 'My point is, the property was nothing to do with her when he wrote this so she has no rights here.'

'Unless your claim were shown to be false,' Jack adds.

Sir Malcolm waves the pledge. 'You have both just admitted, there is nothing false about it.'

'Then why did you not claim High Stoke at the time, over a year ago?' Alice asks. 'If it was legally yours that night, you could have moved in immediately. Why didn't you?'

But the coroner is not easily foxed. 'Compassion for a fellow gentleman in difficulty.'

'So you renounced your claim and returned that pledge to my husband?' Alice asks.

'Do you think to make mock of me?' the coroner demands.

'I am trying to find out how you think the pledge appeared in my book. If you did not give it back to my husband, who did you give it to?'

'God's blood, Egerton,' the coroner objects, 'are you going to allow this woman to play the virago?'

'Mistress Jerrard is not answerable to me, Wipley,' Jack answers. 'It was a fair question, one I myself would have asked. Who did you renounce it to?'

'I didn't renounce it to anyone. Jerrard must have stolen it.' It is a clever move, Alice recognises. On the back foot, the coroner can still think quickly enough to produce the sort of answer that in no way impugns his honour. And he has managed to accuse Henry in the process.

'If Henry had it, he would have burned it,' she says. 'Master Tillotson—' and stops herself just in time from reminding him that Frederick Tillotson accused him of cheating. 'Master Tillotson possessed himself of the pledge.'

'I gave it to Tillotson,' the coroner says as though correcting her.

'A minute ago you said you didn't give it to anyone.'

'You split hairs, madam.' The coroner is rattled at last. 'I *offered* it for safekeeping to Frederick Tillotson.'

'Why would you need to do that?' Alice demands. 'You are a powerful man with your own body servants to protect your property. I'm not aware Master Tillotson had any such protection.'

Sir Malcolm momentarily hesitates and Alice is about to follow up her advantage with the dice when Jack interposes, 'That's a name we all respect. A man to look up to, Tillotson was. Wouldn't you agree Wipley?'

'A close neighbour and a particular friend of mine,' the coroner agrees. 'But this is nothing to do with—'

'I recall you were especially anxious in the weeks after his death to establish whether or not there was foul play,' Jack goes on.

'In the case of such a prominent man, I was duty bound to make doubly sure of my verdict.' The coroner is fluent, assured, a man back on safe ground.

'Indeed, I heard you were most diligent in your search, even setting a member of the Tillotson household to report to you.

Sylvia, wasn't it?'

The coroner shifts in the backstool. 'I may have asked her if she had found anything suspicious.'

'Like going through his pockets?'

The coroner's face darkens. 'Don't start, Egerton. I'm no thief on the lookout for stray pennies.'

'Pity. You might have found what you were looking for,' Jack says.

For a moment, the coroner hesitates, then he collects himself. 'Evidence of foul play, you mean? In the matter of Tillotson's death?'

'Evidence of foul play, certainly.'

'Well, if you knew something, you should have informed me,' Sir Malcolm declares. 'Your duty as a justice—'

'The evidence you sought was not in the matter of Tillotson's death,' Jack suggests.

'And we know what that evidence was, don't we?' Alice cuts in. 'Master Tillotson challenged your win. That was why he possessed himself of that pledge.'

'Now she is entering the realms of fancy.' Sir Malcolm smiles. 'You see why I will have no truck with her, Egerton. You have seen my claim, you cannot deny it is legitimate.'

'You have the right of it.' Jack raises a staying hand as Alice opens her mouth to object. She bites down the impulse to drive home her accusations as the coroner directs a smirk at her. 'However,' Jack continues, 'Let me appeal to your generosity of spirit. Given that you have no need to dispossess—'

The coroner scoffs. 'What are you up to, Egerton? You've never yet acknowledged I had any generosity of spirit.'

Jack shrugs. 'Call it what you like, it was you who spoke of your compassion for Jerrard. I appeal, let us say, to your sense of fair play. Why not drop the affair here and now?'

'I'll tell you why not.' The coroner looms forward, but now he is addressing Alice, poking his cube-like head at her. 'Your husband consented to play, he knew what he was doing. If I generously gave him leeway at the time, I never promised to cancel the debt. Any moral obligation on me is revoked by his death and I claim my right.' He continues to stare and she is silent, bereft of arguments to a man who will not right his crime even when he is given an honourable way out.

'Allow me to suggest this,' Jack says. 'We know the pledge was found in a household book here.' Silently Alice thanks Jack for keeping Henry's name out of it – the coroner need never know that Henry wrested the pledge from Sylvia on the Long Down.

Jack continues, 'We could reasonably surmise that Sylvia slipped it in there to hide it, intending to retrieve it later. You did, after all, set her looking for it in Tillotson's house last autumn.' Before Sir Malcolm can gainsay this, Jack continues, 'It is unlikely Tillotson intended it to get into other hands. If Sylvia had not found it, you would be no worse off than you are at this moment.'

'Fine words, Egerton, but I am unmoved.'

'By renouncing the fruits of this late-night sport, your sense of fair play will be confirmed by your act of generosity.' The coroner shrugs as Jack continues, 'His Grace of Canterbury as we all know is not averse to a little sport himself, and would likely look with favour on one who renounced his winnings to help another of God's creatures.'

The words have a powerful effect on the coroner, who has opened his mouth to speak and now clamps it shut. Alice recalls Henry's description of the opening of Archbishop Abbot's hospital, the vision of Sir Malcolm edging in close so as to be seen near His Grace. It is not fairness or godliness that drives Sir Malcolm, it is social advancement.

Sir Malcolm sits back, his steepled fingers tapping his chin and his eyes glazing as he considers. The fire crackles, flames dancing up from the piled logs and casting a pleasant warmth in the room. At that moment the sun breaks through the cloud, flooding bright spring sunlight across the parlour. The coroner looks round, smiles. 'But you know, I rather like this place, it will be an interesting venture to re-glass and re-tile, throw out a wing. I believe I have sufficient credit with His Grace, Egerton, I don't need your persuasions.'

'A pity,' Jack says. 'Tillotson would be disappointed too.'

'Well, he's dead,' Sir Malcolm says in matter-of-fact fashion, and remembers to add, 'poor man.'

'He told me.'

The coroner frowns at Jack. 'Told you what?'

'Oh, that Henry and you had a long and ill-tempered session at the Red Lion.'

'If there was ill-temper, it was all Jerrard's.'

That's right, Alice thinks, *blame a dead man.*

'Tillotson watched from the shadows as the night wore away—'

Sir Malcolm leans away in his seat. 'Tillotson had no part in the game.'

'You're saying he wasn't there?' Jack asks.

'We didn't even know he was there until the game was over.'

'He studied your play, Wipley. He thought you were switching dice.'

'Just the meanderings of an old man. He was asleep all the time.'

'How would you know that if you didn't know he was there?' Alice interrupts.

The coroner steps round that by continuing to address Jack. 'His eyesight was failing, poor old fellow.'

'He waited until the final throw and challenged you.'

'In all honesty, Egerton, I have tried to keep Tillotson's name out of this. He saw nothing amiss, merely thought he did.' Sir Malcolm is all reasonableness, hands spread in appeal. 'You must understand I am unwilling to malign a man who can no longer defend himself. I even accompanied him home afterwards.'

'He told me you both saw him home. You offered first, then Jerrard accompanied because he feared you might try to wrest the pledge from Tillotson.'

'Jerrard had good reason to want that pledge for himself. I was shielding Tillotson.' Sir Malcolm, the protector.

'If Master Tillotson was that vulnerable, I am surprised you asked him to keep the pledge for you,' Alice points out.

There is a short silence during which the coroner fails to find a retort. Jack is the next to speak.

'In the circumstances of doubt, and out of common humanity, it would be generous in you to show your fair-mindedness by giving up your claim. It would not be forgotten.'

'There are no circumstances of doubt.' The coroner's voice is smooth and confident as he responds. 'I have a legitimate claim, you have admitted it before my man here. Why would I give that up?' He indicates Alice with a jerk of the head. 'I have no need of favour from her sort.'

'You need to be careful about stories getting out. You know how these things take hold of susceptible minds,' Jack warns him.

The coroner leans forward, fixing Jack with narrowed eyes. 'You would be unwise to let it "get out" that I had forfeited my claim when I have not. We live in an age of proofs, and empty threats will be punished.'

'Not empty.' Jack's cold tones match those of the coroner. 'There are these.' His hand comes out of his pocket palm upwards. Suddenly it seems Sir Malcolm is jolted out of his self-assurance. He pulls himself slowly straight in his chair.

Alice leans forward, takes the dice from Jack's hand and rolls them on the hearth, rolls them again, and a third time. 'Fulham dice, Sir Malcolm. A two and a six every time.'

'Frederick Tillotson came to me the day after he took possession of these and the pledge,' Jack says. 'He was fearful of what he held and recognised the need to split them up. He retained the pledge and I agreed to hold the dice.'

Alice holds her breath in the silence that follows. Nearly there. Jack has played a clever game. He has offered Sir Malcolm all manner of face-saving ways out and has been turned down on all counts. Sir Malcolm has thrown away his chances of an honourable resolution and must now deal with the consequences. In the pause, the room suddenly dims as a purple cloud obliterates the sun.

Then Sir Malcolm scoffs. 'That proves nothing. There is naught to connect me with those dice.'

'Do you deny you used them periodically throughout the game?' Alice demands.

'I used dice throughout the game. It was a dice game,' the coroner says, speaking as though to one of simple understanding.

'Including those dice?' Alice asks, carefully avoiding direct accusation.

'Never seen them in my life.'

'How do you know when you have not taken a close look,' she asks.

'Very well.' The coroner leans forward, then back again immediately. 'Never seen them in my life. Satisfied?'

And now Alice realises why Jack warned her against relying too heavily on this. They might all know it is true, but if Sir Malcolm simply keeps denying it, there is nothing they can do. There is no proof, nothing written down, nothing to connect the dice to Sir Malcolm, nothing but hearsay.

'You!' Sir Malcolm turns to his man. 'Disregard all this, it is slander and falsity. In fact, go and wait in the hall until I call you.'

'Stay where you are,' Jack countermands. 'If you leave, I shall be constrained to publish a broadsheet throughout Surrey.' Alice almost gasps.

'Jesu, Egerton!' the coroner protests. 'You're a justice!' His confident air is tinged with panic. 'Do you want to be sued for slander?'

'What slander would that be?' There is a pause as Jack holds his ground and Sir Malcolm gathers himself.

'That ... that you accuse me of using loaded dice! I declare it a foul lie and there is no proof.'

'Who said I accuse you of that?'

'You just—'

'It would be no slander to state that in discussions about a disputed property, you told your own man to leave the room.'

Excluded from the discussion, Alice is free to think, and is thinking at speed. She has to concede that Sir Malcolm is right, there will be no win without proof. There is no living witness and nothing in writing to connect him with those dice.

After a moment's thought, the coroner sits back shrugging. 'It'll be your word against mine.'

'Perhaps I am prepared to take that risk,' Jack challenges him. 'Are you?'

No, Jack, she thinks, I cannot allow you to take on a man like Sir Malcolm. With his connections he would ruin you. You, and Olivia, and all at Freemans who have given me so much friendship.

'So, a broadsheet, no doubt combined with a whispering campaign,' Sir Malcolm sneers. 'I'll have you know, Egerton, I shall go to Justice Townsend and let him know about those dice you could have confiscated from any vagabond who's come up before you!'

Nothing in writing.

'And I will have you know,' Jack answers, a first tinge of anger in his voice, 'I neither start, encourage, nor connive at whispering campaigns. What I do shall be above board. I shall use only those witness proofs that I have.'

Nothing in writing?

And suddenly, Alice has her answer. 'Sir Malcolm,' she cuts in, 'I'm going to suggest a compact.' It is highly risky, depends on her scant knowledge of the knight and of his man.

Once again, Sir Malcolm addresses Jack. 'She's not in a position to offer me a deal. I didn't come here to do deals, Egerton. My time is precious.'

Even as she quails within, Alice relishes adding, 'You should attend well, sir, because I shall offer it only once. What say you?' She has said it now, she cannot retreat.

Jack puts in, 'Mistress Jerrard wishes to make you an offer, Wipley. It will take very little of your precious time, since it will be offered the once.'

They wait. A muscle works in the coroner's slab cheek as he looks hard at Alice. The smooth shine of his face is rucked in a frown of dislike. Alice returns his look with one of waiting enquiry.

Eventually, Sir Malcolm nods shortly. 'Go on.'

Alice turns to Jack and tries to inject meaning in her eyes as she addresses him. 'Master Egerton, I know I said earlier that I wanted to keep this out of our dealings with Sir Malcolm, but now I wish to revise that decision. Would you please hand me the paper you brought here.'

He pats the chest of his doublet. 'You mean—?'

'Yes,' she answers quickly before he can say more. 'Please bear with me. I know what I wish to do.' Even so, her heart hammers against her ribs at this bold foolhardiness. Even Jack might call a halt when he realises what is afoot. But it is inconceivable that he should put himself in the firing line to help the High Stoke household.

Nothing ventured …

Jack draws out the folded document from between the buttons of his doublet. She rises from the stool and steps across and he hands it to her.

'Sir Malcolm,' she addresses the coroner, and as he reluctantly looks at her, she unfolds the sheet and regards its clerkly writing. 'What if an Information was laid?' She looks up. 'An Information as to what took place in a dice game between two men at the Red Lion, one October night in sixteen twenty-four?'

'An Information?' The coroner's eyes dart to Jack's suddenly impassive face, to the dice, back to Alice. 'If Jerrard laid an Information, madam, it is invalid, given that he was involved in the game.'

'Did I say Jerrard?' Alice asks.

'Tillotson?' The coroner frowns.

'It certainly wasn't the landlord of the Red Lion,' she says.

'Tillotson,' he breathes, 'the bastard.' His face is greying over.

'This should be settled here quietly amongst us,' she says. She takes a deep breath. 'Here is what I propose, sir. You give that pledge to Master Egerton and I give this document to your man and together they throw both on the fire. For good measure we will burn the dice also and that is the end of the affair. What say you?'

'Give it here,' he says, beckoning impatiently with outstretched hand.

'Oh, no!' She pulls the paper close. 'You kept me at a distance from my husband's pledge, I do the same. You may view it from where you sit.' She turns the paper towards him, her elbow clamped to her side to hide the trembling. Either this will work, or she will be so deep in trouble she dreads to think of the type of justice that will be visited on her.

The coroner's thoughts are writ clear on his face as he struggles to find another way. 'This property,' he says, 'I won it—'

'Once only,' Alice reminds him.

Holding out a shaking finger to the document in Alice's hand, Sir Malcolm turns his wrath on Jack. 'You drew this up?' he thunders.

'I drew it up, as commanded,' Jack confirms.

'You think to play games with me by concealing this and dancing around the point?'

'Sir Malcolm,' she replies, 'I demand that you choose. Here. Now.' She knows a malicious pleasure in commanding this brute of a man.

'You dare to make mock of me, madam? You country wife from God knows where!'

'I take it from your response you decline my offer,' Alice says, folding up the document. 'Master Egerton, I think we know what to do,' wondering what on earth they *are* going to do.

'Wait!' The coroner holds up a staying hand. 'You deny me the chance to consider, madam.'

'We have given you every possible chance to consider, sir,' Alice declares. 'I never envisaged using this and I am quite sure Master Egerton did not, either. He brought it here because I asked him to. I offer you one last chance.' This is tearing at her nerves, the uncertainty as it drags on, the growing likelihood he will uncover the deception. It has to be dealt with quickly, before he realises. 'Decide now,' she orders him. 'Does this go to the fire, or do I show it to Justice Townsend?'

'By Christ's nails, this is not the end!' Sir Malcolm storms. His rage threatens to turn his face the same crimson as his doublet. 'You!' he calls his man over. 'Throw that on the fire,' indicating the paper Alice clutches, but she steps back. 'The pledge to Master Egerton, please?'

Jack holds out his hand for Henry's pledge. At the same moment he receives it, Alice passes Sam's Adoption document to the coroner's man. All four watch as the flames consume both, and Jack tosses the dice on top.

44

'You appealed to his good nature and he has none,' Alice murmurs. 'He is well served.'

She and Jack stand at the door attending Sir Malcolm's departure. They can talk quietly here, out of earshot. The sun has come out again, and the cropped grass of the clearing quivers brightly in the breeze. Above, the clouds have been chased away, all but high brushstrokes of white which give the sky a clean, washed look. The trees across the clearing shimmer in full spring green. Alice leans against the stone jamb. The trembling is worse than ever and her tight lacing does not help, she feels lightheaded. Reaction, she tells herself, that's all, you cannot swoon here. But she hopes they will be gone quickly.

As soon as he is in the saddle, Sir Malcolm grabs the reins from Joe. He jerks the animal's head for home, and his man and Joe step back sharply, exchanging a look.

She says, 'I thought he would capitulate when you spoke of the archbishop. Instead, his man now knows the truth about his master.'

Beside her, Jack nods. 'Wipley has only himself to blame.'

'I wonder how long his man will remain in his present position.'

'If Wipley's wise, he will keep him close, or that whispering campaign may well start.'

Joe is saying something to the man, indicating the coroner's retreating figure. The man glances round at Alice and Jack, shrugs to Joe and holds out his hand for his reins. Clearly he is not going to talk here. But Joe frequents the Red Lion, as Alice now knows, and so does Sir Malcolm, and sooner or later his man and Joe will meet again. Well, she thinks, it must take its course as it will. The man scrambles into the saddle and feels for the stirrups.

'I really thought the dice would be enough on their own,' she says, and smiles at herself. 'How foolish of me.'

'The dice need never have been mentioned if Wipley had taken the chance to give up his claim,' Jack says. 'But he was right, on their own they were not evidence.'

Yes she thinks, I was foolish, I already knew him for a risk-taker. He reckoned the odds and knew they were heavily stacked in his favour.

Wipley's man kicks his horse into a canter to catch up with his master who is already entering the trees across the clearing. 'Thank you, Joe,' Alice calls and he raises a hand in acknowledgement as he heads back for the stables. Alice and Jack re-enter the house. She closes the door and follows Jack into the hall.

'It was only as we were talking of proof that I came up with the idea of using Sam's adoption paper,' she says, sinking down on the bench by the hall table. The relief of no longer prevaricating. 'I nearly had a seizure, fearing you would try to stop me. What is the sentence for bearing false witness?'

'I'd better not tell you. In any event, you are not guilty of it. By the time I saw what you were planning, I realised you were telling not a word of a lie. You worked on Wipley's awareness of his own guilt, and once that took root he was blind to all else. That said, I nearly had a seizure myself when you held up the document. It was obvious that was no Information.'

Alice smiles. 'But I knew he could not clearly see what was written on it. The night he was here, he misread the title of my book at that distance.'

Jack chuckles. 'Ah, the power of knowledge,' he says. 'Even so, you didn't know if his man could read.'

'I had to take a chance on it, but that was less of a risk. He was brought up in a very poor household; that night they brought Grace back, he didn't even know what a hot brick was. So the chances of his having had schooling were at best …' she recalls a phrase of Henry's, 'vanishingly possible.'

'So that's why you made it a condition that his man took the document to the fire?'

'It was the fairest way, he destroying the document on Sir Malcolm's behalf, you destroying the pledge on mine.'

He sits down beside her on the bench. 'Olivia and I have felt our share of blame that we knew of this dice game and agreed not to speak of it, even to Henry. It was a wrong decision.'

'No, Jack, you must not blame yourselves.'

'When we realised, we resolved to do whatever we could to save High Stoke. Little enough I have done, but I was keen to be here to bargain on your behalf.'

'You were a great help,' she tells him. 'It was right to offer Sir Malcolm some ways out. Better for him had he taken one of them.'

'Well, let's hope it's over.'

She looks at him. 'Yes,' she agrees, 'let us hope.' She is grateful that he has avoided empty reassurances, and she leaves the tacit thought hanging.

With one of Sir Malcolm's stamp, it is likely to be very far from over.

ABOUT THE AUTHOR

GEORGIA PIGGOTT is a former business systems analyst in retail, airlines and telecommunications. Her specialism is tailoring IT systems for non-technical Users. It is this passion for translation and language that has inspired her to explore seventeenth century England.

Georgia lives in Dorset, where her first novel *Just Causes* is set. *A Hazardous Game* is her second novel.

Contact: georgia.piggott@outlook.com

LOOK OUT FOR THE THRILLING NEW MYSTERY FROM GEORGIA PIGGOTT COMING SOON

THE ALICE CHRONICLES
BOOK 3

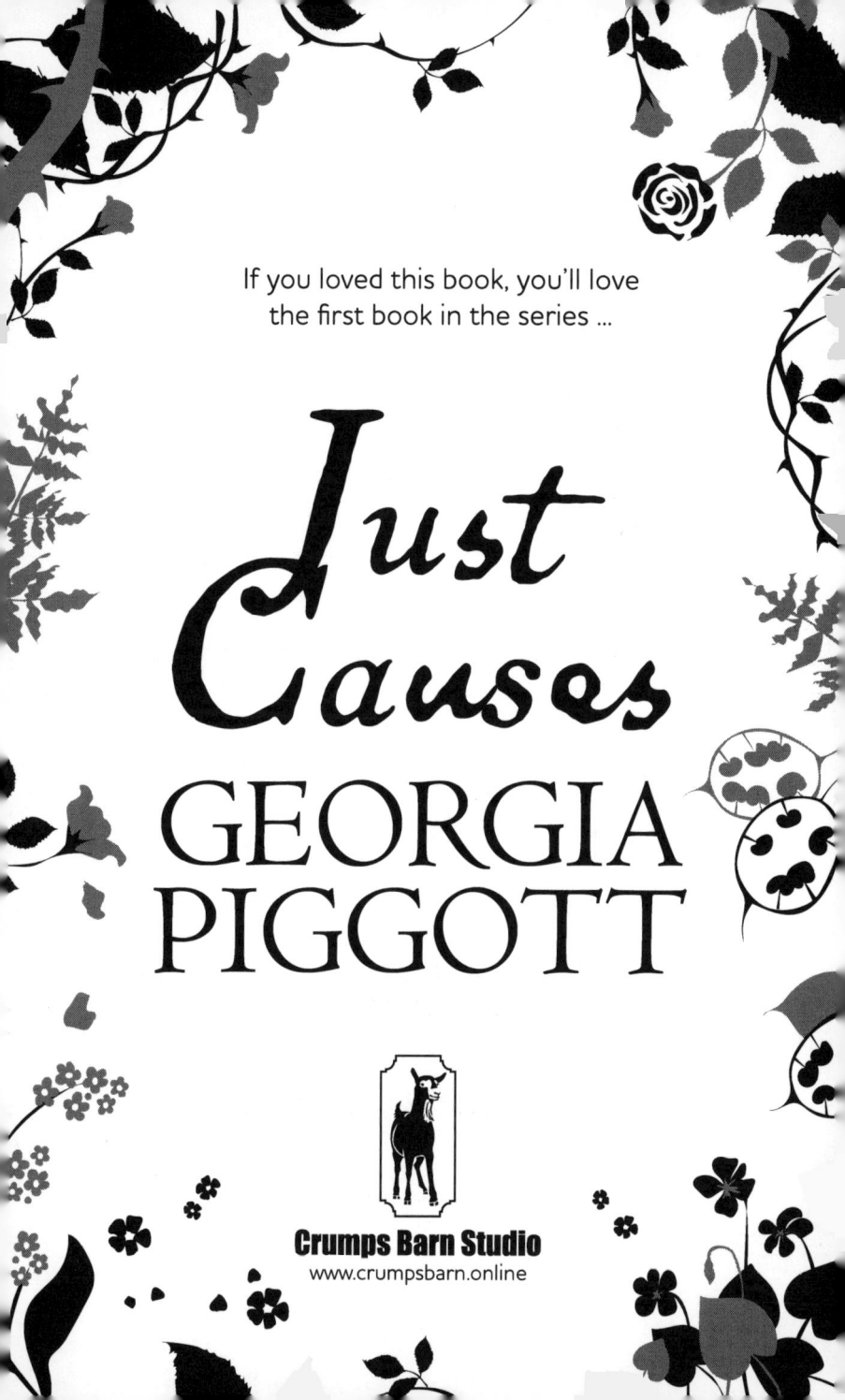

If you loved this book, you'll love the first book in the series ...

Just Causes

GEORGIA PIGGOTT

Crumps Barn Studio
www.crumpsbarn.online

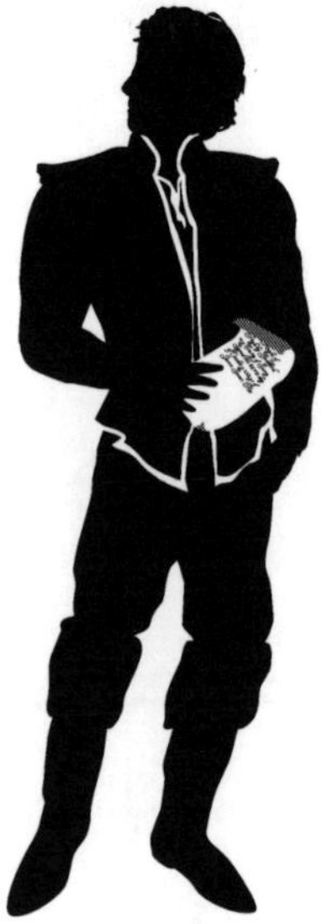